OLEANDER

A GREAT EXPECTATIONS REIMAGINING

SCARLETT DRAKE

PLAYLIST

Get a fuller experience by listening to the
uniquely curated Oleander Playlist.

Scan QR Code to listen to the playlist

DISCLAIMER

The material in this book is for mature audiences only and contains graphic content and themes of an adult nature. It is intended only for those aged 18 and older.

Scan the QR code if you wish to view the full list of Content Warnings. (Contains spoilers)

For Cara, who loves Cas as much as Jude does.

PROLOGUE

The house rose above the trees like a great mythical beast. A neo-gothic nightmare that lived in memories and dreams. Time withered and aged everything, but this place would live forever. I never thought I'd set foot inside this place again.

But he was dying.

I know you hate me. I know I do not deserve your forgiveness, Jude. But please, if you ever loved him – come. Let me say to you what I must, before it's too late.

It's been close to eight years, and I'm still dancing to his tune. But I'm not the boy I was then, weak and innocent as a newborn lamb. Together, they'd made me over into something crueller and less trusting. Whether that means I'm prepared for what lies in wait inside, I don't know.

But I'd never been able to stay away, not then and not now. This house, like its inhabitants, called to me; it always had.

Something he knows only too well.

The rain falls in sheets, heavy and relentless as it pounds the windows and roof of the car. The flight from Gatwick had been delayed because of the storm, and it seems to have followed me over the channel. It makes dark, deep rivers of the gulleys at the side of the road and drowns out the radio station pumping out disco music from the hired car. I hadn't bothered working out how to fix it.

I almost drive around to the back of the mansion to the private resident car park, but instead, I pull the rental car up past the front entrance and into the paved area reserved for visitors and turn off the engine.

There are a few lights on inside and around the front entrance, which should make it seem less imposing and threatening, but it doesn't.

I'm not sure how long I sit there before there's a knocking on the passenger-side window. I don't hear it immediately because of the rain, but I startle at the sight of a hooded figure gesturing for me to roll down the window. I have to turn the engine on to do that, but then it's down, and I think he's trying to decide whether I might be insane or not by the way he's looking at me.

"You Jude?" he asks.

"Um, yeah?"

He smiles a kind white smile that goes all the way to his eyes. He looks to be about my age, maybe a couple of years older, early thirties perhaps.

"He's been expecting you for a month. And since no one else comes, I figured."

"Right."

It's still raining pretty hard, but the guy doesn't seem to notice or care.

"I'm Jasper. The nurse."

"Right," I say again. Of course, he has a pretty male nurse.

Jasper laughs a little and glances up at the sky.

"You coming in? I like the rain, but not this much."

"Yeah. Yeah, I'm coming in."

He doesn't hang around as I take my time getting out of the car; instead, he bolts on long legs back into the shelter of the house.

With a deep breath, I grab my overnight bag and jacket and step out into the downpour.

Jasper's waiting just inside the vestibule, and he closes and locks the huge door behind me as I step inside Deveraux house for the first time in almost a decade. I'd been back a couple of times since Oxford, but that seemed like a lifetime ago now, and nothing appeared to have changed in the years since. I knew he'd started some renovations to the upper floors, but that hadn't carried on down here. Not a single thing is different to how it was then. There's some comfort in that, I find. Some sort of morbid nostalgia that I assumed had died in me a long time ago. It unsettles me. Makes me feel like a stranger in a place I know almost intimately, a place that felt as much a part of me as the heart in my chest.

It occurs to me suddenly that I'd never once come in through this door. I'd always come in through the back entrance, the service entrance, every time.

Jasper, still smiling, takes my jacket and hangs it inside the boot room off the entrance foyer.

"Can I get you some tea or coffee...?" he asks, coming back. "Something to heat you up?"

I look at him. Tall, pretty, dark-haired. Just his type.

"You his nurse or his butler?" I ask. It comes out ruder than I mean it to.

Jasper only chuckles, completely unperturbed.

"I do a bit of everything around here." He shrugs. "He's pretty much beyond the point of doing anything on his own now."

The thought slips into my brain before I can stop it: *Good.*

"Coffee. Black. Thanks."

"Sure thing. Decaf or?"

"Or."

He smiles again. "Got it. He's in the music room." That he doesn't direct me to it, that he knows I know exactly where that is, makes me wonder. How much does he know about what happened here?

"Hey," I call out when Jasper is halfway down the hall. I have to force the words past my throat. "How bad is he? I mean, is he sensible?"

"Oh, his mind is still sharp as a knife. He probably looks a bit different from when you last saw him, though." Jasper's mouth turns sad, the smile he's been wearing since I rolled down the window melting away now.

Sharp as a knife. Yeah, that sounded about right.

But no, Gideon wasn't the knife; Caspien had been that. Gideon, the hand that wielded it.

Me, the soft, yielding flesh.

I don't move immediately toward the music room. I stand there in the great hallway, looking at the closed doors. The rooms behind them are alive with memories: The library, the arboretum, the staircase leading up to his bedroom. I'm certain if I strain my ears hard enough, I'll hear his voice somewhere. Certain that if I inhale deeply, I'll still be able to smell him. He lives and breathes in these walls still, and I can't fucking bear it.

It's why I shouldn't have come.

I'm about to turn and run, drive back to the airport and await my flight back to London on Monday morning when I hear it:

"Are you out there, Jude?" Gideon's voice is changed but still recognisable. Distinct and elegant, as though spoken from a dais above me. "Oh, do come in. I don't have long left, and there's an awful lot to talk about."

I press my hand against the wall to steady myself, breathing deeply for a few moments. When I feel ready, I push off the wall and step inside.

The piano sits where it always has, where I'd first heard Cas play it, where I'd held and comforted him. And later, where I'd kissed and pleasured him, where I'd felt the sharp pieces of him break apart under me. Part of my mind cracks open, just a small opening and the memories pour out with all the strength it had taken to lock them up in there.

It's taken me years to hear a piano played and not feel like my heart was being torn from my chest. Now, I watch his videos online to feel that very thing because something is better than nothing at all.

A violent cough wracks through the room, and I'm almost jolted from my body. I turn toward the noise.

One end of the huge space has been transformed into a grandiose kind of hospital room. A hospital bed with machines standing around it like an audience to the figure within. A couple of high-backed antique chairs at either side. Two tall, ornate chests bracketing the head of the bed. One is stacked with books and a table lamp; the other holds a bright bouquet of flowers. I wondered if they'd come from the arboretum. An enormous TV is set up at the foot of the bed so that it obscures the person lying in it.

It's as though someone has come to die in a museum.

When I move closer and get my first look at him, all of the anger and rage I expected to feel…disappears, evaporating like rain on a hot pavement. A feeling completely unwelcome rushes at me instead pushing tears out from the corner of my eyes. I'm certain I'm about to break down, and I will not allow him to see that again. I turn my head and try to centre my breathing as I wipe at the tears threatening to overcome me.

He probably looks a bit different from when you last saw him.

Death sits on Gideon's chest like Fuseli's Nightmare. It clings to every inch of his skin, fighting him for every breath. And they are terrible, desperate breaths. Painful and raw. His once vibrant, healthy skin is now a palette of grey and blue. Dark eyes that had once gleamed with life are as dull as mud water.

He'd been handsome – an elegant, refined kind of handsome that people would describe with words like 'dashing' and 'debonair' – and now he was a rotten, dying thing. It humbles me in the way I'd been afraid it would. I want to scream and demand he get up and show me he was the same man he'd always been – capricious and cruel, the mastermind of all my misery.

"Hello, Jude," he says.

"Gideon."

"I didn't think you'd come."

"You knew I'd come."

He coughs again and gestures with his hand for me to sit down. I sit.

"You look dreadful," I tell him.

"You still don't mince your words, I see." Gideon grins, eyes gleaming again with cunning. Cas showed me a photo of him once as a child, aged seven or so, and he'd had that same look in his eyes even then.

I glance down at my hands, let the silence swell between us.

"I say, you turned out quite extraordinarily good-looking, didn't you?" he says.

I lift my head to find him looking me over appraisingly.

"Cas always had a thing for your freckles, did you know that? And that dimple on the right side of your mouth. You have grown into them both quite marvellously."

"Is this why you invited me here, Gideon? To flirt?"

He chuckles, but it transforms into a coughing fit.

"Are you in pain?" I ask when it passes.

In a roughened voice, he says: "I have been in pain for as long as I have been alive; this is just a different kind. More immediate, more ghastly to look at."

"I'm sorry," I mutter uselessly.

"Me too, my boy. I'm sorry too." It's weighty with meaning, his eyes horribly sincere, and it hits me with all the force of a punch to the gut. I'd never imagined I'd hear him say it, not really, not properly, and it feels awful now that he has. It sits there between us, ugly and loud.

I look at my hands again so I don't have to look at his decaying face.

"They say I do not have long. A few weeks, perhaps."

It was his pancreas; I knew that much. It had been too late by the time they found it.

Jasper enters carrying a tray with a mug of steaming hot coffee and a bowl of what appears to be soup. He hands me the coffee first before setting the soup tray on a tall trolley table that he wheels over so that it sits in front of Gideon. Lifting a cable, he presses a button and Gideon is raised into a more upright position so he can eat. Lastly, he switches on a light above the bed, flooding Gideon in harsh artificial light.

"Do I need to force you, or are you going to eat that?" Jasper asks Gideon bossily.

"I'll eat it," he placates, picking up his spoon.

Jasper looks at me. "Make sure he does, will you? He's a nightmare."

"A nightmare that pays you very well, so hush."

"Money isn't everything, Gideon, I've told you that."

I watch as Jasper checks the drip hanging by the bed, the one beneath the blanket draped over Gideon, and serves him a concoction of tablets from a little plastic cup.

The familiarity between them feels almost intimate. Jasper gives me a small conspiratorial smile and then disappears from the room, leaving us alone again.

"He's a godsend..." Gideon muses as he stirs his soup around.

I blow over the rim of my coffee.

"Locked away here with me while his friends travel the world, get married and have children. I'm certain he thinks I'm going to leave him everything."

"Are you?" I lift my coffee to my mouth.

Gideon grins. "If he marries me, perhaps."

"You've asked him?"

"A dozen or so times. He threatens to sue me for harassment in the workplace. But he never leaves."

I laugh, and he guides a spoonful into his mouth.

I drink my coffee while Gideon eats his soup in neat little sips from his spoon. It's a comfortable silence, easy almost, despite the years since we last did it.

When he's finished, he sets the spoon in the bowl, moves it away from him, and settles back into his pillows.

"You're not going to ask how he is?" Gideon says at last.

My breathing falters, my fingers tightening around the cup.

"If there was something wrong, you'd have told me the second I got here." I take a deep gulp of coffee. "So I assume he is the same as he always is."

Gideon sighs as though he's trying for patience. As though I'm a misbehaving child.

"This is...not right, Jude," he announces. "Shutting him out like this. When was the last time you spoke to him?" he asks.

"I don't know," I lie.

"Have you met someone else? Is that why you won't see him?"

I give him a look, one that says there has never and will never be anyone else. A look that tells him I don't want to have this conversation.

I mean it, Cas, we're not doing this again.

But this is what we do, Jude. It's what we've always done.

Not anymore. It's over. Don't come to me again. Don't call me again.

And he hadn't. It's as if something in my voice or my eyes that night told him that this time, I meant it.

"It was a lie, Gideon. He was a lie, as were you." I give him a pointed look.

"No. You were the truest, most real, most untainted thing he ever had."

"He made his bloody choice, Gideon!" I snap. "Over and over again, he made his choice, and it was never me."

Gideon gives me a look like I might be the one dying.

"It was always you. He chose you in the only way he knew how."

"By leaving me? By moving to another fucking continent and marrying *him*? That was Caspien choosing me? Christ, Gideon, you still lie so easily; it's frightening."

"He's only ever loved you, Jude. Surely you know that."

I look at him, incredulous. "He doesn't know what love is; you made sure of that! We weren't...*that* wasn't love." I sound certain as I fire it at him, but the truth is, I have no fucking clue how love worked or what it was.

Luke loved me, my parents had loved me, but romantic love was as unknowable to me as the universe. Love in that sense, love in that all-consuming, life-affirming, passionate, glorious sense, had come and gone with one person only, and he'd taken it with him when he left.

Sex and the fleeting kind of intimacy that came from it was something else altogether.

At uni, it had been easy with Finn. Being with him felt, sometimes, like being with Cas, which was why I'd ended it. Then there'd been Nathan. Nathan, who I could barely think about without feeling overcome with emotion so bittersweet that it ached. After uni, it had been celibacy, the occasional Grindr hook-up, and a lot of porn. There'd never been anything approximating the kind of love I'd nurtured for Cas.

Gideon nods, a grim kind of look on his face.

"I've had a room readied for you; you're welcome to stay as long as you wish."

"I can only stay the week," I mutter, blood still hot. "I have to get back on Friday." It's a lie – mostly. I have an engagement party on Saturday that I'd RSVP'd for and no one would care if I missed it. I had nothing to get back to except an overpriced, cold basement flat in Bethnal Green, but I didn't want Gideon to know that.

"Will you write something while you're here?" Sparks of excitement flicker in his bleary eyes now.

"Unlikely. Been a bit blocked recently." It had been fucking hell. Sat in the chilly spare room for the last month, pushing out words in stuttering constipated misery. Yes, I'd come to see Gideon after putting it off for so long, but I also hoped there might be some sliver of inspiration to be found in a corner somewhere here. Surely there was something more than ghosts and the echoes of heartache within these old walls?

"There really is quite a lot to talk about, but I wonder if you wouldn't mind if we start it tomorrow?" Gideon says, already looking drowsy. "These tablets are wonderful for the pain, but they really do destroy my concentration."

"That's fine," I say. "It's late anyway."

Gideon nods, a private little smile on his face as he looks at me. "I'm so glad you came, Jude, really I am. I feared I'd never see you again, that I'd never get the chance to tell you..." His eyes were closing over, lids heavy. "Jasper will show you to your room."

"I know my way about, Gideon."

"Yes, yes, of course. Of course, you do."

A moment later, he was asleep, or something like it. I watch him for a couple of minutes before standing and wandering out of the room. I find Jasper in a chair just outside the music room, reading a book. He has the cover bent back, so I can't see what it is.

"He's asleep," I tell him.

He stands and gives me a sort of searching look.

"You hungry?"

"Not really, no."

Jasper shrugs.

"So, where am I sleeping?"

"Oh, yeah, I'll take you up."

I feel like saying to him that I know this house as well as he does, maybe better, but I'm tired and can't be bothered with the conversation it might invite, so I let him lead me up the stairs.

"You're not what I imagined," he says as we go. "When he talks about you – which is a lot – I imagined someone different."

I'm unsure what to say to that, so I keep quiet and focus on where he is leading us. Though, it was bound to be only one of two places.

Jasper pushes open the door of Cas's mother's bedroom and walks inside. He'd already put my bags on the bed and closed the curtains. A small electric heater sits in the centre of the room, fighting against the chill. For a moment, I see the two of us on the floor, limbs entwined and mouths exploring. It could have been worse; Gideon could have given me Cas's room. There was a time when he would have and perhaps the fact that he hasn't means he has changed a little at least, though it will take a lot more to convince me.

"I switched it on after you arrived; it'll heat up eventually," says Jasper. "I've given you some extra blankets."

"Thanks."

"Bathroom's just down the hall."

"I know."

"Any special dietary requirements?" He is smiling a little now, and I have the peculiar feeling that he might be flirting. "For breakfast? I normally make porridge for him; I do a mean bowl with cream and honey."

The feeling fades. "Um, no. Porridge is fine, thanks."

"You got it," he says before striding out of the room and leaving me alone.

I plug my phone in to charge, though I have to pull out a side table and unplug the lamp to do it. Then, I lie back on the bed and stare at the ceiling.

He was really dying.

Some deep mistrusting part of me had thought that perhaps it was a ruse to get me here; to ensnare me back into the web I'd escaped eight years ago. But surely he knows, as well as I do, that I'd never really escaped. This place, him, Cas, all of it, live inside me. I am as much a part of the web as they were the creators of it. The way a plant or a tree can grow through solid stone if given time. There is still the possibility that he's brought me here to torment me to the last but I'm prepared this time, in a way I hadn't been then.

These walls and the two men inside had swallowed me whole once before, so when I emerged from the belly of the beast, I staggered into the world blinking and raw. This time, though, I have come armed. This time, I've come with sharp edges, blades, and a warrior's hardened heart, and I'll cut myself free without a moment's hesitation.

PART ONE:
THOSE FLEETING, FIERY SUMMERS

"You are in every line I have ever read."

Charles Dickens, Great Expectations

ONE

It was a bright, burning Tuesday in August when Caspien Deveraux broke my heart for the first time.

The news said it was the hottest day on record, though there have been hotter ones since. The weather map on TV showed red warnings, and there were reports of melting train tracks and things spontaneously combusting. My parents had been dead for seven years, and I could barely remember their faces.

It was hard to imagine there even was a time before. Before the Deveraux mansion and the two wraiths that haunted it. Before that summer, when everything was on fire, and I knew what it was to be consumed by flames.

But there was.

I had existed before.

I'd once dreamt dreams that were not about him – dreams that were not about his skin, his hands, or his lips which were always twisted with mockery and malice but which would, later, part with want and desire - though I could not now tell you what they were.

Dreams of my parents most likely. Of a life outside of the small island I'd called home since my parents' deaths. Oxford, probably. Then London. On other, bolder days, Italy, New York.

The year I first met him, I was fifteen. School was done for the term, and the summer break stretched out before me like a cat in the sun.

It was a Tuesday. Life-changing things rarely happened on Tuesdays – or so I had thought. On weekdays, Beth left for work even before I got up; she had to drive to her sales job on the opposite side of the island, and since Luke made his own hours and I clearly couldn't be allowed to stay home reading all day, I was told I was going to work with him.

He'd tried to make it sound like an adventure; uncaring that my adventures were inside the pages of the book I'd stayed up until 3 a.m. reading. They didn't involve crumbling old houses and annual delphiniums.

Luke had been born with green fingers, he said. Once, when I was five, he'd said he'd been born with 'green fingers,' and I hadn't known for a long time that he didn't mean this literally. He knew more about plants and gardens than I knew about Terry Pratchett books. He knew more about plants than most of the garden experts on TV. He talked to plants. Covered them with blankets in the winter. Left the radio on in our greenhouse sometimes for the seedlings he was sprouting. Radio Four: because they liked voices more than music.

That morning, at the sound of him bellowing cheerily up the stairs (Luke never raised his voice in anger), I'd come downstairs, my eyes gritty and my bones still asleep. Yawning, I sat at the kitchen table while he set down a cup containing two boiled eggs, butter, salt and pepper. Buttery toast landed next to it a few moments later.

"Eat up; you'll need your energy today," he said around a mouthful of mushed-up egg.

I glared. "It's child labour, you know."

"Well, it's not. Since I'm not paying you." He thought this was funny and smiled wide. "Well, not in money anyway."

They were buying me a new laptop the week before school if I stuck to this 'arrangement'. My stomach flipped with excitement when I thought about it. I could write on it. I could write. Properly. The one I used now was about ten years old and struggled to load two web pages at the same time.

"Three days a week?" I checked.

He nodded. "Eight until three."

"No Saturdays or Sundays?"

"Not a one. Not unless you want to. I'll give you double for a Sunday, though."

"Double of nothing is nothing." I pointed out.

Luke's eyebrows rose. "So you aren't as bad at maths as Mrs Edmunds says, then? Interesting."

I grumbled as I bit down on an edge of toast. It was still warm, and the butter dribbled over my lip, the scent of the peppery egg making my stomach growl. I'd been hungry before I'd fallen asleep last night.

"How late did you stay up?" His brown eyes softened.

I shrugged.

"Well, I'll try and go easy on you today. Lots to do. First day on the job is always the most important."

I shoved a spoonful of egg in my mouth and stifled a satisfied moan. I'd take his word for it.

Showered and dressed in my oldest pair of shorts and a 'Green's Gardening Group' t-shirt a size too big, I flung my backpack into the footbed of Luke's van first, before climbing in after it. The van was loaded up with spades and forks and an array of gardening tools I felt exhausted just looking at. Luke whistled, happy – excited even – about the prospect of reanimating the long-dead gardens of

Deveraux House.

I pulled out my book as he drove, folding back the cover and losing myself between the pages while he sang along to the radio. It was a forty-minute drive out of Gorey to St. Ouen in the north-west.

Luke hadn't stopped talking about this job for the last month. He'd won the contract over a larger firm in St. Aubin to resurrect the gardens of one of the oldest properties on the Channel Islands: Deveraux House. Built and owned by the Deveraux family, its current inhabitant was Lord Deveraux: by all accounts, some crazy old queen who was as mad as a box of wet cats. I didn't know much about him, and I didn't much care either, but he was a source of morbid curiosity for the island as far as I could tell.

That day though, Luke was happy. Excited like a kid on his way to a theme park. He wasn't thinking of anything except what this contract could mean for him, Beth, and me.

Back then, they fought a lot about money. Or rather, Beth did. I assumed myself to be the cause of that. Me, a kid neither of them had asked for but had been obliged to take in. My parents – mine and Beth's parents, I should say – had been hit from behind by a truck driver on their way home from a friend's wedding, making us both orphans in the blink of an eye. Beth and Luke had been babysitting me that night. Mum and Dad were going to take me with them before Beth had offered – last minute, as I'd heard it told – to allow them a night out together. A night that had turned out to be their last night alive. A night I think now must have been filled with awful pop songs, terrible speeches, and mediocre food.

I think about that frequently. About what I'd want my last night on this earth to look like.

It would be us, of course. Caspien and me, someplace warm. A night spent with our limbs tangled together, nice food and wine in our full bellies as we took that other more intoxicating pleasure from each other.

But my parents had been at the wedding of a distant cousin. A ten-second lack of attention by an overtired truck driver and every-one's lives had changed forever. My mum and dad became a story in the Honiton and Devon News, and Beth and I became orphans.

Ten seconds.

Beth had become a parent and an orphan at the same moment. Luke wasn't a replacement for my own father, but it felt strange to call him my brother. And so 'uncle' seemed like some middle place that suited us both. I'd always been a little difficult as a child, moody and insular, and prone to bouts of deep self-pity. And now I wonder if Gideon and Caspien had smelled that on me. Like sharks in the water. My heart, a soft and fleshy thing that was vulnerable to their poison.

Over the years, that soft fleshy thing has hardened, broken, bruised and scarred over but pierce through the hard outer shell, and there it was. Unchanged at its core.

That day, we pulled up to the gates at Deveraux House before 8 a.m. Another Green's van was already there, waiting. Luke got out and walked up to the gate, two rusted hunks of metal that looked as though they hadn't been opened in years. I learned later that they hadn't. Everyone left and arrived via the service gate on the other side of the estate.

Luke stood around for a bit, chatting with Harry and Ged, gesturing at the gates and looking through it. You couldn't see the house from here. It was situated at the end of a long, twisting, tree-lined drive, which was a curtain of green at this time of the year. In the end, Luke pulled out his phone and made a call, the recipient presumably telling him to come around to the west side service entrance or simply pull open the gates. Luke decided on the latter. With some effort, he and Harry prised open the large gates before sprinting back to the vans and driving through, Ged getting out to pull them closed behind us.

With the window down, I leaned my head out and then my arm, snatching a handful of green as the leaves brushed the side of the van. The house flickered into view through a break in the trees as we drove, but the moment it was revealed in full, I sat bolt-upright in my seat and gaped at the thing. It was a behemoth of a building. A brownish-red brick mansion with over a hundred windows and

a stone-covered wraparound veranda on one side, a large glass conservatory on the other, a turreted section, and around ten chimneys.

It sat slightly raised, as though on a dais of green, with acres of
overgrown garden spilling out from its walls. In the heat of the day,
it had an almost dream-like quality, a mirage in a desert. There
was something unmistakably English in its architecture, something
found nowhere else, but it was this same quality that made it distinctly sinister in the darker months. As though some screaming
madwoman lingered in its upper rooms, wailing late into the night.

As it was, no women lived in Deveraux House and hadn't done
so for more than fifteen years. The full story of why would turn out
to be tragic and fateful, and one I wouldn't hear until the following
summer.

Luke drove the van up to the front, slowing to get a look at the
wide, arched entryway. The large double door was closed, so he
followed the curve of the stone drive around the house towards
the back into a small courtyard. The gravel under the van sounded
extremely loud as we crunched around the building. We passed
the glass-domed conservatory, dirty and unused, with overgrown
weeds in a tumble behind the glass. A few even poked out through
a few shattered panels.

Finally we pulled up on the northern side of the property. The
courtyard was U-shaped, with a row of low buildings on one side
and the house on the other. A single solitary figure stood by a door
in the far corner of the courtyard.

"Wait here," Luke said, giving me a nervous smile before climbing
out of the van.

I nodded, happy to be able to stay outside of the thing – the place
did not scream 'visitors welcome.' As Luke met with Harry and Ged
at the back of the van, I glanced in the wing mirror to see that the
figure standing by the door was a boy. I couldn't see him properly
from where I was, but I was certain he wasn't any older than I was,
maybe even a few years younger. Bright blonde hair to his shoulders like a girl, he wore khaki-coloured shorts and an oversized,
short-sleeved shirt. He stood oddly still while waiting for my uncle

as though he were guarding the place.

We were close enough that I heard him speak when Luke approached.

"You are the gardener," the boy said in a very polite voice.

Luke stuck out his hand. "Luke Green."

The boy didn't shake it, and Luke dropped his hand. He gestured to Harry and Ged. "This is Ged Davis and Harry Foote. Um, is your dad home?"

"My uncle Gideon is inside. Follow me," he announced before spinning on his heel and disappearing inside. Luke glanced at the others and shrugged before following him inside.

It was stifling in the van, even with the windows down, so I opened the door and turned my body sideways so my legs were outside. There was little shade to be found in the courtyard, but I spotted a sliver of shadow on the side near the row of low buildings, grabbed Terry Pratchett, and made my way towards it. I had no idea how long they might be in there talking about annuals, perennials, and pruning, and I wasn't willing to sit in Luke's metal sweatbox and wait for death. It was illegal to leave dogs in hot cars, so I supposed it was illegal to leave fifteen-year-olds in there too.

I sat down with my back against the wall and my knees pulled up and opened chapter five. I'd just started chapter six when I heard a soft crunch on the gravel. Expecting Luke, I raised my head from the book.

The blonde boy was walking across the courtyard toward the row of low buildings – toward me. He was no longer wearing slippers. He wore brown leather boots that stopped at his ankles, and white socks pulled up to his knees. I was half hidden between two brick columns, and so he didn't see me at first, allowing me to observe him as he strode purposefully toward me.

The way he walked was strange. He didn't walk the way boys usually walk. The way other boys ambled, dragged their feet, and scuffed their shoes, this boy walked as though each step was a considered movement. A careful motion of his limbs and body forward toward a very precise destination. He carried something under his arm that I couldn't see. He was almost upon me when he finally sensed my presence, his eye catching me in its periphery.

He didn't startle, not a single gesture that would indicate shock to find a boy curled up in a dark corner of his courtyard reading.

He stopped moving and turned to face me fully.

The shock that should have been his was mine.

A jolt hammered my chest as his eyes locked with my own. I couldn't make out their colour from where I sat, the sunlight pouring over his shoulder, blinding me. All at once, it was the most important thing in the world. The colour of his eyes.

I rose to my feet quickly to face him, a rush of pleasure moving through me at the fact that I was taller. By quite a bit. Half a head, at least.

His eyes were a pale, ice blue.

"Who are you?" he asked in a sharper tone than he'd used with Luke. It somehow had the ability to sound both soft and hard as stone at the same time. "If you're one of those gypsies here to beg again, we don't have any work for you." He drew his gaze down my body and back up, distaste evident.

My ears burned with embarrassment.

"I'm Jude." I got out.

"I don't care. Now leave. There's no work for you here."

My eyes nearly bugged out of my head. I wanted to hit him. Burst his stupid, weird nose. My cheeks felt hot, and my breath quickened from anger.

"Luke's my uncle," I said, breathless with anger. "I'm waiting for him."

His pale eyes narrowed. "Who's Luke?"

I frowned at him. Was he slow? He'd literally just met Luke. I glanced at the house.

"Oh," he said. "The gardener."

I nodded dumbly.

"Right. Well, fine." He looked me up and down again. "You look like one of those begging gypsies."

He turned away and walked to what I soon understood was a

stable. A few minutes later, he emerged, leading a huge cara-mel-coloured horse by a strap across its mouth out into the bright August sunshine.

It was the first time I met Caspien Deveraux, and I loathed him with a passion I didn't know I was capable of.

And though I didn't know it then, I'd soon come to love him with the very same ferocity.

TWO

I hadn't been aware I'd been waiting to see him again until I watched him return his horse to the stable.

The second day, he came out to tell us that his uncle had said we could sit in the kitchen to eat our lunches if we wanted.

On the third day, he sat under a tree on the far side of the garden and read a book. I wanted to know the book title so badly that it was ridiculous. Why did I care what he was reading? He was a stuck-up prick who said I looked like a gypsy.

Since I was only working three days with Luke, I stayed home the next two, reading Pratchett and trying not to think about the weird-nosed boy – Caspien – at Deveraux House.

The following Tuesday, he rode the horse again, past where Luke, Harry, Ged and I hacked and cut at what felt like a hundred years' worth of weeds. I hated gardening. I hated it more in the painfully hot sunshine. I tried to think of my laptop, the reason I was doing all of this. But that, for some reason, made me wonder what kind of laptop *he* had. A MacBook Pro, probably. I hated him.

I watched him from the corner of my eye as he trotted past us and down the incline, head held up and a snooty expression on his face – as though everything were beneath him, including me. When he reached the flat, he kicked his heel into the horse's side and lowered his body just as the horse took off at a sprint. I watched them until they became a small blob in the distance.

"He's training for the Olympics, apparently," Luke said, huffing from exertion.

"Who?" I said, whacking a particularly stubborn bracket of weeds.

"Caspien."

I made a snorting sound. His name really was ridiculous. Caspien. Who on earth called their kid Caspien? I didn't like how Luke said it, either. Like he knew him. When he'd first told me his name on the way home that first Tuesday, I'd felt a weird sensation in my gut. A fluttering. Like nerves or fear. Which I didn't understand because I wasn't afraid of him. I could take him easily.

I learned a little more about Caspien each day I went there. And sometimes, even when I hadn't gone there, Luke would come home and offer some new and incredibly predictable fact about him: he went to school in Switzerland, because of course, he did. He spoke three languages. Not only was he good enough to ride his horse at the Olympics, but he could also play tennis like a professional and was excellent at fencing. *Fencing.* Fencing was for James Bond films.

On the fifth day, Luke sent me to the large conservatory on the east side of the house and asked me to take some photos and clear out anything 'that hadn't ever been alive'. Now, there was a distinction, which I'd been taught early on. Some plants died off in the winter months and looked dead, but would grow back in the spring. I needed to leave these be for now, and Luke would decide what should go when we were replanting.

The position of the conservatory meant that it was in the sun for the first portion of the day. It was almost brutal until I flung open the French doors at the far end. Then, the place became almost pleasant to work in.

I was going to use the small toilet beneath the kitchen stairs when Caspien appeared in front of me. He had his nose stuck in a book and a half-eaten apple in his other hand as he walked out from a room to my left and almost into me.

I managed to see *The Count of Monte Cristo*. It was an aged hardback with a navy cloth-bound cover. I hadn't read it, and I hated that I hadn't.

Before we collided, I stepped out of his way.

He stopped, lifted his pale gaze from his book, and fixed it on me instead.

I was covered in dirt, sweat, and grass stains while he stood looking immaculate in another big shirt, shorts, and those brown house slippers—also too big.

"Oh, it's you," he said before taking a bite of his apple. He sounded almost bored, but his gaze was sharp and terrible. I felt like an insect under a microscope.

"Hey," I replied. It was the weirdest sound I'd ever made. "I'm in the conservatory today," I said as though to prove to him I knew actual words.

"Arboretum," he said.

"What?"

He smiled with one side of his mouth and bit into his apple again. It felt like he'd caught me doing something I should be embarrassed about, but I'd no clue what.

"It's called an *arboretum*, gypsy."

He skirted past me and headed toward the stairs. When I turned to look at him his head was lowered, reading again. Christ, I loathed this boy. Hated him. Hated the way my voice shook when I spoke to him. The way my body trembled nervously at his closeness. Hated the way his eyes made me feel small and insignificant. I hated *everything* about him.

"Don't forget to wash your hands after," he said without looking back.

I had an image of charging after him, grabbing him by the hair and forcefully slamming him against something until he cried. Instead, I watched as he turned a corner and disappeared upstairs.

When I turned, I almost pissed myself. A man stood in the entry-way of the room the twat had just come out of.

Then, I'd taken him to be in his fifties, perhaps even older. It was a child's way of guessing the age of adults, because Gideon was forty-one when I met him. His hair was dark with some grey at the temples, and he stood tall with angular, sharp cheekbones and a long-pointed chin. Navy eyes glittered like sapphires, and his red slash of a mouth smiled strangely at me.

"And you must be Jude," he said and came toward me. "Finally we meet."

Neither his expression or tone was unkind, but there was something in his eyes that made me feel slightly uneasy.

"I'm Gideon." He stretched out his left hand. "Gideon Deveraux."

This was the mad queen of Deveraux? I knew that he was a lord, though he never took his seat in the house, and that he was rich, though he'd let the house fall into some disrepair. I knew he lived alone in a mansion that had his name with only his nephew. This last was something people liked to talk about in town though I'd rarely paid it any attention, imagining the nephew to be a young child. My own mind being that of a child, I didn't really understand the implication of the rumour at the time.

Lord Gideon Deveraux was dressed impeccably in a three-piece morning suit with a brocade waistcoat – the kind a groom might wear to a wedding. I'd rarely see him in anything else in all my time at Deveraux. Knowing what I came to know, I wonder if it was indeed the suit he'd imagined himself being married in.

I stared, a little open-mouthed. I'd never seen a picture of him and had imagined him to be some old, grey, stooped man. But he wasn't. He was young and handsome; dark hair cut neatly, and blue eyes that always seemed to be smiling.

"Hi, sir, Lord, Deveraux," I tried, stammering like an idiot. I was so glad Caspien wasn't here to witness it. I tried again. "I'm Jude, sir. Luke's nephew."

He smiled wider. "Nice to meet you, Jude, Luke's nephew." He shook my hand firmly. His own was ice cold. "And I see you've met mine." He gestured in the direction the twat had just gone in.

I tried to keep my face impassive as I gave a nod. I suspected I'd failed when Gideon laughed.

"He can be very sharp-tongued," Gideon said, before lowering his head so that he could whisper. "Would you believe that he really is a sweet boy underneath?"

"No." It was out before I could stop it. My cheeks burned. My bladder ached.

Gideon laughed louder and placed a hand on my shoulder.

"I like honesty, young Jude. It's so rare these days. Caspien is rather dreadfully insincere." This was said as though it was an admirable quality. "Tell me, how are my gardens coming along? Your uncle promised he could restore them to their former glory. Did he overpromise?" He looked out in the direction of the gardens.

"Luke is the best gardener in The Channel Islands, Sir Lord Deveraux."

"Oh, Gideon is fine," he said, waving me off. "Is he now? Well then if anyone can bring this dead old thing back to life then it is the best gardener in Channel Islands." He looked at me. "*And* his nephew."

I gave him my most enthusiastic smile. "We'll try our best, sir – Gideon."

I left him staring out at the garden as I skirted past him quickly to the bathroom emptying my overfull bladder into the rose-pink toilet bowl.

We were driving home when I asked Luke: "Do you think it's weird that they live there together, just the two of them?"

Luke was the nicest person I knew. I could count on one finger how many times I'd heard him say anything bad about anyone. And that was because some guy refused to pay him for a month's work on a holiday cottage down in Brown Bay. He took him to court and got the money but it took almost a year. Even then he hadn't called the guy a wanker with the same fervour that Caspien Deveraux had called me a gypsy.

"Well, do you think if something happened to Beth – god forbid." He patted his head. "That it would be weird for you to live with me?"

"No."

"Exactly. So I don't think it's weird, no. People like to talk about all sorts of things that don't concern them. Most of the horrible stuff people say is just in their own twisted heads."

I thought about that. "Is that what happened then? Did something happen to his mum?" I couldn't bring myself to say his name.

"Yeah. I'm not sure of the full story, mind you. Again, lots of nonsense people have likely made up. But after she passed away, Caspien lived with his uncle. She was Gideon's sister. So it makes sense from where I stand." He shot me a warm smile.

"What about his dad?"

"No one knows," said Luke. "Well, someone knows. But not me. I'm not one for gossip. We're just there to fix his garden."

I nodded, thinking about Gideon Deveraux and how desperate he sounded when he asked if we could bring his garden back to life. I really hoped we could. I tried not to think about how similar Caspien and I were; of how we'd both lost our parents and how we went to live with our uncles, and how if he wasn't such a horrible snooty twat, we might have had something in common we could talk about.

We might even have been friends.

"I met him today," I told Luke as I stared out the window. "Lord Deveraux."

"Yeah? He's nice enough, isn't he?"

"Yeah…nice enough."

That night at dinner, Beth told Luke she was pregnant. They both cried while I smiled and ate my spaghetti.

THREE

Back then, I was sure my sister hated me. I was certain the resentment she felt at having to look after me when our parents died was a little too all-consuming for her to love me properly. She'd been married to Luke just over a year when the accident happened. They'd just moved into their first home - Luke was born in Jersey and they'd met online before she'd moved here to be with him. They were newlyweds looking forward to starting their own life together and then I, a moody, bookish eight-year-old who'd just lost his parents, was foisted upon her.

I was a 'surprise' to my parents, born the year after my sister left home for university. I'm not sure what they were thinking, or if they'd been thinking at all; they'd just gotten rid of one child and now here was another one to tie them down for a further eighteen years. Since I'd popped out when my sister was eighteen, our relationship had never been a usual sibling one. We'd never lived in the same house and we had no shared childhood memories. She'd stopped being a child long before I came along and so when I moved into the house she shared with Luke, I was like a blood relative she didn't know very well.

If my sister had been a different sort of person, our lack of a sibling connection might have made it easier for her to fall into the role she'd been expected to take up. But my sister wasn't a very maternal person. It wasn't a failing, it just didn't seem to be in her genetic make-up at all. She wasn't warm or particularly loving and in fact, there was a distinct coldness to her that made little sense to me since my mother had been almost overbearing in her affection for people. At least, that's how I remember her. Smothering, but kind, open-hearted and generous.

So my sister's teary emotional reaction to being pregnant was a bigger shock than the news itself.

Also, it meant we would have to move.

Luke and Beth still lived in the quaint two bedroom house they'd had since they got married and now we needed a nursery. They spoke about it over dinner, about how they could have the cot in their bedroom for a little while, but obviously not long term. My sister had given me a look that made me think she was going to ask me to move out, but then Luke reached across and grabbed my hand and squeezed it.

"You're gonna be a big brother, Judey. How you feeling?"

"Uncle," I corrected. "I'm gonna be an uncle."

"Now you'll know how it feels." He grinned. 'You scared? It's fine if you are."

I didn't know what to say. How *was* I feeling? I was definitely a little scared. Unsettled. Anxious. Sort of too big for my own skin as my sister stared at me and mentally redecorated my room into a nursery.

"I'm looking forward to it." I settled on, and Luke squeezed my hand again.

"We can start looking at places tonight," he said, turning to Beth.

"I'm sure there's enough equity in this place by now. And if not, I can leverage some against Green's."

Beth nodded, biting her lip. "Well, now that I'm pregnant, my chance at promotion is stymied until I'm back from maternity leave, at least. And the holiday will need to be off. We'll need every spare penny we can save, babe."

Luke nodded and shovelled a forkful of spaghetti into his mouth.

I had one thought in my head and it wasn't babies or holidays or nurseries. It was whether this meant I wasn't going to get my new laptop.

Three weeks later, the answer to everyone's prayers came from a most unexpected source:

Caspien.

The sun wasn't as hot as that first day we'd come, but there was little wind and even less cloud cover, so it wasn't far off it. When it was lunchtime, we retreated inside out of the blaze to eat in the house's large, mainly unused kitchen. Stone walls and floor and high windows kept the space cool, and I slunk onto the bench and pressed my back against the cold wall.

Luke was talking about the baby, about names and his hopes that if it were a boy, he'd like dinosaurs and space, and how if it were a girl, she'd look like Beth when Caspien walked in. Today, he was wearing a striped blue and white linen shirt – too big as always – and white shorts some way above the knee. His long hair was twisted up into a knot like a girl's, though some wisps of blonde tangled about his face. He wasn't wearing his slippers today but strode towards the fruit bowl, feet bare and smooth legs lightly tanned.

He looked …ridiculous.

No boy I knew would be seen dead dressed like that. Not in front of another boy. Men, even.

But Caspien looked relaxed. Cool and clean and refreshed. He looked French or something.

He snatched up a bright green apple, tossed it into the air, then took a bite of it. When he turned, Luke swallowed his mouthful of tea and lifted his hand in a friendly wave.

"Caspien, how's things?" Luke asked in that same friendly tone he used with everyone.

I hadn't seen them interact before and didn't know how Caspien might react. I braced myself for some scathing comment.

I almost choked on my water when he smiled. I'd never seen him smile before – properly smile – and it made my stomach feel funny.

"Fine, Mr Green, trying not to expire in this disgusting heat. It must be hellish out there."

"I've told you, it's just Luke. And we're used to it, aren't we, lads?" Luke smiled amiably. Harry and Ged mumbled their assent through their sandwiches.

"Make sure you take regular breaks out of the heat and help yourselves to the water in the fridge," Caspien was saying. *Kindly.*

My eyes were wide, my mouth too. Who on earth was this person?

"Will do, will do. Thanks, lad."

Caspien smiled and moved to pour two glasses of water himself before turning to offer us one. When we accepted, he walked over and refilled all our glasses from a jug with ice and lemon, with calm, steady hands. Even mine.

He didn't look at me as he did it.

"Oh, Luke has some news," Ged said to Caspien. Like they were friends. Like he might care. Like he was a normal person who could hold a conversation without biting like a small, blonde, venomous snake.

"News?" Caspien asked, eyebrows raised in interest. He glanced expectantly at Luke.

I was still staring at Caspien like he had grown a second head. I honestly did not recognise this person as the same one who'd spat *gypsy* at me outside on the first day, or the word *arboretum* at me last week. They were two distinctly different people, and I didn't understand why I hadn't been allowed to meet this one when Luke, Ged, and Harry had. Something hot and bitter simmered in my veins.

"Yeah, Beth's pregnant," Luke said, face undeniably filled with joy and happiness.

"You're going to be a dad?" Caspien said, eyebrows raising. "That's amazing, Mr. Green. Congratulations! You'll be smashing."

Smashing. I almost snorted. Who said 'smashing' like that? What was he, fifty?

"Ah, thanks, thanks. We're excited." Luke glanced at me. "Means we have to move, but it's time we got a bigger place anyway."

Caspien frowned. "You're moving?"

"Well, not yet. But we've been looking. We'll have to go a bit out of town to get something for our budget, but we'll make it work." He was smiling wide, but I felt guilty all over again. For taking the room that should have been a nursery. For existing.

Caspien was biting his lip thoughtfully. "Will that mean you can't work for Uncle Gideon anymore?"

"God, no, 'course not. Just means we have to drive a bit longer in the mornings. Which is no bad thing, Judey is great company first thing."

My head snapped towards Luke, who winked at me.

"Judey," Caspien repeated, eyes darkening with something I didn't like. "Is he now?"

"Nah, he's a bit of a grump first thing, truth be told. Takes him at least an hour to wake up."

My cheeks felt hot. From the fact that Caspien knew anything about how I woke up, that he knew Luke called me Judey. That we had to move a little out of town because Luke couldn't afford a bigger house in Gorey.

I slid a weird half-smile at Luke and stood. "Need the toilet," I said and tried not to run as I put distance between me and the pony-tailed boy at my back.

The moment Beth got through the door, Luke had told her. Beth listened intently, confusion growing with each word.

"I don't understand," Beth exclaimed a little breathlessly.

Luke was grinning wide. "It's crazy, right? But it's perfect, babe.

Wait until you see it."

"He's just...giving it to you, rent-free?"

"To us." Luke seemed to remember I was there and turned to where I sat on the sofa, gripping the second-hand copy of *1984* in my lap. "I mean, it needs some work, but nothing I can't do myself. He said if we accept it, he'd get contractors in straight away to check the essentials: electrics, water, heating. The decoration I can do when I'm not working. It's perfect, Beth. You'll love it."

"Why would he do this?" Beth shook her head, genuinely confused.

I couldn't blame her. I was, too. I'd seen the cottage, and it was in fine condition. It would rent for a fortune if he'd wanted to do that. Four bedrooms, a large living room, a generous garden at the front, an even bigger one at the back that looked out onto a lake. A lake. And Lord Sir Gideon Deveraux was offering it to Luke and Beth, and me, to help us out.

It made no sense. But it was happening. It had happened.

Before we'd finished up for the day, Gideon called Luke in for a chat about the contract while we waited in the vans. I half wanted Luke to come back and tell us Gideon was unhappy with our work and that we should finish up at the end of the week. That way, I'd never have to look at Caspien Deveraux again. Of course, that would be a disaster for Luke, Beth and the baby, and I didn't want that.

Not really.

As we drove back, Luke told me what Gideon had said. He was offering Luke a job, and it wasn't the one we'd come here to do. He was offering Luke the job of head groundsman at Deveraux House.

He said there hadn't been a live-in groundsman at Deveraux House for almost twenty years. Luke had told him that he owned Green's Gardening Group and that he'd not want to give up his own business. Gideon had an answer for that, too. He'd invest in Green's to allow Luke to hire a regional manager if he wished. Maybe they could even set up a satellite branch on the mainland.

Then Luke could help restore Deveraux, which would look great on the company testimonial page while keeping Green's running,

too. The icing on the cake was that it was a live-in position. It came
with a four-bedroom, two-storey stone cottage about a mile from
Deveraux on the eastern side of the estate. This was all incredibly
fortuitous and completely unbelievable to me as I sat there, stunned.
But the most incredible part was still to come: Gideon had said
that my living on the estate meant I could be of some company to
Caspien. Caspien, who didn't really have any friends in this country
and who could benefit from hanging out with someone his own age.

"No way. I hate him," I told Luke when I finally lifted my jaw
from the van's footbed.

"Oh, come on. He's a little posh, sure, but he's got a good heart."

I glowered at Luke. "Actually, I'm not sure he has one at all, Luke."

"Judey," he chided. "You know, I'm sure it was his idea."

I laughed at that but it came out sounding all weird. "That we be
friends? I doubt it; he bloody hates me."

Luke glanced at me sideways. "Thought you hated *him*?"

"Well, it's both. We hate each other. We're not gonna be friends,
Luke."

"Hmmm. Well, let's see," said Luke diplomatically. "But no, I
meant the cottage. I think he was the one who suggested it to Deveraux. It had to have been. How'd Gideon know we needed a new
place to live for the baby?"

This made a strange crawling sensation move over my chest.

"Well, maybe he just mentioned to his uncle about the baby, and
it was Deveraux's idea." I'm not sure why I hated the notion that
Caspien had done something…thoughtful. Something that had
helped us out. Something nice for someone. I thought about the way
he'd spoken with Luke, all soft and sweet and polite, and I hated
that too. He didn't fool me. He was a nasty little shit, and if he had
been the one to suggest it, then I was certain there was something
underhand in it.

Except right now, I couldn't figure out what that might be.

"He said we can drive up and see it tonight. Or tomorrow, whatever you want. But it's perfect, Bethy. I think you're gonna love it,"
Luke told her. He was literally shining with joy. Beth was uncertain,

like she wanted to let go of the edge and fall into full-blown joy but was scared to.

"What did you think of it?" she asked me.

I was so shocked that she cared what I thought at all that I just blinked at first, thoughts trying to scramble into something I could voice. *Neighbours* with Caspien? Seeing him more than I already did? Even when school started again, and I didn't have to work with Luke, there was gonna be the potential to see him every day. I hated the thought of it. It made my gut ache.

But if we moved there it would mean they didn't need to use all their savings on a new place, and she'd maybe hate me less, and I probably wouldn't have to change schools.

School.

Caspien went to school in Switzerland.

When school started, he'd leave. I wouldn't have to see him for months, if at all.

He'd leave, I'd still get my new laptop, and things would go back to the way they were before. And it *was* a nice cottage.

"It was nice," I said finally. "I liked it."

Beth smiled, biting her lips. Then she nodded. "Okay, let's go see it tomorrow."

I wonder now just how different things would have been had Beth hated the Groundsman cottage. I'd likely never have seen Caspien again after that summer. He'd have been a boy I'd had some weird feelings about when I was fifteen. That would have been it. But she hadn't hated it.

She'd taken one look at its ivy-covered walls, white window trims, and stone path leading up to the front door, and almost squealed.

Gideon got contractors in that same week. Luke would do some work on it when he could this summer, and we'd move in when school stopped in October – that way it wouldn't interfere too much with my schedule.

It did mean that there was a possibility Caspien would be there while we carried our stuff into the house. He'd probably sneer at our furniture from his horse. I could only hope fancy schools in

Switzerland had different holidays from normal English ones.

FOUR

It was my last day working at the house before school started. A Friday.

It was a day as warm as all the others that had come before it. The next day, we were due to go to town to buy my new laptop and I was fantasising about it. About the stories I could write and the games I could download. It was for school, but the memory on it would mean I could use it for way more than the old model of Beth's I'd been fighting with for the last two years.

I was still in the arboretum in the afternoon when the sun was highest. I had been five days in there while Luke, Harry, and Ged punched and rolled over soil. I'd worked hard though, and the place was almost clear; the dead stuff was gone; the old tools and pots had been thrown in the skip, and I was weeding carefully around a circular bed in the furthest corner.

Something was alive here, and I didn't

want to kill it. Luke always said that killing plants was like killing animals and you should avoid it unless you couldn't. They had feelings, apparently. It had sounded like a stupid notion to me at first, but at some point, I'd taken it on as my own.

I was singing quietly to myself when I sensed a presence in the arboretum with me.

I turned to see Caspien standing at the opposite end of the large space, a few feet inside it. He'd voluntarily entered the room I was in, and the notion made my hands tremble. He was staring at me hard – or so I thought. Actually, he was looking behind me, an odd, far-off look on his face. So far, none of our interactions had gone well, and so I expected no different from this one.

Just being in the same room as him made me feel tense, nervous, and faintly sick.

I decided that the best thing to do would be not to engage. So I turned back to the plant and scraped about at its base, trying to dig out the weeds surrounding the roots so I could lay some fresh soil on top.

The glasshouse was already airless and hot, but with him inside, it felt like a vacuum. Sweat pooled at the back of my neck and trickled down my spine, spider-soft.

"My uncle said this was my mother's favourite room of the whole house," he said.

I was so shocked that he'd spoken and that it wasn't an insult, I was momentarily stunned.

Caspien continued, "He said she was obsessed with flowers and plants. Like Luke, I suppose."

Was this...a conversation? It sounded like one, but the idea of it was so alien that I really wasn't sure. My brain scrambled for something to say. Anything. Intelligent or otherwise.

Momentarily, I considered being as cruel to him as he had been to me. I should tell him I didn't give a shit about his dead mother, that she could be nothing like Luke if she had given birth to the literal spawn of Satan. But I couldn't do it. His voice was soft. Softer than I'd ever heard it, small and soft as a child's.

I hated how it made me feel, hated that it made me feel anything at all. Because I *hated* him.

But then, without conscious thought to the words, I was talking.

"Well, maybe when we're done, you can plant something she'd have liked," I said. My voice sounded dry and scratchy. It was from the heat.

Caspien blinked as though coming slowly out of a trance. He'd been lingering just inside the threshold of the glasshouse like he was afraid to come inside, but now he walked towards me in that strange way he did. Determined and precise. A predator, I thought suddenly, a predator stalking forward to me, the prey. *That* was how he walked.

His hair was down about his face, one side tucked behind an ear. Ears that looked small and kind of girlish. I'd have to look at some more ears to decide if they were girly or not, but they looked delicate with their soft pink lobes. His nose was still the weirdest one I'd ever seen. A little flattened dip in its point that drew your eye.

Derailing my thoughts about ears and noses, he stopped, closer than he'd ever been to me by choice. I was still kneeling by the circular bed, so I glanced at his feet first. Golden pink toes peeking out of those slippers. They were fine-boned and dusted with faint golden hair. I stood, and the scent of something floral fluttered in the space between us. Something sweet and hot that wasn't coming from the flowers but from him. That scent and his proximity caused my stomach to cartwheel wildly.

He stared at me for what must have been a whole minute; my eyes and then my mouth, the base of my throat and then back up to my eyes again. I felt peeled raw and exposed.

"Our uncles think that now that you will be living here on the estate, we should be friends."

"Yeah, I know."

"What do you think about that?"

I thought about it for a moment. Or rather, how to reply to it. I already knew what I thought about it.

But he hadn't said anything awful to me in about three minutes and I felt a little exhilarated from it. Hopeful and stupid.

"I'm pretty sure to be friends, we'd have to like each other."

Some light went off in his eyes and his mouth tilted up very slightly.

He said, "Do you not like me, Judey?"

I considered telling him that no, I fucking hated him. But we were going to be living in his garden, working in his house, and if he was the reason his uncle had offered Luke and Beth the cottage, then perhaps he had the power to have the offer withdrawn too. And it would be my fault if he did.

"Don't call me that."

"What should I call you then?"

"My name," I said, and he gave me an expectant look. "Jude."

He gave a half shrug. "Fine. Answer my question, *Jude*. Do you not like me?"

"Why do you even care? You hate me too."

He smiled at that. A cold, half-formed thing.

"I never said I cared. I asked if you did."

This made something hot flare up inside me. Through clenched teeth, I said. "I think it's pretty obvious we're not going to be friends. We hate each other."

"I didn't know your name until ten seconds ago. How can I hate you?" He shook his head like it was the most ridiculous thing he'd ever heard.

"Whatever." I dropped to my knees again and returned to the plant, reaching out to pull at a particularly stubborn stem that had tangled itself around one of the window frames. "I think we should just stay out of each other's way."

Without warning, Caspien's hand wrapped tightly around my wrist. With a strength that surprised me, he yanked my arm back away from the stem.

I turned to glare at him.

"You are an idiot," he hissed.

"Yeah, well, you're a horrible, stuck-up little prick. So..." I tried to pull my hand out of his grip, but it was surprisingly strong.

"*Oleander,*" he hissed, like it explained why he was about to snap my bloody wrist.

I blinked at him, confused.

"It is a plant toxic to humans. Though I wonder if that would even apply to you." He gave me a disdainful look. "Didn't your uncle teach you anything?"

I looked at the raggedy stem and stepped back from it.

"I...didn't know."

"Did you touch it before I got here?"

"I...don't think so."

"You don't think so?"

"I didn't. I was..." I looked at it. Then at the pile of weeds I'd pulled up. They weren't the same. "I didn't touch it."

"Did you eat it?"

I looked at him. "Of course, I didn't eat it."

He looked unconvinced like I might just be that fucking stupid.

"Then you probably aren't going to die," Caspien said.

"Probably?" My heart was beating too fast in my chest. I felt faint and a little dizzy. Was I dying? *Had* I touched it?

"Come with me," he said, pulling me by my wrist up and out of the arboretum.

He led me through the house to the kitchen and the huge sink, where he turned on the taps. He left me standing there as he disappeared into the storage cupboard and returned with bleach, a bar of pink soap, and a dishtowel. He poured some bleach onto the towel and scrubbed my hands, front and back and between the fingers. Then he lathered up the pink soap – it smelled awful as the suds started to form – and washed my hands for me.

He never spoke. Just diligently scrubbed the potential poison from my hands, rinsed, and then repeated. He did it three times, then told me to wash them myself with the antibacterial handwash that sat on the sink tray.

I did as instructed while he returned the bleach and threw away the soap. When he came back with a glass of water, he ordered me to drink it all.

When I had done it, he asked how I felt.

I still felt a little dizzy, my head a little big, and my body a little tight and breathless, but I was certain it was not because I had toxic plant poisoning.

"Fine," I said.

"I'm going to get Luke," Caspien said. "It's his call whether you should go to the hospital or not." He moved to go.

"Uh, thanks for that," I said.

Caspien stopped, looking uncomfortable. I expected him to say something predictably dick-ish.

"It would have been inconvenient if you'd died in my uncle's arboretum," he said before disappearing out of the backdoor and into the sunshine.

Luke was livid. With himself. He said he should have inspected the greenhouse before sending me in there. These plants were native to the Mediterranean and he hadn't even considered that they might be in there, but he should have checked.

Caspien told him in a very responsible and calm voice what he'd done: he'd checked that I hadn't eaten it, that he'd washed my hands with bleach first and then carbolic soap, and that there were no signs of a rash or irritation.

Luke asked me again how I felt, and it was then that Gideon had arrived.

"I am so desperately sorry, Luke. I had no idea. Seraphina had all sorts of seedlings imported – I never considered it could have been anything poisonous."

"It's not your fault, Lord Deveraux. It's mine," Luke said.

Caspien looked at me. His eyes said it wasn't Luke's fault either; it was mine.

"How are you, young Jude? You look well?" Deveraux asked me.

"I'm fine. I feel fine."

"He didn't eat it," Caspien said.

Gideon nodded.

"Caspien's looked after him," Luke said, shooting a grateful look at my saviour before inspecting my hands again. My forearms and my face. "I think we had a lucky escape. You'll tell me if you start feeling sick? Any pain in your stomach?"

"I didn't eat it," I said again.

Luke ruffled my hair and swore with relief.

"I've got a contractor I deal with for toxic plants. I've called him. He can be here tomorrow to remove it."

Gideon told him to add whatever it cost to his invoice. I was told to sit and read my book for the rest of the afternoon, where Luke could see me in case I went into cardiac arrest. It all felt very dramatic, but I wasn't too annoyed at not having to do any more work that day.

I sat there looking as though I was reading, as though I was taking in a single word on the page, but I wasn't. I was instead thinking about what Caspien had done. How quickly he'd rushed to help me. How carefully and thoroughly he'd washed my hands, and how he'd almost looked concerned about whether I might die.

It would have been very inconvenient if you'd died in my uncle's arboretum.

Inconvenient.

Well, I'd thanked him, and that was that. I didn't owe him anything else. But it annoyed me that I was sitting there thinking about him and whether it meant I had to be nice to him now. I wanted to go right back to loathing the posh twat.

I was lost in those thoughts when the most beautiful sound I'd ever heard began to flutter out of Deveraux House. It was faint, as though being carried to me by the breeze that had travelled in with the lowering of the sun. It was coming from the other side of the house.

It was a piano; of that much I was certain. It didn't surprise me that there was a piano in there; it wouldn't surprise me if there was a whole orchestra in there. I rose, closing my book and wandering in the direction of the noise. Around the side of the house was a covered stone patio that ran the length of this side, and about halfway down were a set of glass-panelled doors that opened outward. The music poured out from inside.

As I approached the open doors, the melody changed, turning into something mournful. Beautiful still, but with a sad undercurrent that pulled me closer to it. I crept quietly, feeling like a trespasser, a thief and a peeping tom all at once.

Inside, Caspien sat with his back to the open doors, his fingers flying over the keys of a large black piano. His head was lowered and focused. The song was urgent now but then slowed again. It meandered, flowing from delicate to chaotic, joyous and then heart-breaking. Looping over and back on itself in a spellbinding cadence. I'd never seen anyone play a piano in real life before, and I couldn't believe what I was seeing. That something so beautiful and delicate and emotional could come from him.

This cruel, horrible menace of a person had done two things today to change the way I looked at him.

I moved toward him without thought, desperate to be closer to the noise and to him, and it was only when he lifted his head that I stopped and held my breath.

The music reached a pinnacle of some kind; a repetitive disconsolate section that made goosebumps rise up on the back of my neck and arms. His head dropped again, and he shook it, his right foot moving furiously but with purpose.

After the crescendo, it slowed again, a light tinkering before it faded to a deafening empty silence.

Caspien wasn't moving.

"You have played it better," said a voice said from my right.

My head snapped around to find Gideon sitting by another open door a little further down. His legs were crossed at the knee and he had a newspaper on it. He was watching me very closely. I stopped breathing.

"Then perhaps you should try playing it instead?" Caspien said, standing. He didn't sound insulted, just mildly bored. "Am I dismissed now?"

"Of course, make sure you take Falstaff for his ride before it gets too dark."

Caspien nodded and slid out from behind the piano, and strode from the room.

Then I was alone with Gideon Deveraux and his calculating stare.

"I'm sorry," I offered when I was certain Caspien was out of earshot.

"Oh, you've nothing to apologise for, Jude." He waved a hand before glancing in the direction Caspien had gone. "He's rather remarkable, isn't he?"

It wasn't the first word that came to mind when I thought about Caspien.

"He's talented."

"Yes. He's exceptional at most things he does. La Troyeux say he could be an equestrian, a professional tennis player, an artist, or a pianist. Achingly beautiful too, which seems extremely unfair. He'll break a thousand hearts, I'm sure of it."

He looked me dead in the eye as he said this. I didn't know what to say. It felt strange to hear his uncle call him beautiful.

I didn't think it was something Luke would ever say about me, though maybe that was because I wasn't beautiful. I wasn't ugly; I knew that. I knew girls liked what they saw when they looked at me. But I also knew I wasn't what anyone would call beautiful.

Caspien was, I supposed, beautiful. If a boy could be beautiful, then yes, he was. Objectively. He had slightly girlish features and soft skin. He smelled sweet and clean. His hands were shapely and pretty with long, elegant fingers. Fingers that could command horses, play piano, and wash poison from my skin.

Gideon was waiting for me to say something. I hoped it wasn't that Caspien was beautiful because that wasn't something I'd ever say out loud.

"I am so happy you're going to be living here, truly, Jude."

"We are, too." It was half a lie. *Luke* was happy. Beth, too. I was mainly concerned about my soon-to-be-normal proximity to his beautiful, talented, exceptional nephew.

"I think you could be very good for him, you know," Gideon said.

My stomach quivered with dread as I glanced in the direction he'd gone. "Um, I don't know if we really..."

"I told you, he's prickly but soft underneath." Gideon cut me off gently, closing his newspaper and setting it on the table by the chair.

"Like a hedgehog then?" I said.

Gideon laughed. "Yes, exactly. And he doesn't have many friends, you see."

I wanted to say: Yeah, and I know why.

"And I think a good, dependable boy like you is just what he needs." Gideon came towards me, a look on his face like he was sizing me up for a task he had complete confidence in me for. I stood taller. "Your uncle says you like to read." He glanced at the book in my hand.

"Yes, sir."

"That you want to write books one day?"

My cheeks warmed. Luke had told him that. Christ, did Caspien know? I felt sick. I wasn't embarrassed about it, but I knew that it sounded frivolous and childlike. Not like wanting to be a doctor, a lawyer, or an engineer. I was sure wanting to be a writer was something Caspien would make fun of.

"I'd like to try, yes." I smiled.

Gideon nodded. "Well, trying is the first part of doing. He gave me an encouraging smile. "Look, we have rather an impressive library here, the biggest on the island the last time I checked." He crossed the room in a different direction from the one Caspien had gone and pushed open a door that was built almost into the wall.

I followed, confused but excited. I loved libraries. There was a small one in town and an even smaller one in school. Stacks of books comforted me – their smell, their weight, their possibility. On a Saturday afternoon, I'd hide in the aisles of Brown's in town and lose myself for hours while Luke and Beth did the grocery shop.

Gideon led the way down a dank-smelling corridor with no natural light before shoving open another door. He pushed it wide and stepped aside to let me in behind him.

My mouth fell open.

It was a library straight from a picture book about what libraries should look like. Rows of books from floor to ceiling, a second mezzanine wrapped around the room's upper part, and which appeared to be accessed via an iron spiral staircase. Behind the staircase to the mezzanine was a little reading nook. A pair of leather couches faced each other in the centre of the room, with a table covered with more books. Two large arched windows on one side of the room provided light, both with comfortable-looking window seats at their bases.

I had an image of Caspien curled up in one, his slippers kicked off and his hair pulled up, and I got a rush of something hot in my chest. Jealousy, I told myself.

"This is...crazy."

"You like it?"

"It's awesome, Lord Deveraux."

"If you're going to be living here, Jude, I really must *insist* you call me Gideon. All this lord nonsense makes me feel like my father."

"Okay...Gideon." It felt strange, but I would get used to it.

"Much better." Gideon beamed, moving into the library. He swept his hand out. "Now, these are all very old books; some have been in our family for years, but this section here is more modern, though Seraphina was more interested in romance and ghost stories. I'm not sure you'll find anything to your liking here either." This was the second mention of Seraphina today and I realised with a shock that this had to be Caspien's mother.

He gestured toward a few low shelves of books beneath one of the windows. "These were her favourites." He turned to me. "How about you make a list of books and authors you like, and I can order some in and update these shelves a little? I would ask Caspien what is popular amongst teenagers, but he reads Russian and French Literature almost exclusively, and there's plenty of that here already."

Russian and French literature. Of course, he bloody did.

"I suppose it's all Harry Potter?" Gideon checked.

I lifted my book to show him what I was reading. "I don't like Harry Potter much," I said.

"George Orwell, huh? Well, there might be some of his here somewhere. In any case, I'm more than happy for you to come up here and use this place whenever you want once you're all in the cottage. It doesn't see nearly enough use these days, like most of the rooms in this house, sadly."

It was a generous offer. This was the biggest library I'd ever seen. I could lose hours in here quite happily. But there was one issue: one blonde, Russian and French literature-reading issue. And I expected it would be enough to keep me away.

"Does Caspien use it?" I asked. I didn't look at Gideon; instead, I cast my eyes along a row of books. I recognised none of the titles.

"When he's home, sometimes. But mostly, he reads in his room."

Caspien's room. I tried to imagine it. I bet it didn't have dirty socks and underwear lying around it. I bet it didn't have sweet wrappers and a row of dirty glasses on the windowsill. He'd likely have a double bed too.

Almost immediately, I averted my thoughts in a completely different direction because I didn't know why I was thinking about his bedroom or his bed.

"I can speak with Luke if you think he'll have an issue with you spending time here without him," Gideon said gently.

I turned to him. His eyes were kind and filled with understanding.

I think I knew what he was implying, but I couldn't be certain. As it was, Luke liked Gideon and was one of the few folk on the island who didn't think Gideon was a pervert.

I smiled. "He won't."

"I should speak with him anyway. Just to make sure. If you think you'll use it, that is."

I looked around the library again. Took a deep breath. The smell of leather, wood, and books was intoxicating. I imagined it in winter, with the fire lit in the large fireplace and the snow falling outside. It's how I imagined the Bodleian library at Oxford to look.

How could I say no to it?

"I'll definitely use it," I said. "I'll wait until school starts though, as I wouldn't want to get in Caspien's way. So when he's gone back to school, I'll definitely be here, a lot."

"Oh, Caspien won't be returning to Le Troyeux this term," Gideon said.

My heart shuddered loudly. "What?"

"He'll be studying here, at Deveraux, with a private tutor." Gideon's hand landed on my shoulder.

My mouth dried up. Caspien *wasn't* going to Switzerland when school started? I tried to keep my face expressionless, but I'm not sure I was very successful when the smallest of smiles pushed at the corner of Gideon's mouth.

"Which is why your company will be absolutely critical for him, I rather think. Gosh, everything is working out quite wonderfully, isn't it?"

I felt sick, but I nodded anyway.

FIVE

Though it had only one small window and smelled of old wood, my room at the cottage was more than twice the size of my room in Gorey. An old fireplace in the corner ran up from the kitchen, which meant I could smell dinner before I was called down for it.

In early winter, that fireplace would blow cold air into the room, but in early September, it was so warm and stuffy that I was grateful for it.

Another positive about the move to St. Ouen was that I didn't have to take the bus to school anymore. Despite being closer, the Deveraux estate wasn't on a bus route – there'd been talk of me cycling the three miles to pick one up – but finally, Luke said it was easier and safer to just drive me there in the morning, which meant I got to sleep in a little longer.

But my favourite thing about the cottage was the garden and the view from my bedroom window out onto the shiny surface of the lake at the end of it. The lake was more of a glorified duck pond, but it was deep enough to swim in and big enough for a rowboat I could lie in and stare up at the sky for hours – which I'd done yesterday.

We'd been living there a week, and I hadn't run into Caspien once. I also hadn't taken Gideon up on the offer to use the library, mainly because my new laptop was living up to its promise and keeping me more than entertained. However, I had pulled together a list of books which I'd give to him when I was helping Luke out on Saturday. Being back at school meant I only needed to help out on the weekends now.

So, despite my Caspien-shaped misgivings, the first week in the cottage was good, and I thought I might actually like living there after all.

I was in second period on the first day back when Alfie – my best friend – slid in next to me and said, eyes wide with disbelief: "Mum said you moved into Deveraux House!"

I'd forgotten Beth went to the same hairdresser as Alfie's mum.

I snorted, pulling my stuff out of my bag. "Not the house, you twat, the cottage. Luke's the groundsman now. Comes with the job." I shrugged like it was no big deal. Which to Alfie, it clearly was.

"Have you met him then? Everyone says he's an old pervert. And his nephew lives there with him, just the two of them." He made a face. "Weirdoooooooo."

I kept my voice level, but felt something hot rise in my chest. "He's not old or a pervert. And Caspien goes to boarding school. He's barely ever there." I wasn't sure why I told the lie.

"Oh, *Caspien,* is it?" Alfie laughed. "Caspien, the friendly ghost."

"That's Casper, you tool."

He ignored that. "Anyway, when can I come round? Always wanted to see inside."

"See inside where?" Georgia flounced down at the desk in front, a plume of something sweet and fruity drifting over us.

"Guess who's got a new gaff?" Alfie tossed a thumb in my direction. "Alcott's moved into a mansion."

"Shut up, Alfred."

Georgia stared at me, and then Ellie came towards us, smiling wide but distinctly not meeting my eye. We hadn't spoken since the night at the beach when I'd kissed her, for reasons that seemed very valid at the time, but I was struggling to remember now.

"Hey, children," she said, sinking down next to Georgia. "I cannot be pissed with this class today."

"You've been back exactly one period, Els." Georgia pointed out. "Apparently, Jude's living in a mansion."

Ellie turned to me. "What?"

"Not just any mansion either," said Alfie. "The Deveraux Mansion."

"Oh, for fuck's sake, I'm not living in the mansion."

"You moved?" Ellie looked hurt.

"Yeah, kinda." I smiled.

"Right, class, I'm here, I'm queer, and I'm ready to teach you everything I know about inheritance, variation, and evolution. Books open at chapter twelve, page thirty-six, please." Mr. Simon's eager voice cut short my friends' questions about my new living situation. Until lunchtime, at least.

"So tell us about the nephew?" Georgia said, blue eyes glittering with interest. "He's our age, right?"

We were sitting at one of the benches outside. Josh was there, too, and less interested in my new address than the rest of them. I took a bite of my sandwich and washed it down with some water, delaying the inevitable – talking about Caspien Deveraux to my friends. The shrug wasn't enough, as Georgia fluttered her hand impatiently.

"Well? Is he?"

I shrugged. "I think so, yeah. Maybe a year younger?"

"He good-looking?" she asked.

Josh and Alfie laughed, but I could see the slight unease on Alfie's face. He'd been in love with Georgia since Year Nine. Had done nothing about it, of course, except whine to Josh and me whenever we'd listen about her perfect tits and hair and eyes.

"How the hell should I know?" I say.

"Ew, homophobic much?" Georgia scowled. "A man can appreciate another good-looking man without being gay, jeez, Jude. Thought you were a grown-up."

"Yeah, Jude, I happen to think you're really fucking hot," Josh said before making a kissing face at me.

Beside me, Ellie laughed. Georgia applauded him, and I tried to decide if Caspien Deveraux was good-looking.

"I'm not homophobic, George. I just don't look at guys like that." I wasn't sure why it felt like a lie. Maybe because I'd already admitted that Caspien was beautiful on some objective level, even if I hadn't said it aloud.

She nodded, more understanding.

"What's he like, though?" This was Ellie. The boys seemed less interested.

"He's stuck up and a bit of a dick," I said honestly. *He did potentially stop you from having toxic plant poisoning, though.*

"Oh, wonder if he's on Instagram," Georgia said, pulling out her phone.

"I wanna know about the uncle," Josh said.

Alfie hit him playfully on the shoulder. "That's exactly what I said! He gives major Saville vibes, man. Old dude with a big house and all that money. My dad says he's a weirdo."

"He isn't fucking old," I half snapped. I wasn't sure why it annoyed me so much, them talking about Gideon like he was an old creeper. I didn't understand why a single guy living alone with his nephew was such a big deal to everyone. Like Luke said, would it be weird for us to live together if Beth died?

"And he's not a weirdo. He's cool, okay? He's been good to Luke and saved us from having to move to God knows where, so just... stop talking about him like that."

There was a heavy silence for a few moments until George said,

"Oh my god! I think I found him."

She shoved her phone at Ellie first, then squealed and stamped her feet like an excited toddler. "Oh, no way! He's gorgeous. He looks like a model; is he a model? Is this him, Jude?" She turned the phone around and held it under my nose. My mouth went bone dry at the sight of the picture. It was him.

He was topless in the snow, hair frozen wet and his nose and cheeks bright pink. His nipples were the same colour, but obviously, I wasn't looking at those.

"Yeah, that's him," I confirmed.

Georgia squealed again. "Oh my god, okay, we need a plan. I need a plan. I want to marry this man."

Josh and I glanced at Alfie, who had forgotten about my outburst and was focused on Georgia, who was scrolling through Caspien's Instagram thirstily. When she said the words "Georgia Deveraux" in a dreamy tone, he stood up from the bench.

"Forgot I need to see Mr. Kinnell about the game on Saturday," he announced and then stormed off in the direction of the sports complex.

Ellie and Georgia didn't look up from the screen as he went.

We were walking to fourth when Ellie caught up to me. "Hey, you."

It was the first time we'd been alone the entire day. I appreciated her waiting until we were to do this.

"Hey," I said as I kept walking.

"Soooo, thought I might have heard from you over the summer," she said, looking ahead and unbothered. "But I didn't. Not a single text. Rude."

"Shit, sorry." I smiled, knowing that it was the sort of thing my smile would make sound less pathetic.

She stopped walking and turned to me. I did the same.

"Properly," she said.

"What?"

"Apologise properly." Her dark eyes glittered not with hurt but humour, and I suddenly remembered why I kissed her that night.

She was gorgeous, yes, but mainly, it was because she wasn't like the other girls in our year. She didn't get upset over silly things.

"Sorry, Ellie. Summer was crazy...I was helping Luke out and moving house. Oh, and I found out I'm gonna be an uncle. It was a lot. I barely even saw Josh or Alfie, either."

She watched me, dark eyes and dark hair shining in the sunlight.

"And what about the night at the beach?" Her voice was soft and quiet, fragile. "Are you sorry about that, too? Cause when you never texted, I thought maybe...you regretted it."

I rubbed the back of my neck, feeling like a terrible person. "That was shitty of me. No. I didn't. I don't regret it."

She let out a soft breath of laughter and hit me lightly on the chest. "God, I'm kidding. You look like I just told you your dog died."

I laughed, relieved.

"Look, I was in Italy basically the entire summer; I hardly even thought about you. And I think, actually, it was me who kissed you. So maybe I was the one who should have texted." She was smiling wide now, and it was contagious. Yes, this was why I liked her.

I grinned. "Equal rights for women and all that."

"You know I'm all about it."

"I do."

She smiled and said nothing, silence swelling between us. I knew what I was supposed to say now. I was fifteen, and Ellie Walsh was one of the most beautiful girls at school, and she liked me. She had kissed me on the beach and called me out about not getting in touch afterwards. She'd put herself out there. I admired it.

What did it mean then that my thoughts were not about Ellie but about a half-naked Caspien Deveraux, pink and cold from the snow?

Truly, I didn't want to explore what it meant. Or why I had memorised his Instagram username, or why I was wondering why I hadn't seen him once since I moved into the groundsman's cottage. So, I pushed all those thoughts aside and forced out what I was supposed to say.

"So, do you wanna come over at some point this week and see my new mansion?" I asked Ellie with a playful grin. "We could study for that Biology exam?"

Ellie's face broke out into a wide, pretty smile.

"Yeah. I would."

Ellie came over on Friday that week. Her dad drove her to mine, Beth going outside to introduce herself, while I waited at the door. Ellie came bounding out of his range rover with her hair down and her lips glossed as her dad shouted he'd be back to pick her up at 9:30p.m.

Beth hadn't been against it when I'd asked if Ellie could come over to study. As long as we kept the door open and she was gone by ten then it was fine. Luke had given me an encouraging kind of smile.

Had I wanted Beth to put up more of a fight? To say no outright? Maybe.

But it gave me the start of a headache when I tried to understand why.

"Oh, it's cute," Ellie said as she dumped her backpack down on my bed and peered out the little window. "There's a boat in your pond."

I laughed. "Yeah, I go out on it and think sometimes."

"Dangerous." She laughed, flopping down on the bed and giving me a mischievous look. "Thinking, I mean. Not boating."

I cleared my throat. "Let me put some music on." I went to the laptop, connected to my Bluetooth speaker, and selected a Taylor Swift playlist from YouTube, who I knew both Ellie and Georgia loved. I didn't think she'd like what I'd been listening to lately, which had been a lot of instrumental piano.

Which I'd found to be great for studying and writing.

"Ah, this is your new laptop," Ellie said, sitting up. She came from the bed to where I sat at my desk and studied it. She was close, the clean floral scent of her hair brushing my cheek as she leaned in. "You got it then. Niiiiice. How is it?"

"Fast. So much faster than the old one."

"No clicking on dodgy links now; that's how you ruin it. And no porn." She gave me a knowing smile.

I laughed and turned the volume up a little. When I turned to stand, her head was close, her lips glittering pink. She smelled of strawberry ice cream and I felt a faint stirring between my legs.

It was a relief, honestly.

It meant I was normal. That I still fancied her. I'd fancied her the night on the beach and I still fancied her now.

It didn't matter that I'd scrolled Caspien's Instagram last night and had a wank in the shower after. It didn't mean anything if I was still turned on by Ellie Walsh.

The door was open slightly, but a creaky stair outside alerted the whole cottage that someone was coming up them, so I wasn't worried.

I took a deep breath and leaned in, and kissed her.

No tongue at first, but then she slid her own between my lips, and I pushed mine against it. Her hand pressed down against my thigh, far from my cock but close enough for it to suggest something else. It took no time at all for me to be hard. Ellie's mouth was hot and wet and tasted lovely. She was lovely.

So bloody lovely.

Before she left that night, she asked if I wanted to go out with her.

I said yes because there was no single reason on earth not to. Before she was home, she updated her Facebook status to 'in a relationship'.

I went to bed and checked Caspien's profile to see if there had been any new posts.

There hadn't been. I had no idea where he was. Perhaps he had returned to Switzerland after all? Maybe he'd had a fall on his horse? I didn't particularly care. It was unsettling, was all. I hated not knowing when he'd appear, sniping or hissing like a snake in the grass.

Since I had his notifications turned on, I got an alert while I read an article about the new Arctic Monkeys album.

It was a photo looking out across the estate from what I assumed was his bedroom window. Not in Switzerland, then.

Tonight, the moon was high, full, and bright, so the picture was well-lit. The grass was rich green velvet, and the shining surface of the lake was like liquid silver.

And in the fainter distance was the bright orange glow from a window of a small, thatched cottage.

A window I knew well. My bedroom window.

SIX

Alfie texted me first thing on Saturday morning:

Alf:

> **You and Ellie? Amazing mate, well done.**

I wasn't sure it was amazing. I hadn't done anything. She'd asked a yes or no question I had no real reason to say no to.

Me:

> **Cheers. You have to ask Geogia out now.**

He sent back the sweating emoji and I sent back an eyeroll. He really did need to ask Georgia. We were sick and tired of listening to him whine about it. And it was only a matter of time before someone else asked Georgia out. Most likely Jason Forrest. He'd been sniffing around her since the school play.

Downstairs, Luke and Beth were talking about decorating, so I went straight to the kitchen, poured some cinnamon squares and stood at the open back door to eat them. It was still hot. Living here limited my freedom a little in a way I hadn't considered. There was no longer a bus at the bottom of the street that I could get into town. Now I'd need Luke or Beth to drive me there, to anywhere really. But with the baby coming and with Luke having so much to do around the house and at work, I didn't like to ask. So my options were pretty limited for what to do today, not that I minded.

I finished my cereal and lumbered back into the living room.

"Anything you need help with today?" I asked Luke dutifully. "Around the house, I mean?"

"We're going out to get some paint and things at B&Q if you wanna come?"

"I'll honestly pass."

Luke grinned. "Fair enough."

"You could unpack those boxes cluttering up your room," Beth said.

"But they make really good tables to leave all my dirty dishes on."

Luke laughed as Beth rolled her eyes, and I headed upstairs for a shower.

"Can you at least hang the washing out?" Beth called up as went. "It's got about fifteen minutes left, and we're ready to go now."

When I didn't answer immediately, she yelled: "Jude!"

"I heard you! Yeah, I'll do it."

"The pegs and basket are in front of the machine, so you don't forget."

"Great idea!" I yelled back.

After showering, I lay on the bed in the hot summer early afternoon and did what most fifteen-year-olds did when they had the house to

themselves: I had a wank. It didn't happen often, so I liked to take full advantage when it did. I even left the bedroom door open.

Then I hung out the washing, eyeing the lake with desire. I wasn't sure if it was safe to swim in, but since it hadn't been one of Gideon's warnings to us when we moved in, and since there was no current, I figured it couldn't be too deadly.

Torn between unpacking the boxes and going for a swim to cool down, I realised I'd have to do one to get to the other. My swim shorts were in one of the boxes marked 'Clothes – Jude', so I upended two on my bed until I found them.

I waded into the cold lake, ha-ha-ha-ing and shh-shh-ing, and pushed out towards the middle, submerging my head to even out the temperature hitting my body. It felt great – perfect. It wasn't very deep, and it was taller than me at the centre, but not by much.

I floated on my back and backflipped under the surface, I swam to one end and then the other and dove to the bottom. Then I swam to the little row boat and climbed in, using the oar to push myself out to the centre of the lake. There, I lay on my back squinting at the sky as the boat rocked gently. I must have dozed off because the sun had moved when I blinked open my eyes. Then, a weird noise pricked at my hearing.

I ignored it at first, but it got louder. Then louder still, almost like thunder getting closer, yet there wasn't a single cloud in the sky.

When I lifted my head, I started at the sight of Caspien on horseback racing towards me. He was at full speed, as far as I could tell, and the sound of thunder was only increasing. It was like he was going to gallop right into the lake.

In fact, he was.

I sat up too quickly, clumsily, and the bad distribution of my weight toppled me headfirst into the water. When I broke the surface, he was turning Falstaff in a circle near the pond's edge as he stared at me.

"Are you drowning?" he asked without a sliver of concern.

"No!" I spat out the lake water and scrubbed a hand over my face as I grabbed for the edge of the boat. "What the hell was that? I thought you were going to come right into the water."

"Well, Falstaff is an excellent swimmer, but he's just had a heavy lunch, so I wouldn't risk it."

Was that...a joke?

I felt like an idiot bobbing there while he looked down at me imperiously from his horse. I wanted to climb back into the boat, but I wasn't sure I could do it with any agility, so I stayed put, scowling at him. His blonde hair was tied back, and he wore beige riding pants with a pale green polo shirt. His cheeks were pink from the ride.

"What?" I asked impatiently. "Why are you still here?"

"I came to speak with Luke." He cast a glance at the cottage behind me.

"He's not here. Beth isn't either."

"They left the baby home alone?"

I glowered. "If you've a message for Luke, I can pass it on. What is it?"

He gave me a long look as if he were trying to decide whether I was trustworthy. I rolled my eyes.

"My uncle wants you all to come for lunch tomorrow. 3 p.m. Do you think you're able to retain that information?"

"Don't know. Might say I never got it."

"And who do you think they'll believe, Judith? You or me?" He smiled maliciously. "Pass it on. Don't be late." With that, he turned his horse, kicked his heel, and took off at a gallop back toward the big house.

I stared at his retreating form for a bit, embarrassed, stunned, frustrated, and with dread curdling my stomach like sour milk.

"Ever heard of a phone?" I shouted after him.

Twat.

For Sunday lunch, we sat outside on the terrace – the same terrace where I'd stood watching Caspien play the piano. That day, Gideon had hired a chef and a waiter to serve us, which was weird. It felt like we'd come out for a particularly fancy meal at a place we couldn't afford.

Caspien sat beside me on my left, Beth and Luke across, and Gideon at the head with his back to the house. There was wine, of which Caspien was allowed a small half glass and which he sipped like hot tea. I hadn't wanted any but wasn't allowed it in any case. I'm sure Luke could have been persuaded, but Beth was having none of it.

I didn't particularly like alcohol anyway – not the wine we'd stolen from Josh's parents' wine fridge or the whisky we'd tried from Alfie's dad's cupboard. I didn't mind beer, but that wasn't on offer here.

Instead, I had a sugar-free 7-up with Beth while the others sipped their wine.

"So, Luke, Beth," Gideon began. "I invited Jude to come and use the library here whenever he wanted – since you told me he's a big reader – but I haven't had a chance to clear it with you both, yet. I know Caspien would love the company, too."

"That's awfully kind of you, Gideon," Beth beamed. I'd never seen her smile so much; she'd not stopped since we arrived. It was alarming. "Jude would love that too."

Jude would bloody well not, and if Beth hadn't warned me not to 'act up,' I'd have said as much.

"Yes, I suppose it'd be good to hang out with someone under forty for a change." It was Caspien who spoke. Not only did he speak, he turned his head and smiled at me. Not the mean, ugly smile he usually gave me. A real one. Pretty and warm. I blinked in shock.

"Don't let Mario hear you say that," Gideon chided. "He's only thirty-two."

"Well, he looks a lot older," Caspien retorted, somehow making it sound innocent and not mean.

"Mario is his tennis coach," Gideon explained. "Nice guy. He flies in from London twice a week. Do you play tennis, Jude? Perhaps you could join them for some lessons?"

"No," I said, hoping it would cover both questions.

"Jude used to play a bit of rugby. Was good, too." Luke smiled at me. "But he got his wrist broken on a hard tackle last year and decided to give it up."

"Which wrist?" Caspien asked me.

"Left."

He nodded, some glimmer of something in his blue eyes.

"It still hurts when I'm writing or typing for too long." I directed this at Gideon, who had a sad look on his face. "Probably wouldn't be great for tennis."

"That's a shame."

Talk moved to the baby, the cottage, and the Deveraux garden revival, which was still ongoing. The Jersey Enquirer wanted to do a feature on it, apparently. The garden, that was.

I was bored, but I was also acutely aware of the body to my left, and that alone had me on the very sharp edge of awareness. I was aware of every mouthful it took, every sip of wine it had, every slight shift it made.

He sat straight and upright and cut his food carefully. He used his napkin frequently like he'd been trained. This caused me to focus on the way I didn't sit straight, the way I slouched, and the way I dragged my food apart with the knife and fork instead of slicing it.

Today, he wore a white cotton T-shirt that looked buttery-soft, navy chino shorts, and white slip-on sandals. His hair was in flouncy golden waves about his head.

As the lunch plates were cleared, I stood to use the bathroom, desperate for some solitude. Desperate for some distance between me and Caspien where I could slouch and breathe and not feel like a dog who'd been allowed to eat at the human table. I couldn't wait to get home.

I was walking back towards the terrace when I found Caspien on his phone in the large sitting room across the hall from the arboretum. I hadn't meant to listen, not really, but when I heard the soft, pleading tone he was using, I froze.

"I can't," he was saying. "Because I'm not alone. Well, I am, but I can't do that here." His back was turned, so I couldn't make out his expression, but his voice sounded so completely different that it was shocking to me. It wasn't the mean one or the bored one he'd used with me; it wasn't even the polite one he put on for Luke. It was something else entirely. "No. You'll have to wait."

I watched as he ran his finger along the surface of a table absently. If he turned his head, he would see me, but for some reason, I couldn't make my feet move.

"Tell me," he said quietly. "Tell me what you would do to me."

He made a low, breathy noise, and a shock of heat rushed between my legs so hard and so fast that I felt dizzy from it. My face got horribly warm.

"Mmmm. Well, that sounds nice." And then he turned. He didn't look overly shocked to find me standing there.

Looking me straight in the eye, he said, "Yes, okay, I can't wait." The next noise he made was obscene, but it didn't match the look on his face. "Speak soon. Bye."

He slid his phone back into his pocket and walked toward me. I sent a prayer upward that he wouldn't look down at what was going on between my legs; I was sure I wouldn't survive that kind of public shaming. The shirt I wore was long, and I'd never cared more about the amount of material that went into making clothes until that moment.

"You know, Judith, it's basic manners not to eavesdrop on other people's conversations."

"I wasn't eavesdropping." I lied. Who on earth was he talking to like that? Did he have a girlfriend? Because there was absolutely no mistaking the sort of phone call that was.

"No? What were you doing then? Just looking at me?"

"Oh, as if." I turned to go.

"He's not going to stop, you know."

I stopped and turned back. "Who?"

"Gideon. He won't stop until we're friends, until we're as close as two little boys can be. You may as well give him what he wants."

I frowned. "I really don't think he cares that much."

"You don't know him."

"Why does he want us to be friends so badly?"

He shrugged. "You heard him; he feels sorry for me."

It sounded like a lie. And I didn't know the truth – though I was certain Caspien did.

"You know, since I don't have any friends."

"Have you ever wondered why that is?"

"Not really."

He sighed loudly and took a step toward me, sliding his hands into the pockets of his shorts. "Look, I think we both know that what he wants is completely outside the realms of possibility, but we could play along. It would at least get him to leave us alone."

"Play along..." I repeated.

The idea of playing Caspien at anything terrified me. But beneath that, I was filled with a nervy anticipation that reminded me of the top of a roller-coaster before that first dip.

"Yes, Judith, play along. Play with me."

"You'd better stop calling me that, or you can play with your bloody self."

Too late I heard it in my own ear. Caspien's eyes lit up and he smiled. It made me think about those noises he made on the phone.

"Oh, I think you are going to be fun, Jude."

I didn't even want to begin to imagine what that meant. Instead, I asked, "Who were you talking to on the phone?"

"No one you'd know."

Maybe if we were friends, he would tell me?

"So, what do you say, Jude?" He stuck his hand out. "Would you like to play at being friends? For Gideon?"

I bit and chewed at my lip, trying to decide why this all felt like a trap. One I could see up ahead and yet was walking into willingly. I looked down at his hand. Hands that would soon come to haunt my dreams.

Carefully, I took it in mine.

"For Gideon."

The smile he gave me then was slow and close-lipped, and it made my heart beat a little faster as if venom was swirling through my veins.

"Marvellous," he said before letting go of my hand and breezing past me.

I could only stare after him, sweat licking at my neck and my hand burning like a brand where I had touched him.

SEVEN

Ellie came over after school on Wednesday. Beth was out at her gym class, and Luke was working in the bedroom down the hall, the one that was to be the nursery. We were on my bed with the door pushed slightly closed, kissing.

We'd made an attempt at studying; our books were open on the page we were supposed to be looking at. But then she'd surged toward me without warning and pushed me flat on my back and pushed her tongue into my mouth. I'd not known how to react right away, though after a minute, all the parts of my body that were supposed to react did.

"I like you," she told me between kisses.

"I like you too."

This made her smile – a shy thing that didn't quite suit her. I wondered if it was an act. Or maybe the other Ellie, the confident, bold one I saw every day at school, was the act. She leaned in to kiss me again, but before she could push me back down on the bed, the phone rang – a brazen shriek from where it was on the wall at the bottom of the stairs.

"Ah, I better get that." Luke was drilling, so he wouldn't have heard it. However, when I was at the door, the drilling stopped. "I've got it," I called to him before flying down to catch it before it rang off.

"Hello," I asked, breathless.

There was a moment's pause. "It's Caspien."

My whole body felt like it had been shot through with electricity.

"Hello," I said again. "Are you...I mean, Luke is upstairs."

"I called to speak to you."

Another zap of electricity. My breath thinned. "Oh, right."

"I wondered if you wanted to come over. To...hang out." His voice sounded strange. Stranger than normal. Stiff and careful, like he was reading the words from a page.

"Hang out?" I repeated. My shock at the sound of his voice on the phone had overtaken my confusion, so it came out as a question. "With you?"

"No, with bloody Gideon," he said. "Yes, with me."

"I..." I wanted to say don't be bloody ridiculous, but part of me was too gobsmacked to get anything out. With horror, I realised I wanted to say yes. I was about to when I remembered Ellie was upstairs.

"I can't."

"Why not?" He almost sounded put out.

"Because my...because I have a friend over." I didn't understand why I hadn't wanted to call Ellie my girlfriend, why I hadn't wanted Caspien to know I even had a girlfriend, but at that moment, I told myself it was because the more stuff Caspien knew about me, the more advantages he had over me, and the more dangerous it made him.

But the truth, of course, was far simpler than any of that.

"Oh, it's the girl, is it?" he said in a flat voice.

I didn't even question how he knew. Maybe he'd seen her arrive somehow. Maybe Luke had mentioned it. Maybe he had cameras in my room.

"Is she your girlfriend?"

I hesitated too long. "Yeah, sort of."

He was silent for a bit. "Okay then. Well, bye."

"Wait," I rushed before he hung up. I didn't understand it; perhaps it was the sheer novelty of him having called me at all - that he wanted to hang out with me was something monumental, too - but I didn't want him to go.

He hadn't hung up and so I grasped at the first thing that came to mind.

"We're going to the beach on Saturday," I heard myself saying. "My friends and me. If you wanted to come with us."

"Is your sort of girlfriend going to be there?"

"Yeah. And her friend. And my other two friends, who're boys: Josh and Alfie. So like, it won't be weird or anything." I had no idea why I was saying this, why I was inviting him. Shit. Alfie. Alfie was going to be seriously pissed off.

"Yes, okay then. I'll come."

"Cool."

"Bye," Caspien said, and then he was gone.

After he hung up, I sat on the bench at the foot of the stairs with the receiver in my hand for five whole minutes, wondering what on earth had just happened.

He turned up early on Saturday morning.

I was still in bed, thinking about wanking, when Luke called up.

"Judey! Caspien's here." I heard him giving him directions to my room and the sound of the stair creaking, and then he knocked on the closed door.

I practically flew out of my bed and pulled on a pair of sweats, glancing around the mess of my room. There were still a few un-packed boxes, a glass by the bedside, some dirty underwear on the floor. I kicked the underwear under the bed and opened the small window wide before shouting for him to come in. He strode in like a gust of fresh, clean air.

He looked fresh and almost glowing in shorts and a crisp white t-shirt. He was wearing white trainers that looked new (and not his ridiculous too-big sandals), and his hair had been cut. Shorter around his ears and face but still longer than most boys I knew wore theirs.

He looked me up and down and then moved to sit on my bed. The sight of him there, on top of my bedcovers, on my bed, made me feel very strange.

"I wasn't sure what time we would be going," he said, glancing curiously around my room. His eyes lingered on my bookshelf before he stood up and went towards it.

"You could have called?"

He scanned the titles as he said, "Shall I go and come back?"

"No, it's fine."

He slipped out a book, flipping through the pages before turning it to read the back. It was my third-hand copy of *Dracula*.

"I'll wait outside." He looked at me. "I'm borrowing this."

Then he was gone, the stair creaking as he descended.

I showered quickly and pulled on clothes, shorts, and a T-shirt that I debated far too long over. I made sure my phone was charged, shoved a towel and some sunscreen in my rucksack, and headed downstairs. Beth was in the kitchen making what looked to be sandwiches for us all.

"You packed sunscreen?" she asked as I put my bag down on the dining room table. When I nodded she asked, "Have you put it on already?"

"I'll do it."

She packed a tinfoil-wrapped parcel into a cool box. She'd made enough for twelve, it looked like.

"He's in the garden," she said. "He came with nothing, bless him.

So make sure you give him sunscreen too. Gideon's a little hopeless with this stuff." Beth had an almost fond look on her face. A look I'd never before seen for other people she considered to be hopeless: her boss, the dental receptionist, the waiter who messed up her order when we went out to eat.

Outside, Caspien was sitting cross-legged on the wooden bench reading. He wore sunglasses now; a designer pair that suited his face. The sun pooled over him, making his hair look like it was made of pure white. He had turned golden over the summer, a bronzed pinkish glow that contrasted against the bleached white of his t-shirt.

I thought of him saying, 'Play with me,' in that very low secret voice he'd used on the phone, and my insides turned watery and hot.

I realised I'd been staring too long when he spoke. Not looking up.

"Have you read this?"

I cleared my throat. "Yeah."

"It's quite boring, isn't it."

"The film was better."

He snorted. "I highly doubt that."

"You haven't seen it?"

"I don't like films."

I frowned. "Like...in general?"

He closed the book and lifted his head. "In general, I prefer books."

I mean, so did I. But I still enjoyed watching films.

"What about the cinema?"

"What about it?"

"Do you...go?"

He thought about it and then shook his head. "I've never been to the cinema, no."

"Not even to see The Avengers?"

He looked at me from behind his sunglasses. "If I were going to go to the cinema, trust me, it would not be to see The Avengers."

"It's not nonsense," I defended. I guess, on some level, it was, but I also enjoyed it.

"What's not nonsense?" Luke said as he popped his head out of the house.

"Caspien hasn't seen The Avengers."

"I never said that."

"You did, you said—."

"I said I hadn't been to the cinema to see it. Not that they didn't make us all watch it in the recreation room at La Troyieux. It was nonsense."

"I agree, buddy. Too far-fetched for me." Luke chuckled at his own joke. One he made frequently about the far-fetched nature of films like The Avengers. "Right, are you two ready to go?"

Caspien stood, still holding the copy of *Dracula*, which it looked like he was taking with him to the beach, despite how boring it was. He followed Luke, and I followed him. Beth handed the cool box off to me as I passed along with the rucksack she'd packed.

"Remember, sunscreen."

"I know, I know. I will. Thanks."

Outside, I put the cool box in the boot of Beth's car, and while I did so, Caspien climbed into the front seat with Luke without so much as a glance at me. I glared at the back of his head. I already regretted inviting him.

I hadn't even mentioned it to Alfie yet, and so when he sent a text to the group chat to say they were already at the beach, I decided to break the news.

Me:

OMW. And...Caspien is here with me.

Then, because I was a coward, I said:.

Me:

Beth made me invite him.

Alfie sent a dozen question marks and a few exclamation points, and Josh sent a few crying with laughter emojis. I typed back for him to chill, and that Caspien was cool. Then I shoved my phone back in my pocket and stared out the window.

This was going to be terrible.

It was terrible. But not for the reasons I expected. It was terrible because they liked him. Because once again, he'd been nice to them. When I introduced them he told them he was glad to meet them and that they should call him 'Cas'. I'd tried to hide my annoyance at that. I'd known him close to three months at this point and had not been given that nickname to use.

Ellie had come forward and kissed me quickly, sliding her arm around my waist to pull me closer – proprietary in a way I wasn't sure how I felt about. Not with Caspien's presence two feet away. It felt weird having her do it in front of the others. She'd been a little handsy in school this past week, but this was more than that, and I couldn't help glancing at Caspien as she laid her head on my shoulder. He wasn't looking at me. Instead, he'd begun pulling off his T-shirt and then his shorts to reveal a pair of navy blue swim shorts with a little designer motif on the waistband. Alfie was a little chilly at first, but an hour later he'd come around and was inviting him to his birthday party in a month's time.

I hadn't known what to expect. I was certain there was another personality buried in there somewhere and that he'd pull it out just the way he had with Luke and then Beth. I'd been right. I just wasn't sure why it annoyed me so much. Seeing him talking with Alfie and Josh and smiling at Ellie and Georgia shouldn't have annoyed me, but it did.

It felt too complicated to understand, too stupid to even articulate, but I hated that I was the only one he didn't act like a normal person around. More than that, I hated that I cared enough to be annoyed about it.

"He seems nice," Ellie said, stretching out beside me.

"Does he?" I said moodily.

"I mean, Georgia thinks so..." She looked over to where the others were.

"Yeah, he's a proper prince charming. Just her type."

"She's waiting on him to ask her, you know."

"Who?"

"Alfie."

Something relaxed inside me. "She knows?" My eyebrows shot up and Ellie gave me a look as if I were stupid.

"Hey, will you put some on my back?" She nudged me with the bottle of sunscreen and then flipped onto her front, pulling her pigtails out of the way of her exposed back. She wore a green floral bikini that tied around the back of her neck. I squeezed a dollop onto the middle of her back, causing her to shriek loudly.

"Jude! You put it on your hands first! It's too cold!" She laughed, throwing a playful glare over her shoulder. After she'd settled, I began rubbing the lotion over her shoulders and down the slope of her back, smooth and already golden from the sun. She had a freckle in the right-hand corner, just above the waistband of her bikini bottoms, and I focused on it. It felt strangely awkward. And suddenly, I had the memory of Caspien washing my hands over the large sink in the kitchen of Deveraux House.

As though my thoughts had summoned him, a shadow fell over us, and I looked up to find him staring down at me. Dripping wet, his cheeks flushed from exertion, his body a glittering golden thing; he looked like a magical sea creature.

"I need a towel," he told me like I was his mother.

It was strange then that I abandoned Ellie's back and reached over to get my backpack, pulling out one of the towels Beth had packed for us.

When he was finished drying himself, he laid it out on the sand next to me and fell on top of it. He'd wrapped up my copy of *Dracula* in his clothes before going into the water, pulled the book out, and started reading it.

"So, Cas, Jude says you used to go to school in Switzerland?" Ellie asked, sitting up. She hooked a hand over my shoulder and perched on it, looking over at him.

"I did," he said without glancing up.

"And now you're home-schooled?"

"Now I'm home-schooled."

"So what do you do for, like, fun?"

"I guess I come to the beach and hang out with Jude's friends."

Ellie snorted at this, but Caspien didn't. His expression didn't change. He kept his eyes focused on his book – my book – and his head turned away from the sun. When he didn't say anything else, she turned her gaze to me and shrugged.

"You coming in?"

There was no reason not to, though part of me felt bad for abandoning him, despite the fact he'd been in there with the others while I'd sat here. He'd be completely fine here on his own. His body language practically screamed for us to leave him alone anyway. I'd been staring at him too long because Ellie nudged me.

"Yeah, let's go," I said and let her pull me towards the water.

Luke picked us up at 6:30 p.m. We shook out our shoes and towels of sand and bunged everything into the boot of the Kia before climbing in.

After asking if we'd had fun, Luke launched into the work he'd done on the south-facing gardens, which included some landscaping and levelling off the lower patio, removing and reinstalling the stepping stones which led from the water fountain and under the arch to the covered walkway. Caspien looked and sounded interested, asking all the right questions and validating Luke's work, but I could see him furiously texting someone on his phone. His knee bounced rapidly, too, and his teeth chewed at his lower lip. I'd never seen him so tense.

"You wanna stay for dinner, Cas?" Luke called over his shoulder as we turned into the long drive of Deveraux House. "We're doing a barbecue."

"Oh?"

I was certain he'd say no. He was like a coiled spring, as though the second the car stopped, he was going to bolt off. Whoever was holding his attention on the phone had him completely on edge. It had to be the person he'd been speaking to on the phone last week. My insides felt twisted and pulled tight, a knot of anxiety I couldn't think past.

"Yeah, you have to try Beth's potato sweetcorn salad. It's something else, isn't it, Judey?"

"Yeah, it's great," I managed.

"Sure, I'll come. I just have to nip back to the house really quick to change, and then I'll come back. If that's okay, Luke?"

"Sure it is. We'll drive up there first and wait for you; how's that?"

Caspien pressed the lock button on his phone, turned it screen down on his knee, and nodded to Luke.

He did bolt from the car when we stopped, saying he'd be as quick as he could before disappearing inside the kitchen door of the large house.

Staring after him, curiosity licking like flames up my spine, I told Luke I really needed to pee and followed Caspien inside. He might have to change, but I was certain that the reason he had to go back to the house had something to do with whomever he had been texting furiously on the drive back from the beach.

The house was relatively dark. Only the lamps in the hallway were lit, and they didn't offer much illumination, given the height of the ceilings. I passed the arboretum, then the music room where I'd watched Caspien play piano, and then the library, where the door was slightly ajar. I leaned into the gap and listened, but it was deathly silent inside it.

Then I heard it. A soft muffled cry that sent my pulse thundering.

I turned my head in the direction it came; the large reception room off the front entryway, and hurried toward it. The doors were closed but not all the way, and when I pushed it open, I could barely breathe. My eyes took a moment to interpret the scene.

A tall male knelt with his arms wrapped tightly around Caspien's middle, his head buried against his stomach as he nosed and rubbed his face against the skin beneath Caspien's t-shirt. With a gentle tug, he pulled him into his lap, forcing Caspien to straddle him as they embraced. I watched transfixed for a moment, the tenderness with which the figure held him, the desperate way he kissed and sniffed at his throat and his hair. There was something almost...fatherly in the way he held him, but then the man made a noise which caused something sickening to twist in my chest and something hot to flood my cheeks. I looked at Caspien's face, hoping to see something I understood there.

He looked...unsettled. But still distant and removed from the situation in the way he often did.

"You shouldn't be here," Caspien said.

"I can't stay away from you, you know that." The man explained, miserably. "I miss you all the time." He lifted his head then, and I caught a glimpse of his profile. A dusting of dark hair brushed a strong jaw and a small, neat nose. Had I seen him before? I wasn't sure. He wore a short sleeved T-shirt which revealed muscled arms with a smattering of dark hair. "Don't you miss me? This is driving me fucking crazy, Cas."

"I told you not to come," said Caspien.

"Cas, he's gone for the whole weekend. A whole weekend alone. How could I resist?"

"I'm not alone," Caspien huffed. "If anyone sees you here, and they tell him, how will you explain it?"

The man laughed. "I'll tell him you seduced me. That I had not a hope in hell of resisting you." He reached up and kissed him then, and Caspien visibly softened in his arms.

I felt as though I had been slapped, hard. My face stung, and I backed out of the room. As I turned, my elbow banged against the sideboard and rattled the antique birdcage on top. I bit back the yelp of pain, scurried across to the music room and hid myself up behind a large sideboard near the door. Here, I crouched, pulling my knees up to my chin and making myself as small as I could.

Outside the room, footsteps grew closer, and then the sound of the door opening, lights flicking on.

For some idiotic reason, I squeezed my eyes closed. This was stupid. Why didn't I hide somewhere else? Why didn't I run back to the car? Then I could have told Luke that some grown man was kissing and touching Caspien.

I knew it wasn't right. I knew it then, and I know it now.

I opened my eyes to find Caspien in front of me, staring at me. He looked furious. But more than that, he looked...frightened.

Before I could say anything, he turned on his heel, walked back out of the door, and flicked the light out as he went.

EIGHT

I got back to the car a couple of minutes before Caspien did, sneaking back out the way I came and sliding into the back seat. If Luke noticed anything was wrong, he said nothing.

When Caspien got into the car, redressed in a clean T-shirt and shorts, he pulled his seatbelt on and apologised for taking so long. He didn't look at me in the rearview the entire journey to the cottage, which I noticed because I could barely keep my eyes off him. I needed to get him alone and ask him about the man in Gideon's house. Was he still there? Waiting?

Throughout the barbecue, my skin itched from the questions bubbling under it. Caspien was cool and calm and entirely placid in the face of my questioning stares and heavy looks. He ate two burgers and a hot dog and picked at his bowl of salad while answering Luke's questions about the beach, Gideon's trip to London, how his studies were with his tutor, and if he missed boarding school.

I watched in awe as he answered them all politely and without any hint that he'd just kissed a grown man in his uncle's reception room as if it were the most normal thing in the world.

"You should stay the night," Luke suggested as we helped clear away the plates. "We have a blow-up mattress. You can sleep in Jude's room. I'm sure Gideon won't mind."

My legs faltered so that the plates I was carrying almost toppled to the floor.

What would he say? *Actually, my older boyfriend is waiting for me at home. I have to get back.*

Instead, in true Caspien style, he shocked me by saying, "That would be nice." He looked at me. "Just as long as Jude doesn't mind."

My face must have done something strange because Luke said, "He doesn't have friends stay over much; that's why he looks like you've just suggested he swim once around the island."

"Why not?" Caspien asked me.

I still couldn't think properly, so my mouth opened and closed like a dying fish for a moment before Beth said, "He doesn't like people in his space." She used her fingers to motion quotation marks around the word 'space'. "Goodness knows what he's gonna do when the baby gets here."

It was true. I didn't like people in my space – I was only just about getting used to Ellie coming over and touching things and leaving her flowery, sweet scent around my room. But having Caspien alone in my room, that was to say, to have him alone where I could ask him about exactly what I saw back at the mansion, was too good an opportunity to miss. And the fact that he'd agreed to stay meant that he must be at least willing to talk to me about it. Because he surely knew he wasn't going to get away with not.

I looked at Caspien with intent. "I don't mind."

His eyes took on a sharp, knowing look as he nodded. "Then I would love to stay over. Thanks."

I helped Luke blow up the airbed while Caspien helped Beth with the dishes. I couldn't imagine what they'd be talking about down there, but their voices were a steady drone coming up through the fireplace.

"I think he's lonely, you know," Luke said in a half-whisper. "Living up there in that big house with just Gideon for company. Needs some friends his own age if you ask me."

"Did Gideon tell you that?" I wasn't sure why I was suddenly responsible for Caspien's social inclusion – but it seemed I was.

I wondered what Luke would think about what I'd seen earlier. I'd not stopped thinking about it, and yet, as the night had gone on, what I'd seen had become far more incredible and unlikely. Had they actually kissed, or had I just imagined it? Had I imagined the noises the man holding him had made? Caspien was my age, fifteen. And that guy had been Luke's age. An adult. It made no sense that they'd have been kissing. But then I thought about what he'd said, about how he'd tell Gideon that Caspien had seduced him...about how he couldn't stay away...about how he missed him all the time.

It made that sick, twisty feeling in my stomach come back.

When the bed was made, Luke disappeared downstairs, and I sat at my desk and quickly checked my socials. Georgia had uploaded some photos from the beach, which I scanned and liked, lingering too long on one of the two girls with Caspien in the background.

In the middle of the afternoon, Caspien had gone for a long walk along the shore on his own, and the shot captured him standing staring out at sea, looking serious and pensive. His hair had begun to dry by then, and it sat fluffy, thick, and golden on top of his head. His blue shorts hung low on his waist, showing sharply angled hip bones, a delicately curved spine, and strong thighs and calves.

"So your friends are predictably boring," came the voice from behind me.

I started; he'd been checking his phone the last I'd looked.

My cheeks flushed at the idea of him having caught me looking at the picture, but then I relaxed. Ellie was in the foreground in a bikini. He'd assume I was looking at her.

I brushed a hand through my hair and sat up, turning in the chair to face him.

"And yours are twice your age and should probably be in prison," I said.

He stiffened before reaching out to close the door, shutting us inside together. He eyed the airbed.

"I'm not sleeping on that."

I shrugged. "Then go home. To your *friend*."

He smiled and moved to sit down on my bed. Leaning back on his hands, he studied me. "Tonight was the second time I've caught you spying on me, Judith. If you aren't careful, I'm going to start thinking you fancy me."

My face heated, but I managed to make a scoffing noise. "Yeah, you're really not my type."

"Stupid, giggling airheads are more your type; I forgot."

"And what about your type? Old perverts, is it?"

He snorted. "Christ, you're such a child."

"We're the same age?!"

"Yes, and it's as much of a shock to me as it is to you, believe me," Caspien said. "Look, ask me whatever it is you want to know. Say whatever it is you want to say – but get it out of your system now because it's not something we are ever going to talk about again." The look he gave me was harder, more threatening. "And it's not something you're ever going to mention to another soul. Not Gideon, not Luke, and not your stupid, idiotic friends. Do you understand?"

Rage and something else rose in my chest. I wanted to defend my friends, but they could be stupid and idiotic, even I knew that.

Anyway, this was more important.

"Fine. Who is he?"

"What does that matter?"

I couldn't think of a single reason why it did. Except that, I wanted to know his name. I wanted to know so that when I was older, bigger, stronger, I could hunt him down and hurt him in some way.

I vowed to myself at that moment that I'd find out his name some other way. "I guess it doesn't..." I chewed my lip as I thought about what else I wanted to know.

"Do you love him?" I asked, completely unsure why and completely certain he wouldn't answer anyway.

He gave me an odd look as though he thought I might be joking, then when it was clear I wasn't, he said, "No, Jude, I don't."

I tried not to care about the soft way he said my name. Softer than he'd ever said it before.

"Does he love you?" It had looked like it. *I miss you all the time.*

"Certainly not."

I frowned at this. At the certainty with which he said it. Then I asked, "Was he the person you were talking to on the phone when I...before?"

He smiled, slow and amused. "You think I have a whole squad of them?"

I raised an eyebrow. If anyone did, it was him.

He rolled his eyes, but he answered. "Yes. He was."

"And do you...like...you know. With him..."

Caspien's eyes narrowed devilishly, lips parting. "Do I what?"

I looked at the floor. "You know..."

"If you want me to answer it, then you're going to have to say it."

I kept my eyes lowered. "Do you have sex with him?"

"I'm fifteen years old. Of course I don't."

When I lifted my eyes, he held my gaze a long time without speaking. I sensed the lie in it, or I thought I did, perhaps because everything Caspien said *felt* crafted and careful, intricate in a way that hurt my brain trying to decipher.

He glanced away, sighing as he added, "He's not a complete idiot."

Did that mean he wanted to?

"He says he's happy to wait." Caspien was staring at my bookshelf.

At first, I thought he meant *wait at the house* until I realised that wasn't what he meant at all. My head filled with noise, and my breathing turned hot and quick again. I felt angry and helpless all at once.

"And you're going to? With him? Some old guy you don't even love?" It was out before I could think about how it sounded like I cared.

His eyes found mine, a mocking look on his face.

"Oh, so you only have sex with people you love?" He said it like it was ridiculous. "Do you *love* her then? Your stupid girlfriend?"

"Stop saying that," I snapped. "She's not stupid."

"She's not very smart either."

"How would you know? You barely spoke to her."

"I didn't have to; it's painfully obvious."

"Well, I suppose if forty-year-old men are your type then you would think that."

"He's thirty-two."

I shrugged. "Same difference. He should be in prison."

Caspien gave me a very serious look. "That's not funny."

"I'm not joking." If it meant he'd be away from Caspien maybe that's exactly where he should be. Behind thick bars and high walls.

He stuck his chin out. "I'll be sixteen in three months."

"And he'll still be a man twice your age. It's disgusting."

He studied me closely, eyes turning mean. "Are you sure it's not the fact he's a man, Jude? Is that really what disgusts you?"

I felt my face screw up. "Eh, no. I don't care if you're gay, Caspien." That he thought I did pissed me off.

But then, we barely knew each other, not beyond this weird tenuous acquaintance we'd been forced to cultivate. He didn't like me; that much was obvious. He also thought I was several social and intellectual levels beneath him. So, of course, he thought I was a homophobe too. I didn't think I was. I didn't know any gay people, except for maybe Charlie Eastman, but I didn't even know if he was gay. It was just something people at school said about him. Actually, I hadn't seen him this term. The thought hit me like a bucket of ice water. "Was that why you left school?"

"What?"

"Because you're gay?" I asked. "Did people at your old school have a problem with it? Is that why you never went back?" The thought of him being bullied over it made me surprisingly angry. He had a vicious tongue and the quickest brain of anyone I'd ever met, so verbally, I knew he could stand his ground, but physically? I drew my eye over his neat frame. He was lean and soft-looking. Delicate in ways boys weren't. He could be an easy target. For an idiot.

"Boarding schools are really nothing like your comprehensive cattle farms. You'd be surprised at how many boys like to stick their cocks into the holes of other boys and call it recreational fun. It's basically a rite of passage at boarding school."

An assortment of images I didn't ask for and didn't want flooded my head, hot, melting heat filling my gut.

I swallowed. Caspien looked amused.

"So you've...done stuff with other boys? At school?"

He shrugged. "It's really not a big deal."

Not a big deal. It wasn't right, I think I knew then that it wasn't right – a child shouldn't be so casual and forward about things like this – but Caspien wasn't like any child I knew. He didn't speak like one or act like one, and when I was around him I found myself drunk on his worldliness. Intoxicated by the things he might be able to show me or teach me that no one else could.

"But not with the person you saw at the house. I've never let him inside, even if I've wanted to sometimes. Many times." He let out a low, breathy noise very similar to the one I'd heard him make on the phone. "It feels like nothing else on earth, you know. Completely overwhelming, like you might die. But then you don't, and it's... well...it's very good."

I wanted to yell at him to shut up. I wanted to say that this was all wrong and that I didn't care what went on in boarding schools in Switzerland or wherever, but here in England, what he was saying and doing was illegal because he was a child, and I wanted no part of it.

But then his voice changed completely. He went from sounding dreamy and breathless to sounding uncertain and a little afraid.

"You won't tell anyone, will you? About him. Really, nothing has happened, I swear." When I said nothing, his eyes darkened a fraction. "If you do, I'll only deny it and make up something awful about you. Who do you think they'll believe?"

"You're probably the most horrible person I've ever met."

"You live on an island with a population of one hundred thousand. You've barely met anyone."

"Oh, it will take a lot to beat you."

"A compliment?" He smirked. "You really are smitten with me..."

I glowered at him.

"Boys, do you want some hot chocolate before bed?" Luke yelled up at us from the bottom of the stairs. I got up, walked over to the bedroom door, and cracked it open.

"We'd love some, Luke, thanks!"

"You got it!"

I closed the door and turned to face Caspien. "I'll keep your dirty secret for you," I told him.

His face broke into a relieved smile that lit his eyes and softened his pink mouth.

"On one condition."

He stiffened, face turning to stone.

"You don't see him anymore. You won't talk to him on the phone or text him or whatever else you do with him. It stops. All of it. Or I'll tell Luke, and trust me, he will believe me."

He looked faintly shocked, like I'd surprised him. He thought about this a moment, then gritted out through his teeth: "Fine."

He flopped back on my bed, pulling out his phone to begin typing. "I suppose your stupid friend Georgia could entertain me for a little while. You know, until I'm legally allowed to fuck whomever I want."

I reached out to snatch the phone from him. He was faster, pulling it out of reach instantly.

"Don't do that," I fumed.

"Why not?"

"Because you don't even like her, and she'll get hurt."

"But I need someone to play with, Jude. And since you've just taken my toy away..."

"Oh, stop being such a dick, will you?"

I was standing over him as he lay on my bed. His T-shirt was ruched up, and I could see the golden stretch of his stomach, hard and flat above the waistband of his shorts.

Suddenly, his legs shot out, and he hooked them around the back of my thighs, locking them together. He smirked as he held me there.

I didn't know who this Caspien was. He wasn't the cold, serpentine boy from the mansion. He wasn't even the stiff, serious boy who'd washed my hands clean of Oleander plant. It wasn't the boy at the beach or the boy who chatted warmly with Luke. This was someone else, maybe even the same person who kissed men in dark rooms and whispered provocative things to them down the phone.

There were so many sides to him. He was a kaleidoscope, one that I couldn't look away from. I was entranced.

I tried to get loose, but his legs were strong. He rode a huge horse every day, I thought. Still, I pulled against them for a bit, trying to use my hands to prise his legs apart, but the angle was awkward. A shift and pull from him at the back of my knees had me tumbling forward onto his chest.

There was a moment, one strange, stretched-out moment, where I could do nothing but stare into the ice blue of his eyes. Then, at his mouth. And then back to his eyes again.

It came from nowhere, but I felt it everywhere. The need to kiss him. I imagined the soft, wet pink inside of his mouth, the taste of his lips, the shape of his tongue. It was an onslaught of want. Loud and hot and violent.

As my senses rushed back in, I felt something hard and warm between my legs. Whether he felt it too, and it's what made him release me, I don't know, but I practically threw myself backwards off him, staggering back into the desk.

Caspien sat up on his elbows and stared at me, his own breathing quick and his eyes alight with something dangerous. He was looking at me as though seeing me for the first time. As though, for the first time, I interested him. But it was a dangerous sort of interest –the sort he might give a bug he'd trapped under a glass.

Confused and terrified, I fled from the room, muttering over my shoulder that I was going to get the hot chocolate.

NINE

Our relationship – or whatever it was in those days – changed imperceptibly after that. I couldn't quite say how, but I knew when, and it had been after that night in my room. The first night I'd felt turned on by a boy.

After leaping away from Caspien, I'd run to the toilet, opened my shorts, and looked at it. It was unmistakable in that bright overhead light. I was more turned on by a boy than I'd ever been when I kissed my girlfriend.

I didn't know what to think about that. Though I suppose, as with most things, it was feeling that came first – my body knew what it felt and what it wanted – it was that my head hadn't caught up yet.

Did I like boys now? Was I gay? Walking backwards through it, I tried to think about what exactly it was that had done it; had it been the play fight? I play-fought with Alfie and Josh all the time, and I'd never, not once, gotten hard from it. Nothing like it.

Had he just rubbed against me in a way that had caused something biological to happen? Had it been the conversation before? What he'd said about it – about sex with a boy – feeling like nothing else on earth. *Completely overwhelming; like you might die. But then you don't, and it's...well...it's very good.*

I thought about Ellie. I liked kissing her. I'd definitely gotten hard from kissing her before, more than once, which surely meant I liked girls. Which did I like more?

I thought about the need I'd felt just moments before; that hot violent urge I'd had to kiss Caspien when I'd been inches from his mouth. There was no point in lying to myself that I'd ever wanted to kiss Ellie even half as much as that.

I'd returned to the room with our hot chocolate and avoided his eyes as I gave him it. He hadn't said a word, but I'd felt something change in him.

I'd lain awake on the air bed for most of the night. Rigid, too hot, and very aware of the boy in my bed – a dangerous path because as soon as the thought entered my head, it consumed everything else in there, tearing through it like a forest fire. What would it feel like to go and lie next to him? To feel him go soft and pliant under me, just like he'd done for the man back at the house. The idea of him gripping onto me like that. The idea of him wanting me like that.

It didn't take long until I was hard again. Uncomfortably so.

Caspien's reaction to the night in my room was different. The jokes stopped; those suggestive comments he'd thrown at me since I found him on the phone, stopped. He was aloof again, distant again. He was the boy in the big sandals and oversized clothes who looked at me as though I was beneath him, again.

I hadn't realised it, but somehow, with my eavesdropping and my agreement to 'play-along' for Gideon that afternoon, we'd taken some tentative steps close towards what might, under some lights, be considered a friendship.

Now, it was like we'd gone back to the way it had been before. He barely looked at me, he never called and invited me over again, and he never again came to the beach with us (I'd asked him twice more).

I didn't like it. The awkwardness, the way he was careful not to touch me, the way he was extra careful not to look at me, and I felt ashamed and embarrassed that it was because I'd accidentally gotten hard while play-fighting with him and he knew about it. It did occur to me that this was the perfect sort of attack for him. My interest in him laid bare. And yet, for some reason, he hadn't used it.

The difference now, though, was that I couldn't avoid him, not now that we studied together twice a week in Gideon's library. Caspien wrote lines of meticulous Latin and sketched from photos he'd taken on his phone while I copied Algebra equations from the online coursework site in my rough, sloppy handwriting.

Neither of us had mentioned anything about that night, in fact, we'd deftly avoided making any reference to it whatsoever – the pervert and the conditions I'd imposed on him included – and so I'd almost forgotten all about it altogether when three strange things happened.

The first was this: a Thursday night, a few weeks after the night in my room, Gideon peered into the library to tell Caspien there was a call on the landline for him.

The way Caspien stiffened caught my attention. I knew immediately that it was his pervert. Standing, Caspien avoided my eye and followed Gideon out into the hall. Everything in me wanted to follow him and eavesdrop again, but I turned my attention back to the question in front of me. *'The inspector thinks Crompton is a lively, cheerful place.'* He doesn't. My pencil shaded the circle denoting the false statement so hard that the tip broke off.

He came back quicker than I expected, striding into the room less than five minutes later and flopping back down where he was before. I watched him pick up his pencil and scrutinise his drawing like it had insulted him.

If he felt my eyes on him, he pretended he didn't.

"That was him, wasn't it?"

"He won't call again," he said without looking up. He tilted his head and began to shade.

There was nothing much else I could say to that. I wanted to ask what he told him to be so sure he wouldn't. Was it that he had to be patient? To wait until a little longer? It was less than two months until his birthday and the thought of what could happen after that made me ill. I wondered who Gideon thought had been on the phone. Who had Caspien told him it was? I guessed that it was lies upon lies, so I kept my mouth shut and went back to my homework.

The second strange thing happened when I turned up on Tuesday evening. Caspien wasn't in the library, which in itself was weird. He was always there when I arrived, his nose deep in a book or scratching away at his sketchpad, but this time, the room was empty and dark, unused. My first thought was that I'd mixed the days up or forgotten something he'd said about not being here. But then I heard a burst of piano through the wall. I dropped my bag and followed its source down the windowless little corridor to the large music room on the other side.

The room was half dark, and the little picture lights on the walls didn't stretch far across the massive empty space.

Caspien was at the piano, barefoot and hair wild. His playing was ferocious and angry, banging on the pedal and the keys as though in a fight with them. I glanced around to make sure Gideon wasn't observing him again, but the room was empty except for us.

I watched from just inside the doorway as he carried the piece through to a devastating, heart-stopping conclusion. When it was over, he stared down at his hands for a long time, almost as long as it took his breathing to return to normal.

I hadn't moved, had barely even breathed, but something alerted him to my presence and his head snapped around. For half a moment, it looked as though he didn't recognise me, like I was a total stranger who'd wandered into his house. Something cold and uneasy slithered down my spine.

Then he blinked.

"What are you doing here?" he asked me.

"It's Tuesday."

He blinked again. "Is it?"

His face looked pale in the dim light of the room, and even from here, I could see faint, dark circles beneath his eyes. I hadn't seen him since Thursday – this wasn't unusual. If I was helping Luke with the garden maintenance, then sometimes I'd see him on Saturday or Sunday around the estate or in the house – but I'd been at the cinema with Ellie on Saturday, and on Sunday, I'd met up with the boys to play football in Harris Field.

I went towards him and he stood from the piano stool, scrubbing a hand over his face and through his hair which looked unwashed. My unease grew.

"Where's Gideon?"

"How should I know?" he snapped.

"Is something the matter?" I asked, carefully.

"What exactly would be the matter?" From here, his eyes looked dull and muddied like dirty sea water. "Go home." He moved past me, but I turned to go after him, reaching out a hand to tug him back by his elbow.

"Caspien, what's going on?"

"Piss off, Judith." He yanked hard, and I released him, and then he was charging away from me.

Something was very clearly wrong, but I had no clue what. Had no clue what to do. Where was Gideon? I let Caspien go and set about the house, looking for him. His study was empty. The downstairs reception rooms were dark, cold, and unlit.

It looked like the kitchen hadn't been used tonight at all. Where was Elspeth? Gideon's housekeeper was usually here most weeknights, pottering away in the kitchen or dusting the downstairs knickknacks.

Luke had a mobile number for Gideon but did I want to worry everyone when I didn't even know what was wrong.

Despite how he looked, this behaviour wasn't entirely abnormal for him. I knew fine well, he could be moody and awful. Perhaps, this was just one of those times. I'd forgotten he could be like this.

After checking the arboretum and the front patios to find no sign of Gideon, I went outside to see what cars were in the back. Gideon drove a Jaguar, a silver XE saloon that wasn't parked outside, so he must be out. There were none there at all. Which, for some reason, I hadn't even noticed on the way in.

I took the stairs up to the bedrooms two at a time. The upstairs was a square mezzanine with doors and corridors leading off it in several directions. I'd never been up here, so of course, I went the wrong way. Down a wide hallway, I opened the door to a gallery room, a few unused bedrooms – dust sheets covering the furniture inside – and turned to find a whole wing cordoned off by a large wooden folding screen. Behind it was dark and unlit, and so I figured neither Caspien nor Gideon's bedrooms would be beyond it. The first set of locked doors I came to on the other side of the staircase, I decided, had to be Gideon's bedroom.

I hammered again anyway. When there was no answer, I went further down the hall. A few more doors were locked, and I did the same here. A few bedrooms weren't locked but looked and smelled unused – cold, dark rooms that hadn't been occupied in months if not years.

The door at the furthest end was slightly open, light spilling into the hall. I knew it would be Caspien's room; the angle of it would have a view over to the cottage, and the closer I got to it, the closer I felt to him. For the briefest moment before I stepped inside, I was terrified at what I'd find. I was terrified he'd hurt himself, that I'd find him covered in blood or worse. I held my breath as I pushed open the door and stepped inside.

A large ornate bed sat in the centre of the room. Not pushed against the wall as most beds were, but right in the centre. Two large antique lamps stood like sentinels on either side of the large bed. Books sat in piles on either side of it, as though unpacked from boxes and just abandoned there. A large fireplace on one end was lined with trophies and plaques; some in the shape of horses, others shaped into tennis racquets and balls, and some a little figure with a sword.

At the foot of the huge bed on a wooden ottoman were stacks of what looked like sketch pads, trays of pencils, and a small Philodendron next to it. Taped around the walls were pages from those sketchpads, random compositions, some of which looked half-finished. Next to those were pages of what looked like music. It was like a great wind had scattered everything in the room, and no one had bothered to tidy it.

Caspien lay on his side in the centre of the bed. His back was to me, so I couldn't tell if his eyes were closed or not.

"Caspien," I said.

"I told you to go home."

I ignored that and came closer. "Where's Gideon?" I asked.

He said he hadn't known downstairs, but I didn't believe for a moment that Gideon would leave without telling him where he'd gone. Gideon was eccentric and strange, but he wasn't completely irresponsible.

"With his newest whore I'd imagine," Caspien said, sounding tired.

"Where's Elspeth?"

"Visiting Family in Norfolk."

Gideon had left him alone without a soul to look over him? Rage bubbled under my skin. When I got to the side of the bed, I looked down at him. He looked small there in the huge bed, small and very young. I had the urge to climb in next to him and put my arms around him.

"Did something happen?" I asked gently.

"No."

There was a bone-deep fear in my body that I didn't understand. I wanted to help him, protect him, fix whatever it was making him act like this, but I was scared too.

"I'm going to call Luke," I said and went to move from the bed.

"Please, don't." His voice was small but fierce.

Gingerly, I sat back down on the bed and shifted across it so I was closer to him.

"Then tell me what's wrong..." I left it hanging there a moment before I added. "I thought we were friends?"

I expected him to laugh at that. Throw it back in my face and say something mean. Instead, he just said, "You're only here because Luke asked you to be. Or because you feel sorry for me. I can't decide which is worse." *That's not what I feel for you.* "No. That's not true."

He scoffed. "No? Come on, Jude, we both know if it were down to you, then you'd be with your real friends or *your girlfriend.*"

I thought about that – not about how bizarre it was that he was saying it – but about whether it was true. Did I come here under duress? Would I rather be with Alfie and Josh right now? Or Ellie? I shook my head even though he couldn't see it.

"Maybe at first. But not now."

He unfurled himself and turned to look at me, studying me, checking the validity of my claim. "Really?"

The frown smoothed away a little and some light came on in his eyes, and I was drawn like a moth to it. I was responsible for putting that light there. It was a heady feeling.

"No." I smiled. "I'm here because I want to be, Cas." It was the first time I'd ever used the nickname. The one I'd never been given permission to use. I prepared myself for the light in his eye to go out. Instead, he surged forward and wrapped his arms around me in a tight hug. It stole my breath and put me into some kind of shock.

Caspien was pressed against me. Of his own volition.

When he buried his face in my neck and took a deep breath, I felt a tremor move through my entire body. He was solid and close. So close. To be this close to him was absurd. For him to be clinging to me like this was so outside of normal that it only compounded the fact that something was very, very wrong with him.

"I'm sorry," he whispered against my ear. I was so beguiled that I didn't even think about what he might be apologising for. A moment later, he pulled back and wiped his face.

My hands hung loose and useless at my sides.

"When did you last eat?" I asked in a strange voice.

He was avoiding my eyes now like he was embarrassed. "I can't remember..."

"I'm going to go downstairs and make you a sandwich. Will you stay here?"

He gave me a look like maybe he didn't want me to leave, but then slid backwards against the headboard and nodded.

"I won't be long," I told him and stood.

By the door I looked at him over my shoulder before bolting downstairs to the library where I'd left my bag and my mobile. My finger hovered over Luke's number. Everything in me wanted to call him. I didn't know what was wrong with Caspien or whether a sandwich was going to fix it, and my instinct in most situations was to call Luke. But then I heard his voice – soft and pleading – 'please don't' and I stopped.

I slid my phone back into my bag and went to the kitchen.

I threw together a cheese and ham sandwich, poured a glass of cold orange juice, and carried it upstairs. Caspien was asleep, curled toward me this time so I could see his eyes were closed.

I sat down on the bed and watched him for a full minute, wondering if he was faking it, though I'd no idea why he would. He looked young while he slept. Small and wisp-like. There was no hint of the viperous, sharp-tongued boy he was when conscious.

Another of those weird protective flares lit up inside me.

Through the open window, I heard the sound of a car and I set the sandwich and orange juice down by the bed and went to look outside.

Gideon's silver Jaguar was pulling into the courtyard, crunching over the gravel. I bolted downstairs. He took too long to get out, but when he did, he was typing something on his phone and didn't notice me standing by the back door. He went to the boot and retrieved a bunch of designer shopping bags from it. He was almost upon me before he glanced up and saw me.

I saw it happen. The transformation in his face. A dark, cruel look lifting from his eyes, and another, softer – more familiar – look settling over it.

"Young Jude! How's things? Keeping Caspien out of trouble, I hope."

"Where were you?" I snapped before I could stop myself.

Gideon halted, staring at me. "Pardon?"

"There's something wrong with him," I said. "I got here and he was acting strange and didn't know what day it was. He hasn't eaten. He looks ill."

There was no reaction on Gideon's face at first; he looked stunned. But then he rushed forward and passed me into the house. I followed him upstairs to Caspien's bedroom, where he went straight to the bed where Cas was still asleep.

He sat the shopping bags down by the bed and perched on the side of it, reaching out to brush Caspien's hair off his head.

"I had to go to London last minute for some urgent business I had to attend to in person." He smoothed an elegant hand over Caspien's cheek.

"Why didn't you tell us? We would have kept an eye on him?"

Gideon looked over his shoulder at me. "I did. I left a message on Luke's mobile – I don't like doing it – he's not a babysitter, but because Elspeth has the week off, I didn't like the idea of him being completely alone. Didn't he receive it?"

Luke was responsible and always checked his texts and messages. I shook my head, confused. Then it hit me.

"Luke switched phones this week."

"Ah, that'll be it." He looked back at Caspien and made a soft noise at the back of his throat. "He is so self-sufficient and yet somehow completely unable to look after himself."

I wanted to say that he was fifteen. I didn't think he was expected to look after himself.

Gideon stood, lifted the bags and ushered me with him out of the room.

"He doesn't sleep well at the best of times, so I think knowing you were here has settled him. He must be exhausted."

I didn't like this. Any of it. Didn't Gideon think to call the cottage when he didn't hear back from Luke? I felt angry and sick and I wanted to scream at him that Caspien needed someone who cared about him properly.

"What about his tutor? Wasn't he here today?"

Gideon gently closed the door to Caspien's room. "Oh, well. He quit. Quite suddenly actually – some personal issue back home, a bereavement, I think – so we are in-between. I am searching for a replacement now to get us to the end of the school year. Next year will be another issue. Perhaps even Kingsland would be suitable."

My mouth fell open. Caspien at Kingsland. At *my* school. The thought was terrifying. I'd see him every day. We'd likely travel to and from school together. We'd definitely have subjects together. It would be either the best or the worst thing to happen since we drove up to Deveraux House at the start of summer.

"Thank you for looking after him, Jude. I'm eternally grateful."

"I didn't do anything..." I made a sandwich and poured some juice. Neither of which he'd touched.

"No, I know that's not true. It would have meant a lot to have you here." Gideon gave me a look. "You're important to him, Jude. I hope you know that."

I could only stare back at him. Important to Caspien? I doubted that very much. But tonight *had* felt different. Very different. My mind was stuck on the way he'd clung to me. Needy and soft, like I *was* important. How he'd felt in my arms. How vulnerable he'd sounded when he'd asked if I really came to see him because I wanted to. I liked that feeling a lot.

Maybe since I'd never felt that important to anyone, not since my parents died, not really. And for Caspien to be the one to make me feel like that was as inconceivable as it was shocking.

TEN

Caspien's sixteenth birthday was the following Sunday. It was a quiet lunch which Beth and Luke (and I, honestly) were surprised to have been invited to. Gideon had extended the invitation on Thursday, so I'd passed it on. *Just a small thing with those closest to him*, Gideon had said. I assumed then that he meant closest geographically.

He was in the library when I turned up for study night the Thursday after his 'episode'.

His nose was deep in a book with a French title and a painting of a young boy on the cover. He didn't look up as I sat down across from him at the table and pulled out my laptop and textbook. All trace of sickness or whatever had been on him on Tuesday evening was gone. His hair was bright and shiny, and his skin a smooth pink gold.

"Are you okay?" I asked when the

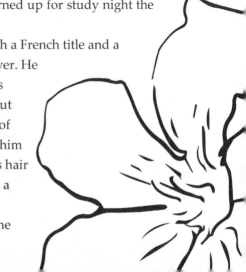

silence got too much to bear.

Over his book, his eyes found mine. A frown creased the space between his brows.

"Why wouldn't I be?" His words were sharp and hard, all trace of the softness he'd had the last time I saw him gone.

I'd wanted to call yesterday to check on him, but something had held me back. And this, I realised, was that something.

I put my bag on the floor and opened my laptop.

"No reason..."

And that had been it.

The three of us walked up from the cottage to the main house on the afternoon of the 30th November. I'd gone into town the day before to get him a gift, and it was only as I walked up and thought about how he might receive it that I realised I'd left it on my dresser.

"I forgot his gift," I said.

Luke shook his head and laughed while Beth tutted before reaching into her bag to give me her set of keys.

"Don't dawdle," she warned.

"With the way you walk? I'll still beat you there," I threw over my shoulder as I jogged backwards toward the cottage.

My gift was where I left it, and I scooped it up and hurried back downstairs.

Those closest people to Caspien were apparently Gideon, me, Luke, Beth, Tarbert and Elspeth and some child of Gideon's cousin who had come to stay for the weekend. Finlay, his name was. A scrawny boy with glasses, a brace, and a shock of reddish-brown hair.

In all the months I'd known them, I'd never heard Finlay's name mentioned once by either Gideon or Caspien. Yet there he was, sprawled on the rug in the main living room, shoving a cupcake into his mouth like he belonged there.

Gideon had already given Caspien a pile of designer clothing, a new iPad, a silver bracelet engraved with his initials, and a new leather saddle for Falstaff. Luke and Beth had given him a voucher for an online bookstore, and now it was my turn to hand him my gift.

I felt stupid and nervous. Why had I insisted on getting him an individual gift? Luke and Beth's voucher would have been more than enough from all of us. I never got Alfie or Josh gifts. And Caspien and I weren't even proper friends. We were something else. It was weird. I regretted it immeasurably the moment he turned expectant blue eyes on me.

I stood up, went to where he sat, and shoved the gift bag at him.

"Um, it was just a couple of things I saw and thought you'd like," I said as he took it.

I sat back down and watched him open the bag and pull out the first tissue-wrapped item. A sheet music book of the best of Studio Ghibli. I loved the Studio Ghibli movies, and as soon as I saw it in the bookstore, I couldn't get the image of Caspien playing something from My Neighbour Totoro out of my head. The second item was a tin of special edition Faber-Castell drawing pencils. I didn't know much about pencils, but the woman in the shop told me they would make a nice gift, and they had come in a rather elaborate-looking tin.

He flicked through the book quickly, as if he were looking for something, and then closed it and set it beside his other gifts. He tore the wrapping paper off the pencils and flipped open the tin to inspect the contents, nodding.

"Thank you, Jude. This is very kind of you," he said, setting the tin on top of the book.

It felt like the entire room was looking at me, watching my reaction to his reaction. Finlay on the floor had this weird look on his face as he glanced between us both. Gideon was beaming wide.

I shrugged. "It's no big deal."

Caspien's eyes narrowed very slightly at that, but he said nothing more.

"I'll bring the sandwiches and cakes through, shall I?" Elspeth said, standing. "If there are any left, that is." She glared at Finlay, who gave her a cheeky grin. Unlike Cas, he wasn't obnoxious with his overt poshness; he was sort of geeky and childlike with it.

The rest of the afternoon was a weird, awkward thing that felt staged, like we were all part of some play I didn't know the lines for. We ate sandwiches – tuna cucumber, egg and cress, and salmon cream cheese – and then cupcakes before Gideon carried through a large chocolate birthday cake with '16' written in white chocolate icing, and we all sang happy birthday.

Gideon let Caspien and Finlay have a small glass of champagne each.

This time, since it was a special occasion, Beth and Luke said I could have one, too. I didn't particularly like it. I thought it tasted like fizzy salted water, but I did like the warm, bubbly feeling that settled over me afterwards. Like how after I'd run or swam really fast, my body felt light and filled with hot air. I gulped it too fast, trying to burp quietly as the fizziness rose up in my chest.

While Elspeth cleared away the cake, Gideon talked with Luke and Beth about some work he planned on doing at the house. Finlay was showing Caspien something on his phone. I took the opportunity to slip away and call Ellie. She wanted to come over that night, but I hadn't committed to it since I didn't know what time I'd be home. And now, sitting on the step outside, I hovered over her name in my phone.

I did want to see her and spend time with her; it's just that I wanted to spend time with someone else more. I was only out there contemplating calling her because the person I wanted to spend time with was inside giving his attention to someone else. It was pathetic. I was pathetic.

Angry with myself, I flicked away from Ellie's number and brought up Instagram instead. I'd followed Caspien a couple of weeks ago, the day at the beach; we'd all followed him in some pretence that we would all be friends. He hadn't followed me back, and he didn't post very often. In fact, he hadn't posted at all since I'd followed him.

So when I went to his page and noticed a new post from earlier, I sat up straighter. It was a picture of his bed, gifts arranged artfully on top, and a single birthday cake caption. I noted the iPad, dark blue Chanel bag, expensive cologne, and the scarf from Finlay. My gifts weren't there, but all of the others were. That's when I noticed it.

Something that didn't belong. Something I hadn't watched him open earlier.

The book had a green antique-looking hardback cover. An early edition certainly with the title etched in foiling on the front. No matter how much I zoomed in, I couldn't make out the title.

Who'd bought him it? Why did seeing it make me feel chilled to the bone?

I tried to reason it out. Of course, given the piles around his room, it was possible that one of his books had found its way onto the bed and into that photo. But something told me that it wasn't an accident. It looked placed there. Deliberate. It sat in the middle of the bed in the centre of a posed photo. It looked like a message.

I stood up and rushed back inside.

I took the stairs as quietly as possible and made my way to the last door at the end of the corridor. It was closed but not locked and the pile sat on the bed exactly as it did in the photo.

Except the book was gone.

Lots of the books that had been lying in stacks the last time I was in here were now on shelves. Some still lay in piles beside his bed, but if my gut was right, then would he really put the book on a shelf like all the others? I didn't think so.

I knelt and looked under the bed which was clear and so clean that the wooden floor shone.

There was a tall chest of drawers by the window, which I went to next, opening each one and rummaging quickly through it. T-shirts, shorts, underwear and socks, but no books. I knew the invasion of his privacy was wrong, but I was too keyed up, too convinced about what I would find and how angry I was going to be about it, to focus on something as pointless as right and wrong. Not when *this* was so beyond wrong.

The ottoman at the foot of the bed had two small doors and three drawers in the centre. Here, I found stacks of unused sketchpads and paper. In the drawers were phone chargers and other cables.

Though I was certain I wouldn't find it, I turned and scanned the shelves anyway. The books were mainly modern, so I looked for any that stood out as clothbound and green.

As a last attempt, I moved to the bed and stuffed my hand under the pillow on his side, then the other. I pulled out a black eye mask, which I stuffed back under. With a sigh, I sat down to think. I'd confront him. Ask him outright. I doubted he cared enough about what I threatened or thought to lie to me. And now that he was old enough, I supposed no one could really stop him. I felt sick. I felt angry. I felt impotent with both. I felt something dig into my thigh.

I stood and pulled back the duvet. It was such an obvious bloody place, and I'd almost missed it. Snatching it up, I studied the cover of what I could now see was a very old edition of *Les Liaisons Dangereuses* by Pierre Choderlos de Laclos. I opened the cover and saw, written in pencil:

" *'A lover is a man who turns himself into a slave.'* "
Caspien, my beautiful boy, let me be yours...
Happy birthday, X

I read it over and over and over. Then I read it again. I felt validated, devastated, and incensed all at once.

"You can borrow it if you like." Caspien's flat voice came from behind me. "It's not his best work; a little verbose for my tastes. His non-fiction texts are better."

I turned, the book gripped in my hand. His eyes dipped to it and then back to me. He was unmoved.

"Were you wondering where I put yours? I'm sure they're around here somewhere." He made a show of looking around. "Unless they got scooped up with the other rubbish."

I tossed the book on the bed and stalked toward him. He took a step back so that he was against the bedroom door, with me crowding him there.

"I told you what would happen if you saw him again."

"Yes, you'd tell Luke, and Luke would believe you. But now it hardly matters, does it? Now I could pack my suitcase and fly off into the sunset with him, and there would be nothing you or anyone could do about it."

This struck a new kind of fear into me. Endless and huge. Caspien going. Caspien leaving. Leaving me. Angry, I pushed my body into his so that he was pinned between me and the door. He made a small noise of surprise in his throat, and his eyes went wide.

"It might be legal now, as of today, but he could still go to prison for what's happened before. And he could still lose his job."

Caspien's eyes narrowed. "What are you talking about? What do you know about his job?"

"You think I don't know who he is?" I seethed.

Caspien looked frightened now.

"I know, Caspien. I know it was your tutor. The one who suddenly had to quit and move back home. I'm not a bloody idiot, and I'm pretty sure once they find out he's been grooming one of his students, he'll struggle to find work anywhere again." I was vibrating with rage, and the words I was saying were so unlike me I didn't recognise myself.

Caspien had turned a strange shade of grey, his eyes hard and his jaw tight. Finally, after many moments when I could practically hear his brain working, he said, "Well. Seems you're not quite as dumb as you look, Judith."

"I'm not dumb at all, but I'll assume you are if I get even a hint that you're seeing him again."

Caspien's eyes didn't leave mine. "You're threatening me?" He sounded impressed.

"No. I'm trying to keep you safe from someone who doesn't care about you."

He scoffed at that. "There's not a soul alive who cares about me, Jude. This isn't bloody news to me." It didn't come out like he was looking for pity, but like some well-known fact he was tired of talking about.

"What are you talking about?" I scowled. "Gideon cares about you." *I care about you.*

He gave me a look that sent a shiver down my spine. "You know nothing about Gideon, Jude."

"What does that even mean?"

He rested his head back on the door with a quiet thud. "Forget it."

I wish I'd pushed him that day. Maybe he'd have told me the truth, or some version of it, and saved us both some of the pain heading towards us like a freight train. If he'd told me the truth, would I even have believed him? How could I have understood something like that then?

Then, I was a child trying to play an adult game. A game I didn't understand the rules of. A game Caspien and Gideon had been playing for a long time before I came along.

Instead, I said something I'd be embarrassed about later. "People care about you, Caspien. I care about you."

"Is that why you're rummaging around my room and threatening me? Because you care about me?"

Guilt hit me square in the chest. I looked down away from his eyes.

"I...didn't mean to...I just..."

"So why did you?"

I swallowed. My mouth was so dry from the champagne and the argument that it hurt to do so. "Because I was angry. I saw the photo and the book, and I knew it was from him, and I was..." I whispered the next words. "I hated it."

"Why did you hate it?" His voice was almost gentle.

When I looked at him, I felt heat rush to my cheeks because I knew he knew why I'd hated it. He knew why, and he wanted *me* to say it.

I wasn't breathing and there was a sound like music in my ears. Like Caspien playing piano. He was so close and so devastatingly pretty, and I didn't know how to say all the things swirling about in my belly with the sandwiches, birthday cake and champagne, but I knew if I did, then everything would change.

Things were already changing. This hot, confusing, frightening thing that got louder and more desperate whenever I was around him had reached some critical point. One I couldn't come back from even if I wanted to. Telling him why I'd hated seeing that book seemed too difficult, too impossible.

So I went toward him instead, took his face in my hands, and kissed him.

ELEVEN

At first, Caspien stood stiff against me. Then, his hands came up to grab hold of my upper arms, and he opened that terrible, vicious mouth.

It was soft and wet and tasted of champagne and birthday cake. It was hot, too, his tongue and lips searing mine as he kissed me back, exploring the inside of my mouth with his own. When he sucked on my lip, I shuddered.

My entire destruction felt possible from that kiss, and I had no desire to fight it. It was what books and song lyrics told you kisses ought to be. It was the end of childhood and the beginning of something else, and I knew I would not be the same when it was over.

The other thought moving through me was this: *This is Caspien. I'm kissing Caspien. He's letting me kiss him.*

It was ludicrous. To be kissing him. For him to be clinging to me like this. To have his tongue in my mouth. I'm sure it was the illogical nature of it that had my dick hard in an instant. I shoved him back against the door and rubbed myself against him. When he moaned softly and rubbed back, I felt something weep out of it, hot and wet.

With a hiss, I jumped back, releasing my hold on him.

He stared up at me, cheeks flushed and eyes dark with excitement.

He licked his wet lips. "Well, well. I honestly didn't think you had it in you."

"I ...what..." My brain was completely offline. When Caspien raised a sharp expectant eyebrow at me, something inside collapsed. "I have to go..."

I threw open the door and bolted downstairs and out the back door. I ran all the way back to the cottage without stopping, my lungs burning and my heart beating so dangerously fast under my ribcage that I was sure I was going to die. Did people have heart attacks at fifteen? I realised too late that I didn't have keys to get inside and that I'd have to wait for Beth and Luke to get home. Beth and Luke, who didn't even know I'd left.

Confusion, panic and shame crawled over me as I sat with my back against the front door.

I'd kissed him.

A boy.

Not just a boy either; him. Caspien.

I didn't even like him. In fact, I hated him most of the time. So why had I done it?

Was I gay?

I liked Ellie. I liked kissing her and being with her. I liked how she smelled and the way she smiled. She was sweet and soft and funny. Everything he wasn't. I wanted to talk to someone about what it might mean, but I had no clue who. Luke would understand; I knew he would, but I wasn't ready for it to be in the house, living with us.

And what did it mean he'd kissed me back? I decided to cast that part aside immediately because there was no reason for anything he did. Or rather, there were a thousand. Each one designed and well-planned. He probably thought it was funny. Something he could take the piss out of me for later.

I'd kissed him. I'd done it. And I knew now that it had been something I'd wanted to do for a while—maybe since the night in my room, maybe even before that. I'd wanted to kiss him, and so I had, and now everything was different. What was I supposed to do now? Who even was I now? Christ, I hated myself for it.

But then, I thought about his mouth and how it had tasted, how his tongue had felt sliding against my own, and I realised I wanted to do it again.

I groaned. How was I going to look at him again?

Okay, I wasn't. That was a plan. I could stay away from him, and then there'd be absolutely no danger of it ever happening again. None. I couldn't do anything like that again if I didn't see him. So I just wouldn't.

Except...it felt like I'd woken something up that had been asleep inside me, and now it was awake and hungry and alive.

I didn't think you had it in you.

God, my head hurt.

I didn't have to wait long. Luke and Beth returned about a half hour later, worried looks on their faces because Caspien said I'd looked sick as a dog when I came out of the bathroom. He'd said it was probably the champagne. That I'd asked him to let them know I'd walked home to get some air.

I agreed with every lie he'd told them and let Beth put me to bed with a headache pill and a glass of water, swearing not to let me touch alcohol again.

Alcohol. That was the reason it had happened. It had to be. It was the champagne. That made sense.

I tossed and turned for an hour or so before the pill took effect, and the adrenaline seeped from my body.

I woke up the following morning to three texts and a missed call from Ellie. There was no point in putting it off, so I called her. She answered on the fourth ring.

"Hello," she said, a little sharply.

"Hey. Look, I'm sorry. I should have called, but it was one of those formal things where I felt like I'd get daggers for going on my phone or something."

"Caspien was on his phone."

"What?"

"I saw his insta. He posted a pic."

Right. The inciting incident.

"Yeah, well, he went to put his gifts in his room, and so he took it then, I guess."

"I'm sure you could have found a way to text me, Jude," she'd pointed out huffily. She was right; I could have.

"Yeah, sorry."

"Did you just not want me to come over?"

"No, it wasn't that. I just didn't know how long we'd be there. Luke and Gideon talk for hours, and I hadn't asked Beth if it was cool."

"Hmm, right."

"I am sorry, Ellie," I said again. When she didn't say anything, I added. "See you at school?"

"Yeah."

She hung up without saying anything else, and I felt like shit. I wondered what the chances were of Beth letting me stay home today if I said I still felt like crap from the alcohol.

I lay there feeling sorry for myself for a bit, trying not to think about kissing Caspien until I heard Luke's voice calling up the stairs.

A bowl of Cheerios was on the kitchen table and a large glass of orange juice.

"How's the head?" Beth asked as she poured her tea into her travel mug.

"Is this what a hangover feels like?" I rubbed at my head for effect.

Luke laughed and bit into his toast, speaking around it. "You'll live. I'll buy you a bacon buttie on the way to school."

I groaned, miserable. It would take a lot more than a bacon buttie to sort my head out; I knew that much.

Ellie barely spoke to me all day. She wasn't downright pissed off with me, just distant and a little sad looking. It only added to the weight in my gut I'd been carrying around all day. Like butterflies, only heavier. I could barely eat lunch, convinced I was going to throw up from overthinking.

I checked my phone for a call or a message even though he didn't have my number. Even if he did, I was certain he'd never call me. I didn't even want to speak to him. I didn't want to see him: that thought terrified me most of all. I felt lashed raw from the kiss, and I feared him like an open wound feared salt.

At lunch, they were asking for volunteers to help organise the Halloween ball for Year 9 and 10 after school the following afternoon. I said yes just so I had an excuse not to turn up to study night. Josh and Alfie had looked at me strangely. I never volunteered for anything, but then Alfie had shrugged and said he'd help out, too. Josh couldn't, as he had rugby practice.

Ellie had given me a bewildered look, too, but said nothing else. Then, her and Georgia left the lunch table and wandered off with barely a goodbye.

The guys pounced on me immediately.

"You have a fight?"

"Did you break up?"

They asked at the same time.

Had we broken up? Since I went around kissing boys now, maybe that meant we had, but I wasn't sure, so I shrugged.

"Come, on, Jude. Sort it out. If you guys break up there's no chance for me and Georgia," Alfie whined.

"Mate, there's no chance for you and Georgia because you're too shit scared to go for it," Josh said without looking up from his plate. He'd covered his chips in cheese and tomato sauce as he always did before eating them very carefully, one by one, with his fingers.

"I'm gonna okay, Halloween Ball, it's happening."

"You said that before the Snow Ball last year," I pointed out. "And the summer fling."

Alfie looked at me, hurt. "Yeah, well, we can't all have girls falling into our laps, mate."

I frowned. "Hardly.

"Oh, come on? Ellie? Katy Phillips before she moved to Bristol. Abbie Driscoll."

"Mackenzie Waller," Josh supplied, shoving a chip in his mouth.

"Who?" I had no recollection of anyone called Mackenzie Waller.

"Oh, yeah!" Alfie's eyes lit up at the reminder. "Mackenzie, she worked at the Beach Hut. She was obsessed with you."

"If you say so," I muttered, looking at my phone again for a text that was never going to appear.

"I do say so. They all take one look at you, and they're like, 'Oh, Jude...you're so tall and nice. I love your freckles. Where's Jude, Alfie? Is Jude on Snapchat, Alfie?' His voice had gone high, and he batted his eyelashes at me.

"Yeah, whatever."

"It's not a bad impression, actually," Josh supplied. "Abbie Driscoll did sound like that."

As they both laughed, I stood from the table.

"Well, Georgie doesn't like me like that, so you don't really have that excuse, do you?" Then, for some stupid as shit reason, I said, "But I'd be quick because I'm pretty sure Caspien likes her."

Alfie's eyes bugged out of his head, face paling with genuine fear. "What?"

I shrugged. "He mentioned something about it." A lie. He had mentioned her, though I was certain he didn't like her. I was certain Caspien liked men. Older men. Perverts, specifically. But if it made Alfie get his finger out and if it meant they stopped focusing on me, then it wasn't a horrible lie. A lie told for the right reasons. *Like the ones you tell Ellie?*

"He mentioned that he likes her?" Alfie scowled. "Seriously? Does she know?"

I shrugged again. "I don't know. But girls are pretty good with this kind of thing." I gave him a pointed look. "Okay, gotta go. Need to speak with Miss Ukede about my biology exam."

I left them in the dining room. Alfie stared after me, his life with Georgia flashing before his eyes.

TWELVE

Of course, Ellie was right to be pissed with me for ignoring her all night, and since I'd also kissed someone else (a boy), I didn't blame her. But I also hadn't done much grovelling either. And that, I soon learned, was what had been expected of me. It was Georgia who gave me that lesson at the meeting for the Halloween ball the following afternoon.

"You should buy her something," she said quietly beside me.

"Huh?" The group were discussing what sort of music there should be; one of the girls had an uncle who did weddings. Another had a brother who was in a covers band. I couldn't be arsed either way but cast my vote for the covers band with a raise of my hand.

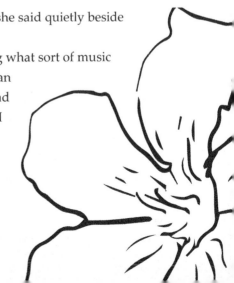

"Buy her a gift. To apologise," Georgia said.

"I already apologised."

This earned me a look. "She likes you a lot, you know."

"Yeah, I like her too."

"No, Jude, like...a lot, a lot. Christ, boys are so...clueless."

She wasn't wrong. I was clueless. Alfie was clueless.

Caspien wasn't, though. He was a boy who had a lot of clues.

And my mind was back on him again, where it had been most of the day. And yesterday. I'd lain awake most of the night thinking about it. Looking at his Instagram.

Had he liked me kissing him? Had he spent the last two days thinking about it in minute detail as I had? Unlikely, since he'd kissed boys before and men too, it wasn't a particularly big deal for him. Maybe that was why he left his school in Switzerland because he'd kissed them all. That particular thought made something blister on the inside of my gut.

No. He hadn't spent a single second thinking about it. He'd probably picked up the phone, called his pervert, and had a good old laugh about how terrible a kisser I was. I forced my attention back to Georgia and her advice on how to get Ellie to stop being pissed at me.

"So, what should I buy her?" I asked, turning to Georgia.

After clearing it with Beth, I invited Ellie over on Thursday evening. On Wednesday after school, I'd gone into town with Josh to pick up the 'apology gift'. Alfie had football and couldn't come, so Josh and I wandered into the make-up store with a screenshot Georgia sent me, a hefty percentage of my pocket money, and a look of extreme bewilderment on our faces.

Men, and most certainly boys, didn't belong in places like these. The mirrors and display cases made me think of those rooms at the carnival, and the number of attractive girls eyeing us curiously was overwhelming.

In the end, I showed my screenshot to a supermodel wearing a lot of make-up – who smiled at me like I was a stray kitten who'd wandered in – and went off to pick it out for me.

Josh and I stood still and tried not to touch anything.

It cost almost a hundred pounds for a small bag that weighed close to nothing. I was certain there was nothing in it. But it was gift-wrapped so nicely that I didn't want to open and ruin it to check. The receipt listed mascara, lip tint, and highlighter, which I assumed were very expensive.

"Hey, what if she thinks you're saying she needs make-up," Josh said as we walked back towards school where Luke was picking us up.

"She won't; she's not like that," I said. At least, I didn't think she was.

I didn't give it too much thought because most of my brain was wondering why on earth I was buying Ellie a gift to apologise for something when I'd done something far worse.

The rest of my brain was still thinking about that far worse thing.

I'd started to wonder if maybe I'd imagined it after drinking that glass of champagne. If maybe it had all been some strange drunken dream born from the same place as the hard-on I'd got the night we'd messed around on my bed. Figments of an overactive teenage boy's imagination.

The irony was that Caspien himself was the only person who could confirm whether it had happened or not. And I was avoiding him.

I was pretty sure I could avoid him forever with some careful strategising.

"Did Georgia pick these out then?" Ellie asked with a small, tempered smile. It was like she was holding back a bigger one.

It was Thursday night and we were facing each other on my bed. She'd torn open the top of the gift bag and was pulling the items out and inspecting them carefully one by one.

Was I supposed to deny it? Was it less of an apology since I hadn't picked them out myself? I had no clue. She looked at me, and her mouth transformed from a smile into something softer.

"Thank you, they're perfect."

"Sorry," I muttered. My skin had felt weird and ill-fitting since we'd come upstairs. Since we'd been alone.

My head was still full of Caspien, even with Ellie in front of me. His pretty mouth, his grey-blue eyes, his vicious sneer. There was comfort in those things. Because I knew my place in front of them. Beneath him.

Here, and perhaps whenever I was alone with Ellie, I felt like I was playing some role. One that didn't suit me and that I clearly wasn't very good at since I kept getting it wrong and missing my lines.

She nodded. "It's okay. I'm over it."

I couldn't tell if that was true or not.

We still weren't allowed to have the door closed, but it didn't stop Ellie from scooting up the bed and planting her mouth on mine.

I kept my hands by my sides at first but then worried that she might read something into that, so I slid my hand into her hair and angled her head closer. Kissing her back as hard as I could. Analysing it even as it was happening.

Familiar, sweet, and safe.

All things the kiss with Caspien hadn't been.

When she pressed her hand between my legs, tentative and gentle, I felt a stirring of something pleasant. But I didn't know if it was because I was thinking about Caspien's mouth while I compared them both.

But soon, he was all I was thinking about, and the pleasant feeling spread down and out, so it was another mouth and some other hand on my dick.

I pulled back quickly, guilty.

Ellie gave me a look of confusion that I tried smiling at.

I was relieved when Luke's voice from the bottom of the stairs crashed through the awkwardness.

"Jude! Come down a minute, will you?"

I gave Ellie a small smile and stood. "Uh, I'll be back in a minute."

She nodded, watching me with big doe eyes.

"The door was open," I told Luke.

Instead of saying anything he just nodded toward the kitchen and then went back into the living room and closed the door. I could hear the title music of University Challenge begin.

Confused, I wandered down the hall to the kitchen and almost shat myself at what I found there.

Caspien sat at the kitchen table, hands clasped in front of him.

Only when I closed the kitchen door did he turn to look at me. His eyes were dark and faintly furious.

"What are you doing here?" My question came out rude. I'd been avoiding him for a reason and now here he was sitting at my kitchen bloody table.

"I could ask you the same thing," he said.

I stared at him. "I live here."

"It's Thursday."

"Right? And?"

"Oh, so you knew what day it was?" His eyes widened. "Because I thought maybe you'd gotten your days mixed up again. Like you did on Tuesday, but no. It seems you didn't."

"I didn't."

"Okay, so then why aren't we studying in the library?"

I blinked. I really couldn't decipher the look in his eye.

"Because..." *I kissed you, and I haven't stopped thinking about it, and I was scared I might do it again.* "I was busy," I muttered, which seemed to incense him further.

"With your girlfriend?" he sniffed.

"Yes, actually."

He stared at me for a long time. Then he stood.

"Is this about the kiss?" he asked.

My cheeks burned so hot I was sure my head was about to burst into flame.

"Do you seriously think you're the first purportedly 'straight' boy to kiss me?" He let out a small laugh and then tilted his head to study me. "Oh no, wait, that's not it. It's because you liked it, isn't it? That's why you're being weird."

"Can you shut up," I warned.

A low thrum had begun to rattle in the pit of me. I wasn't sure if it was because I wanted to hit him or kiss him.

He took a step closer, and the low thrum turned to a loud thump.

"We can do it again if you like," he said with a sly smile. When he reached for me, I caught his wrist, holding it out from my body like it was a poisonous thing. "It would be far more interesting than watching you sigh your way through your biology homework."

I trembled at how close his mouth was. It would be nothing to just move my head, lower my mouth toward his, even if just to shut him up...

"Jude?" Ellie's voice came from the hallway outside.

I practically threw him away from me and watched as a look of pure delight swept over his features. Stepping away from the door just as she pushed it open, I turned to face Ellie, who looked surprised at the sight of Caspien.

"Oh, hey, Caspien." She glanced at me before giving him a small wave. "I didn't know you were here."

"Hello, Jude's girlfriend." He gave her a smile that sent a chill down my spine.

Ellie smiled back at him, a little confused. "Happy Birthday, by the way," she said to him.

He gave her a close-lipped smile.

She sidled closer to me and asked him: "Are you...staying, or?"

Caspien and I spoke at the same time.

"No."

"No."

I wanted him to disappear immediately.

I was certain then that she knew. And if she didn't, then she would soon, she would be able to guess the longer we were in the same room together.

"I suppose I'll get going," Caspien said. "Let you two do...whatever it was you were doing before I came along." He gave me a grin that I could only describe as unhinged.

When he was a few steps out into the hallway, Ellie called out, "You should hang out with us again soon."

"Sure, why not? Jude has my number." He gave me a pointed look.

Then he was gone. And I could breathe.

When we were alone, she turned to me. "What was he here for?"

My head scrambled. I decided to stay as close to the truth as possible. "We normally study together on Thursday nights. I forgot to cancel."

"Rude, Jude." She grinned playfully.

My phone buzzed in my back pocket as we made our way back upstairs.

Unknown:

Come over on Saturday. I need you for something.

I typed back quickly.

Me:

How did you even get this number??

Unknown:

Luke gave it to me. You know, since we're 'friends' now.

I ignored him until Ellie left – though my phone sat like a silent siren on my bedside for the next two hours. I could barely hold a conversation with her, my mind obsessing over what he might be sending me while I sat there and let Ellie kiss me.

When I finally looked, there was only one new message from earlier.

Caspien:

Come over by 12 on Saturday.

Me:

I can't. I'm busy.

I had brushed my teeth and was getting into bed before he replied.

Caspien:

It wasn't a request, Jude.

Then:

Caspien:

I'd hate for your girlfriend to find out how much you like kissing boys.

I froze. My blood boiling in my veins. I could imagine him smirking as he lay in bed, enjoying every minute of making my life a living nightmare. I shoved my phone back into my pocket and resolved to ignore him and his threats.

Ignoring him lasted until I woke up on Saturday morning. There was another text from him.

Caspien:

I found your girlfriend on snapchat. I think I should message her and tell her what we did.

I was all the way awake in an instant, my fingers typing furiously, heart thumping wildly.

Me:

As if you would.

Caspien:

It's amusing you think I wouldn't.

My heartbeat quickened, panicked.

Me:

Leave her alone.

The three dots appeared a few moments later.

Caspien:

Maybe you're the one who should leave her alone. Since you like boys.

My cheeks flamed and my mouth dried. Of course, I wasn't going to answer that. Or refer to it whatsoever.

Anyway, I was pretty sure I didn't like boys. I just liked one boy. Who I in fact hated. My head hurt.

Me:

Are you seriously this bored?

Caspien:

It's not boredom, Jude. I just really like playing with you.

I loathed how my body reacted to that. My dick took notice instantly and I shoved the phone away from me and stuck my hand down my boxers.

Caspien:

I think I'll start with 'Hey Ellie, I feel shit about this, but there's something you should know about Jude: Surprise! He likes boys!'

Me:

Are you psychotic? Like, is that your thing?

It would certainly explain a lot.

Caspien:

> I bet you'd like to know all about my thing, wouldn't you, Judith?

Me:

> Fuck off

I threw my phone down on the bed again. It was another minute before it vibrated again. Another five before I felt brave enough to look at it.

Caspien:

> You have until 12 to get here or I'm messaging her.

THIRTEEN

Though I was pretty sure I was going to be doing more murdering than studying, I shoved my biology textbook and my laptop into my bag and headed out of the house. Luke and Beth had gone out earlier to some farmer's market on the other side of the island and wouldn't be back until later.

I dumped my bike at the back door, noting that Gideon's car was in its space, and made my way to the library. It was empty. I was passing the sunroom when I spotted Gideon standing at the far end, where the Oleander plant had been before Luke's specialist contractor had ripped it out. He was staring at the one we'd put in its place; a Brugmansia Aurea. It took calling his name twice before he turned around, blinking as though coming awake.

I noticed then that he wasn't dressed properly, wearing a smart shirt and what looked like striped pyjama bottoms. He looked out of it – like he was drunk. His hair was mussed, and a light stubble coated his jaw.

"Oh, Jude, hi. You'll be here to work, I'll get out of your way." He brushed a hand through his hair, dishevelling it further.

"No, I'm here for Caspien," I told him. "Have you seen him?"

"Who?"

Concern rose in me. "Caspien. He wasn't in the library."

"I'm here," Caspien's voice sounded from behind me. I turned to see him sitting on the top step of the staircase. It looked like he'd been there a while watching Gideon.

As Gideon came toward me, he smiled. On his feet, he wore outdoor shoes.

"Christ, every day you look more and more like him…" he whispered, looking at Caspien. I felt his hand on my shoulder.

His voice was even quieter when he spoke, a whisper meant only for us. "I am certain he was sent here to torture me until the end of my days," he said before wandering down the hallway into one of the sitting rooms, the door closing with a gentle snick behind him.

"What's wrong with him?"

"He's in one of his moods." Caspien didn't sound particularly concerned.

I rounded the stairwell so that I stood at its foot. He still sat on the top step. He was wearing shorts and a T-shirt, his feet bare, and his hair a sleep-rumpled mess. At the sight of him, all the anger that had carried me here disappeared like a fog in the sun's warmth.

"And what sort of mood is that?"

Caspien studied me. "Have you ever had your heart broken?"

I never had any clue what he was about to say, ever, but this was completely beyond anything I could have expected. I had no clue how to answer. Whether I even should. What would he do with that kind of information? But then I was thinking about my parents. About how much I'd cried and how alone I'd felt in the weeks and months after. Was that heartbreak? It had felt like something inside me had broken, never to be fixed again.

I didn't feel it as intensely now, not with any consistency, but there were still moments when the longing for them was so strong and fierce it would suffocate me.

"Yes."

His gaze sharpened as if my answer intrigued him.

He considered something for what felt like a long time. Then he said, "I think it's easier for hearts to heal when they're still young. Gideon's was fully grown and weaker than most when it was broken. It will never heal."

Something hung unsaid in the air between us for a moment before I glanced again in the direction Gideon had gone. I returned my gaze to Caspien.

"Well," I asked him in a firmer voice. "What did you need my help with?"

Caspien stood, let out a sigh, and turned.

"Come," he said, disappearing down the upper floor corridor.

Anticipation buzzed under my skin like a swarm of agitated bees.

With a surge of trepidation, I followed him up the stairs. I could hear sounds down the hallway in the opposite direction of his bedroom, along the 'closed-off' wing, so I followed them. There was only one door open, one about halfway down the corridor.

Inside the room, the sheets had already been removed from the furniture, and he was pulling up the sash windows on one side of the dual-aspect room. The room itself was in much the same style as the rest of the house, but there was something distinctly feminine about it. Where the downstairs décor had notes of burgundy, green, and navy, this was done in pinks, creams, and purples.

Caspien was by the window, an easel set up in front of it and fiddling with what looked like a box of pencils.

"You can sit there," he said, pointing to the window seat diagonally opposite where he stood. He'd already set it up with a cushion.

"Why?"

He stopped what he was doing and stared at me as though I was an idiot. "I'd have thought it obvious, no? I'm drawing you." He went back to arranging his pencils.

I stared at him in shock. "You want to draw me?"

He flicked his gaze up from under his messy blonde hair. "It isn't really a matter of wanting; it's a matter of necessity. I have to submit a life portrait for my art exam and since there is very little life around here..." He looked around the room specifically. "You'll have to do."

My mouth dried up as I gripped the strap of my bag against me to steady myself. This wasn't even close to what my mind had come up with when I'd wondered what he'd needed me for.

"What about Gideon?"

Without looking up, he said, "Gideon couldn't sit still if his life depended on it."

"I'm not..." I wanted to say 'model material' or 'not going to make a good model', but instead I said "... doing it."

Caspien sighed. "Yes, you are. Sit down, Jude."

"You threatened me. Now you want me to *help* you? That's not... that's messed up, Caspien."

"Oh, well, if we're going to be doing that, then technically, you threatened me first."

I opened my mouth, then closed it. "That...wasn't the same thing."

"No?"

I huffed my way across the room towards the window seat. "I mean, couldn't you just ask me to sit here for you like a normal person? Like a friend?" I already knew what he was going to say before he said it.

"We're not friends, Jude."

"No. We definitely aren't." I walked to the window and threw my bag down first before slumping into the window seat. "We're playing at it; for Gideon and Luke."

He levelled a look at me. "That's correct."

I glared angrily out the window for a few minutes until he said, "Didn't you bring a book?"

I turned to glare at him. Of course, I did. I always had a book in my bag, something he knew well enough. Something he'd found surprising at first given my 'airhead-looking face'.

"I mean, you can read if you like. That's sort of how I imagined it."

Well, now I wouldn't read. Not if it was how he imagined it. Instead, I pulled my knees up on the seat, wrapped my arms around them, and stared out the window.

With a soft sigh, Caspien began to draw.

I rested my head on my knees and stared out at the grounds of Deveraux; honeyed autumn light poured over its surface. You could see the lake from this window, our cottage too, but at a different angle from the window in Caspien's bedroom. The breeze was pleasant and soft, the sound of birds hypnotic, and with the gentle scratch of Caspien's pencil lulling me off, I felt my eyes begin to close over. I was on the cusp of sleep when I heard his voice, soft as a feather against my skin.

"You'd have said no," he said.

My eyes snapped open, and I lifted my head to look at him. "What?"

His shoulders dropped, and he rolled his eyes. He motioned with one finger for me to turn my head back around, and I complied.

"If I'd asked you to come over and model for me, you'd have said no." His voice wasn't as soft, but there was still an edge of vulnerability that I hadn't heard before – not since that night I'd found him alone, but that didn't count. That night existed in some weird alternate universe where this Caspien didn't live.

Would I have said no? Everything was strange now after we'd kissed. After *I'd* kissed him. It wasn't as if things had ever been normal between us. Caspien was like no one I'd ever met before, but before the kiss, it had been manageable, at least. We had been making small incremental steps toward something that might have, under some definition, be called a friendship. Until I'd ruined it.

Christ. This was actually my fault.

"I'm sorry," I said.

I could imagine him frowning but I didn't dare turn my head. "What for?"

"For kissing you, I guess," I muttered, embarrassed. I was glad I couldn't see him. "I don't know why I did that."

"Oh please," he scoffed. "You did it because you wanted to. The real mystery is *why* you wanted to. Given you purportedly hate me. Given you don't like boys. And given you have a girlfriend."

I did turn to look at him then. "Why are you like this?"

He lowered his pencil. "You'll have to be more specific."

I waved in his general direction. "Like that, this. You're always so bloody..." I shoved myself off the seat and stood. "You make it so hard. You're literally impossible to be around. No wonder you have no friends."

"Who said I needed friends?" He shrugged. "Friends are useless."

"*Useless...*"

"Yes."

"Have you ever even had any? How would you know?"

He stared at me, and for once, it looked as though he had nothing smart to say in return. I thought about the night in his room again, where he'd said I was only there because Gideon and Luke had made me. I thought of how he'd hugged me when I'd said I wasn't. How fragile he'd seemed that night. Where was that Caspien? Who was that bizarre version of Caspien? The craziest part was that I was a lot more comfortable around the one in front of me now.

He was just so bloody confusing to me. To *every* part of me.

"I need the toilet." My body was stiff and sore from sitting, and that weird, jangly feeling was back beneath my skin. Like the crackle of thunder before a lightning strike.

"You can't run away every time something gets a little difficult, you know," he snarked as I reached the door.

My cheeks were hot. Because I had run; I'd run to the bathroom the night I'd gotten hard, I'd run to the cottage after I kissed him, and now.

"I'm not running; I'm going to the bathroom."

"Sure. But you'd better come back."

I didn't answer him, walking out of the bedroom without looking back. I took the stairs nearest this side of the house, an old servant stairwell, I assumed, which twisted down and along a dark stone corridor for a bit until I ended up on the far side of the kitchen. Elspeth was doing something violent with dough on the large wooden countertop, and she gasped in fright when she saw me.

"Jude! My god! I thought you were a ghost!"

"I am. I haunt this house on the weekends, didn't you know?"

"Ha, oh, hush you," she laughed. "What on earth are you doing coming from that way?"

I wasn't sure what to tell her, wasn't sure Caspien would want her to know we were in some unused bedroom while he drew me. "Um, we were studying in one of the other rooms today, the one on the other side of the house." I pointed upwards in the general direction I thought the room was.

She gave me a sad kind of smile. "Ah, Seraphina's..."

I froze, a chill prickling over my whole body. He'd taken me into his mother's room? His *dead* mother's room. A shiver ran the length of my body.

Elspeth wiped her hands on her flour-dusted apron and came toward me, clearly concerned about what she saw on my face.

"He must think a lot of you to let you in there. He doesn't let any of us in, not even to clean it or change the bedsheets after he's slept in there."

He *slept* in there?

"I didn't know..."

She pressed her lips together and nodded sadly. "She was such a beauty, such a sweet, sweet girl."

"You knew her?" I asked instead.

Another sad nod. She looked like she was about to burst into tears, and I wasn't sure what I'd do if she did.

"Saw her grow up. Sad business what happened." I didn't know what had happened, and though I desperately wanted to ask, desperately wanted to know anything that might explain why Caspien was the way he was, I didn't dare.

"Oh, I shouldn't be talking about that stuff with you; sorry, love."

Her face softened into a gentler smile, less haunted. "I'm so glad he has you, Jude. That boy needs a good bloody friend." There was something very specific in her tone, in the expression on her face that I didn't understand then but which, of course, I do now.

Obviously, I wanted to tell her that we weren't friends, that he'd made it quite clear he didn't want or need any. Especially me. I wanted to tell her that I'd tried, that I'd been trying for weeks to be his friend, and at every opportunity, he'd thrown it back in my face.

But then I thought about it...

Had I really tried? Or had I decided I hated him the moment he'd hurt my feelings back at the start of summer and resented his presence in my life since then? How much of an effort had I really made?

Christ, friends didn't go about kissing other friends and getting hard by rubbing on them. Shame and guilt flooded over me. What sort of friendship had I offered, really? He might have threatened me to come here today, but I'd threatened him long before that. He was right. I'd done it for his own good, but I'd still done it. I hadn't offered support or advice, not the way I would, were it Josh or Alfie. I'd never even tried – properly – to get to know him.

Yes, he made me feel strange and odd. I might have wanted to kiss him every time I looked at him, but all of that was my problem. It didn't change the fact that despite what he said – forcefully – Caspien did need a friend.

I let Elspeth make us a cheese sandwich, and I carried it on a tray with two cartons of juice and a couple of apples back up to his dead mother's room.

I was *going* to be nicer to him.

I was *going* to be his friend, whether he let me or not.

FOURTEEN

He looked surprised like he truly hadn't expected me to come back.

"Elspeth made us some lunch," I announced with a stupid, cheery tone.

"Do you want to eat in here or somewhere else?" The room felt sacred now, not a place to eat cheese sandwiches, but I wasn't going to mention that.

"Here is fine," he said, looking suspicious.

I set the tray down on the floor next to my backpack and carried the plate and juice over to him.

He didn't say thanks as he took it, just watched me mistrustfully.

He placed the juice on the window ledge before setting the plate on his lap and picking up his sandwich.

We ate in silence, me sneaking looks at him when I thought he might not be looking at me. He never was. I was pretty sure Caspien never looked at me when I

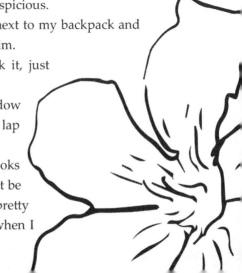

wasn't looking at him. There were always more interesting things for him to look at, though unfortunately, that was not the case for me.

"I wouldn't have said no," I said after a lengthy silence.

He turned to look at me, pale blue eyes narrowing ever so slightly.

"I mean, if you'd asked me to come over. If you'd said you needed me for something, I wouldn't have said no."

He put down his sandwich and turned his body fully to me. Suspicion still swam in his eyes. "Did you get a personality transplant while you were in the kitchen?"

I shrugged. "Maybe I was just hangry."

"Maybe." He didn't look convinced.

"I didn't get a chance to eat before I came over, you know, with that whole blackmailing thing." I took a bite and gave him a playfully pointed look.

"I told you last night I needed you here by noon," he said. "You should have gotten up earlier."

I swallowed my mouthful and chased it down with a long drink of juice. He really was the most perplexing person I'd ever met. Every side of him thorny and prickled – a hedgehog had been the perfect description – even the pretty sides. And he was pretty.

Terrifyingly so right at that moment.

Bathed in sunshine, sleeves rolled up to show off delicate wrists and finely tapered fingers. Bed shorts riding high on long lean legs that were far stronger than they looked.

I picked up my other sandwich and looked out the window, where it was far safer for my eyes. It was a bright December afternoon, with a gentle breeze dancing off the trees and a clear, cloudless sky for miles. With food in my stomach and my new resolution to try and be an actual proper friend to Caspien, I settled in to read.

It was just after four in the afternoon when he stood and declared he was finished. I'd read most of La Morte D'Arthur over the afternoon and wouldn't have minded if it had taken him another hour so I could have finished it.

I stood, groaning a little as the blood rushed back to my butt and legs, stretching my arms over my head to adjust my spine.

I watched him pack away his pencils – I still wasn't certain if they were the ones I'd bought him for his birthday – into a large wooden box, organising them just so before closing and latching the box. He lifted the large sketch pad and was about to flip it closed when he caught me staring.

"Do you want to see it?" he asked stiffly.

"Yeah. If that's okay."

He shrugged and held the pad out to me. Nerves fluttered in my stomach as I took it. I'd no idea how Caspien saw me. I mean, I had an idea, given the things he said and did, but how had he drawn me on the page?

I didn't even know if he was any good at drawing. That would almost be worse. As I took his sketch pad, I prepared myself to say something kind no matter what. Even if he'd drawn me hideously.

I held my breath and looked down.

Deep down, I suppose I'd known he wouldn't be bad. I'd yet to find something he couldn't do, especially if it involved his hands, but nothing prepared me for just how good he was.

In beautifully realised pencil detail, I sat in the window with my head buried in a book and my face etched in furious concentration. He'd picked out the wisps of hair that curled at the back of my head and around my ear, the freckles across my nose and cheeks, the dark shadow of my eyelashes.

Outside, he'd somehow caught the glimmer of sun on the pond as well as a few birds soaring into the sky. There was the intricate de-tailing of the window frame and the strip of sunlight cutting across the wooden floor beneath me. The composition had an unfinished quality, with the edges fading into the white of the page.

It was exceptional. I felt moved in a way I hadn't prepared for.

I realised my mouth was open. He stood with his box tucked

under his arm and a faint frown on his face as he looked at his own work.

I knew he didn't need praise, certainly not mine, but I gave it to him anyway.

"You're really good. This is so good."

His gaze flicked to mine and I saw the faintest glimmer of something in the corners. Like he was pleased.

He looked back at the portrait.

"It will be better when I fill it in." He took the pad and folded it closed. "You weren't as terrible a model as I thought." He set the box on top of the pad and moved to close the window.

"Is that your way of saying, '*Thank you, Jude? You sat for hours in a really uncomfortable position for me, and I'm grateful.*'"

"Of course not." He had his back to me now, climbing up on the window ledge to pull closed the little latch on the top. It gave me a ridiculous view of the tops of his thighs and the curve of his arse. I tried not to look. I was about to turn away completely when he twisted weirdly and began to fall.

I rushed toward him and threw my hands up, meaning to catch him, but the gravity was too much and I stumbled too, but backwards, both of us falling into a heap on the floor. Me on my back and him on top, chest to chest, face to face. His mouth was so close that if I reached up just a little...

I couldn't.

Wouldn't.

Not again.

He stared at me, a half-embarrassed, half-angry little frown on his face. I waited for him to lash out with an insult about my clumsiness or stupidity, about it being my fault he fell in the first place.

But instead, he kissed me.

He pressed his lips onto mine, shoved his tongue into my mouth and ravaged it.

Then my hands were in his hair and holding his head in place because the thought of him stopping was the worst thing I could imagine.

I would die if he stopped now; I was certain of it.

His mouth was as warm and wet and perfect as I remembered, and I explored it like the paradise it was. Greedy and dizzy from the pleasure it offered.

When he pressed his body harder against me and moved, I saw pure white light, parts of us rubbing together that caused my whole body to sing loudly. Fireworks sparked behind my closed eyes and heat building so quick and urgent that I thought I was about to be incinerated from the inside.

He made a noise then, some desperate whimper that I knew I'd spend the rest of my life thinking about, and tore his mouth from mine to look down into my eyes.

His cheeks were flushed pink and his mouth a bright strawberry red and I thought I might cry from how beautiful he looked.

It was the sort of beautiful great art and literature was created for. Fragile and delicate and destructive. I would write about it the very instant I was alone, and if the words didn't exist to describe it, then I'd create new ones. I reached my lips up, seeking his again, and he took pity on me and kissed me again. As he tilted his angle and moved again, a jolt of pleasure raced down my spine to my balls.

"Cas…" I moaned, moving one hand down to his arse and gripping his cheek hard, using that grip to move him over where I needed him. We kissed and moved and breathed together, minutes or hours or days of tasting him, of chasing that edge of pleasure that would take me to the end of the world.

Before I could stop it, I was over the edge, falling.

With a deep groan, I bit out against his mouth as I crushed him against me.

Caspien followed me a few moments later, or at least I thought he did. It was quieter, and he held his mouth pressed against mine, breathing into it as his long limbs trembled. Then it was over. He dropped his head to the crook of my neck and breathed me in.

It was me who spoke first.

"I'll break up with Ellie."

He sat up and stared down at me.

"Whatever for?"

"Because..." I gave him a look that said it should be obvious. It *was* obvious. To me, at least.

He climbed up and off my body, leaving me feeling bare and exposed. Cold and very wet too. He'd lain on me for approximately two and a half minutes, and somehow, my body had gotten used to his weight on it. I felt like I might be blown away.

"Because of *that* you want to break up with your girlfriend?" He snorted like it was the most absurd thing he'd ever heard. "Don't be such a child."

I had never felt less of a child in my life. I rose to my feet.

"I don't know what it's like at boarding school, but here *children* don't do that." I pointed at the floor where we'd just done the most intimate thing I'd ever done with another person. "Christ, Cas, I've never done that before with anyone." I wanted him to know what that meant.

He blinked, and then his eyes grew dark, like a predator whose prey had just shown some fatal weakness.

"Is that your way of saying you're a virgin? What, can't you get it up for her?" His smirk was cruel, and I felt it like a needle in my chest. "Why do you think that is?"

I hated him again. Rooted around for something to say back, something shaped cruelly I could throw at him. But then I remembered the promise I'd made myself: be his friend. Even if he didn't want it. Even if he made it impossible. *Make an effort.*

"You don't need to act like this, you know," I said calmly, though my heart was thundering behind my ribs. "Like nothing means anything or like everything's a joke. You don't need to act like that with me."

His face did a strange thing, like he was trying very hard to keep something from showing on it.

"But it didn't mean anything. We got off together, for Christ's sake. I've done it a million times before. It doesn't mean we're in love, Jude."

Love. The word was huge and loud and threatened to flatten me. I felt my entire body heat up from my toes to my hair.

I hadn't been implying that. It hadn't even crossed my mind. I didn't love him, for Christ's sake. I was pretty sure I hated him. Or at least, what I felt for him was complicated and took up a lot of time and space and energy in my brain but it wasn't love. It wasn't anything like it.

Avoiding his eyes, I crossed to where my bag was and grabbed it up off the floor.

"I have to go." I started toward the door.

"Oh look, Judith's running away again."

I stopped and turned back. His eyes were hard as marbles, sparkling in the dying sunlight.

"You know, if you don't want me to go, you could just say that." It was bravado, spoken from some senseless place I'd never even been.

I imagined some alternate reality where he said don't go, Jude, and I wouldn't. We'd clean up and lie together on his bed and talk. Maybe about books or films or music or something else. Maybe later, we'd do that all over again. Slower, less fevered.

And as he said nothing in response I deluded myself that he was imagining the same. When it was clear he wasn't going to speak, I pulled my bag over my shoulder and said, "I'll see you on Tuesday."

I left him standing there in his dead mother's bedroom, not knowing that winter would come and go, the leaves of the trees would be turning, sprouting the green of a new spring before I saw him again.

FIFTEEN

As I walked out of last period on Tuesday I checked my phone to see a message had come through at 2:46p.m.

It said:

Caspien:

> I'm going back to La Troyeux today. Don't bother coming over.

I'd stopped still in the middle of the corridor and read it over and over.

He was leaving. Leaving Deveraux. Leaving the island? I felt the bottom drop out of my stomach, a rush of loss and a swell of something like panic.

A body nudged into me from behind.

"No watching porn on the school grounds, Judey," Alfie snickered.

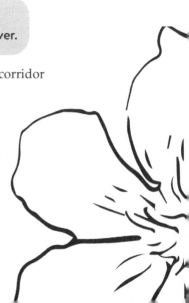

Georgia was leaning into him with her head on his shoulder. When I'd been getting off with Caspien, Alfie had somehow found the balls to ask her out. Had gone to her house with flowers and everything – I'd been seriously impressed. Now they were a thing.

Now I knew we would be expected to do things as a couple, something which had begun to hang over me like a fat rain cloud since I heard about it on Saturday night.

But right now, none of that mattered. Right now, Caspien was leaving.

"I have to go." I shoved my phone in my pocket and legged it down the stairs and out of the building.

Ellie was waiting for me outside and she turned to smile.

"Sorry, Ellie. Emergency at home. I'll call you later."

She stood with a wide-eyed look on her face as I rushed past her towards the school gate where Luke's van was parked in its usual spot.

I threw myself inside. He turned to me looking worried.

"What's—"

"Is Cas going back to Switzerland?" I asked as I pulled on my seatbelt.

He shook his head, then shrugged. "I've no idea; was out at St. Helier today."

"But you were there yesterday. What did he say?"

"Never saw him, Jude, what's the matter?" He looked worried about me.

"I just need to speak to him before he goes. It's really important."

I could feel Luke's eyes on me as I pulled my phone out and texted him back. I'd planned to be cool. I'd thought of nothing else but seeing him for two and a half days. How I'd act when I saw him tonight, what I would say, what I wouldn't. Now I cared about none of that. Now I only cared about stopping him from leaving.

Me:

I'm on my way home. Can you wait for me? Please.

He never responded, and when Luke drove me up the long drive to the back door of Deveraux I already knew I was too late.

I found Gideon in one of the downstairs sitting rooms. He was sipping a glass of whiskey and writing something in what looked like a journal. He glanced up as I came into the room.

"Jude, there you are," he said as though he'd been expecting me and I hadn't come bursting unexpectedly into his house.

"Is he gone?" My voice was twisted tight like a knot.

Gideon gave me a sad little smile. "He left this morning. His flight into Zurich landed..." He looked at his Rolex. "Oh, about twenty minutes or so ago."

Of course, he'd sent me the text after landing then.

I felt the strength leave me. Impotent fury curling my fists. This was my fault. I shouldn't have run away on Saturday. If I'd stayed. If I'd called or texted or come to see him on Sunday...maybe he wouldn't have left.

I sank down onto the closest couch and put my head in my hands, exhausted suddenly.

"Why...?" I breathed out. I hadn't meant for Gideon to hear, but he had, and he got up from the desk and came to sit next to me. He put a comforting hand on the back of my head, ruffling my hair gently.

"Why do you think?"

I lifted my head to look at him and his hand fell away.

"I don't know." I shook my head.

Gideon had the strangest expression on his face as he said, "Oh, Jude, I think you do."

I shook my head. "I don't. You said he hated it there. Why would he go back?"

"Cas is a bit of a masochist at heart." Gideon seemed almost amused by this. "He likes to prove to himself he can do anything, stick out anything. But, well, I do know that he would have stayed had he thought there was something worth staying here for." He levelled at me the most calculated look I'd ever seen on a human. It chilled me to the bone. "Did something happen between you two?

Did you have a fight?"

I shrugged miserably. "We always fight. But I wanted..." I trailed off. "I hoped I'd get here before he left...to tell him..." I couldn't order a single thought in my head so that I might explain it. Though truly, I had no idea what I was trying to tell Gideon. Or what I'd have told Caspien had I got there in time.

Of course, it wouldn't have made any difference. I know that now. But I was stupid then. Naïve. I was Sisyphus and Cas the mountain.

Gideon said nothing for a long time, but then he reached into his pocket, pulled out a handkerchief, and handed it to me. I was embarrassed to find I'd been crying.

The handkerchief was pale grey and had the initials G.L.D monogrammed in darker grey. For Gideon Lorcan Deveraux, I would learn later.

"I was in love once, too," he said.

I started with shock.

I shook my head again. "I'm not. That's not what I—."

"Not even with your girlfriend?" He cut in easily. "Lovely young lady by all accounts. Pretty, too." His mouth twitched with something resembling distaste, but I was distracted as his sharp stare left mine and drifted across the room. I followed his eyes to where a portrait of his sister, Caspien's mother, hung. She wore a yellow dress, the neckline hanging off her shoulders to show off a long, elegant neck. She had his eyes, a crystalline stare that pierced through skin and bone, but her mouth was softer. A hint of a smile pulled at the corner. I could imagine her laugh.

"Love is often painful. I think it's rather the very nature of it."

"What happened to her?" I heard myself asking. I'd meant to ask something else. Something about love and pain and why he was so sure the nature of one was the other.

But I suddenly wanted to know about Seraphina Deveraux. I'd heard stories. Everyone who lived on this island had. Some stories had her locked in the attic of this house still. Some had her alive in a hospital in London, feral and unhinged. But most believed she'd died by suicide because the husband she gave up her name and her inheritance for left her for another woman. I wasn't sure which one I believed or hoped was true; all of them were equally as tragic.

"She fell in love too," he said obliquely before turning from her image and looking back at me. "You could write to him," Gideon said, standing. He was walking back to his desk.

"Write?"

Until then, I'd written exactly one letter in all of my fifteen years. To a boy in 1942. For a history project a few years ago, they'd made us write to our imaginary counterparts in occupied Jersey to ask them how they felt about the Nazis and tell them what lessons had been learned from the second world war. Jacob – the name I'd invented – had not written back.

"Caspien has such an old soul; I think he'd appreciate a letter rather than a text or an email."

"A letter," I repeated stupidly.

A few minutes later, he came back from his desk with a sheet of headed notepaper with what I assumed to be Caspien's dorm number and address in La Troyeux written on it.

"I don't know. I don't think he wants to hear from me." I was folding the piece of paper anyway. Once and then again into a small cream square.

"Of course he does," Gideon said, putting his hand on my shoulder. "You're his only friend in this world."

"Cas hates me, Gideon."

At this, Gideon threw his head back and laughed. "He said that?"

"Not in as many words, but he's made it pretty clear, yeah."

"Well, then he definitely cares about you, that's certain."

I frowned at that. "I don't understand."

Gideon seemed a little disbelieving that I was being so slow about this. "If Caspien didn't care, then you'd know, trust me." Gideon smiled. "His ambivalence is much crueller than his animosity. If he acts as though he hates you, then it's very likely he feels the opposite."

There was a gleam in Gideon's eye that day that I took to be a sort of shared joy. Something well-meant and benevolent. Like he was imparting some kind and helpful wisdom that would help me navigate what was to come.

But, of course, nothing could have been further from the truth.

After dinner and a shower, I went to my room and dug around in a box until I found a notepad. Then I sat at my desk to write a letter to Caspien. Gideon knew him best of all, so if he thought he'd respond to a letter – he'd completely ignored my text earlier – then I would try.

> *Dear Cas,*
> *I'm writing this because you left. Why did you leave? I thought you hated that school?*

I tore the page out and crumpled it up. If I was going to write to him, then it had to at least hold his bloody attention. I'd been writing for years, squirrelling away on a fantasy story set in a small island town I never wanted anyone to read. But still, I knew I could write better than what I'd just written down.

I had no clue what to say. How honest to be. I decided to write it as though he'd never read it, the way I wrote my fantasy story.

> *Dear Cas.*
> *You left.*
> *I can't believe you left.*
> *I went to the house today to try and catch you before you did, but I was too late. It felt different without you inside it. I think that's how my life is going to feel now. Sometimes, it feels as though you've always been here; I can't remember what my life was like before this summer. Before you.*
> *I'm guessing you left because you didn't want to*

look at me after what happened, and I suppose I get it. I've been scared for days about looking at you, too, scared about what I might do when I did. I haven't stopped thinking about it.

You're everywhere: in my head and my dreams, and I'm not sure what it all means.

I meant it when I said I'd break up with Ellie. I would have. If you wanted me to, then I would have. I shouldn't be with Ellie. Not when I feel the things I do about you. Things that scare me. I'm not scared that I might be gay or anything; I don't think I care about that. I'm only scared of you not feeling the same way and what that might make me do.

I'm sure you don't feel the same way. I'm still pretty sure you hate me – though when I said that to Gideon, he said that's the proof that you don't. That you have to care to have said anything at all about your feelings.

But you've gone back to a place you hate because it's preferable to being here, with me. So, I don't know what to think about that. What if I'd promised never to kiss you again? Never to touch you again? Would you have stayed then?

I think that would almost be worse. To see you and be close to you and have the memory of what it felt like to...to be with you like that and not be allowed to do it again.

But really, I just want you to come back.

I'll do whatever you want me to do as long as you come back.

Please,

Jude.

I almost tore the page out again. More than once. But in the end, I didn't. I slid it under my mattress and decided to sleep on it – literally. I'd read it and see how I felt about it then.

Except that didn't happen. The following night, as we were setting the table and Beth was standing by the stove cooking chicken stir fry, she'd let out a horrible scream before doubling over in pain.

Those minutes after were sharp with alarm as Luke rushed in from the living room and wrapped her in his arms.

And then I saw the blood. Blood where even I knew there shouldn't be.

It was the most terrified I'd ever seen my sister. The most hysterical. She was saying 'no, no, no, no' over and over as tears streamed out of her eyes.

Shaking and pale, Luke was trying very hard to sound calm as he told me to fetch a bunch of towels from the upstairs press. Next, I was to take the key to Beth's car from the hook and lay the towels out on the passenger seat.

When I'd done that and come back to the kitchen, he had Beth up and standing, though she was still doubled over and holding her stomach while crying silently into Luke's chest. I've never forgotten the look he gave me over her head, desperate, lost, and already grieving. Because he knew. I think maybe he knew everything that was to follow. The dreadful chain of events that would happen after that awful December night.

SIXTEEN

In some ways, the loss of Luke and Beth's baby should have been easier to cope with than the death of my parents.

I didn't know the baby; I hadn't even seen it beyond a grainy black-and-white scan attached to the fridge. Honestly, I'd barely thought about it much at all. But the effect it had on Luke and Beth and the easy, comfortable life they'd built around me was tectonic. Like some great shifting of the earth beneath my feet. What had been a solid, predictable, and untroubled home life turned into something else overnight.

The first week after, Beth never left her bed. Luke would come home from work and cook dinner – he wasn't good at it, so I'd help him peel carrots and pota- toes and cook simple, tasteless meals for us at night, which she didn't eat. He tried to smile at me, but it never quite reached his eyes, and I watched helplessly as strands of grey whispered through his once-dark hair. Death and misery moved into the house with us and refused to adjust to our way of life.

So instead, we adjusted to it.

For the first couple of weeks, it was as though Beth had been the one to die. Luke cried, the house felt cold and quiet, and I never saw her once. If she did venture out of her room, it was after I went to school, and though I could hear soft murmurs and quiet sobs through the walls at night, she felt like a ghost that was haunting the cottage. I suppose I was surprised by how she was coping – or rather, not coping. As I said, my sister wasn't a very emotional person, but after the baby died, it was like some other person had emerged from inside her, and they were filled with feeling.

I thought about going to speak to her, to tell her how sorry I was, but I was scared I was the last person she'd want to see. The child she hadn't wanted while the one she had was gone.

I felt loud and clumsy, as though I was intruding just by existing, so I tried to be as quiet and invisible as possible. It was a familiar pattern; it was the one I'd fallen into when I'd first come to live with Beth and Luke, so it was easy to revert to again.

It was a miserable time and even the weather seemed to agree; the world turning tearfully damp and grey. Jersey rarely saw snow, even in winter, but the rain was a constant pour that seemed to go on without end.

I tried calling Caspien a couple of times that first week, but each time, it would ring a few times before switching to voicemail. There were never the same number of rings, so I knew that he was avoiding me on purpose.

My voicemails were embarrassing. Pathetic. And I would have been ashamed about them except that I missed him so much. All I wanted was to go up to the house and have him snipe, bite, and say something cold to me because that would mean he was here and nothing had changed. That would mean anger and resentment could douse the achingly sad loneliness inside me.

Worse was how Ellie was with me. Asphyxiating me with attention. She treated me like I was some small broken bird she'd found by the road. Talking to me in soft tones, fetching my lunch for me, offering to carry my bag, and levelling big, concerned eyes at me during every class we shared. I didn't understand it; I felt guilty about it.

Of course, I was sad about the baby. Of course, I was sad for Beth and Luke, and of course, I wished it hadn't happened, but the weight of sadness lying in the pit of my stomach wasn't truly about the baby. It was the disappearance of the person haunting my hopes and dreams from my life as suddenly and completely as though I'd lost a limb and was trying to adjust to a life without it.

It did, however, serve as a good cover, and I would often find myself thinking of him, longingly and would glance up to find Ellie giving me one of her doting looks.

By the end of the second week, everything changed once again.

It was Saturday – it also happened to be my sixteenth birthday - and I'd lay in bed until almost noon.

There'd been nothing planned, of course. I would have been surprised if Luke had even remembered (it was always Beth who remembered things like birthdays and anniversaries), and I wasn't expecting anything.

I was going over to Alfie's later for a party he'd arranged for me. He'd invited the girls, a few others from our year, and a few lads from Josh's rugby team. His mum and dad – notoriously relaxed about this kind of thing - were staying overnight at some fancy hotel in town for a Christmas party.

But as I hauled myself out to bed and toward the bathroom, the door to Beth and Luke's bedroom was pulled open, and Beth emerged.

By that point, I hadn't seen her for almost two weeks, and the sight of her was a shock.

I stopped still in the hallway, unsure of what to do or say. I wanted to disappear, but since that wasn't possible, I considered taking a few steps backwards into my bedroom and closing the door. She stared at me with a strange look on her face for a few long, terrible moments. The look wasn't hostile, which was, I suppose, what I'd been expecting. She was sad, but the way she looked at me was soft and surprisingly tender.

Then, all at once, she moved toward me. Four or five strident steps, and she wrapped me up in a tight hug.

"I'm sorry, Jude," she whispered. "I'm so sorry."

I found myself pressing a hand to her back, warm under her pyjama top. I didn't know what I was supposed to say. I didn't know what she was apologising for.

"I'm sorry too," I said, and I felt her hug me a little tighter.

"I love you, okay? I'm sorry, and I love you."

I said, "Okay." And then, "I love you too." I wasn't sure we'd ever said it to each other before.

She kissed my head, though since I was as tall as she was, it was a sort of kiss on the side of it. She pulled back to look at me thoroughly.

"Happy Birthday. Sixteen, huh? You're basically an adult now."

"You're going to send me down the mines tomorrow, aren't you?"

"Nah, not on a Sunday. First thing Monday, though." She gave me a wink and let me go, edging toward the bathroom. "I'm going to take a quick shower. Tell Luke to put the coffee pot on, will you? Then I'll make us some bacon and pancakes. How about that?"

I blinked, then nodded.

"I'll bring your gifts down in a bit. Go put some clothes on, birthday boy."

And with that, she disappeared into the bathroom. I stared at the closed door for a minute, though maybe I was waiting and listening to see if she'd break down again as soon as she was alone. I didn't hear anything except the sound of the shower being twisted on and the spray hissing into the bath.

Beth told me some years later that when she'd been lying in bed all those days, wondering and thinking about why this had happened to her – to them – she'd concluded that she was to blame. When I asked what she even meant by that, she said that every day since our parents died, she'd had the chance to be a mother to me. She'd had the chance to step up and prove that she could be a mother to someone who needed one. She'd concluded, and the universe had apparently agreed, that she hadn't done a very good job of it. Therefore, she couldn't be trusted with a baby of her own.

It was nonsense, of course. But I think it helped Beth in some strange way. To feel like she could, one day, be good enough.

Luke had given me a hesitant smile, as though afraid to hope that she'd turned a corner when I'd gone downstairs and told him Beth was in the shower and she'd asked him to put the coffee pot on. When she came down, she looked fresh and well-rested. She'd kissed him on the cheek and went immediately to the pantry cupboard for the flour.

It felt almost normal as we sat down to eat crispy bacon and pancakes, both drizzled with the last of the syrup.

"These are delicious; thanks, Beth." My mouth was half full as I spoke, which would normally have annoyed her. This time, though, she just gave me an indulgent smile and took a sip of her coffee.

"So, what's your plans today? Doing something nice with Ellie?" she asked, face bright.

I looked down at my plate. "Ah, yeah, I'll see her later. A few of us are going over to Alfie's later to stay the night. We're gonna watch some films and play pool."

She nodded. "Are his parents okay with it?"

Technically, his parents were okay with it. But normally, when I stayed at Alfie's or Josh's, Beth or Luke would call their parents to check if it was fine. Check what time I should be dropped off and picked up, check that we weren't actually going out on a murder and rioting spree across the island. I'd cleared it with Luke already, and he knew Alfie's parents weren't going to be there. He knew because he'd also been invited to the same Christmas party they were going to – it was for small business owners across Jersey – and they'd spoken about it on the phone. He'd taken a bit of coaxing but agreed in the end, fears allayed by whatever Malina (Alfie's mum) had told him. Beth was usually much harder to convince. I didn't expect any difference this time. And I didn't want to ruin her mood by having an argument about it.

Dread curling in my stomach, I looked imploringly at Luke.

"They're going to the Lavine Christmas Party," he said. "But they've assured me they'll be checking in and they've got their neighbours keeping an eye out."

"That's tonight?" she asked and Luke nodded, before taking a large gulp of his coffee. "Oh, thank Christ, we don't have to go."

"Yeah," he muttered, sounding relieved.

Beth looked at me again. I decided that if she said I wasn't to go over, then I'd accept that.

"So you and the boys and the girls at Alfie's house, unsupervised."

"The girls aren't staying," Luke supplied before I could.

"They're not," I confirmed. "They'll be there for a bit but Ellie's dad will be picking her up later. He'd never let her stay over."

"Hmm," Beth said. "No, but Georgia's parents might and if they think Ellie is there."

"I swear, they're not staying." And they weren't. George had a midnight curfew so they would be there late, but they weren't staying. This whole thing seemed ridiculous to me since what they were afraid might happen between a bunch of horny teens left unsupervised could just as easily happen between 6 p.m. and midnight.

"Okay," she said at last. "I'm trusting you. It's your birthday – you're sixteen now – and you should be able to have a good time with your friends. Be sensible though, please. Don't let us down."

I gave her an appreciative smile. "I promise, I won't."

"Okay, hurry up and finish that and we can open your gifts," she said and stood up to carry her plate to the sink.

My gifts turned out to be an iPad, a pair of noise cancelling headphones, and a book voucher. I was a little stunned, stammering out my thanks before giving them both a hug and disappearing upstairs to set it up. There was a voice message from Ellie on my phone, singing me happy birthday and telling me she couldn't wait to see me later.

Alfie's read: '*Happy Birthday Dickhead*' and Josh's was just a birthday present and beer emoji.

I thought about Caspien. Would he have bought me a gift had he been around? I didn't think he knew when my birthday was;

couldn't remember it ever coming up in conversation. I went to his Instagram and checked for anything new. Nothing. The last post was his own birthday post over a month ago. It had 656 likes. I wondered if the pervert was amongst those 52 comments.

Surely he wouldn't be stupid enough to comment on an Instagram post of his underage boyfriend, lover, whatever he was? Curiosity crept, spidery, across my brain. I wanted to know more about this pervert tutor of his.

I glanced down the comments, clicking on any usernames that stood out, anyone who sounded like a teacher or a pervert. I had that same trembling rage I had whenever I thought about him, about how disgusting he was, how he should be in prison or, at the very least, not teaching students privately.

I wondered again whether I should tell someone, Gideon, at least. Had he suspected anything at all? What would he do if he knew?

What had Caspien said to him that day as I'd listened? *If he sees you here, if anyone sees you here, and they tell him, how will you explain it?*

How would they have explained it?

My whole body drew up, a sharp realisation narrowing to a pinpoint.

If that was his tutor, then that remark made absolutely no sense. His tutor's presence in the house could be explained quite easily. Perhaps there'd be some difficulty with it being a Saturday, but it wouldn't be entirely implausible for his tutor to be in the house altogether.

I thought back to when I'd confronted him in his bedroom before I'd kissed him. The fear in his eyes when I'd said I knew his identity, but more importantly, how that fear disappeared when I knew it was his tutor.

It wasn't him. I'd been wrong. It's just that Caspien had let me believe that I wasn't. His words took on an entirely new meaning then: *If he sees you here, how will you explain it?*

Did that mean Gideon and he knew each other? It could have been a generalisation, that he meant 'if anyone sees you here' it would be hard to explain, but some spidery inkling in my head told me that it was the first; Gideon knew this man. This man knew Gideon.

It was killing me not knowing the identity of this fucker. This man who had so easily wrapped his arms around Caspien and pulled him close, who Caspien had allowed to do that. Now I knew the feeling I got in my chest whenever I thought of it: jealousy.

I thought of the note inside the book again: *Caspien, my beautiful boy, let me be yours.*

Love, X

I felt it like an electric shock to the chest then, that 'X'.

What if it wasn't, as I'd assumed, the 'x' someone puts on a birthday card? What if X was his name? I sat up and looked at the comments again, scanning each one for something that would tell me if X was a name and if this X followed him on social media.

My heart sank when I saw there were a lot of followers with X in their usernames. I checked all of them. He didn't appear to be among them.

I needed a new plan.

I had no clue what I was going to do once I found out who he was; maybe I wasn't going to do a thing. But not knowing who he was was driving me crazy, and with Cas completely gone from my life, it seemed as good a way to spend my time as any.

SEVENTEEN

I'd not enjoyed the champagne I'd drunk at Caspien's birthday, but I found that vodka coupled with something sweet and fruity could achieve that perfect, blissful, drunken state. One I'd become very accustomed to at university.

Josh had brought a bottle of something shockingly green and tongue-numbingly sour that he'd convinced his older brother Gareth to buy for him. There was talk about having to wash his car every Sunday for a month; I wasn't really listening.

We mixed the vodka with Red Bull first, which, after three large glasses, caused a weird buzzing to start under my skin and in my chest, which I think now was just a caffeine overdose. And when the Red Bull ran out, we used the girls' lemonade and cranberry juice. By 8 p.m., we were drunk.

Ellie sat on my lap on Alfie's den sofa, smelling of the apricot and strawberry drink her and George were drinking from wine glasses, while Georgia lay stretched out on the other end with her feet on Alfie's lap. She was creating what she called 'Jude's Birthday Playlist' with the concentration of a mathematician.

Josh and a couple of the rugby guys he'd brought with him took shots in the kitchen.

I'd taken one shot, Beth's warning plea to be sensible still ringing in my ears.

Alfie's den was on the basement floor of his parent's huge six-bedroom, three-storey detached house and looked onto a massive garden with an outdoor pool. A projector streamed YouTube on the wall at one end – currently playing a Calvin Harris video – and a kitchen and breakfast bar sat snugly at the other. Aside from Caspien, Alfie was the richest person I knew. His parents owned a large number of properties as well as lots of land across the island, and since Jersey was small and there wasn't a lot of either, they'd become extremely wealthy from it.

They'd brought a cake down shortly after I got here, which Alfie's parents had arranged, and sang happy birthday at the top of their voices. They gave me gifts too, which I honestly hadn't been expecting. Ellie had intimated that she'd bought me something, which had turned out to be a heavy bottle of expensive–looking aftershave in a clear bottle, a navy Ralph Lauren hoodie, and a custom–made card with pictures of us together on the front. Josh gave me a terribly wrapped rugby top, which he'd left the price on. And Alfie and Georgie bought me, jointly, a Fairisle Christmas jumper, a reindeer made of Chocolate, and, terrifyingly, a packet of extra-large condoms.

This had elicited a shrieking laugh from Georgia, who'd said Ellie had told her what size to get – something Ellie vehemently denied.

I thanked everyone, a little embarrassed by the generosity (and the condoms), and proceeded to get more drunk. I was in the kitchen pouring everyone's drinks when Ellie found me. She looked exceptionally pretty. Her eyes were dusted with glitter, her lips red like the dress she wore, and sharp dark lines swept out from her eyelids, making her look cat-like.

I leaned in to kiss her. She made a very soft, very feminine noise and sank into me, and for a moment, I forgot all about Caspien Deveraux and how much I wanted him. Blood rushed south, stirring me with want. We kissed until Josh shouted for us to hurry up with the drinks.

Ellie pulled back and threw a glare at him while I went back to pouring too much vodka into tall glasses. Behind us, the music went up a notch.

"I hope you know that was a joke with the condoms, " Ellie said. "I definitely didn't tell George about your...you know."

I laughed, pleasantly buzzed. The earlier embarrassment I'd felt was a distant memory. Lost in a daze of vodka and gratitude and good vibes. "So you don't tell each other everything?"

She gave me what I thought was a caught–out look. "I mean, we do. Mostly. But not about that, I promise."

I was pouring along a line of seven glasses, two seconds of cranberry juice in each; then I'd do four, or maybe two, of lemonade. "So then...Georgia hasn't told you about Alfie's?" I held up my pinkie.

She burst out laughing. "Um, no comment." She went to the fridge and pulled out the lemonade. "I'm sure guys tell each other plenty too."

"Um, we don't tend to talk about girls' tits all that much," I said honestly.

We talked about films, rugby, and whatever PS5 game Josh and Alfie were playing. I was the weirdo among them who didn't really get video games. I never had. When kids were playing computer games, I was reading. Sometimes, I'd come round to their houses and do just that while they played.

It was probably a miracle that I was never bullied at school for being the weird, bookish one. I think I had Alfie – the richest, most popular kid at school, and Josh, the sportiest and all-round nicest kid at school – to thank for that. By virtue of them, I became untouchable. And yet, they never made me feel like I didn't belong or as though I was bathing in their shine.

Later, at Oxford, I'd think back on this friendship as juvenile and transitory – a stepping stone on my journey to building the sort of friendships that *would* last years. I always knew we would drift apart. That our lives would split off into completely different directions; Alfie staying in Jersey to work with his father, Josh to some small town rugby team in the UK proper, while I lost myself to a bigger city like London or Manchester. I wonder now if my friendship with these two boys who knew who I was before Caspien was somehow the most authentic I've ever had.

That night, I saw all of this spread out before me; the fleeting nature of friendship and childhood. I was grateful to them for being a part of my life, and I was determined they always would be. With loud, fervent proclamation, I hugged them both and told them just that. Josh laughed and poured me another shot while Alfie looked like he would burst into tears.

"Mate, when I think about how you lost your mum and dad and then had to start a new school," he was rambling, drunkenly, breath smelling like cranberries. "I just, I just think you're great. You're my best friend. You and Joshy. I love you both."

"Love you too," mumbled Josh. "Love you too, bud."

I was emotional and grateful and very, very drunk. It's how I found myself upstairs on the balcony on the first floor – or was it the second? – dialling Caspien's number. It went to voicemail as expected.

"Isssme," I slurred. "Again. I mean 'mshure you know that. ANYway...it's my birthday today, happyfucking birthday to me I guess..." I tailed off, sliding down the metal balustrade a little before righting myself. "And hereiam out here freezing my dick off talkin' t'yu. But, you knowwwhat? I feel greatttt. Vodka is actually really great. MUCH better than shhhampagne anyway. I hate shsssham-pagne. And I hate you. Yeah, I actually decided that tonight, I hate you. Gidyeon saidyoudint hate me but he's verrrrry incorrect about that, but I wanted to make shhhure that you know I hateyoumore."

I paused and took a very deep breath. The air seemed to hiss and sizzle inside the heat of my chest before bursting out in white, boozy plumes.

"I hateyou forleaving me with this. This thinginsde me that never goes away." I was quiet for a minute, morose. "But whateverr. I'm probably going to lose my virginity tonight." This I found hilarious for some reason and broke off into a fit of laughter. "Anyway, I hopeyourehappy. In swit-ZER-LAND. See you never I guess."

By the time I'd hung up I was sitting on the ground of the balcony, my arse numb from the cold. I could hear dance music playing from below, through the open balcony door. I'm not sure how long I was there before Ellie appeared and let out a loud gasp as she dashed toward me.

"What are you doing out here!? You'll freeze to death!"

She somehow managed to get me off the ground and into the house, levering me upstairs to the spare room Malina had earlier given me. I tumbled onto the bed, and Ellie disappeared. She returned some unknowable amount of time later with a bottle of water and some white tablets she forced me to swallow.

"'msorry," I said.

"You don't have to be sorry," she said, smiling fondly. "It's your birthday."

"Timezzit?"

"Uh, just before ten. Why don't you sleep it off for a bit, and I'll come wake you up before I go?"

I nodded, and the entire three-story house tilted on its foundations.

When I woke again, it was morning. Foul, grey light stabbing through the crack in the blinds. I felt a body pressed next to me and turned to find Ellie half-naked with an arm slung over me.

I felt every trace of alcohol left in my body evaporate instantly. Sobriety rushing at me like a steam train. I sat up immediately and looked down. I was only wearing boxers. I was also hard, painfully so. I glanced around the room for some evidence of what might have happened – did we...? Surely I wouldn't have. Christ, surely *she* wouldn't have? Not when I was in that state.

If we had, were we careful? *Be sensible, please. We're trusting you.*

Ellie's red dress was nowhere to be seen, though her black shoes lay where she looked to have kicked them off by the foot of the bed. My mouth was sour and dry, my tongue coated with the hide of some dead animal.

A half-full bottle of water was by the bed, so I drained it and slipped out of bed, the room swivelling sickeningly. I looked for my phone to check the time: the house was deadly silent, and it felt early by the murky light I could see outside. My phone wasn't by the bed or under it, so I tried to remember when I'd last seen it. Or used it.

In the ensuite, I emptied my bladder, painfully, given how bloody hard I was. The stream was a lurid amber colour and smelled like rotten fruit. I ran the tap and washed my face with cold water, then I looked at myself in the mirror, searching my eyes for some clue as to whether I was still a virgin or not. Surely, if I couldn't remember doing it, then I wouldn't have been able to? What *could* I remember doing?

I remembered the gifts. I remembered the pizza. I remembered playing pool, badly. Josh and Alfie and me singing. I remembered kissing Ellie upstairs on the living room couch. Why had she stayed? Finding some toothpaste under the sink, I rubbed some over my teeth to try and clear the taste of alcohol.

In the bedroom, Ellie was still sleeping. I sat down on the bed and stared at her, terror swimming in my mind and gut at the thought of having forced her or hurt her in some way. Surely, I wouldn't, regardless of how incapacitated I was.

I thought about us being stupid and not using anything and the consequences of that. No, she was sensible. Smart. I knew she was. And if I'd hurt her, then surely she wouldn't have gotten under the blankets and held me while I slept?

Reaching out, I gently shook her awake. She moaned softly before cracking open her eyes. I waited a beat for her to come more awake, for some expression to move into her eyes that I could try and decipher. She sat up, frowning. I couldn't stop my eyes from dipping down at her exposed breasts. They were perfect. Nipples darker than I'd ever seen in any picture or in any film.

"You okay?" She reached out and brushed her hand over my shoulder and down my arm.

"How come you're here?"

"I came up to wake you, to say I was leaving, and you threw up all over me."

"Fuck," I said, horrified. "I'm so sorry."

"Alf wasn't much better, and Josh was already asleep. I didn't want to leave you in case you threw up in your sleep or something."

"Did George go?"

"Yeah, she asked to stay, but her dad..."

I nodded in understanding. Georgia's dad was terrifying.

"What about you? Your parents thought you were there? Aren't they gonna know?"

She shrugged. "I'll deal with it when I get home. I just wanted to make sure you were okay."

I felt such a rush of gratitude for her then that I almost burst into tears. Instead, I pulled her into a hug. Took a deep inhale of her hair.

"I'm sorry about your dress."

"It's fine," she said, rubbing my back. "I probably wouldn't have worn it again anyway."

"It was really pretty though," I said miserably.

She laughed softly. "Okay, I'll buy another one."

I said. "I think maybe I'm not cut out for drinking."

"I think maybe it was all the 'birthday shots' the boys were forcing you to drink."

"I think maybe I need to take responsibility for my own actions."

"Well, that's very grown-up of you."

We sat like that for a bit, her arms wrapped around me, her nakedness pressed against me until I felt almost human again.

"I thought maybe we'd...you know. Last night." Now I was certain we hadn't.

"Jude, you were comatose."

"Well, maybe I was really irresistible covered in sick and comatose, maybe you couldn't resist me."

She sat back to hit me lightly on the chest. "You wish!"

The softness in her eyes was such a relief that I felt almost dizzy from it. I tackled her to the bed and buried my face in her neck. At first, she shrieked, but then, as my hands roamed up her body, she went quiet, her breathing turning quick.

I didn't touch her bare breasts; it felt too serious, but I did skim my hand up the side of her thigh and over her hip as my playful growls turned to soft kisses. When she turned her body and arched into me, I knew what she wanted. I asked anyway.

"Can I...touch you here?" I looked at the perfect round tits and the quickly hardening nipple, and my mouth watered. I'd never wanted her as much as this.

"Yes, please, Jude."

I moved down her body and closed my mouth over it, instinct telling me to suck and kiss and bite just a little. Ellie gasped, and I flicked my tongue over it. Then her hands were in my hair, and her skin was in my mouth, and I wondered if it was over, the madness that had taken hold of me this summer. It was her who reached for her knickers and began to push them down.

I leaned up and looked into her eyes, finding her smiling, tender and soft. I pushed my own boxers down, and her breaths turned quicker.

Naked, she spread her legs and let me between them.

"The condoms," she panted to me. I froze, embarrassment heating my cheeks. She *was* sensible.

"Where are they?"

"In my bag," she gasped, sounding nervous, as she gestured over my shoulder. I climbed off her and went across the room towards the chair, my whole body feeling large and hollow with only my heart beating inside of it, a thunderous echoing thing.

My hands shaking, I tore one from the strip and made my way back to her.

"Get another in case it breaks."

I didn't understand this but did it anyway. As I pulled the first one around the head with clumsy, unskilled fingers and the rim tore away from its sleeve, I understood. I started again.

Time froze as I carefully rolled the sheaf of rubber over myself and lowered myself back down between her legs again.

When I pointed it toward the hot space between her thighs, jabbing it against her, she winced.

"Sorry," I said, barely able to hear my own voice over the sound of my heartbeat.

"It's fine, it's okay." She was smiling at me so fondly, so full of complete and utter (misplaced) trust that I felt overwhelmed, and the words slipped out.

"Ellie, I love you," I said.

She looked like she would cry and reached up quickly to kiss me. I know I must have tasted of vomit and terror, but if she noticed, she didn't show it.

"I love you too, Jude," she whispered, clinging to me.

EIGHTEEN

Sex, for me, has never been the mindless pleasure-filled paradise my peers would have me believe. It's never been that simple animalistic act driven by lust and need that people often describe it as. For me, it's always been accompanied by some great complex maelstrom of emotion.

There is some pleasure, of course. Beautiful, transcendent, and glorious. But it's fleeting. Guilt and regret, shame and remorse; those feelings always linger long after the pleasure has receded.

I felt all of those things in the moments after that first time.

I'm not sure what Ellie felt. Maybe she felt regret too, it was possible. But she'd looked happy.

Ellie, who I cared for, but didn't love.

I was ridden with guilt because I'd said something I didn't mean. Regret,

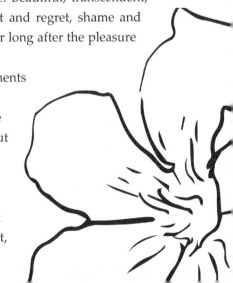

because I wished I hadn't. Shame, because I'd turned myself into one of those boys who lied to girls to get them to have sex with them. Then there was the remorse for all of that.

Maybe because of how my first time was, this has laid the foundations for every sexual encounter I would go on to have thereafter.

After, we cuddled silently for a bit before Ellie's phone started ringing from across the room. She picked it up to her mother shrieking down the phone. I couldn't hear the words, but the sounds of a tinny, angry parent reached me. Ellie said very little to her mum. She didn't argue, raise her voice, or deny anything. At the very end, in a very childlike-sounding voice, she apologised before hanging up.

"She's on her way." She came back to sit on the bed by me, looking entirely unbothered that she was likely grounded for the foreseeable future.

"I'm sorry," I said. "Is it gonna be bad?"

She shrugged. "She'll be annoyed for a bit, pretend I'm grounded, then get sick of me moping around the house, and that'll be it." She leaned in and kissed me again, smiling against my lips. "Totally worth it."

My cheeks turned hot. "What time is it?" I asked.

"Just after ten. When's Alfie's parents due back?"

"About twelve, they said."

"Sorry, I'm not gonna be able to help you clean up downstairs." She didn't look sorry in the least.

"They told us not to bother. They have a cleaner coming tomorrow."

"God, Alfie's a spoiled brat. It's sickening."

I nodded in agreement.

We sat there for a bit, and though everything felt different, changed, a little frightening, I felt the morosity begin to lift from my chest a little. Finally, she let out a sigh and stood. I watched her pull on her red dress before I realised.

"Ellie, you can't put that on – it's covered in my sick."

"I wiped most of it off," she said, nonchalantly. "But I will borrow this if that's okay?"

It was the hoodie she'd bought me for my birthday. I nodded, and she proceeded to slip on her black shoes.

"I should get up too." I sat up feeling exposed and vulnerable, naked but for the duvet pulled over my lower half.

"You'll probably need to borrow something of Alfie's. Your shirt looked sort of ruined."

"Great." How would I explain that to Beth? *Be sensible.*

I'd had sex, but I had used a condom. Was that sensible?

After Ellie left, I showered in the ensuite and wrapped myself in a towel. Then I went looking for Alfie, Josh, and my phone. In Alfie's bed, I found Josh, fully clothed, mouth wide open, and dead to the world. I pulled out a pair of sweats and a tracksuit top from Alfie's tallboy, put them on, and ventured downstairs.

By some miracle, we'd managed to restrict the chaos to the Den; the living room looked almost untouched except for a stray beer bottle and a glass with some pinkish liquid at the bottom. Outside, a strong wind was rattling the balcony doors, which hadn't been closed properly.

As I went to shut them, I spotted my phone on the concrete, face down with its bright blue rubber cover facing up. As I reached down to pick it up, I was kicked in the face by the memory. I was the one who'd been out here. I'd been out here on my phone, in fact.

A chill spread out from the base of my spine and over my entire body, leeching it of all warmth. Somehow, my phone was undamaged and still had some battery left.

With mounting horror, I went to my recent calls.

Caspien was at the top with the word 'outgoing' and a number (4) beside it. I'd called him *four* times? I wanted to die.

I remembered the voicemail with painful little detail. I only knew it had happened, but when I tried to think about what I'd said a chasm of nothingness opened up in my brain, white and bottomless.

I knew what I *might* have said. What I *could* have said. What I *probably* said while under the influence of alcohol. I'd managed not to throw up, but bile rose now. I folded myself over the balcony railing and groaned.

Alfie found me like that a short while later.

"Mate, I feel the same," he said, clapping a hand on my back. "How much did we drink?"

"I honestly lost count."

"What time did the girls go?"

So he didn't know George had gone home without Ellie. Or couldn't remember. He would find out eventually. Despite what Ellie said last night, I didn't believe that what had happened this morning would not reach Alfie by way of Georgia. Then he'd feel crappy about my not telling him.

"Ellie stayed," I told him. "She just left. Her mum was pretty pissed."

Alfie stared at me in silence for a beat, his alcohol–poisoned brain taking in the information. Then his eyes went wide. He covered his mouth with his hands and leapt back a step.

"Judey!! *Judey, my dudey*!! You finally gave it up!! So proud of you, so fucking proud!!"

"Mate, can you stop shouting for the love of god? My head."

"Fine, fine," he said, quieter. "So, how was it? Tell me everything."

"Piss off. As if."

"Oh, come on, don't be like that! Happened in my house didn't it? Wait, not in my bed? Please tell me not in my bed."

"Josh is in there."

"The room my grandma sleeps in then. Cool. Cool." He burst out laughing, the sound scraping and scratching at my hangover.

I rolled my eyes and bent my head, focussing on keeping the bile down.

Christmas came and went without much fanfare that year. The big house was quiet. We'd heard Gideon had gone to his house in London, and I assumed Caspien would go from Switzerland to there and back again after the term ended. The three of us cooked and ate at home, staying in pyjamas for most of the time.

Beth was still in this strange new phase of being, which mainly meant more hugs and far more generous gifts. As my birthday was so close to Christmas I always had one lesser and one greater gift. I assumed the iPad to be the greater but when Luke pulled a Cannondale road bike out of his van on Christmas morning I could only stare at it, stunned.

I felt a little embarrassed by what I'd bought them: a voucher for the French restaurant in town they liked. But they'd hugged me and thanked me as though it was enough.

Mocks were set for the last two weeks of January, so I had to at least pretend to study during break. (We'd do mocks in both upper and lower 6th and I'd scrape through both which scared me so shit-less I'd pulled out something miraculous in my A's.) Along with this was, though a year early, the start of our prep for Uni applications. Ellie was applying to Edinburgh to do Veterinary medicine – she'd had pictures of the city on her wall for years and posted those aesthetic Instagram reels daily of its cobbled streets and hilltop castle, so there was no question of it being her first choice. There'd never been any assumption that I'd follow her there, and though she'd never said it directly, I knew she planned for us to carry on seeing each other long–distance.

In my case, St. Andrew's had the best English Literature degree in the country, but the entry requirements were insane, so I was eyeing Durham, Warwick and Oxford. Warwick was the least demanding in terms of entry; achievable certainly. Durham was the north of England, further from home, more alien, more daunting; I'd never been further north than London, and Oxford felt part fantasy to me. I'd always dreamed of going, but it would rely on my results being better than even my teachers thought I'd achieve. Even if I somehow did get in, the expense of living and studying there might be too much for Luke and Beth.

But I felt better having narrowed it down. And the entry process for Oxford was akin to some herculean trial, so it was probably good that I'd started preparing for it now.

The Monday after New Year, Luke returned to work, and Elspeth told him that Gideon was due back the following day.

So, on Wednesday – the day before school started back – I called the mansion. Elspeth answered, and she wished me a happy new year, asking if I'd had a nice Christmas, before she went off to find Gideon.

"Young Jude! How nice to hear from you! Did you have a wonderful Christmastime? And it was your birthday too – how charming!" He sounded so feverishly cheerful I wondered if he might be drunk.

I asked how his Christmas was.

"Lord, it was exhausting. Far too many soirees with friends, you know?"

I didn't, but I said yes anyway.

"Truthfully, I much prefer my own company. Glad to be back in the old mausoleum." There was a pause. "You'll be calling to ask about Cas, I suppose?"

The sound of his name felt like a warm breath on my neck.

"Um, eh, no, I wasn't," I said but I immediately regretted it. I did want to ask about him. Of course, I did. It just wasn't the reason I'd called. I tried to decide how embarrassing it would be to ask about him. Had Gideon spoken with him? Did he know about my drunken call the night of my birthday?

"I actually have something here for you that he asked me to give you," Gideon said.

Everything in me drew up sharp. I couldn't breathe. "He...you do?"

Gideon let out a little chuckle. "Yes, head on up whenever you can."

I wanted to drop the receiver and bolt right up there. Cycle my new bike as fast as I could. Instead, I took a breath and said as calmly as I could, why I'd called, "Actually, I wanted to ask a favour."

"Anything I can do, young Jude, you know you need only ask."

"Well, Mocks are coming up – they start on the 19th – and I just wondered if you wouldn't mind me coming up to use the library for the next few weeks. Probably every night. It's just here is a little—"

I hadn't finished speaking before he dramatically explained that he was mortally offended that I should think I had to ask. He'd given permission for me to use it months earlier and hadn't rescinded it. He'd even bought books for there that I'd recommended. I was *always* welcome at Deveraux.

I thanked him and told him I'd come the following day after school.

The entire day, my stomach leapt and lurched as though I were on a boat amid a stormy sea. I'd barely been able to sleep the night prior. Cas had given me a gift. He had bought me a birthday present. Then I thought about Gideon's *exact* words as he'd spoken them: *I have something here that he asked me to give you.*

Maybe it wasn't a gift. Maybe it was something I'd loaned him or left behind in his room. Had he given it to Gideon before or after my drunken phone call? The phone call which over the last few weeks had come back to me in terrible little fragments of misery.

I hate you.

I hate you.

I hate you for leaving me with this.

After my party at Alfie's, Ellie had been grounded. And since she spent Christmas in France with her Dad's family, I hadn't seen her (except via a video call) since that day. That morning.

I'd spent the days after the incident waiting for Ellie's parents to call Beth and tell them everything that had happened: how we'd been drinking and I'd been sick and Ellie and I had stayed together and how we'd likely slept in the same bed, maybe even had sex. But it never happened.

It turned out Ellie told her mum I'd gotten really upset about my parents and the baby and begged her to stay with me, which she'd done because she cared about me. She'd apologised and taken her punishment and pleaded with her mum not to tell Beth because Beth, too, had been through a lot.

It worked.

The longer I went without seeing Ellie in the flesh, the more distance that came between me and her and it – the sex – the more it faded from my memory. Inside, I felt exactly the same as I had before it. What lingered was those feelings of guilt and shame; anytime I gave them the floor, they crept into the spotlight and refused to leave the stage.

Ellie had come into first period that morning looking bright with happiness and like I alone was the source of it all. She waited until we were in the corridor to tug me into a doorway, reaching up to kiss the underside of my jaw.

"I missed you soooo much," she whispered, edging her lips toward my mouth.

"Me too," I replied, closing my eyes.

"Guess what? I'm only grounded until after exams."

Her parents had originally told her it was for the entire term.

"Amazing."

She nodded, a shy, tempting look coming over her eyes. She took my hands and leaned up to whisper into my ear. "I can't stop thinking about it."

"Me too," I said again.

Cruelly, I wanted to forget it had happened at all. I hated how irreversible and permanent it felt. I hated that I spent every day checking my phone for contact from Caspien. I hated, too, that despite everything I felt about what I'd done and was doing to her, how much further I was prepared to hurt her the very moment he walked back into my life.

But still, I longed for that moment.

I rushed dinner down that night so quickly that I almost choked on it. Then I slung on my backpack and cycled the Cannondale to the big house. It was bitterly cold, the winter air sharp and glittering as a knife, but I never felt it. My blood was warm from nervous anticipation.

Elspeth was in the kitchen stirring a large pot of something that smelled delicious. She gave me a hug and offered me a bowl of soup.

"I've just eaten, but thank you, maybe later," I told her.

She said she'd put a bowl aside with a dinner roll in case and told me Gideon was in the red sitting room if I wanted to say hello.

I found him reading on one of the armchairs, long graceful legs crossed at the knee and wearing his gold circular reading glasses. The light was low in the room; only the wall lights and a small glass reading lamp on a table beside him turned on. He sat up as soon as I came in. He placed a bookmark between the pages and closed it, set it on the side table, and stood.

"Jude, hello, there you are."

"Hi, Gideon," I said.

He paused and tilted his head, studying me. "You look different; what did you do?" He waved a hand in front of me. "Did you get taller?"

"I don't think so."

"Hmmm, there's definitely something different about you. I'll figure it out."

He gave me a small secret kind of smile, threw an arm around my shoulder and steered me out of the room. As we went towards the library, he twittered away about how London was dreadfully loud, dreadfully wet and dreadfully cold. I was trying to figure out how to ask him about Cas's gift and not sound desperate but I didn't have to, because when he opened the door to the library I saw the parcel. Large and flat and wrapped in dark blue paper with gold ribbon, it sat propped up on the table in the centre of the room.

There was a white envelope next to it.

"I'll leave you to open it by yourself," Gideon said with a serious sort of voice. He gave me another soft pat on the shoulder and shut me in the room with Caspien's gift.

The fire had been lit and crackled softly behind the guard as I approached. I had an inkling of what I *thought* might be inside, but it didn't prepare me for what I found when I peeled off the thick paper.

My own face, fey and dreamlike, stared up at me.

He'd filled it in with watercolour, a palette of pinks, greens, and blues. Light caught on my rosy lips and cheeks, and sunlight poured through the window. Behind me was a view out onto the estate, rolling dips and hills which I knew led all the way to the sea. He'd added something too, something that wasn't in the room with us that day: a delicate pink flower that sprouted from deep green vines curled around the composition so that it stood in as a kind of frame. The art itself had been mounted inside a thick, white ornamental frame, giving it a sort of delicate grandeur. I stared at it for a long time, imagining his hands moving over the curves of my skull and the bone structure of my face. His delicate fingers tracing each eyelash and freckle. I thought about what I'd have said or done had he given me this in person, and I was suddenly glad he wasn't here.

At the very bottom, in the smallest, most elegant script, it read: *Jude in the window, by C.L.D.*

Everything I'd tried to ignore suddenly fell away, and I wanted him, again, desperately, ferociously. It made every loose, easy, calm thing inside me turn hard and pointed and violent. I lost myself in that ocean of feeling for a few trembling moments before I tore open the envelope.

Jude,
Happy Birthday.
From,
Caspien.

NINETEEN

My first exam was at 9 a.m. on a Tuesday. History. It was the one I was dreading most.

But a strange kind of focus came over me the second I sat down. I spent the next two and a half hours weaving a convincing argument about the three sources they'd given us, and their usefulness to a historian studying responses to religious change in the reign of Mary I. The Tudors were my least favourite monarchs. I preferred the Angevin kings; I'd always been drawn to Richard the Lionheart more than Henry VIII.

A couple of hours later, I walked out of the exam hall feeling dazed, as though coming out of a trance, relieved it was over. Ellie was waiting for me by the main entrance; her own chemistry exam had begun at the same time but finished fifteen minutes earlier. She kissed me quickly on the lips and slipped her arms around my waist.

"How'd it go?"

"Good, I think."

"Told you. I think you could have taken my chem one for me too. Oh, to be naturally brainy like you," she sighed.

"I'm really not."

"You are, though. You're hot *and* smart. I'm super lucky."

I shifted, awkward under the praise. "Is your mum picking you up?"

"Dad. I think he's outside now," she groaned. "Only two weeks to go. I feel like a bloody prisoner."

"Yeah, two weeks will fly."

She leaned up on her tiptoes.

"I can't wait to be alone with you."

I knew Ellie wanted to have sex again. She'd mentioned as much in our text chats while she was in France – on Christmas morning, she'd even sent a topless photo. *'Merry Christmas, Jude x'* it had said. It had done its job. I was a 16-year-old boy, and I quickly learned that I didn't have much control over these things. No matter where my heart and mind lay.

The first time she'd asked for a photo back, I'd made an excuse about not being at home and then pretending to forget. The second time, though, I gave in. And though I'd been embarrassed and nervous, I'd still pulled it out and photographed my semi-hard cock and sent it to her. I'd felt it was the decent thing to do.

"Yeah, me too," I muttered.

"How can you still be shy?" She gave me the face she did sometimes, like I was a small, adorable puppy. "God, you're so cute."

When she kissed me again, a little deeper this time, I tasted cherries and apples. A few people in the corridor whistled.

Every night that week, I cycled up to Deveraux, sat in Gideon's library, and stared at the painting. Every night, I thought about calling him. Even if it was just to thank him. But the longing in my chest was a constant thing, the absence of him almost as all-consuming as his presence. I knew if I called him, I'd only embarrass myself again by begging him to come home.

He'd long ago begun to feel like a ghost, some figment I'd conjured out of loneliness. I'd have been convinced he wasn't real if it wasn't for Gideon.

Gideon would swoop into the library like a moth to remind me of him, as if I were in danger of forgetting.

"Gosh, it is a wonderful likeness," he'd said about the painting that first night. He'd come in to offer me a cup of hot chocolate, which he'd made himself. After that, he would bring me one every night at the same time. "I think he captured your heart in every stroke."

"He said you were quite angry with him that day," he said the following night.

I'd been about to deny it because I only recalled the fervid, burning moments on the floor. The white exquisite pleasure after. But then I remembered how I'd arrived, how angry I'd been with him and his threats to tell Ellie everything.

The night before my English Lit mock, he set the hot chocolate down next to *Dracula*; I'd chosen it for tomorrow's exam. It was the same battered copy Caspien had taken to the beach that day. "I say, did you ever write him the letter we spoke of?" He sat down and gave me an encouraging smile.

I shook my head. "I tried. I just...I couldn't think of anything I thought he'd like to hear about." I remembered the letter I'd written and stuffed under my mattress. I'd forgotten all about it.

"I don't think that is the purpose of letters, Jude." He took a sip of his hot chocolate.

I frowned at this. "What's the purpose of letters then?"

Another of his encouraging smiles. "Well, to say things we might not be brave enough to say face to face."

I looked down at the page of *Dracula* in front of me. The passage that stood out was so apt that I felt a shiver run down my spine: *I am all in a sea of wonders. I doubt; I fear; I think strange things, which I dare not confess to my own soul.*

"I say this only as I'm going to see him tomorrow," Gideon was saying. "I fly out early, and I could take it to him personally. If that's something you'd want me to do."

He was going to see him. Envy pulsed through me. Christ, what I'd have given to see him.

But I forced myself to think about the letter. Perhaps I could thank him for the painting and apologise for my drunken call. I could ask when he'd be home and make those promises I'd made in the letter under my mattress – *I'll do whatever you want me to, please just come back.*

Perhaps I could even tell him about the strange things I dare not confess to my own soul.

Gideon let me use his desk in the corner of the blue sitting room. There was the Deveraux letterhead on rich white embossed paper, envelopes, and an array of pens in the small narrow drawer under the large desk. He patted me on the shoulder, gave me a proud smile, and went whistling out of the room.

I began it like I always did:

> **Dear Cas,**
> **You left.**

Maybe it was the paper, the pen, the desk, or the room, but after that, the words flowed easily and came out with less despair than all the other times I'd tried to write to him. This time, they were shot through with quiet rage. I hated him for leaving – I'd meant most of what I'd said on that call.

I hated him for not answering my calls and for disappearing from my life. But most of all, I hated him, loathed him, for infecting me like he had. For slipping under my skin and into my blood and finding his way to my heart. I blamed him for the guilt, shame, and remorse I carried around about Ellie because I knew all the things I was supposed to feel about her; I felt for him instead. That was *his* fault.

I hated the tall, dark-haired pervert who haunted my dreams and whose face was always just turned away from me, identity forever concealed. I wrote that I knew he'd lied that day, that I knew it wasn't his tutor, but that I wouldn't stop until I found out. I told him that some days, I felt as though I'd never take a full deep breath again until I knew his name.

If not for him, I told myself, then Caspien would be mine.

I only needed to know his name. Then the power would shift, as though knowing it and uttering it would destroy him completely.

I froze.

Epiphany swept over me as I took in the whole of Gideon's desk. There were a couple of leather journals stacked to one side next to the tray containing the Deveraux stationary. A small wooden box of business cards with '*Lord Gideon Deveraux III, Deveraux House, La Neuve Route, Jersey, St. Ouen, JE8 6BL*' written in neat gold font. A few letterheaded notepads. I ran my eye along the leather-bound books. One was smaller than the others, and my heart jumped as I spied the worn lettering on the spine that read: Address Book.

As I slid it from its spot between the tray and the other books, I sent a wish up that Gideon was both diligent and methodical about his contacts and put all of them in here. I took a guess that X was his first initial and so flicked immediately to the back of the book, paging forward until I reached the X's.

My heart stuttered. Surely it couldn't be this easy.

There was only one name written here.

Xavier Blackwell. Blackwell, Havisham, and Pryce.

There were two numbers and an email address.

Trembling with adrenaline, I copied them out quickly onto a piece of paper, folded it, and put it in my pocket along with the letter I'd written. Then I slid the address book back, making sure it was facing the same way I'd found it.

On a new piece of letter paper I wrote;

Dear Cas,

You left. I'm sorry if it was something I did. I really hope
to see you soon. Actually, I think I might.

P.S. Thanks for the painting.

Jude.

I folded the piece of paper, stuffed it into one of the envelopes, and sealed it.

When I walked out of the sitting room, Gideon was across the hall in the red parlour, reading again. He stood and came to meet me.

"Ah, a lad who knows what he wants to say! I like that."

I smiled and held out the envelope to him. He took it, holding it between his long fingers as though it were something precious.

I shrugged. "Thanks. I'm not sure he'll even read it."

"Oh, I'll make sure he does, don't worry."

I gave him a grateful smile. "I think I'll head off. Kinda tired." I faked a yawn that I wasn't entirely sure was convincing.

He tilted his head, mouth turning down. "Of course. Will you be okay on the bike? I can always take you back in the car."

"Nah, I'll be good. Thanks though. And thanks for letting me come again, and the letter, and well, everything."

Gideon's smile was tender. But ever since Caspien's words that day about how I knew nothing about Gideon, and since that night when I'd found him here alone and acting strangely, I'd never quite taken Gideon's smiles to mean exactly what he wanted me to think they did.

"Do not mention it, young Jude. Anything you need, anything at all."

I wasn't sure what made me ask it, but I said, "If he wanted to come home, would you let him?"

A strange look passed over his face, darkening his already dark eyes. "*Let* him?"

"I just mean, I wondered if maybe you'd sent him away or something. If maybe he'd done something he shouldn't have. I don't know. And he won't answer my calls so..."

Gideon shook his head as he came towards me.

"He simply woke up and declared he was going back to La Troyeux. No explanation, no discussion. I rather thought it was something to do with you, in fact."

I wasn't going to answer that, though I could tell he wanted me to.

"So then if he wanted to come back, if he told you when you saw him that he'd changed his mind and wanted to come back, he could?"

"I'd have him on a flight that very day. Jude, Deveraux is Caspien's home, and he will always be welcome here. I miss him terribly. Elspeth does too. And I'm sure you do."

I gave him a guileless smile. "I have a feeling he'll be back soon."

Gideon's expression sharpened ever so slightly and I was glad I'd put nothing in the letter that might have condemned me.

The moment I got home, I opened my laptop and typed 'Xavier Blackwell' into the search engine.

I could hardly believe my eyes. Could hardly believe it had been so easy.

There was page after page after page of him. Caspien's pervert was some kind of celebrity lawyer. He was thirty-two, though he'd started his own firm at twenty-six. There was a picture of him with a famous actress who had sued a British film studio for equal pay, pictures of him with footballers and politicians, even one with a prince.

I wanted to laugh. It was almost too bloody good.

But suddenly, I understood that Caspien's fear hadn't solely been about himself being found out; he was afraid for Xavier Blackwell's career—a career that would most definitely be ruined by the fact that he'd been messing about with a fifteen-year-old boy.

A career, as it turned out, I cared nothing about.

I pulled out my phone, typed two words into a text, and hit send.

This time, I only had to wait four minutes for him to call me back.

TWENTY

"What on earth do you think you're doing, Jude?" Caspien's voice was a shard of black ice.

All of my bravado disappeared the instant I heard it. I tried to breathe, tried to find a voice that was stronger and more assured than I felt.

"Oh, hey. Nice to hear from you," I said. "How's Switzerland?"

"Cold. Now, what are you playing at?"

"I'm not playing at anything," I said. "I wanted to test out a theory, and I guess it's confirmed."

He made a thin snorting sound. "Don't be absurd. Nothing's been confirmed. I'm simply tired of your pathetic, stalker behaviour. I'd have thought my leaving the country would have been enough to stop your stupid infatuation with me, but clearly not."

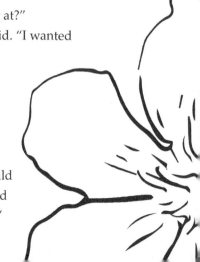

It stung. Sharp and hot. But I barrelled on nonetheless. "Hardly. But you know who is infatuated with you? Xavier Blackwell. Senior Partner at Blackwell, Havisham & Pryce. *'I can't stay away from you, Caspien,'*" I mocked. *"'I miss you all the time.'"*

He was silent, and I felt the frigid ire of his rage across the sea. Whereas my anger and fury toward him were always hot, his ran cold as the ocean floor.

"You don't know what you're talking about."

"Is that so." I thought about this. Maybe I didn't. Maybe I'd miscalculated, abysmally. But I really didn't think I had. His reaction was already moons away from how he'd reacted to my previous guess. I could hear how quick his breaths came. "Guess it won't mean anything if I send him a message then. You know, just to confirm that I don't know what I'm talking about. I'm sure his email address is here on his company website..."

"What is it you want, Jude?" he hissed.

At that moment, there was only one thing I wanted, and I wasn't about to pretend otherwise.

"When are you coming home?" I said.

He was quiet for a long time. If not for the quick flutter of his breaths, I'd have thought he was gone.

He said, "Where are you?"

"At home."

"In your room?"

I didn't understand. "Yes, why?"

Caspien said, "Put your camera on."

"What?"

"Just do it."

I hesitated a moment before I pulled the phone from my ear. Before I switched mine on, he turned on his own. My heart did a lurch in my chest when I saw him. He was dimly lit and beautiful and fresh from a shower. His hair was wet and pushed back from his face, his skin damp and glittering. I hit the button to turn on my own and shrunk a little from the deadly weight of his glare.

"Well, are you happy now?" he said.

"What do you mean?"

"Isn't this what you wanted?" He ran his tongue over his lip. My eyes traced the movement. "To see me."

"Wh—what are you talking about?"

He rolled his eyes. "I truly thought my leaving would help you figure out what it was you wanted, but evidently, you're still behaving like a child."

"I'm not a bloody child," I pouted.

"No," he said, and his eyes gleamed with something. "No, you're not anymore, are you? How was your journey into manhood? Was it all you hoped it would be?" His smirk was callous and a little sly. "Did you hear angels singing when you slipped it inside? Some say it's quite profound."

My entire head seemed to catch fire, burning bright and loud, a beacon of shame and embarrassment. It had been too much to hope that my memory of telling him I was going to lose my virginity on my drunk phone call was questionable. I'd hoped I hadn't said it. Hoped my mind had been only showing me the most embarrassing possibilities so that the truth would be more manageable.

I was too humiliated to answer, so he went on.

"You know, some also say that one hole is very much like the other. Merely a warm wet place to stick your cock."

I didn't even need to wonder where and how he'd learned to speak like this. I already knew. And I hated Xavier Blackwell more than the driver who'd killed my parents at that moment.

I gritted out, "Well, if that's what he says to you, then I feel sorry for you."

A strange look crossed Cas's face.

"And you told her you loved her, I suppose?"

Something in my face betrayed me, and of course, he pounced. "Oh, my god. You actually did. Jesus Christ."

"Look, you don't know anything, okay? We're—"

"Oh, for fuck sake, Jude, stop lying to yourself, and me, it's bloody exhausting." Caspien's voice was sharp as a blade. "How many times have you gotten off to the thought of what we did in my mother's bedroom?"

I couldn't breathe. I wanted to hang up and never have to look him in the face again, but that thought lasted less than a second. Instead, I glanced away from the phone.

"If you tell me the truth," he said. "I'll let you ask me something in return – something I promise to answer truthfully."

I looked back at him. He was serious. Beautiful and deadly and serious.

"But if you lie about it, and trust me, I'll know because you're a horrendous liar, I'll hang up, block your number, and you'll be lucky if you ever see me again."

My bones trembled beneath my skin, alive with panic and terror. These past few months had been bad enough. Never see him again? It was unthinkable. I knew I could threaten him, threaten to expose his lawyer; wasn't that what I'd come on here to do anyway?

But deep down, past the madness, I knew I didn't want that.

I didn't want to threaten or force him to see me. I wasn't sure this was any better, him forcing me, but it certainly came with less guilt.

I closed my eyes and counted.

My voice shook a little when I said, "I...can't remember."

"Try."

I'd thought about what we did more times than I could remember: in class, as Luke drove me to school, while kissing Ellie, while thinking about the essay I was writing, the film I'd just watched, or the song I was listening to.

But he'd only asked how many times I'd *gotten off* to it. Still, it was a lot. I was a teenager. I closed my eyes and thought about it. I'd imagine it was him with his hand around me. I'd imagine the curve of his lips or the shape of his hands. I'd remember his kiss and his tongue and the sounds he'd made when he'd come. I'd think about how the inside of his mouth had felt and tasted. I was almost fully hard by that point and I gripped the end of my dick to try and calm it down.

When I opened my eyes to look at him, he was smiling a little, clearly pleased with himself. His eyes looked dark in the light of his dorm room, his mouth a lush ruinous thing.

I remembered that mouth open and filled with mine.

"A lot, okay," I said with a heavy sigh.

"I thought so."

Sweat had begun to dampen my forehead.

"Cas, look, I don't...I don't know what I want, okay? I wish you were here so I could see you, so we could talk and see..." I didn't know what I was saying or where the next words would lead me. "I just wish you hadn't left."

The self-satisfied look on his face melted away. Something softer and more sincere moved into his eyes.

Later, I'd come to understand that he knew how sincerity affected his features. It was why he so rarely showed it. Sincerity gave his face an almost fragile quality. Delicate and exquisite. His beauty was always striking, but when he was tender and gentle with it, he became almost painful to look at. Magnificent and terrible as an angel. Divinity made flesh.

"You're making things very difficult for me, you know," he said quietly.

"Sorry." And I was. I was sorry about a lot of things.

It felt like a long time before he spoke again. When he did, it was with a measure of defeat.

"I will be home at the end of March for two weeks."

"*March*?" It was January. I was certain I'd go crazy if I had to wait another two months to see him.

"Yes. Then there is one more term before I can say goodbye to this overpriced prison in the Alps for good." He looked around the room with disdain.

"Is it that bad?"

He shrugged. "It's no worse than any other school, I suppose. It's just that everyone who goes here is a sociopath. The child of a millionaire or oligarch or diplomat; sometimes all three at once."

"Sounds awful," I said.

"It is. But I'll likely have to see half of these idiots again at Oxford."

"Oxford? You're going to Oxford."

Another shrug. "It's where all Deverauxs go. It's where Gideon went. And my mother before..." He trailed off. "Anyway, he's already paid my tuition. I've had a place reserved there since the minute I was born, I think." This was said with a measure of derision.

I couldn't remember having a conversation as normal as this with him before. I listened, hungry for whatever he would feed me next.

"But truthfully, I'd like to go to the Lervairè Conservatory. It's a music school in Boston. They only admit thirty students per year; it's quite prestigious."

"Thirty per year?" There were more than that in my registration class.

"Costs a fortune if you aren't awarded a scholarship," he said. "Not that money is the issue, of course. It is the skill I lack."

"You have plenty of skill."

The side of his mouth lifted a fraction as though he might smile, but then it was gone. "I have a degree of it, but not enough for Lervairè."

"Well, Lervairè sounds like a wanker."

He let out the first laugh I'd ever heard from him, and it very nearly stopped my heart.

He was about to say something when there was a rap on his door, then someone shouted in French. Or whatever other language they spoke there.

"They're putting the lights out," he grumbled. "They insist on treating us like criminals. We're fed like them, too. I mean, the food is passable, but it's the herding of us into the dining hall at one and six like prime cattle that is the issue. Some of us like a late dinner."

I caught myself smiling because hearing him talk like this, as though I were a friend he could just talk with, gave me a pleasant warmth in my stomach I never wanted to go.

"Gideon is coming to see you tomorrow?"

He nodded. "Though not by choice."

"What do you mean?"

"There is some kind of parental mediation session. He has to attend it, or they'll attempt to expel me again."

My eyebrows shot to my hairline. "*Expel you?* What did you do?"

"This time or the last time?"

I laughed. "Um, this time?"

"I broke the Austrian ambassador's son's nose with a Lacrosse stick." When he saw my expression, he added. "I hadn't properly warmed up, and my grip was loose. It was an accident."

"Right."

Caspien said nothing.

"Do you have to go?" I asked, remembering the lights-out call.

"I should. I have a 7 a.m. skiing class."

"Can I...call you again? Tomorrow?" I held my breath.

He stared.

"Yes," he said at last. "If you like."

I bit back my smile. "Well, I guess I'll let you go, then."

"Haven't you forgotten something?" he said.

"Um, I don't...have I?" I looked around, thinking.

"I promised you a truth. In return for yours."

My cheeks warmed from the reminder of mine.

"Oh, yeah, that's right." I tried to think of something. It wasn't that I didn't have things I wanted to know the true answer to – I had plenty. It was that I didn't know which I wanted to know the answer to more.

I wasn't going to ask him anything about Xavier Blackwell. I wouldn't waste this kind of opportunity on him.

In the end, I went with something I had asked myself over and over and over these last few weeks. Something only Caspien would be able to answer. Something I'd tried to ask him in my many letters and something I had asked him in my texts and voicemails but which he had failed, as yet, to answer.

"Why did you leave?" I asked.

I could tell I'd shocked him. Maybe he'd been expecting something about Blackwell. Maybe he'd been expecting something along the same vein as what he'd asked me.

He stared at me, and I thought maybe he wouldn't answer. He looked so unsettled by the question that I was sure that when it did come, it wouldn't even be the truth.

Finally, he said, "To protect someone."

"What does that mean?" I frowned.

"One truth, that was the agreement. Goodnight, Jude."

And then he was gone, and I was left with those three words rattling around my head for hours until I finally fell asleep.

TWENTY-ONE

My English Literature mock was the following afternoon. I'd flown through the critical appreciation question with enough praise for Percy Bysshe Shelley's *St. Irvyne* to fill eight sides of paper.

The second question, on whether the most fascinating characters in Gothic Literature were its villains, I'd managed to, quite miraculously I thought, compare the spectre of Dracula haunting the pages of Harker's diary with the unravelling psychopathy of Frank in *The Wasp Factory*.

Whether it was the nightly calls with Caspien – and the way they'd filled the huge gaping void that had stopped me concentrating fully on anything else – I didn't know, but the last two (French and Maths) had gone pretty well, too, I thought.

Caspien had made fun of the note I'd given to Gideon, though he was happy I hadn't written anything obscene in it because he was sure Gideon had opened it and read it before giving it to him. He'd brushed off my praise about the painting, calling it a 'very low-effort undertaking'. The low-effort undertaking now had pride of place on the shelf above my bed. Though, I took it down and put it in the wardrobe whenever Ellie came over. I wasn't in any way equipped to deal with the questions that might arise from her seeing it there.

Now that her grounding was over, she came over twice a week. On Saturdays, we'd have sex while Luke and Beth were out. Each time I got better, she got a little louder, and I felt a little less guilty about telling her I loved her.

I didn't always say it, though I was normally inside her when it would slip out from between my lips, gasping and unbidden. I was beginning to think that I did, in fact, love her, but in a way that felt easy and normal and completely unimaginative. I was sixteen, and she was my high school girlfriend, so, of course, I loved her. It took no thought or effort to love Ellie.

What I felt for Caspien was more bewildering, labyrinthine, and like a cryptic puzzle that changed and evolved every time we spoke. More adult, more serious, more frightening.

It was on our fourth or fifth call when he first asked me about sex with Ellie. At first, I'd wanted to lie about it, to deny it was even happening, but I remembered his words on the first call. I *was* a horrible liar.

Then I thought that sharing it with him could maybe go some way to smoothing over the lines that had been drawn between my feelings for him and Ellie and how they could continue to exist at the same time.

"What...do you want to know?" I asked.

"I don't know," he said casually. "How it feels? If you enjoy it? If she enjoys it. Whatever."

"I think she does." I shifted on the bed.

"You think?" he said. "God, I feel sorry for her already."

"Shut up. She does okay. I know she does."

He smirked. "Do you, though? They can fake it rather well, I hear." He'd already said enough for me to know that he'd never had sex with a girl. These things he'd always heard from 'some' or 'they'; the sort of knowledge boys picked up by social osmosis rather than personal experience.

"She doesn't fake it." I wasn't certain about this, but I did know she wanted to have it more than I did. I figured that if she weren't enjoying it, then she'd be less intent on us doing it so often.

"Then that means you're skilled or just big. Which is it?"

"Maybe I'm both?" I said boldly. I wasn't sure I was either, but I clung to the boast like a limpet to rock.

Caspien studied me, a light dancing in his eyes that made me feel pinpricked all over. "I suppose I'll have to take your word for it."

I felt the weight in his words like a weight on my dick.

"I suppose you will," I got out.

He recovered quicker than I did, and then we were talking about the film they'd made them watch in the recreation room after dinner.

A week later, he asked me, "So, do you enjoy it, then? With her."

I was lying in bed. I hadn't gotten dressed after the shower. I'd masturbated while thinking about him again; I'd taken to doing it on the nights we were due to talk so I was calmer and less agitated and more prepared for whatever state I'd find him in when he answered the phone. That night, I was wrapped in only a towel and still loose-limbed and hot from the wet heat of the shower. My brain was sated and unguarded.

"It's okay," I said.

"Christ," he exclaimed. He was eating red grapes, slipping the dark rounds into his mouth, biting them with one side, before chewing quietly.

I sat up a little. "Look, I don't know what it's supposed to feel like. I mean, it feels good when I...you know, and it feels nice when I... when it starts..."

"Jesus, your descriptive abilities are astounding; Oxford will be lucky to have such a wordsmith in their midst." He rolled his eyes. "Please tell me you have access to more of your vocabulary when writing words down."

"Shut up," I said. "I don't write about sex."

"And evidently, you don't talk about it either."

"No, I just have it. A lot."

This shut him up. He stopped chewing and stared at me.

I began to feel awkward under the scrutiny of his gaze. "I mean not a lot, a lot. Just...like a couple of times a week. Not that often, really. Alfie says Georgia comes over every night and wants to do it more than once a night. Which is—"

"Would you still break up with her if I asked you to?" he said right over me.

I stiffened. He put another grape into his mouth, bit down, and then began to chew.

"What?"

"You said once, after I made you come, that you'd break up with her if I asked you to."

I remembered, of course. But my mind was stuck on the arrangement of those words: *after I made you come*. After *he* made *me* come. It felt hugely significant.

He waited.

I swallowed. "Why would you even ask that?"

"It wasn't my idea, Jude. It was yours. Remember."

"Of course, I remember; that's not what I'm asking."

"What are you asking?"

I hesitated. "Is...do you? Is that what you want?"

I could not, in that moment, comprehend the idea of him saying 'yes'. Or rather, I could, but it seemed so absurd to me that he may as well have asked me if I wanted to move to the Himalayas with him and become a Tibetan monk. What was also absurd was how certain I was that I'd do it if he asked me to.

He put another grape into his mouth. "I just want to know if you would still break up with her if I asked you to."

If you lie, I'll know. You're a horrendous liar.

"Are we playing truth for a truth again?" I asked, stalling. "Because if I answer that, then I'll be wanting one of my own."

I thought I was being very clever. That I'd outsmarted him. But then he smiled that small cool smile of his and I knew even though

I hadn't said it out loud, I'd given him the answer.

"Never mind," he said.

He never asked me again.

A few nights after that was the first time we did more than talk on the phone. I'm not sure how I was ever clear-headed enough to hold a conversation with him, given how desperately I longed for a repeat of what had happened the day before he left. But when we took things to that next stage, it felt so entirely natural and inevitable, that I could see it was always going to happen. This was the pre-determined destination.

It started quite innocently.

We hadn't even been talking about Ellie and our sex life, there was no obvious warning for it at all, and so I didn't even know that it would lead there until it was far too late to stop it.

It started like this:

"I had to fight him today," Caspien said.

We'd been talking about Costa Rica before, and so I was confused. He did this, jumping from subject to subject like a gymnast across a spring floor—gracefully and with skill. My own skill was in keeping up with him.

Most of the time, I was only half-listening, hyper-focused on the side of his neck, the way his hair flopped over those small girlish ears, or that tormenting point at the end of his nose. I had decided that all noses should be shaped like this; I didn't quite understand the biological engineering of a nose, but the end of it should have a maddening little divot on its point like Caspien's did.

"Fight who?" I blinked, turning my attention fully to his words now.

"Hannes."

I searched my brain. Had he told me about someone called Hannes before? Forgetting something we'd talked about was always a fear of mine because I never wanted him to think I didn't listen. Then he'd stop calling. I'd never see him again.

All of my fears then led directly back to the same place: Never seeing Caspien again.

He put me out of my misery. "The Austrian ambassador's son."

I remembered. "The one whose nose you broke with the hockey stick."

"Lacrosse. Yes, Hannes. Hannes Meier."

"You fought him?"

"In Fence."

Fence he'd told me about. Fence I'd only seen in movies. They wore masks and all-white clothing and held rounded-ended swords, which they thrust at each other in very specific moves with very specific names. I'd Googled it after he'd hung up that night.

"Making you fight him with a sword after you broke his face doesn't seem like a very sensible idea."

"No, probably not. Except I'm sure that was the point because he's better at it than I am."

"He beat you?" I couldn't imagine Caspien being beaten at anything.

"Yes. He had me on the floor with his Épée at my throat, and the weirdest thing happened; I got hard."

My cheeks burned, and I felt a low familiar thickening between my legs.

"I suppose it was something about being on my back on the mat with him standing over me. I don't know." He shrugged. "But I liked the feeling of it."

"Of being on your back?"

He smiled a little. "Of being on my back. Of being...bested. It doesn't help that he has the nicest cock I've ever seen."

I coughed, choking on my hot chocolate. I sat up. "You've seen his cock?"

"Of course. Communal showers. Not that I look, well, I mean I look in so far as I have to have my eyes open, but he struts around with it out constantly because he knows how nice it is."

"There are nice ones?" I asked. I wasn't aware until that moment that cocks were supposed to be anything other than utilitarian. That they were more than just appendages that fulfilled a variety of tasks. I didn't know, beyond the usual discussions about size, that the aesthetics of cocks were even a thing.

He gave me a look as though I were the dumbest creature he'd ever known. "Do you consider all pairs of tits the same? Forget it; of course you do." He rolled his eyes. "His cock is nice, yes. And he knows it. And this is exactly what I was thinking of when he was stood over me with his Épée pointed at my throat. If we'd been alone I'd have likely offered to suck him off, but we weren't, and so it's been on my mind all day."

I felt a curl of something hot and sour in my stomach. The image was exciting and tormenting at the same time.

"But you hate him."

"What has that got to do with sucking his cock?"

I remember feeling foolish for thinking that it had a lot to do with it.

"Oh, I suppose when she does it for you, she's looking up at you with those big stupid loved-up eyes and telling you how much she loves you. But it is possible to have your mouth full of someone's cock and loathe them with ninety-nine percent of your conscious brain. The other one percent is hard and ferally turned on."

Ferally turned on.

At that moment, I could not have remembered a single instance of Ellie sucking my cock had any kind of sword been pointed at my throat.

I swallowed. "Right, well. I need to go." I needed to go because things had gotten very serious down below, and I was in danger of embarrassing myself to a point I wasn't sure I'd be able to come back from.

"Where are you going?" he asked, frowning.

"Um, nowhere. I just need to go. I'll call you tomorrow."

"Jude," he said and it was in this quiet, weighty voice that froze me in place. "Are you hard?"

When I couldn't respond, the very corner of his mouth softened, a light flicking on in his eyes. I let out a slow breath.

"Show me," he said.

"Excuse me?"

There was a beat, and then another, and then Caspien was shifting. His dick appeared on the screen a few moments later and I sank back into my bed and stared. He wore black shorts but he'd pulled the waistband down and hooked them beneath his balls. He was half hard. He wrapped his hand around the base of it and stroked it a few times. I kept staring. A moment later, it was gone, and his face was back.

"Now, your turn."

It had been easy to convince myself that what Caspien and I did on those calls was no more than what other boys did when they compared each other's dick sizes after P.E. It was also very like what I did when I was alone, and so having another person witness those things seemed no more than a novelty.

But after the second call, where Caspien and I watched each other stroke ourselves until we came on our stomachs, those moments we shared began to consume me.

Every time I looked at my dick I thought about how Caspien had seen it, and how he had told me, sounding quite impressed, that it was bigger and prettier than Hannes Meier's. I wasn't sure if what I was doing was considered cheating on Ellie, but the idea of her finding out – of anyone finding out – what Caspien and I did together terrified me so much that I knew it couldn't be entirely innocent.

Still, I made no move to put an end to them.

TWENTY-TWO

It was the middle of March when Ellie asked me what I had planned for summer. We were all lying on blankets; it was an unusually hot day for March, the sort of day that made me lazy and tired and made the earth seem like it was inside a huge greenhouse, airless and stuffy.

Alfie and Josh had come over, and we'd kicked the ball around on the stretch of grass on the other side of the lake until it got too hot even for that. Josh had gone to meet some rugby friends, so the four of us were lying on the grass, half-dozing. Ellie was on her stomach, freckled shoulders exposed and pinked with a pair of white-rimmed sunglasses perched on the end of her nose.

"Are you guys going anywhere on holiday this year?" She said without looking up from her phone.

"They haven't mentioned it. Doubt it." I was reading an article about a movie adaptation of *All Quiet on The Western Front*. I wasn't particularly paying attention. Not enough to have been prepared for what came next.

"You could come with us to Bergamo," she said, turning to me. This got my attention. I looked over at her. Whatever she saw on my face had her saying, "I already asked my dad."

There was a quick flutter of panic inside my chest. I had already spent a lot of time daydreaming about summer, about Caspien and me this summer. I'd dreamt of sweltering afternoons like this one, lounging right here by the lake, reading on the western patio, cooling off inside Deveraux. Other nameless things which I'd never utter aloud. In any case, none of my daydreams had involved Ellie. And they should have, if we were boyfriend and girlfriend then they would have to.

I realised it then: Ellie would need to feature in every daydream I had forever unless I ended things. It wasn't arrogance to say that I was certain that I was a prominent feature in Ellie's daydreams of summer in northern Italy.

"I don't know if Beth would say yes," I said, though it was a lie. Beth had been far more lenient and far less intractable with this stuff. "The money," I explained.

"Well, you wouldn't need much, just pocket money, really. The house is always fully stocked when we get there, and we drive from Cherbourg, so there are no flights to pay for." She was sitting up now, excited by the idea.

I glanced at Alfie and Georgia, who were sharing AirPods and watching something on Alfie's phone screen. I bit my lip and glanced over her shoulder at the big house.

"I'll ask," I said, smiling nervously.

She misread it for something more like enthusiasm because she squealed, fell on top of me and began babbling about all the things we would do in Bergamo.

That night, when I called Caspien, he didn't answer. I couldn't imagine where he'd be on a Saturday night. I already knew he had no friends there; he'd told me often enough how much he loathed everyone at that school. How they were rich and boring and stupid. How no one there had a single interesting thing to say.

It didn't stop me from thinking of him with Hannes Meier, though. Of Caspien on his back with Hannes Meier above him, thrusting his pretty cock into his open and willing throat.

I was eating toast and making tea the following morning when Luke strolled in, whistling happily along to some pop song on the radio.

"Morning, Judey," he sang.

"Morning," I mumbled around a mouthful of hot toast.

"Don't suppose you fancy helping me out for a bit at the big house today? Ged's on holiday."

I groaned. "It's going to be boiling – do I have to?"

"Well, no. You don't have to, but there might be some cash in it for you if you do. Which I hear you might need for a little Italian trip you're thinking of taking this summer." He winked.

"How did you hear about that?" I asked, far sharper than was appropriate.

Luke frowned. "Scott mentioned it last night when he came to pick El up. What? Why is your face like that?"

"Nothing. So what did Beth say?"

"She said we'd speak to you about it. But she's not completely against the idea. Figures you deserve a holiday, same as us, and we were thinking that if you're with the Walsh's for a few weeks, then me and her can get away somewhere for a break. You know, change of scenery."

"You could still do that even if I don't go. I'm sixteen, which is old enough to be at home on my own."

He was still frowning, like there was a complicated maths equation on my head he didn't understand.

"What's going on here? Thought you'd be begging and pleading us to let you go to Italy?"

I had nothing. There was nothing I could think of to say that would make any sense. He was right; I should be begging. Why *wouldn't* I want to go to Italy with my girlfriend for the summer? I swallowed. Behind me, the kettle popped off the boil, so I spun around and busied myself with making tea instead.

"Judey, you know you can talk to me about anything, right?" Luke was closer to me, and his voice careful. He laid a hand on my shoulder.

I tried to imagine how I might say it, how I might tell him what was going on inside my mind. But I wasn't sure what words I would use to explain something I didn't really understand myself.

There was something I could say, though, something he might be able to offer some advice on. Something that didn't need to mean anything more than just what it was.

"I'm thinking of breaking up with Ellie," I said so quietly I didn't think he could hear it over the stirring of the teaspoon.

"You are?" Luke asked, sounding confused.

I nodded. "I just don't think...I mean...I think maybe that she..." I turned to Luke and picked my way through the tangle of thoughts in my head. "I'm sure she likes me more than I like her. I feel like I'm lying to her; I mean, I have lied to her, and every time we're together, it's like I'm lying to her over and over again."

The words, once they were out, wouldn't stop. I didn't know how to stop talking, and so on and on I went. Luke listened intently, soft eyes rounded with concern.

"But I told her I loved her, and I didn't mean to; it sort of just came out the first time. Which I know is wrong, but I didn't know how to take it back either. And I've told her a few times now so she thinks I love her, and I don't think I do. And like, if I did I'd be more certain about it, right? I mean, I care about her, and I think she's great and funny and pretty, but I don't think I love her. Because I don't think about her all the time and have daydreams about her and stuff, which I think maybe I should. But now she's asked about Italy and I didn't know how to say no to that either because if I had, then she'd want to know why, and then I'd have to tell her about how I don't think I love her. And I'm so scared of hurting her, Luke, and of everyone hating me for it. I mean, Georgia would hate me, and then maybe Alfie would too because he likes her so much, and so instead of all that, I just said I'd ask you guys about Italy. So now it's like it's too late and..."

Luke had pulled me into him and wrapped his arms around me. I understood it was because I was crying. I'd somehow broken down and was breathing quick and panicked breaths into his shoulder as he rubbed comforting circles into my back.

"Hey, it's fine, buddy. Everything's going to be okay. *Shhhh*, it's fine; don't worry about it."

"I think there might be something wrong with me, Luke," I mumbled against him.

"There's nothing wrong with you, mate. Nothing at all."

After, Luke sent me upstairs to get changed into work clothes, and we headed up to the big house. It was planting that was to be done, which I didn't mind half as much as weeding or pruning. I liked seeing the fresh soil turned over, soft and new; the earthy scent of it was always grounding to me. In a way, that reminded me distinctly of Luke. We were laying a row of new pink and white rose bushes along the front of the house to compliment the turquoise Festuca Luke had planted there already. I could already imagine the end result. The intense blue grass shrub would burst up along the upper level, and the pale pink roses sprouting up and around the lower tier to make it look like icing around the base of a large stone cake.

"She'll be hurt no matter what you do, you know," he said when we were elbow-deep in the third trench. "I reckon you're right about her caring a lot about you, and the longer this goes on the more hurt she'll be when it does end. Especially if you could have ended it a lot sooner."

"I know," I said gloomily.

"But she will be okay." He reached out to pat my shoulder. "I know everything feels like a life-changing event when you're young, but most things aren't."

"I'm sixteen," I pointed out.

He held his hands up. "Well, my point stands. Both points."

And he had been right. I rarely think about Ellie now, not with any deep sentiment, at least. Memories of her, fleeting and faded, would pass through my mind every now and then. A girl I'd see in a cafe who reminded me of her, a stranger's laugh I'd hear that sounded like hers, and a soundless blurry memory would rise to the surface before sinking back down again. Come and gone in a fraction of a moment.

But some things *were* life-changing. I knew that, too.

My parents' deaths had changed everything about my life.

And I knew, even then, that Caspien, too, was one of those things.

I'd thought then about telling Luke. Soil scattered about our knees, the sun beating down on our necks, and the scent of not yet sprung flowers blooming around us. It would be easy to tell him. To give voice to the thing blooming inside me; he'd take it and treat it with care, I knew that. I couldn't tell him about what Caspien and I now did on those calls late at night, but I could trust him with the rest, I was sure of it. The thoughts that went everywhere with me, the reason I suspected I didn't love Ellie, the reason I spent more and more time in Gideon's library skimming books by Wilde and the works of Sassoon—Gideon had, as it turned out, had a lot of queer literature on his shelves. My most secret hope was that Luke had similar thoughts at my age. That he'd reassure me this was just some by-product of adolescence, the forming of our sexual minds and desires.

But all I said was, "I'll talk to her soon. I promise."

"It's not a promise you need to make me, Judey," Luke said gently. "It's to yourself. You're not the kind of person who leads girls on and hurts them, that much I know." The smile he gave me was encouraging and it sent a spiral of guilt through me because as I'd known for months, I was exactly that kind of person.

The following Tuesday evening, I was in Gideon's library – Elspeth had told me he'd been in his study when I arrived, meeting with someone important from London– and so I settled in and made an attempt at an old A-Level English paper: 'Censorship of the arts can never be justified – discuss.'

I was going rather well when the door to the library burst open, and Gideon strode in with another man at his back.

"…copy is rather old. And I think the fourth edition has a preface by Isherwood. Jude! I hadn't known you were here." He was beaming at me, warm and pleasant, but my whole body had turned to stone as though I'd looked at Medusa herself. "Xavier, this is our neighbour, Jude. He and Caspien are quite close. Jude's studying for his A-levels; he's an exceptionally bright boy." He said this last part as though it were something of a novelty.

Xavier Blackwell stood about a meter away from me, so close I could smell his aftershave. Rich and woodsy. Sickening. He wore a three-piece suit, though he was carrying the jacket in large loose fingers. The waistcoat showed off a broad chest and wide shoulders but a trim, well-defined waist.

He held out his hand to me. "Hi. Xavier Blackwell," he said. His eyes were so dark they were almost black; I could see the flickering gold light of the wall lights in them. He was tanned with a perfect smile and a haircut I guessed was more expensive than my entire wardrobe. "Nice to meet you, Jude."

Though the pictures I'd seen of him online captured his good looks, there was something else to him. An energy, charisma, which I suppose is what some would call it, that gave him the air of a celebrity almost. Though maybe this was just what my mind had done to him.

I didn't stand but stretched my hand up to meet his.

"Nice to meet you," I managed, though I was certain my voice sounded half-strangled.

"Xavier is my lawyer," Gideon explained. "He's looking to borrow a book, which I am certain is right here…"

I couldn't stop staring at him. His hair was dark like his eyes, but there were copper touches in it where the light touched. He was almost violently handsome, like some Spartan had wandered out of The Iliad and into Gideon's library. He was good-looking in the opposite way Caspien was; where Caspien was all pale fragility and dusky pinks, Xavier was black eyes and sharp jaw. Hades and Persephone.

He hadn't moved, but he alternated between watching Gideon rummage through his shelves and darting glances back at me, curious.

"So, you and Caspien are friends?" he asked.

There was something in the way he said 'friends'– a tiny inflection – which I thought changed its entire meaning. I'm certain no one else would have noticed it, but I was fixated on him so closely that I could probably tell how many eyelashes he had on each eye.

My instinct told me to pretend I hadn't noticed. So I shrugged and said, as nonchalantly as I could, "We've hung out a few times."

He breathed a soft little smile and nodded.

"Here it is!" Gideon exclaimed. "Oh, this is the second edition. I was certain it was the third. Still a great read," he said.

Blackwell took the book and leafed through its pages. "I'll give it a go," he said, patting the book with his palm.

Gideon was staring at him with a weird mooning sort of look.

"Do, do, I'd love to discuss it with you. Now, can I get you a drink before your car arrives? You know you are welcome to stay, there's more than enough room."

"I hate to put you out, Gid, really the hotel is fine."

"Nonsense. You know I'm always happy to have you." The undercurrent in his words made my cheeks feel hot.

Blackwell looked at me. "Nice to meet you, Jude."

I nodded, wordlessly.

"Sorry to disturb your studies, we'll try and keep the noise down." Gideon giggled like a girl.

Blackwell smiled indulgently and shook his head. Before the door closed behind them I saw, very distinctly, Gideon throw a longing stare at Xavier Blackwell's arse.

I'd thought hard about whether I would bring it up to Caspien that night. Did I want to remind him that Blackwell existed? That I suspected Gideon had a crush on him? That I'd met him? He'd never been particularly open to any conversation that involved Xavier Blackwell, and part of me wanted to be the one to tell him that Gideon was very clearly into his pervert, and would, in my view, make a far more palatable lover for him. Another part of me was terrified about what his reaction might be. Would he be jealous? Furious? Or worse, would it cause Caspien to run back to him?

I was still debating on whether to mention it when he video-called me just after ten. I was in bed, reading with just my booklight. The window was open and the moon shone a bright sheet of white onto the wooden floor.

He started with, "You know I'm convinced the reason Switzerland was never attacked during either war was because it is quite simply the most boring country on earth and no one wanted to set foot in it."

"I've always thought it looked quite nice there."

"Nice? Is that how you choose your holiday destinations? On how nice they look? Are you someone's grandmother?"

He was in a mood, I could tell.

"I don't choose holiday destinations at all. I've never been abroad."

He looked positively horrified. "What? Never?"

I shook my head.

"Christ," he said. "Quite the little homebody, aren't we."

"Not by choice," I said what I said next because I wanted to see his reaction. "Ellie's invited me to Italy with her this summer. Her family spend a few weeks there every year."

I could see no discernible reaction on his face, and my stomach sank.

But then he asked, "What did you tell her?

I shrugged. "I said I'd ask Beth and Luke."

"And what, you haven't yet?"

I hadn't thought this all the way through. I shrugged again.

"Italy is beautiful in summer, though it depends where you are.

I'd avoid Rome entirely, and Florence. Unless you like the sensation of being boiled alive in a human soup."

"What are you doing this summer?" I asked in what I hoped was a nonchalant tone.

"I haven't given it much thought."

"Right."

There was a stretch of silence before he said, "I suppose I'll be at Deveraux. I miss my horse. And my books." Now, this *was* said nonchalantly, but the way he avoided looking at me entirely made something hopeful bubble up in my chest. "Gideon mentioned something about taking a cruise on the Nile, I think, but I couldn't think of anything I'd want to do less."

"Yeah, that doesn't sound all that fun, to be honest."

"Exactly."

"I called you on Saturday night," I said. "You didn't answer."

He gave me a hard look. "I was busy."

"With Hannes Meier?"

He didn't react. "And if I was?"

"Were you?"

"I actually don't think that's any of your business, do you?"

I wanted to say that yes, it was, but I didn't dare. It was on the tip of my tongue then to mention Blackwell, to tell him that he and Gideon looked rather cosy when I left and that I wouldn't be surprised if he were busy with him right now. But apart from some hollow momentary satisfaction, I couldn't really see what good it would do.

"I was at a double feature in town," Caspien said, though he sounded a little embarrassed by it. "They're doing a week of Studio Ghibli films."

I had to bite back the smile that threatened to spread across my heating face.

We spent the rest of the call talking about *The Cat Returns* and *Tales from Earthsea*.

TWENTY-THREE

Caspien's homecoming, scheduled for the last week in March, began to feel like a countdown. A countdown to the starting point of the rest of my life; when everything I was confused about or which kept me up at night, would finally be resolved.

As soon as I saw him again, I imagined some great shift would happen inside me, like a big boulder would be rolled away to reveal the answers to the questions I'd been torturing myself with for months.

I thought about how it had started between us in the summer and wondered, not for the first time, how we had ended up here. How had I gone from loathing his every molecule to hanging on his every word? How had I gone from plotting his murder to dreaming about the scent of his skin and the shape of his hands? The wanting of him had grown so immense that it had the power to stop me in my tracks.

Caspien was an altarpiece, Deveraux his reredos, and I came to him in blind idolatry.

I'd planned to break up with Ellie prior to Caspien's returning home to Deveraux. But the week he was due back, she'd called to say her grandfather had died. Old and apparently quite senile, he'd been living in some elderly home in Norwich. She'd cried quite inconsolably over the phone while I'd said things like 'At least he wasn't in pain' and 'He knew how much you cared,' though I had no way of knowing either was true. Before hanging up, she'd said she loved me and would call me when she arrived. I'd said it back because not saying it then wasn't an option.

I'd gotten around the Italy question by saying Beth and Luke were considering it, and it would depend on how hard I studied for my A-Levels (my mock results had been decent) and how much I helped Luke in the lead-up to summer. Conveniently, both of these meant I'd have less spare time to spend with her. The guilt at spinning these lies lasted only as long as I was with her. After, as surely as the wave always returned to the shore, my thoughts would return to Cas.

We'd spoken only once on the phone the week he was due home. On Monday, he called to say he'd beaten Hannes at Fence with a 'very clever point-in-line' and then a 'disengage.' He was as excited as I'd ever heard him.

"What time are you due home on Saturday?" I'd cut in when I'd heard more than enough about Hannes Meier's superior swordplay.

"The car is collecting me at 8:30; my flight leaves Zurich at eleven." He hadn't video-called, so I couldn't see what he was doing, but it sounded like he was moving around. Packing, maybe. "What are your plans this weekend?" he said as though my entire month, year, hadn't been leaning toward this point, as though it was even slightly feasible I'd made any other plans except wait for him to call.

"Not sure," I said. "Do you want to do something?"

There was a short silence before he said, "Something?"

A jolt of delicious heat shot straight between my legs.

I swallowed. "Yeah, whatever you want."

"Whatever I want..." he dragged it out.

I breathed out.

"What if," he said, "I want you *not* to come until I get home? Do you think you could do it?"

A thousand-volt electric shock would not have had a more violent effect on my body.

"Why...would you want that?" I managed.

"Do I need a reason?"

"If you want me to do it, then I wouldn't mind knowing why, that's all." It sounded terrible. Painful even. But I knew if he asked me to, I would do it. He didn't need to give me a reason. I wasn't even sure why I'd asked for one.

"Forget it," he said, sighing.

"I don't...want to."

I could practically hear him smirking. "Very well. Then do it because I want you to. No other reason."

I licked my tongue over my teeth. My cock was already hard and a little painful. The thought of four more days without easing that, even a little? Well, I wanted to throw up.

But there was something in his voice, something very similar to how he'd spoken to Xavier Blackwell on the phone that day, and that alone drowned out everything else.

"I'll think about it," I said.

"I'm willing to bet that *thinking* is going to become quite the challenge by, let's say, Wednesday evening."

I snorted. He laughed softly.

Saturday arrived with the most excruciating need I'd ever felt. My entire body trembled with it. Tight skin over jittering bones. A pulsing in my legs and hands and balls. But I'd done it. I'd done what he'd asked for no reason other than he'd asked. I was sure the moment I set eyes on him, I was going to hurt him.

I smashed a cup in the kitchen, burnt my toast, and left the pot with the eggs boiling so long the shells had turned black and the pan smelled like the metalwork department. I was pretty sure, at my age, there was a health risk in going this long without masturbating. I'd Googled it but hadn't found anything conclusive.

His journey was Zurich to Heathrow and then Heathrow to Jersey. As far as I could tell, it was about five hours in total, so I was expecting him to be at Deveraux by dinnertime. He hadn't said a thing about seeing me, but I'd already decided I didn't care. I'd go over to see him regardless. In fact, I distinctly hadn't mentioned anything about going over because I didn't want him to say no.

I needed to see him as much as I needed to come. Perhaps even more. So if he hadn't called me by 6:30 p.m., then I was going to cycle up to the house.

"Gideon said Cas is due home today," Luke said after dinner.

I was lying on the couch trying to force myself through the chapter I was reading. He said it as though he might be imparting some vaguely interesting piece of information to me that I may or may not have cared about.

Luke didn't know we spoke on the phone.

"Yeah, Gideon mentioned it to me too," I replied.

He was flicking through his phone on the other sofa. Beth had gone into town to meet her friend for a bottomless brunch.

"Was gonna head up and see him later."

"Cool," he said without looking up. "I'm heading out to meet the boys for a couple around six. I'll meet Beth out, and we'll come back together later. Not too late, though."

"No worries."

My phone buzzed with an Instagram notification. Ellie had posted a picture of her and her grandfather. He was wearing a bright green Christmas jumper and one of those paper crowns you get inside crackers. She was in a headband shaped like reindeer antlers. It read: *Miss you, Gramps x*

I sent a heart and locked my phone again.

By 6 p.m., Caspien hadn't gotten in touch. Luke had left in a taxi to meet his friends about twenty minutes before, and so I'd finally been able to stand and go to the kitchen to watch the road. He was sure to be home by now. Unless there'd been a delay. Unless he'd missed the connection.

My fingers itched to text him. I pulled my phone out to do just that when a text came in.

Ellie:

Miss you 😵 x.

I was about to respond, debating too long over the words, when another came through.

Caspien:

what are you doing?

Was he serious?

Me:

I'm at home.

Caspien:

That's not what I asked.

Me:

I'm not doing anything. Are u home?

Caspien:

Yes.

My hands trembled as I wrote:

Me:

Luke and Beth are out

Caspien:

How lovely for them.

Me:

if u want to come over

There was nothing for so long that I thought I might just go out-side and drown myself in the lake. The speck of pride I had left wouldn't possibly allow me to turn up there now.

But then:

Caspien:

all right.

I ran upstairs first and made sure my room was clean. Which it was since I'd cleaned and mopped it earlier for something to do. I opened the window and squirted some of my cologne into the air.

I went to piss and check my reflection in the bathroom mirror. Then I brushed my teeth. Then I worried that brushing them might indicate that I'd been expecting to kiss him, so I grabbed a bag of Skittles from the sweet cupboard, threw a handful into my mouth and chewed.

I switched the TV onto something I thought would look as though I'd been watching instead of what I'd actually been doing. A rugby union match was on, so I turned the volume up and made to settle into the couch to watch it.

I could not have told you what teams were playing or who was in the lead; my brain refusing to move past *Caspien, you're going to see him, you haven't seen him in the flesh since September.*

Six bloody months. It felt like years. It felt like yesterday. It felt like I was going to—

The doorbell rang.

My blood was popping and bursting like there were fireworks beneath my skin, my heart vibrating wildly behind my ribs. I went to go answer the door.

He stood with his hands in the pockets of his navy chinos. He wore a strange cord jacket in dark grey, a darker grey woollen shirt beneath it, and a deep wine-coloured scarf around his neck, though it wasn't particularly cold.

His hair was shorter than it had been when I'd last seen him. A messy tangle of blonde that looked like spun silk. I realised I'd been staring too long without saying anything.

"You know I don't actually need an invite to come in," he said. "We own this house. It's just a matter of manners."

"You sure you're not a vampire?"

"Why, would you like me to suck you dry?" he said and stepped inside.

He sat on the couch. I offered him a drink (Don't you have anything stronger than this?). Skittles (They will ruin your teeth, you know?). Food (Elspeth prepared an entire tasting menu for me—I needed to walk it off).

He'd taken off his jacket and scarf and was sitting on the opposite end of the sofa with his legs slightly spread, long fingers settled on his thighs. I wasn't sure if he was actually watching the rugby. Or just pretending to like I was.

All I could smell was him, fresh air, and something sweet, and there was a battle inside myself not to throw myself on top of him and rut against him until I came.

His eyes were still on the TV when he said, casually, "Did you do it then?"

There was absolutely no emotion in his voice. He might have been asking what I had for dinner (a single roast potato because I couldn't stomach a thing). But still, I knew what he was asking. I took a long drink of my Coke. Hoped my throat wasn't dry so that words would sound normal.

"What if I did?"

I saw him shift his body a little, tongue dipping out to trace his lower lip.

"I'd ask you to prove it."

I made a weird snorting noise. "And how exactly would I be able to do that?"

He turned his head then and looked between my legs. Then he shrugged. "You could show me it."

"How would that prove anything?" I tried styling it out because the thought of taking out my dick to show him how hard it was, was causing my brain to derail slightly.

"I've an aptitude for this sort of thing." He was smiling now, a pretty sharp thing that felt like a knife at my throat.

I was suddenly afraid. What if this had all been some terrible joke to him? What if the moment I pulled it out, he'd stand up and point and laugh? Despite what we'd done over the phone for the last few weeks, this still seemed like the sort of thing he might do.

So I said, "You first."

He stared at me a few long moments then rolled his eyes and pulled out his dick. It was half-hard, pretty and pale like the rest of him. It was longer than it had looked in his hand on any of our calls, and the end a deep pink. He pulled at it lazily while he raised an eyebrow at me, expectant.

I unzipped and manoeuvred the stiff aching thing out of my jeans. Even this was torturous; every graze and shift of fabric making it vibrate with shocking sensitivity. Caspien's eyes on it felt as good as him touching it.

"Christ, it really is quite something," he said, looking at it.

My chest puffed up. "Thanks," I smirked.

He met my eye, something wolfish in his gaze. "Does she like it? Your girlfriend? I bet she does."

I stopped breathing.

"Do you shove it down her throat?"

I wasn't certain what was happening, only that my mind was

recoiling even as my dick throbbed.

"I like being choked on someone's dick like that," he told me. "The bigger the better, really. I like it to feel as if I'm going to die."

I let out a strangled groan and felt something pulse out of the head of it.

Caspien was alternating between looking at my dick and my face, conductor-like concentration in his eyes. He stroked his own without urgency.

"Would you like to do that to me, Jude? Shove that…" He indicated it. "…so far down my throat I can't breathe? Choke me with it?"

"Caspien," I warned.

He smirked. "Tell me what you'd like to do to me."

"I…" I wasn't even touching it, and it was pulsing, a stream of liquid leaking out of the tip. "I'd like…to kiss you again."

He blinked a few times. Surprised.

"Well, do it then," he said.

I leapt across the couch and pressed him into it with my body. His bare dick chafed against mine as I shoved my tongue down his throat. I moaned, deep and satisfied, as I tasted him.

There are things I've tasted since – the burrata from that café by the Tiber in Rome, the croissant from that café in St Mark's Square, the hot chocolate from Angelina's on the Rue de Rivoli – that I'd describe as little pieces of heaven on earth. But his mouth, laced as it was with grape and watermelon, altered my brain chemistry in a way that I've never been able to undo.

He let out a little huff of breath at first, but then he was kissing me back. Our first kiss had been a strange thing, our second a rushed desperate chaos of lips, but this, I decided, would be something else. I kissed him slowly, deeply, I tilted my head and sucked and bit at his lips in gentle motions. I drew my tongue over his and curled it around it. Caspien sank into the couch deliciously submissive, his body softening and hardening at the same time. When I felt him grab my dick I thought my body might erupt in flames.

He stroked my dick with his long, elegant fingers, his touch a searing brand. His mouth, a warm, wet paradise I never wanted to leave. I lasted less than ten seconds before I gasped, bit down on his lip, and poured great floods of white over his hand.

After, I sat up and muttered an apology, but he just wrapped his hand, still covered in me, around himself and stroked.

His eyes never left mine as he did it, and I watched, bewitched, my brain popping and fizzing like champagne as he made himself come. His own orgasm was gentle and restrained, and it slipped out of him in a series of small gasps. He scooped up his own mess – mixed now with mine – and sucked them into his mouth to lick them dry. Then he leaned across to kiss me, pushing our come into my mouth with his tongue.

My head spun as my dick twitched back to life.

I kissed him back eagerly, not at all minding the thick sour taste of us inside his mouth.

I was already desperate to do it again.

TWENTY-FOUR

I moved through those spring days in a trance. My sleeping hours were filled with dreams of us together, warm young bodies tangled, scents and smells, and nightly expulsions that would wake me before the sun was up, wanting him.

The music room, the Arboretum, the boat that bobbed in the lake outside my window, on the deep grass inside the wood that ran on the furthest side of the grounds. In all of these places, he'd kiss me and touch me, opening himself up to me like the petals of a flower. I dreamt of him, of us, everywhere.

The awake hours were worse.

Because in these, I was fully conscious and able to direct my thoughts where I wanted them, and I wanted them on him. Back then, he was the beating heart inside my chest, the hopes and dreams I harboured in my soul. I existed only because he perceived me. He lived inside me then, in a different way to how he does now – like some exotic disease I was infected with in my youth and of which there is no cure.

And I wanted to live inside him too, crawl under his skin and settle there.

In the shower the morning after the night before, I'd closed my eyes and run my hands over myself, imagining they were his. I'd ejaculated against the tiles before wiping it clean with my hand. Then, as I stared at it, curious, I brought my hand to my mouth and tasted it.

I didn't like it, but I couldn't forget the memory of him having sucked the mess into his mouth like it was some delicious treat.

I cycled up to the mansion before lunch that Sunday and found him in the stables with Falstaff. He was brushing the horse's coat in long, slow strokes while feeding him chunks of bright red apple with the other. I watched him for a bit from the door without announcing my presence.

He hadn't invited me, and part of me feared his reaction to my being there. Maybe he wouldn't want to see me. (I lived in constant fear that one day, he would decide he was done with me and shift his attention elsewhere.) He wore his usual riding outfit: tight beige trousers, black knee-high riding boots, and a fitted navy polo. His hair was still wet from the shower, slicked behind his ears.

When he moved around the horse, he caught sight of me standing by the open stable door. He said nothing, but neither did he look unhappy to see me.

"Did he miss you?" I asked him.

He let his gaze linger on me a moment before he went back to brushing the horse. "It looks like it," he said.

"Are you taking him for a ride?"

"No. I'm out here for the invigorating conversation."

I walked a little toward him. Toward the horse. I had always been a little afraid of horses; their size and strength and power. I'd read something once about someone being kicked in the head by one and their skull cracking open like an egg. Brains pouring out. It wasn't hard to imagine it.

Falstaff was huge, with polished black eyes and a great chomping mouth. He eyed me cautiously as I approached. I could feel the heat lifting from him. Caspien watched me as he continued to brush before holding a chunk of apple out to me.

"Hold your palm flat, almost inverted," he instructed. I was certain he could tell how terrified I was, but if he noticed, he chose not to mention it. "His teeth are blunt but strong. He could easily take your fingers off."

I swallowed and held my palm out beneath his large mouth. He snuffled at it, hot breath ticklish against the flesh, before he scraped up the apple with his teeth and tongue and began to munch.

"Do you know of the old birdwatcher hut?" Caspien asked casually, still focused on the horse. "It's on the far side of the estate, just off the long drive."

I knew where it was. I'd stumbled upon it one day about a week after we moved here. It was a small wooden space with a bench inside, nestled in the trees and long rectangular openings cut into three sides.

"I know where it is."

"I'm going to take him out for a run," said Caspien, moving the brush into the leather pouch hanging on a hook on the stable wall. "Meet me there." He didn't bother waiting for my answer before leading the horse past me and outside.

He didn't need to wait for my answer. Because it was very clear, even then, that I was always going to do whatever he told me to.

It was a good twenty-minute walk to the hut from the stables. I never saw him as I went, but I took a different, less obvious path to it.

I headed through the woods and followed the stream, crossing it in a couple of places when the edge became too challenging. It wasn't a deep thing, just a small pebbled trickle which went all the way to the edge of Deveraux, under the wall, and beyond.

As I got closer, I began to consider why he'd wanted to meet there, in that small cramped darkened place. I suspected it was for one reason, and like having a sudden fever, my brain started to grow white, hot, and suffocating inside my skull.

It was hard to ignore the thoughts and images my brain presented me with, and as the hut appeared through the trees, solitary and vigilant, my breath had reached a frenzy. A small latch held the door closed, and it seemed as loud as a gunshot when I snicked it open.

Inside was as I remembered it, except for one thing: the promise it now held. The air was stale and a little hot, but aside from that, there was no sign that anyone had been here for some time. I didn't think anyone used it for birdwatching anymore. Two slim bench seats ran along either side, and I sat down on one of them to read and wait for him.

It was another half hour before the sound of the door being pulled open drew me out of the pages. I'd heard nothing outside, but I'd slipped into my usual 'readers trance' while I'd waited.

Caspien stepped into the hut, breathing hard, his cheeks flushed from his ride. I sat up and closed my book, watching as he pulled across the snib to lock the door from the inside. When he turned to me, there was a look of fierce determination on his face. He took a step towards me, and to my utter surprise, he dropped to his knees on the muddy ground and reached for the button on my jeans.

I blinked at him in shock before leaning back to let him undo the button and then the zip. He pulled me out carefully. There was not a single moment of hesitation before he sucked me into his mouth.

I wasn't hard, not at first, but it didn't take long at all. He took me to the back of his throat, and I felt something tighten around the head like a fist. I gasped, overcome with the sensation, and felt my cock go all the way hard. He released me and began to suck and lick, clinically almost, competently certainly, and I dropped back against the wood behind me and tried not to come as quickly as I had last night.

I couldn't look away. The sight of it in his mouth was extraordinary. I could see it and feel it, and yet my brain was unable to accept it was happening. Pleasure raced up my spine, flooded my chest and squeezed at my heart. His eyes were open, focused and calm as he watched me watch him. When he pulled off and licked at the saliva that had collected on his wet lips, I groaned.

"Have you thought about this?" he asked, his voice rougher than I'd ever heard it.

Words weren't possible, so I nodded.

"I thought about it too, while I was riding. About what it would feel like in my mouth, about how it would taste."

He took me back into his mouth, and this time, he used his hand, too, twisting while he bobbed his head. My brain was on the verge of implosion, my dick too. His fingers curled and stroked and caressed while his mouth moved over me with expert skill. I thought: how did he learn how to do this so well? Who taught him how to do this?

I imagined Xavier Blackwell, Hannes Meier, and countless faceless rich boarding school boys whom I loathed and wanted to thank profusely at the same time.

"Caspien...I am going to..." I whined.

He pushed me down his throat again, then tickled his fingers over the soft, sensitive skin of my balls, and I was done. I reached for his head and thrust into his warm, tight throat, holding him there as I finished. When it was over, I fell back again, panting and soft-limbed and swimming in more bliss than I knew what to do with. My eyes were closed, but when I felt him rise and come to sit next to me on the bench, I opened them to look at him, awed.

Everything about him awed me.

I was bewitched in the truest sense of the word. I felt his spell hanging over me like a veil, the world hazy and white whenever I was near him.

I loved him. I was as certain of that as I was my own name, both universal truths. *I am Jude Alcott, and I am in love with Caspien Deveraux.*

"Stop looking at me like that," he said, tucking a stray strand of hair behind his ear. It had dried on his ride and now sat curled and golden on his head.

"Like what?"

"Like that."

"Don't all the boys you do that to look at you like this, after?" Maybe it was a pathetic attempt to find out how many boys there were, or maybe it was an attempt to make myself look less...less in love. But his eyes grew very serious as he looked at me.

"No," He said. "No one looks at me the way you do."

I felt those words like a burn. My cheeks flooded with warmth.

Embarrassed, I sat up, tucked myself into my jeans, and buttoned them.

"I don't mind it," he said obliquely.

"What?"

"The way you look at me." His gaze was very intense suddenly, his eyes holding my own in their pale grey snare. "Everything you think and feel is in your eyes, you know. When you hated me, I could see it. When you didn't, I could see that too." His voice was horribly self-assured. "It's rare. Most people try to hide what they truly feel. But not you, Jude Alcott."

He knew, then. How I felt about him. He could see it in my stupid face every time he looked at me. I couldn't think of anything more humiliating.

"Is that what you do?" I asked him. "Hide what you feel?"

"You think I have feelings? My, how times have changed." He was smiling a little.

"Oh, I always knew you had them. I just figured they were mainly about how best to murder me and hide my body, how much you resented my entire existence. That sort of stuff."

A dimple appeared on his cheek as he smirked.

"As if you never had similar thoughts about me. More black and murderous by far."

I laughed. "Yeah, that's true. I pretty much wanted to murder you the first time I saw you."

"Oh, I know."

"You were pretty awful," I admitted.

"I still am."

"You're not so bad. Or maybe I'm just used to you now."

"Perish the thought." He moved to stand. "I'm hungry. Elspeth is making bean crock – it should be about ready."

I stood as well, swiping up my book and stuffing it into the back pocket of my jeans.

"Okay, well, I'll see you later, then I guess."

He turned. "Don't you like bean crock?"

It was as much of an invitation as he'd ever given me. I nodded, smiling like a fool.

"I do, actually."

I walked back the way I came while Caspien rode Falstaff. Falstaff, who he'd left grazing near the stream, bridle looped around a low-hanging willow branch while he'd done what he'd done to me in the hut. He'd told me that by the time he'd brushed him down and fed him, we'd be in the kitchen around the same time.

A warm buzz of pleasure had settled over me as I walked, as I played over what he'd just done to me, the sight of me in his mouth, the look in his eyes. I realised with a jolt that I hadn't even kissed him.

Neither had he gotten off. What would I have done if he'd asked me to return the favour? Would I have gotten to my knees for him? Let him grip my hair and thrust into my mouth? As heat shot up my spine and between my legs, I knew that I would.

But then Ellie's face appeared in my mind, and the warm buzz turned to a chill.

I wasn't hungry anymore.

TWENTY-FIVE

The smell of the pork and bean stew hit me as I reached the back door. Elspeth was humming to herself as she chopped something green and leafy on the large central workspace.

"Jude, sweetheart. Come in, come in. I've made some bean crock, and there's plenty to go around. Is Cas with you?"

"He's in the stables; he'll be here in a minute." I told her I was going to wash up and slipped from the kitchen towards the downstairs cloakroom to wash my hands.

Gideon was coming down the grand staircase as I passed.

"Young master Alcott! How are you this fine day?"

I glanced up, trying to gauge his mood by noting what he was wearing: a three-piece suit. "I'm good, thanks, you?"

"Marvellous, just marvellous. Are you looking for my nephew? I think he went riding this morning, but he should

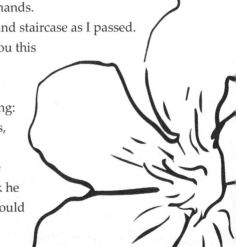

be back any minute now." He came down the stairs and drew a
look over me. "Did you two have fun last night?"

My cheeks grew warm. "Um, yeah, we watched a movie. Hung
out." I shrugged. *Everything you think and feel is in your eyes, you
know.* I skirted my eyes away from his.

Gideon's eyebrows rose. He seemed bubbly, almost and as eager
as a child. "Oh, Cas said you watched the rugby."

"We did, yeah, then a movie. I don't think he was very into it. It
was sort of on in the background."

"While you talked?" he said. "You must have had a lot of catching
up to do. Between you and me," He leaned in. A vaguely sweet,
boozy smell emanated from him, half-hidden beneath his cologne.
"I think he missed you."

"I don't know about that," I said, though I was secretly delighted.

"And I know you missed him too, didn't you?" At this, he tilted
his head and gave me the sort of look you would give a baby.

"I—"

"What are you doing, uncle? Don't you have some port to bathe
in?" Caspien's voice blew in like a chill wind.

We both turned to him.

"Darling nephew. You didn't fall off your horse then?"

"Afraid not," Caspien said. "I am going upstairs to shower and
change. Bring the stew to the library, will you?" he said to me as he
pushed past us and leapt up the stairs two at a time.

We both watched him go.

"Normally, he's in a better mood after his ride," Gideon mused after Caspien had disappeared down the upper-level corridor towards
his bedroom. "Anyway, I have some work to do. You two have fun
now." He patted me good-naturedly on the back and floated off.

I wasn't sure what 'work' Gideon did. There seemed to be a lot
of signatures required on wads of paper being ferried in and out of
Deveraux by courier. Hours spent on the phone with him talking
animatedly in French or Italian. German sometimes, too. I assumed
it had something to do with investments or shares but it was murky
to me. A vague thing that never much interested me.

Elspeth had made up a tray, and I took the two bowls of stew, small bread rolls fresh from the oven which she'd smeared with jersey butter, and two glasses of squash into the library and waited for him to return. My appetite had returned as soon as I'd smelled the bean crock, and I was so ravenous that I picked up a roll and bit into it before Caspien arrived. I managed another five minutes before I picked up my spoon and began shovelling the soupy bean and pork stew into my mouth.

By the time Caspien arrived, showered and redressed in a pair of blue pyjama bottoms and a white long-sleeved T-shirt, I'd finished my bowl.

"It'll be cold," I said, indicating the bowl. "Do you want me to ask her to heat it back up?"

"It's fine," he said, sitting on the sofa next to me. He lifted the bread, tore off a piece and dipped it into the rich gravy. Rather than watch him eat – his mouth doing entirely innocent things forced more perverted notions into my head – I got up and perused the shelves. Before long, I found myself at the rows Gideon had told me belonged to his sister, Caspien's mother. I wasn't surprised to see clothbound copies of things like *Wuthering Heights*, *Anna Karenina*, and *Rebecca*. There were also a string of worn paperbacks with Mills & Boon printed on the spine. *The French Lieutenant's Wife* and *Lady Chatterley's Lover* were by far the most well-read. They were both in multiple parts, yellowed pages flaking off the spine and the covers detached in loose sheafs.

"To think that all I know of her is her collection of tawdry romance novels," he said in a tone I couldn't place.

I gently slid the copy of Lady Chatterley back in and turned to him. "Gideon never talks about her?"

"Oh, incessantly. But I'd never believe anything he says about her." He had finished eating and was lying out on the sofa with his head propped up against one end. "I rarely believe anything he says about anything."

"What happened to her?" I ventured.

His eyes turned to me sharp and cold, and I immediately regretted it.

"Shall we trade?" he said icily. "How did your parents die?"

"Car accident. They were hit from behind by a truck." There was nothing glamourous or mysterious about it. It happened every day all over the world. Seraphina Deveraux's story, from what I'd gathered, was far more exotic. Something more like a story from one of those novels she'd loved so much.

"Did the person who killed them die too?" said Caspien.

I shook my head. "No. He went to prison for three years and got banned from driving for two." He hadn't been drunk or under the influence, just tired and overworked, apparently.

He stared at me. "Fucking tragic. The law in this country is a joke. Manslaughter is what it is, and he used a three-ton weapon to do it. Are you angry?" His own voice sizzled with anger, and I felt a weird sense of gratitude to him for it.

"Not really," I replied. "Not anymore."

I *had* been angry. For a few years after it happened, I was mainly sad, but then, when I turned fourteen, I couldn't remember feeling anything but anger. I'd been old enough then to understand that someone's carelessness had destroyed my entire world.

But one day, I woke up and realised I didn't feel that same anger anymore. I could still find it inside if I looked, packed away under other memories and feelings I'd grown out of. Sometimes, I'd pull it out and shake it off, holding it against me to see if it still fit.

Cas was quiet for a long time. Then, he said, "She killed herself."

There was absolutely no emotion in his voice. It wasn't cold or anything like it, just entirely indifferent. I went toward him and sat on the opposite couch.

"You can wipe that look off your face, too," he snapped. "I don't want your pity, Judith. It's no worse a tragedy than yours. In fact, it's less so."

He avoided my eyes, and I knew why. He *was* angry. I imagined having a parent kill themselves would be a far harder kind of anger to shelve away. To know that not even you, their own child, was enough to keep them tethered to life.

"Do you know why? I mean, was she sick or..."

"Gideon says she was depressed her entire life, that part of it was an affinity with melodrama and morbidity. They were both sad creatures by all accounts. I don't know if it was that their parents – my grandparents – didn't believe in mental illness or if it was that she never asked them for help. Sounds like her father doted on her most of her life." His voice had turned languid with what sounded like longing. "When she got pregnant, it was a scandal apparently as he was some local boy *'without money or good breeding'*. When her parents found out they locked her up here, then forced her to birth me."

I sat forward, horrified. "Gideon told you this?"

"This, I found out from her diary," he said. "I'd never have be-lieved it had he said it. I needed to read it with my own eyes. But yes, she rather hated me by the sounds of it; from the moment she was aware of my existence, she loathed me." He looked straight at me. "She jumped from the cliffs at Sorel Point. "

I was slack-jawed, unable to comprehend having to live knowing your mother hated you, and had killed herself. No wonder he hated the world.

I hadn't a clue what I was supposed to say, so I sat silent and still for a long time. I wanted to refute it, tell him it couldn't possibly be true. That there must be some other interpretation to be taken from a depressed woman's diary that wasn't this. Though there seemed to be no words I could summon that could go anywhere close to trying to comfort him, and though I'm certain he didn't want it, I still tried.

"She was ill. I'm sure that's not how she felt at all, not really."

His eyes turned hard and cold as a frozen planet. "And you know the inner workings of my dead mother's mind; how exactly?"

I looked away from him to my hands, then back up at him. "What about your father? Did she talk about him?"

"Daddy dearest. Ah yes, she talked about him at length. She loved him with as much ferocity as she hated me. I think she blamed me for his leaving her. Gideon says he doesn't know who he is, but naturally, I think he's lying. He's always had a rather aberrant relationship with the truth."

I remembered something then. The afternoon I'd come here after Caspien had blackmailed me to sit for him. Gideon had been acting strangely. *Christ, every day you look more and more like him,* he'd said, looking at Caspien. Had he meant Caspien's father? A shiver trilled down my spine. He *was* lying.

Carefully, I said, "Would you want to know? If Gideon *was* lying and he did know? Would you want him to tell you?"

His gaze turned sharp, and I wondered if he suspected something. Though I didn't know how he would. "No," he said after a moment. "What would I do with that? What do I need with a father at this age? As a child with those kinds of inclinations, yes, perhaps it would have been novel, but now I have no need of him."

And so, I said nothing about what Gideon had said that day. I shelved the words from that day like I had the anger over my parents' deaths. If Caspien had no need of them, then neither did I.

Over the years, those words were forgotten, dust-covered and unused in the cellar of my memory. Until one day, over a decade later, when the truth of them would tumble out. Gargantuan and shocking as a dead whale beached on the shore.

Monday came with a weighty dread that filled my entire body. A heavy, solid thing that clung to my bones and threatened to pull me under. There was no good time to break up with Ellie, but the week after her grandfather's funeral seemed particularly cruel. But then, so did what I was doing with Caspien behind her back.

I'd tossed and turned the entire night and managed to scrape three broken hours of sleep at most. On Sunday, I'd ignored her calls and lied about being at the cinema. I'd answered her texts with weird platonic words that I'd been sending to Caspien six months ago. Caspien, who I was instead sending texts that made me hot, fumbling, and aroused.

The entire world seemed to me then to be upside down.

There wasn't much time to talk until lunch, but I got the sense that she could sense something was wrong between us.

"So, how did it all go?" I asked her the moment we sat down, alone away from the others. I'd given Alfie a look that he'd understood, and he'd moved off to sit with Georgia and Josh at a table a few rows down the dining hall.

"I mean fine, but it was just all so...sad." I was sure she was about to cry again. "I went in to see him after, although Mum said I should only do that if I was sure because I'd never get the image out of my head. That it might be how I end up remembering him, and Christ, Jude, I just wish I hadn't done it." She shook her head as if clearing the image. "God, I'm sorry. I feel so selfish talking like this when he was like my grandparent who I saw twice a year, and you've lost like both your mum and your dad."

I frowned at her, confused by this. "What's that got to do with anything? You lost someone you loved. You're allowed to be upset about it, El."

She gave me a watery smile and nodded. "I missed you so much. Do you want to come over tonight? My parents are out."

I stuffed a forkful of chips in my mouth and said around them, "Yeah. Okay."

The weight lifted a little. I had a few hours reprieve.

Caspien called me the moment I got home.

"Gideon has gone to London for a few days. Do you want to come over?"

"Tonight?" I asked, stalling.

"No, next Tuesday. Of course, tonight."

"I can't," I hesitated. "I'm going over to Ellie's."

There was a pause. "Wow, you're really going for shagger of the year, aren't you?"

My cheeks caught flame. "*What? We* haven't shagged?"

"Hmmmm. As good as. At least, I'm sure that's what Ellie would think if I told her."

"Not this again." I sighed. "You're not going to tell her."

"No, I'm not. I wouldn't have told her before either, you know. I'm not that awful of a person."

"That's still under debate," I said and he snorted.

"You like me now, let's not lie. You especially like when I take you down my throat and choke on your dick."

I groaned, rolling back onto the bed and grabbing said dick. I thought he might continue with this, but he didn't. I opened my eyes and let out a deep breath.

"Look, if you must know, I'm going to break up with her tonight." The words hung there in the air like an unwelcome stench.

"Why?" he asked.

"Why do you think?"

"How on earth should I know the interior design of your mind palace, Jude? It's why I asked."

I didn't know what to say. What I should or shouldn't tell him, what he would and wouldn't want to hear. So I told him exactly what I told Luke.

"She cares about me too much. More than I care about her. I don't think that's how relationships should work."

"Actually I'd say that's how most relationships work," he replied. "One person always cares far more than the other. I don't think you're doing anything wrong in acknowledging it."

"And what about what we did on my couch, or in the birdwatcher hut, or the library? Is that wrong?"

"You know I don't think it is." His voice was sharp suddenly.

"I meant while I'm with Ellie," I said. "That feels wrong. Especially when she's telling me she loves me, and I feel guilty when I say it back."

"Why do you feel guilty?"

"Because it's a lie."

A brief pause. "Christ, Jude. Do you think you have any idea what love is at your age?"

He was using the voice he used when he'd tell me how Russian Literature was greater than both English Literature and the 'toilet paper' that was American Literature. Imperious with a lacing of condescension. It was how I always heard him in my head, when I thought of our conversations in hindsight, when hours later I'd think of something smart to say to something he'd said or asked. It was as though we weren't merely months apart in age and more like he were some wizened old sage with a wealth of experience beneath his cloak and beard.

"I think," I said. "I think I know what it isn't."

Another pause. Then:

"I'm honestly not sure you do."

TWENTY-SIX

I wasn't going to be persuaded. Regardless of Caspien's less-than-helpful advice and attempts at convincing me not to do this, I'd already decided. I had to do this. It had already gone on too long, far too long.

I should have broken up with her after the day in his mother's bedroom. I'd known then that my feelings for him were entirely different, more potent, than my feelings for Ellie had ever been. I'd known in a scattering of moments on that floor that I'd never feel anything for Ellie that came close to what I'd felt for Caspien.

What I felt for him now.

He'd peeled back a few layers and shown me what lay underneath, and I wanted him more than I ever had before. It was those incremental steps toward each other that occupied my mind as Luke drove me to Ellie's after dinner.

"I'm going to break up with her," I told him as he pulled up outside her house in St. Brelade. The lights of every room were on inside, the blue light of the TV bouncing off the walls in her brother's room upstairs. A ribbon of nerves danced around my stomach. "Do you think...I mean, I don't think she'll want me hanging around for long. After."

"Oh, buddy." He made a sad clucking noise. "Yeah, sure. I need some petrol anyway. And I suppose I could use the jet to wash the car. Give me a call when you're done, okay? I'll come right back."

I nodded, grim.

He put his hand on my shoulder. "It'll be okay, Judey. You're doing the right thing."

"I know. I just feel shitty about it."

"I'll bet. But Ellie's a strong girl. I mean, you're pretty great and all, but she will get over you. Eventually." He smiled at this last part.

I rolled my eyes. "I'll call you in a bit."

I had to ring the doorbell twice before she answered. My chest ached as she pulled it open with a bright smile and an expression that bordered on adoring. She was wearing short shorts and an oversized sweatshirt with '1989' on the front. Her dark hair was bunched up in a high knot, cheeks flushed, and legs lithe and long.

She threw herself at me, wrapping her arms around me in a tight hug. The kiss she placed on my lips was gentle and tasted of peach and vanilla.

"You should have just come in." She smiled and grabbed my hand to try and pull me into the house. I watched her face fall when I didn't move.

"Just...I thought we could go for a walk."

"A walk?"

"Yeah, down to the beach maybe?" I looked up at the sky. The night was clear and pleasant. Mild enough that she wouldn't have to change.

She eyed me suspiciously. "Um, sure...okay. Come in while I put my shoes on."

"It's cool, I'll wait here."

Her expression faltered a little more, but she nodded and went back inside, leaving the door open while she went. I looked at the inside of her house, which had always felt warm and welcoming to me, knowing that it was the last time I'd ever get to see it.

It was as awful as I'd expected it would be. I'd been stumbling and vague and unable to give any reasonable explanation. She'd accused me of cheating on her while she was in Norwich at her grandfather's funeral – which I'd denied – or liking someone else at school – which I'd also denied, but more comfortably – and stormed off angry and confused, calling me names I more than deserved, but it was done.

Luke picked me up at the pier, a sympathetic glance at me as I got in the car that I was sure I didn't deserve. He never asked me how it went or how she took it; he just drove us home. Silent and supportive from the driver's seat.

When we reached the estate, I asked him to drop me at the big house. He'd given me a look but nodded and kept driving.

"I'll be home shortly," I told him before getting out of the car.

The moment I stepped inside, I heard the piano, and I rushed to the music room. I remembered the last time Gideon had left him alone, when I'd found him strange, wild, and fragile at the piano, and panic fluttered behind my ribs.

He sat upright and elegant at the piano, fingers moving artfully over the keys. The song this time was mournful and slow, meandering through low notes and high. I recall thinking that it sounded like heartbreak.

My emotions were not as easy to define then. I knew them only as loud, chaotic things which burned a path straight through me without clarity or warning.

But I know now that what I felt for him that night was empathy. Acutely and painfully, I felt all of Caspien's losses as if they were my own. I hadn't expected to feel more pity for him than I'd ever managed to find for myself. (We'd both been foisted upon family members who had never expected to have to make space for us in their lives.) But while I had Luke, solid warm grounding Luke, Caspien had Gideon. Gideon, who was a walking puzzle of a man, and who seemed as unknowable to me as the moon. Their relationship was jagged, openly hostile, and with the barest glimmers of warmth now and then. I'd been lucky.

I'd never thought of myself as lucky before. No one who loses their parents at a young age knows what luck feels like. But I understood something then, and it was that, for the years I'd had them, my parents had loved me. Intensely and unconditionally. Cas had never had unconditional love. I suspected Gideon incapable of it. Xavier Blackwell's intentions, too, were not borne of love; I was certain of it. They'd come instead from a place of deviance and twisted desire.

So in that moment, Caspien was transformed. Or rather, how I perceived him changed so permanently that I saw him only for what I *wanted* him to be. Vulnerable and lost and in need of something only I could give him.

Love. Unconditional.

Only *I* could love Caspien how he deserved to be loved. And so I would.

I'd love him in spite of everything he was and everything I knew he could be. No matter what he did, no matter how much he hurt me, in this I would be constant.

As long as Caspien Deveraux breathed, I would love him.

I've often wondered if I hadn't made that prideful promise to the universe when I was still a child, if things would be different now. Would *I* be different now? Would my life have followed a different path? Would I have been able to love someone else?

He turned, his playing coming to a discordant end.

"It's over then?" he asked, standing up. "Is that why you look so miserable?"

I strode across the room, purposeful with my promise, and took his face in my hands and kissed him. I fell upon him with the same force I always did, as though he were moonlight and I the shore being pulled into him. The keys clanked as he fell back against them, as I brought him to me to taste his jaw, his throat, and the nodes of his collarbone.

I dropped to my knees, nudging the piano stool out of the way with my body, and then I pulled down those loose pyjama bottoms he always wore and drew him into my mouth. He was soft and warm, and the scent of his skin was crisp as a winter's night. He gasped, in pleasure or surprise – I wasn't sure – but his hands were suddenly in my hair, gripping tight, urgent.

I moved on instinct, clumsy and awkward in my attempt to make him hard. Every second that went by, I expected him to throw me off, but his hands only gripped me tighter. Revelling in his need, I looked up at him and sucked him deeper, deeper so that I could feel the sensation of him growing hard into my throat. Then his mouth fell open, pleasure whispering from between his lips. My tongue curled around him, and as I pulled back to draw breath – it hadn't occurred to me to use my nose for this – out came a long string of saliva. I sucked in a breath and let him guide me back over him, enclosing him, harder now, between my lips.

He watched me work, focused as a watchmaker, shapely mouth parted in what I wanted to be awe.

I was hard, desperately so, but I ignored it. It didn't exist. All that existed was Caspien; his cock and my mouth and the weight and warmth of his body against mine.

"Jude," he said in an urgent voice. I pulled off, choking around the thick pool of saliva flooding my mouth. He gripped himself, stroked once, then again and came with a breathy little moan over my face. I realised with a shock that my mouth was still open. The taste of him landed on my tongue and lips, and I gulped at it hungrily. "Now you," he said, a little breathless. "I want to see you come."

I obeyed. Still on my knees and painted with him, I stroked myself fast and rough while he watched. I came with a crashing intensity that made my ears ring and my heart feel like it would burst out of my chest.

When I fell forward, it was into him, and I folded an arm around his waist and buried my head in his abdomen.

When his hand settled on my head again, fingers sifting almost tenderly through my hair, I had the strangest urge to cry. From pleasure and fear and the overwhelming sensation that I was nothing unless I was allowed to be this to him. Have this with him. I could not imagine a life outside of this. It would be as void and empty as death itself.

The words sat on my tongue for hours after, the immense and terrible truth of them: *I love you. I don't want to remember a time when I didn't. I love you. And as long as I am able to draw breath, then I will love you with every single one. I love you.*

I walked home that night feeling dazed and slow, a weight in my chest so dense and unwieldy that I could barely get my legs to move. I stopped multiple times to stare up at the moon, feeling the weight of it too, waxen and gargantuan, pressing down upon me. Symbolic to me, I thought, of my feelings for Caspien. Far too powerful for me to comprehend.

TWENTY-SEVEN

Caspien still had another week at home before flying back to La Troyeux for his final term, so it felt like a cruel and unusual punishment to have to keep going to school knowing he was home at Deveraux.

I wanted to be with him more than I wanted to skip school. Though, I'd also never wanted to skip school more in my life. I was again dreading it. Ellie hadn't mentioned it on her socials, but Georgia had posted some vague inspirational quote on her page late the night before that I assumed was aimed at me: *Hurting someone is as easy as throwing a stone in the ocean; but you will never know how deep that stone will go.*

I didn't get it.

Alfie had texted me around the same time:

Wat the fuck, bro?

I'd ignored it.

I'd begun to feel the coming apart of the relationships that had defined my high school life up until this point. In a year, I would be in another city surrounded by strangers and possibilities, and it was this that I clung to as I walked into registration.

Ellie seemed to have been watching the door avidly, though looked away quickly when I entered. I sat down next to Alfie and made a determined attempt to ignore the glare he aimed at the side of my head. He couldn't exactly say anything with the girls at our backs, but as soon as we were out and heading to History, he all but dragged me into the toilet. He threw a loaded look over his shoulder at Georgia, who was dragging Ellie off in the opposite direction toward the arts building.

"What the fuck, Jude?" he said, eyes wide. "You broke up with Ellie??! Before the prom?"

I went to the drinking tap in the corner and bent my head. "The prom was the last thing on my mind at the time, Alfred."

"Then what was on your mind? I don't get it? Why'd you do it?"

"Because I didn't want to go out with her anymore. Why else?"

This seemed to completely blow his mind because his eyes became even wider, blonde eyebrows hitting his hairline. "That doesn't even make sense, mate."

"Doesn't it?" I said. "Why do you care so much, Alf? Focus on your own girlfriend, yeah?"

He stalked toward me. "Yeah, well, my own girlfriend is acting like it's my fucking fault or something."

"Well, that's just stupid. Why would it have anything to do with you?"

"That's what I said. I think she thinks you're seeing someone else or something and that I knew about it or whatever."

"Well, tell her it's not true."

"Eh, I did!"

"Then, I don't know what to tell you. Or what you want me to do about it?"

He blinked at me. "What is even going on with you, mate?"

"Nothing. There's nothing going on with me. Leave it alone. " I pushed past him and out into the hall. He came after me, of course. Unable to let it go. Unable to understand that it wasn't any of his business.

"Look, I know this year has been a bit crazy," Alfie was saying, walking with me down the corridor. "Moving to Devs and working with Luke and then Beth's baby and mocks and prepping for A's, but like, Els and you were great."

I wanted to stop and hit him, and I probably would have if I thought it would make him shut up. But I knew it wouldn't. He'd still be shortening words and rabbiting on and acting like he knew everything about everything when in fact the entire wealth of Alfie's knowledge extended to Rugby Sevens, his PlayStation 5, and the John Wick films. Some perverted part of me wondered what he'd do were I to turn around, and say very slowly and clearly, that I'd broken up with Ellie Walsh, the hottest girl at school, because I preferred having Caspien Deveraux's cock shoved down my throat to kissing her. This, I knew, would have shut him up.

I slowed my steps and turned to him. "Look, Alfie, we're both going to Uni next year. Me to Warwick and her to fucking Scotland and everyone knows long-distance relationships don't work. I'm doing us both a favour. She's hot and smart, and she'll thank me that she's single when she gets to Edinburgh. Even if she does hate me now."

I let the words sink in, saw his expression turn, and then I added. "If you want me to talk to George for you – explain that this has nothing to do with you – then I will. Though I doubt she'd believe me. I'm sure she hates me as much as Ellie right now."

Alfie smiled suddenly. "More mate. I think she hates you way more."

Lunch was awkward. I sat with Josh and a few of his rugby friends a few tables away from Georgia, Alfie and Ellie. My sandwich tasted like wet cardboard, and behind me, I could feel Ellie's hateful glare boring into my head.

I wanted to be home already. I wanted to see him. Kiss him. Hear his voice. It was worse knowing he was at Deveraux and not in another country, knowing that I could be with him now if I wasn't here listening to chat about which girls the rugby lads wanted to take to the prom. He'd be going back to Switzerland in six days, and I resented everything that kept me from him.

I thought about skipping fifth and taking an Uber to the house, but I couldn't be confident I wouldn't see Luke on the way in. He worked on the grounds three days a week now, today being one. And there was no way I would be able to explain my presence there at this time of the day.

As I was leaving sixth, there was a text from him.

Caspien:

> I've no idea what I used to do all day around here before you came along to entertain me.

Me:

> read pretentious Russian literature and ride your horse.

Caspien:

> I've already done both of those today.

Me:

> well, I've studying to do. Not all of us had our place at Oxford confirmed when we were 5.

This wasn't a lie. I *did* have studying to do, but we had agreed to do it together in the library later. But I wanted him to ask if I was still coming. I wanted to know that he wanted to see me. It was an urge I never grew out of; I would always leave plans we made open-ended, would always ask him things in a way I thought would induce him to tell me what I wanted to hear. It rarely worked.

Caspien:

You know as well as I do that if you want to get into Oxford, then you need my help to do it.

Me:

You're offering to help me?

Caspien:

I might be. I'll want something in return though...

I smiled.

Me:

Maybe I don't need your help.

Caspien:

We both know that's a lie.

Me:

What is it you want?

I was stopped in the middle of the common outside the front of school, completely absorbed in the small flickering dots on the screen.

Caspien:

> I think you know what I want, Jude.

I felt my dick harden in response to that.

Me:

> Gideon home yet?

Caspien:

> He's due back tonight. About 10.

Me:

> I'm just leaving school now. I'll be there in an hour

This time, when I asked Luke to drop me straight at Deveraux, he opened his mouth to say something, and closed it, his eyes skipping very briefly from the road to me.

Finally, he said, "You and Cas are getting on pretty well these days, huh?"

There was a small flurry of panic in my chest, a manic beating of tiny wings. Luke's face was easy, relaxed; nothing unkind or suspicious in it. Merely curiosity.

"Yeah," I said. "He's alright, I suppose."

Luke smiled, that same warm upturn of his mouth he always gave me when I did something that impressed him.

The door to the library had barely closed before Caspien had me pushed back against one of the wooden shelves and was kissing me hard. I dropped my bag on the floor and dug my hands into his hair. He scraped his teeth over my lip, bit and gnawed at my jaw and sucked what I felt would be a bruise into my neck.

"Did you miss me?" I asked.

"I told you," he said against my skin. "I was bored."

"You must have been really bored," I panted.

"Extremely," he said, kissing a path across my throat. He slid his hand over me, making an appreciative noise when he felt how hard I was. "Is this for me?"

"Of course it is." The noise was building in my head, building to that place where it would turn white and loud. Pleasure sparked out everywhere, a million little firestorms all over my body.

"Did you think about this today?" he asked between sweet kisses.

"All day," I managed.

He went to his knees, and I could do nothing but endure the inferno as it consumed me.

As distracting as he was, he was also an exceptional study partner. He posed interesting questions, reviewed texts from viewpoints I'd never have considered, and made fascinating arguments. He had a way of looking at the world that always brought everything into sharp, lucid focus. I was mesmerised. Spellbound. And by the end of that week, I had never been more in love with him.

I'd catch myself gaping in wonder at something he'd say or how quickly he'd be able to define the meaning of some overly wordy passage or poem and have to force my features into something more subdued. Less enthralled. His brain fascinated me. As much as every other part of him fascinated me.

He was then the smartest person I'd ever met. I thought of the boys I sat with at lunch talking about girls, sports, and video games, and I couldn't understand how he could possibly be the same age.

Each day that week, Luke dropped me off at the big house after school, where Caspien and I would use our mouths and hands on each other first before committing solidly to studying.

It worked.

I'd never been more focused on revision, felt more prepared for an exam, or enjoyed schoolwork as much as I did that perfect week in April.

As we drew closer to the end of the week and his leaving me, a buzzing began under my skin and between my bones. A yawning pull that only made me more desperate for him, so I grew rougher with him.

On the Saturday before he left, I noticed two round symmetrical bruises on his hip bones where I'd dug my thumbs in too hard as I'd taken him in my mouth. The day before, I'd bitten his lip so forceful-ly it had bled onto my tongue.

He didn't seem to mind these little stamps of desire, but they scared me. The ferociousness with which I needed him and with which I couldn't bear to part with him, terrified me. I barely slept the night before he left for Switzerland.

The car was picking him up at eleven on Saturday morning, and he'd agreed to meet me at the birdwatcher hut at eight. I'd gotten up early and pulled on shorts and a T-shirt, telling Luke and Beth I was going for a run. And I had run. All the way across the estate to the hut, so I was dripping with sweat by the time I got there.

This time, he was waiting for me, perched on the bench with his knee propped up as he scrolled his phone. He took one look at me – I held my breath, certain he'd refuse to touch me given the sweating, dripping state I was in – but a feral sort of look came into his eye, and he lunged at me.

"Christ, Jude. You taste so good," he told me as he licked and sucked at the sweat at my throat and inhaled the damp hair curling at my neck.

We tumbled to the ground and tore each other free of our trousers, our impatient and hungry mouths devouring. I was on my back, and he was on top, and he wrapped his hand around us both and began to stroke.

I saw stars. Bright blinding lights of rapture sparking behind my eyes.

"Cas...fuck, that feels..."

"I know. I know." He was moving his body on me like he did when he rode his horse, a powerful tightening of his thighs, the fluid movement of his arse up and down. "I love how hard you get for me, Jude. This big dick is always so fucking hard for me."

"Shit..."

Caspien didn't swear often, not as much as Josh or Alfie or other boys at school, or other girls at school, even, but when he did it was always in moments like this, when he was turned on and loose, his restraint unravelling. I loved when he spoke to me like this while he touched me; the scent, sound, and feel of him overwhelming every one of my senses.

He leaned forward and dropped a large, hot, mouthful of spit on our cocks.

"Have you ever gotten hard for another boy, Jude?"

I shook my head fervently.

"You know I haven't."

He smirked, looking pleased. "This beautiful dick only gets hard for girls and me. How peculiar."

I wasn't sure the former was even true at this stage. I didn't even want to find out.

"*Caspien.*" It was a warning.

He still had us gripped in one hand, stroking lazily, but with the other hand he was digging the edge of his thumb into the slit, something that always drove me insane. Poking back and forth and around, almost like he was trying to widen the hole there. The sensation had been odd at first, but I'd grown to crave it. I even played with it when I was alone now, trying to understand the magic of it.

"When I come home again, I think I'll let you put this beautiful thing inside me. Would you like that?"

Need pulsed out of the hole he was playing with.

"Fuck," I said and thumped my head back against the mucky ground.

"Would you?"

"Yes. Fuck, Cas, yes. Fuck."

"Would you fuck me hard and rough or slow and soft, do you think?" He spat onto our dicks again and began to move his hands faster, both together. "Tell me."

"*Hard.*" I glared at him, that violent desperation taking over me again. I dug my hands into his thighs and moved my body in time with his, imitating the act I so badly wanted to do. "I'd fuck you so hard, Cas. So fucking hard you wouldn't be able to sit on that horse for a week."

He came, erupted, in a glorious white fountain all over me. His body arched as though he'd been shot through with an arrow from behind, all the grace and beauty of a dying Greek hero.

I came an instant later, pleasure moving through me quick and bright as my orgasm pulsed out over our hands and softening cocks.

When it was all over, I wanted to pull him to me, hug him tight and profess everything I felt inside, but I knew it would only ruin the moment. He shot me a sly, seductive smile and stood up. The weight of him lifting off my body felt like the dip of a rollercoaster.

He pulled two handkerchiefs out of the pocket of his riding pants and threw one at me. C.L.D was stitched prettily in navy into the cream cotton.

"What does the L stand for?" I asked as he began wiping himself down.

He shot me a look. "Lucifer."

I rolled my eyes and stood to wipe myself clean of our expulsions.

When he was finished and had tucked his used handkerchief back into his pocket, he said, "I don't know."

"What do you mean?"

"I mean, I don't know what the L stands for." He smoothed his hair back and avoided my eyes. "My father's name began with an L. Or at least, that's how she referred to him in her journal. The mystery was her parting gift to me."

"So she did care about you then," I said a little too energetically. "If she loved him and named you after him, then she must have cared about you."

He gave me that look he sometimes did, the one which suggested he thought I was the stupidest person he'd ever met. But then I saw it, the tiniest glimmer, a dance of light behind his eyes. Innocent hope. It was snuffed out in an instant.

"Christ, I would like to live in your world for a day, Jude," he sneered. "Is it summer all the time? Are the rivers flowing with chocolate? Unicorns prancing around?"

My cheeks flamed. "I was only pointing out th—"

"Don't," he snapped.

I didn't want him to go on this note, not after this week and just now and because of everything that I felt and wanted from him now. I moved toward him.

"Okay," I said placatingly. "Okay, I'm sorry. I won't bring it up again." I bent my head to kiss him. His lips were cold, mouth unmoving. "Please. I'm sorry."

His mouth opened like a flower, the inside warm and sweet, and he let me kiss him.

"I have to go," he said when I pulled back. "I've not finished packing."

He moved to go and I looped my hand around his wrist. "You'll call me tonight? When you get there?"

"Yes, Jude."

Letting go of him physically hurt.

"Cas," I said as he pulled open the door.

He paused.

"I'll see you in six weeks, okay?" I said.

Six weeks felt like a lifetime to me then. Impossible and vast.

"Yes. Good luck with the rest of term."

"Thanks, I'll need it." I'd meant that getting through the rest of it without him here would be so brutal that I could barely let myself think about it. But if he guessed that's what I meant, he didn't react in any way.

I drank in every inch of his face – the perfect, elegant structure of it, the slope of his nose, the graceful way he seemed to breathe – as though it might be the last time I ever saw him.

In many ways, I wish it had been.

TWENTY-EIGHT

Despite his strange behaviour the day he left, he called me when he returned to school just as he'd promised. He looked tired, a little deflated at being back there, I supposed – but it was nothing that worried me. He was how he always was on the phone; moody, sharp-tongued and occasionally flirtatious, and soon we were back to our usual arrangement.

Except that this time, I knew what it was to have him. To hold him and kiss him and touch him. This time, when we did those things on our calls, the absence of him was far harder to bear.

I longed daily for summer; summer meant he'd be home, and the planning of the rest of our lives could begin. I still studied in the library at Deveraux, and occasionally Gideon would pop his head in the door asking if I'd heard from Caspien, if I was hungry, or if he could disturb me a moment while he

grabbed a book. I never saw Xavier Blackwell at the house again. In fact, I hadn't thought about him in weeks. I'd never mentioned it to Caspien in the end, I never wanted his name uttered between us ever again if I could help it.

And so it was with a cold startle of shock that Gideon was the one to bring him up to me one Saturday afternoon about a fortnight after Cas had returned to La Troyeux.

He'd come breezing in wearing a light-coloured suit – I'd rarely seen Gideon in anything but a suit. Normally a three-piece, the rich fabric tailored so well to his body as though he were dressed for his wedding. That day, he wore only the waistcoat and the trousers, almost white, with a cornflower blue linen shirt that was open at the neck. The only change between his summer and winter wardrobes was the absence of a tie. He looked well. Handsome and well rested, but nothing about him that suggested he was in one of his merrier (intoxicated) moods.

"Jude, how are you this fine day? How is the revising coming along?" he asked with a dramatic sigh. "Gosh, I loathed revising. Truly."

He had a stack of books in his arms, which wobbled precariously. I jumped up and rushed over to help him.

"Oh, fabulous, perfect, the right man for the job, I see."

I helped him stack them. He seemed to know exactly where each of them went. Pointing me to the right shelf and slot so that they were back in the correct indexed fashion.

When we were finished, he asked me to join him in the blue sitting room, where Elspeth had laid out some tea and scones. He was in the mood for company, he said, and it was important to take a break from revision.

I joined him, sitting down on the uncomfortable sofa across from where he sat and watching him pour our tea from an ornate brass teapot.

"I shall be in London this weekend with Xavier, whom you met a few weeks ago."

I tried to keep my face as neutral as possible, my voice steady.

"Your lawyer?" I asked.

"Yes, though truthfully, we are much closer to friends." His smile turned almost simpering before he blinked it away. "Anyway, you are completely welcome to come to the house while I'm gone. Luke has a key."

"Right," I nodded.

Gideon's gaze settled on me, studious. "So, you must be missing Cas terribly by now."

I choked slightly on my mouthful of scone, reaching forward to lift my tea to wash it down. The tea was too hot, and it burned my mouth before eventually going down. Gideon was still watching me, that familiar smile in his eye now. A private joke only he knew the punchline of.

"You haven't told a soul, have you? That you like boys as well as girls."

My entire body went white hot, then very cold suddenly. I felt it at the base of my skull, a peeling away of a layer to expose the raw pink heart of me.

I opened my mouth to speak, closed it again. Then shook my head.

"My father was exceedingly old-fashioned," Gideon said, lifting his teacup. His wrist was slim and elegant, and the gold of his cufflink glittered in the sunlight. "He didn't believe it was possible for a man to love another man the way men are *supposed* to love women. But neither did he think it a sin to have relations with them; boys' schools are quite the hive of homosexual experimentation, you see, and he had no issue with the principle of the thing. I'm certain he experimented just as I did, just as most of us do; he just didn't want me getting ideas of making a life with a man. After all, who would carry on the Deveraux name? The line?"

I couldn't move, I sat with my mouth open slightly eager to hear the story he was telling.

"Seraphina would marry, and since her child would have their father's name, it was impressed upon me that I alone was responsible for the lineage. But, as it turned out..." Here Gideon shot me a conspiratorial kind of look. "It was very much possible for a man to love another man. And I did, quite completely. I loved one so fiercely that I was prepared to give up my title and my fortune for him. For what are either of those things against the magnificence of love? Against the scent of another's skin in your lungs, or the sound of their pleasure in your ear; that great fire of lust in their eyes when they look at you. It's like nothing else on earth – money and title do not even come close. But you, Jude, you are lucky, for you have neither. You have nothing to lose but your heart, and I think you have already given it away, haven't you?"

I saw little point in feeling insulted by that; he was right. I had neither money nor title. He was right too that I had already given my heart away; I saw no point in lying about that to Gideon of all people.

"What happened?" I asked instead of confirming it. "With the man you loved?"

Gideon went stiff as a cat, as though he hadn't expected me to ask. "He loved my money and my title more than he loved me. Without it, I wasn't such an attractive prospect."

"It sounds like you had a lucky escape."

He stared openly at me for many moments. "Caspien is lucky," he said. "Because I don't think you care a jot about his fortune, do you?"

I shook my head.

"But I also think you care terribly about your own." I frowned, not understanding what he meant by this since I didn't have one. "You want to make something of yourself, leave this island and live a life somewhere else. Go out into the world and prove that you can do something more than what Luke does."

Heat rushed to my cheeks, my stomach turning inside out from shame.

"I see how you look at him, the shame and embarrassment that crosses your face when you think no one's looking."

The shock and shame burned their way through my chest. I shook my head. "That's not..." Tears welled up behind my eyes. "I love Luke; he's like a big brother and a dad to me – I love him."

And I did. More than Beth, more than anyone. But this treacherous, treasonous thing was something I kept hidden in the darkest part of myself. How, for example, I wished for once he'd dress properly at parents' evening, like Alfie's and Josh's dad. No turning up in shorts and a worn Green's Gardening Group T-shirt, or how I wished that he'd make sure to clean the dirt out from under his fingernails when we went out for dinner, or how I wished he'd talk about something other than plants or soil quality to Cas when he saw him.

Gideon moved around the small coffee table and put his arm around me, fatherly and comforting.

"Oh, goodness, sweet Jude, no one is suggesting you don't love him. Of course you do. Luke is a wonderful father figure to you and a very good man – there aren't many of those around, trust me, I know. It's clear how much you love him."

I'd managed to keep the tears in, but the humiliation and guilt made my mouth loose.

"He's talked about me going to work for him, about how the business was his dad's and how he wants to keep it in the family and how I'm his son, but I..." I shook my head. "It's not what I want. It's not the life I want."

The life I wanted was something I couldn't begin to make Luke (or Beth) understand. I wished I could explain to them how I wanted to be a writer, live in London, and spend my weekends tangled up in bed with Caspien before dragging ourselves out of it to visit bookshops and see movies. They didn't even know I wrote. I'd never told anyone except Caspien because somehow it didn't feel as silly to say it to him; it even felt like something he might be impressed by. And he had been, I thought. He'd given me a look he'd never given me before: a slight speculative raise of his eyebrows and a glint of approval in his eye.

I didn't think Luke and Beth would judge me for wanting to be with a man or stop loving me because of it, but it did seem like the life I wanted was worlds away from the life they wanted me to have. Which was, ostensibly, here on the island helping Luke for the rest of my life like I owed it to them for taking me in.

And who knows, maybe I did. Maybe I was being selfish for wanting something else.

Something I considered then to be better.

"No, no, a smart boy like you wants something more than this island can offer," Gideon soothed. Then he said, in an almost whisper, "You want to become something you think will make him see you as his equal."

I almost gasped at the bare, stunning truth of it. I pulled back to look at him, stricken and open-mouthed.

The denial didn't come.

"It's nothing to be ashamed of, Jude. Love cultivates within us the most farcical of notions. It's a dangerous thing, really. And gosh, you are quite desperately in love with him, aren't you?" He gave me a commiserative look.

I could only stare at him pleadingly. I often think about how I must have looked to him in that moment; vulnerable and defenceless as a kitten in a box. The look, whatever it was, was all the confirmation he needed.

"Oh, Jude. You poor thing. You poor, poor thing."

I couldn't understand at the time why his apology sounded so strange and discordant, like an out-of-tune piano. But now I know it was because he was pleased. My misery – the misery he knew would come inevitably – pleased him.

"He's going to break your heart, you know. And still, you'll love him. He'll break it over and over again and you'll continue to love him."

"You think he'll...break my heart?" I asked as though I didn't fear that very same thing with every single breath I took.

"Oh, he won't mean to, not entirely, but he doesn't quite have it in him to love the way you do, the way I used to be able to. In a way, I've done quite well with him. I've made him far smarter than either of us."

"I don't care," I said naively. I don't care if he can't love me the same way I love him. I'm still going to." Unconditionally, for as long as I could breathe.

Gideon's eyes glittered. "Yes, I think you will, won't you?"

He pulled me into a tight hug that smelled of violets and fresh moss.

TWENTY-NINE

I didn't dare tell Caspien about the talk with Gideon. Even at that point, their relationship and the boundaries of it, were far beyond my understanding, and I was terrified about what he might say or do if he knew I'd been discussing him with Gideon at all.

Over the years that followed, my feelings about Gideon have metamorphosed. Though I knew that Caspien thought him a liar and that their relationship was fractious and twisted, he had never been anything more than kind and generous with me. He was eccentric and odd in ways I could never put my finger on, but he'd never been cruel to me – not overtly, at least. Then, he felt like the only person in the world who knew and understood me fully.

He knew the deep parts of me I'd never shown anyone else. Parts of me that I'd never even admitted existed to myself. In those weeks leading up to summer, I saw him as a confidant and confessed my sins to him like he was my priest.

At first, I'd been worried that Gideon might tell Caspien about our long talks about the nature of love, about Caspien, and about the future I saw for us far from this tiny island. But now I know that he wouldn't have dared. Because for everything he was, Caspien did not always play the game by Gideon's rules, and Gideon could not win a game unless he were in complete control of it.

I came to understand that they trusted each other as far as two snakes in a basket might.

Caspien was due home the last week of May, and I'd already decided I would tell him I loved him. I suspected he was already aware of it – I look back now and think that almost everyone around me was aware of it. I wore my heart on the outside of my body, bright as a beacon. It was no wonder it was pierced right through.

My love for Cas was too big to contain then, and I didn't want to contain it any longer; I wouldn't. I'd tell him. I'd show him. I didn't need him to say it back, but I did need him to know that I was here, that I always would be, and that I'd love him unconditionally no matter what.

I wasn't stupid enough to think that he loved me back, and that wasn't only because Gideon thought he was incapable. It was because I hadn't yet shown him that love was something achievable, something that *could* exist between us. I knew he'd likely meet other more interesting people at Oxford next year, but those sorts of people he'd known and been around all his life, and he'd never loved any of them.

I was unique in this alone. I was happy to be the orphaned boy from his hometown because it was what connected us. This house connected us: the library, the arboretum, and the birdwatcher's hut. We'd make more memories this summer so that if I couldn't follow when he left for Oxford, then at least he'd remember how happy I'd made him here. We'd always have this, no matter what happened next.

I'd gotten rid of Blackwell, and I'd do the same with anyone else who thought they could love him better than I could. It was an embarrassingly childish notion, but I believed it in the marrow of my bones.

I'd be his constant. This summer, I'd show him that. I'd be everything and anything he needed me to be.

He was capable of love, and I'd prove it.

It was the Saturday the week before Cas was due home, and I was in the garden helping Beth hang up the washing. Luke was home for lunch, pottering about loudly in the kitchen behind us. It went quiet, and a few minutes later, he stuck his head out of the back door.

"Judey, can you come inside a minute? Beth, you too."

Both of us looked over at the same time. The tone of his voice had pricked my attention – serious and polite, like the tone he used with my teachers or at the bank. I looked at Beth.

"Bit busy, Luke," she huffed before going back to the pegs. She hadn't picked up on the tone.

"I know, babe, but there's a solicitor here to see us."

This got her attention. She froze, looking back at him.

"What?"

"Can you come inside, please?"

There was a tilt of panic in his voice now. He usually deferred to my sister when dealing with professionals: doctors, police officers, solicitors. She dropped the pillowcase in the basket and started toward the house.

"You too, Judey," Luke said.

Bewildered, I followed.

The solicitor's name was Francis Moreland. He was from Moreland and Wright, a London-based legal firm that specialised in trusts and estates. After apologising for coming on a Saturday without warning – he hadn't had a contact number for us – he said he'd been approached by a client who wished to remain anonymous but had asked them to set up a trust for a third party. Here he looked at me.

"In the name of Mr. Jude Alcott."

Moreland was a tall, long-limbed man with big hands, so he looked almost doubled over in the loveseat by the window. He had a rather large mole on his temple that I was staring at so hard I momentarily didn't hear him say my name.

"Jude's?" said Beth, looking at me.

"Yes," Moreland confirmed. He lifted his briefcase onto his lap and flipped it open, pulling out a sheaf of papers held together with a thick paperclip. "I can't say it's something we've ever handled before, might be a first actually, but all within the letter of the law. This..." He searched for the word. "...benefactor has deposited quite a generous sum into an ancillary account set up in the name of Moreland and Wright, but which is to be for the sole use of Mr. Alcott. There are some conditions to the trust which I must advise you of. There will—"

Beth cut in. "I don't understand what you're talking about. What trust fund? Is this to do with our parents' life insurance?"

Moreland blinked, then looked at the papers as though he may have missed something. Then he shook his head. "Ah, no. Not at all."

Beth looked at me and then at Luke. Luke was as confused as I'd ever seen him about anything.

"You'll need to explain this properly, so I understand it," Beth said.

"Of course, my apologies, Mrs. Alcott."

"Green," she said. "Jude's my brother."

"Of course, of course, my apologies. Mrs. Green." Moreland was more or less calm, but there was a sliver of impatience as he explained the thing for a second time. "A benefactor has instructed Moreland and Wright to set up a trust in which Mr. Jude Alcott of The Groundsman Cottage, Deveraux Estate, St. Ouen, Jersey, The Channel Islands, is the sole beneficiary."

It was after this that Luke finally spoke.

"Gideon," he gasped. "It has to be. Gideon! Of course."

I glanced at Moreland, who remained stoic and expressionless. If it was Gideon, then he either didn't have that information in front of him or was an exceptional poker player.

"If I might go on to explain the conditions of the trust to Mr. Alcott?" he asked mildly.

The generous sum he'd spoken of was to cover my university fees so I wouldn't need to apply for any loans, all three years and a fourth if I chose it. There'd be a monthly amount deposited into an account of which I alone had to be the sole holder. A ridiculous amount for an 18-year-old. There was a separate sum, apportioned off and to be used for things like private health care (including dental), gym memberships, and any extra study costs I might incur. I could access a portion of the trust from the date I received my provisional driver's licence for driving lessons and a car.

I listened to it all without saying a word. I felt like I was in a dream or some weird reality show where the host would jump out at any moment with a camera laughing his head off at me.

"Do you have any questions, Mr. Alcott?" Moreland asked when he was finished.

"Um, so, you really can't tell me who this person is?" I asked.

"I am afraid not; the confidentiality clause is wrapped up pretty tightly."

"Can I say no?" I asked. "Refuse it?"

Beth was coiled tight as a spring beside me. She almost went off at that but held herself still.

Moreland looked at me as though I'd lost my mind. "I mean, yes, of course you could. No condition of law would force you to take it. And I should have mentioned this earlier, but this is in no way a loan of any kind. There is no requirement for this to be repaid. Ever."

I nodded. My mind was a quiet chaos as I tried to organise my thoughts. Who would do such a thing for me? Gideon was the obvious answer; we'd grown close these last few weeks since Cas's departure. Since I'd told him about how I felt. Gideon alone under-stood what I wanted from my life and what I needed in order to get those things.

But why keep it a secret? Was it that he didn't want Caspien to know? Did he think I'd refuse it if he offered, not wanting to be a charity case? I knew Gideon could be generous, and he had been to both Luke and me in the time I'd known him. But something about this made me uneasy, something I couldn't quite see or understand yet.

"Can I think about it?" I said.

Moreland blinked behind his thick glasses.

"Yes, yes, of course. And it wouldn't do any harm to have your own solicitor look it over." He reached into his briefcase again. "I'll give you my business card. I am flying back to London this evening, so there's no rush. Please take your time."

Beth shot me a look which I resolutely ignored. Luke stood, and we all followed. Moreland shook all of our hands before handing me a copy of the document, his business card slid under the paper-clip on top.

"I think this is the most altruistic thing I've ever seen in all my years working as a solicitor," he said, the layer of professionalism rubbed away slightly now. "All the way over on the flight, I thought about what I would do were I offered this."

"And what would you do?" I asked.

He smiled, small and kind, and I saw a glimpse of the man behind the suit and the glasses. "Sign it in a heartbeat."

THIRTY

If I counted all the little ways he broke my heart, totalled them up, and set them on a scale, I doubt they would even come close to that first, deep break. The one that felt like a crack tearing through stone and earth, through things that had existed since the beginning of a life, to alter it irrevocably.

That was the thing about heartbreak – mine anyway – it didn't feel like a complete shattering, like something that could never heal. It felt more like a deep fracture over which, in time, things could grow over. The tear could never be completely mended, not so that it was as it had been, but with enough work and time it could fool the eye into thinking there'd never been a crack there at all.

After, I spent a lot of time thinking about words Caspien himself had said to me the day he drew me in his mother's bedroom. (The painting that hangs now inside the cupboard where I keep other things I don't want to look at; the treadmill I used for three weeks after I turned twenty-five, the overpriced protein shakes I'd bought from an Instagram ad, my parents' ashes.) The day he'd asked if I'd ever had my heart broken.

When I'd surprised him by answering yes.

He'd said, *I think it's easier for hearts to heal when they are still young.*

He'd said nothing of the same heart being broken over and over again, sometimes in exactly the same place, sometimes slightly to the left, sometimes slightly above. That surely would weaken the entire structure until one day, the thing would crumble to dust.

But at the time, that first, deep break had felt like more than just a fracture. It was a great chasm cleaved through the heart of everything I believed; riven so deep and so devastating that I wasn't sure anything could grow there again.

I remember the day vividly: fragrant, bright, and milk-warm. Like the earth was heating up slowly from within and by August it would be unbearable and broiling. I remember how I'd felt, too: joy, euphoria, hope. I was a bird flying far above the clouds on a clear blue day.

I just didn't see the rifle pointing up at me from the ground.

I hadn't contacted Moreland yet, despite it being almost a week since his visit, despite Beth and Luke hovering around me incessantly. Luke had a client who was a solicitor, and he'd asked him to look over the paperwork.

According to him, it was all above board and legal. Highly unusual, he said, stunned, but legal. His advice was to sign it immediately before whoever this insane person was changed their mind. He had a fax machine I could use. I'd shaken my head and said I wanted to think about it some more.

On Monday after school, I'd cycled straight up to the big house and burst in on Gideon in the red sitting room. ("Blue for business, red for repose," he often said.) He was as I usually found him: reading, a glass of dark wine on the side table and wearing his gold-rimmed reading glasses. He closed the book on his knee and slid his glasses off.

"Jude. To what do I owe the pleasure?"

I held out the sheaf of paper to him.

"Is it you? Did you do this?"

He'd started with shock before sliding his body forward to perch on the end of the chair. He reached for the papers. Sliding his glasses back on, he began to scan the pages. I'd watched his face closely for clues for something that would give away the truth of it, but there'd been only a slight lift of his brow, which had disappeared a moment later.

Finally, he handed me back the papers, his gaze incalculable.

He said, "Well, that is quite something."

"Well, is it? Are you the 'anonymous benefactor'?"

He was perfectly still for a moment before he set his book aside and stood up.

"Perhaps it's best not to poke at these things too hard; who knows what might fall out. Besides, you know what they say about curiosity. It seems to me like someone wants to see you do very well for yourself, Jude." He pointed at the paper in my hand. "And has all but given you the means to do it."

It wasn't a denial. It wasn't an answer. But it was all I got.

I had to assume that it was him and that he simply didn't want Cas to know. But why? I couldn't understand. Neither could I understand my hesitation to accept it. What was I waiting for? I knew the offer had no expiration date, but it still sat on my desk the entire week like a glowing treasure chest just waiting to be opened.

I wanted to speak to Caspien about it. But not over the phone. I wanted to show him the paperwork and have him pour scorn over it and tell me to burn it, or tell me I was the biggest idiot on earth not to have signed it yet.

He was due back that Thursday night; his last teaching day had been on Tuesday, but he had a Fence tournament on Wednesday evening that he had to stay at school for. He had to beat Hannes Meier in the final for a gilded replica of a trophy which was over 100 years old. I wished him luck and told him I'd see him on Friday night. Gideon was again in London (I remember wondering if he was meeting Blackwell again), so it meant we'd have the house to ourselves.

That Friday, Luke had a big contracting job on in Beaumont and couldn't leave the site to pick me up, so that morning I'd taken the bike to school. The ride home had taken me around forty minutes, the last part quite heavily uphill, but I'd arrived home energised and sweating from the workout.

Caspien had arrived home late the night before; I'd seen the car come up the drive just after ten. Still, I'd waited a half hour before I'd texted to ask if he was in bed yet. I wanted to sneak out and go to the house to see him, and if he'd given me any indication it would have been welcome, then I would have. I missed him like an ache, a deep knot in my chest that I knew would only release when I saw him.

He hadn't texted back until after midnight.

Caspien:

About to sleep. Come over tomorrow night.

Me:

did you beat him?

Caspien:

Yes. 15 to 11

I'd gone to bed with a proud smile on my face.

Since he'd told me to come over in the evening, I showered, made myself a sandwich, and tried reading a book for an hour or so. I was distracted, agitated, and excited to see him, my stomach and chest in complicated knots. That was the moment I realised, with startling clarity, how tightly my mood was linked to Caspien.

I thought about those months when he was cold and abrupt with me; how difficult I'd been. How unpleasant to Luke I'd been on those days he'd asked me to help out at the big house, specifically because I knew Caspien would be around and I hated being so small and insignificant to him. I thought of how lost and uncertain the world felt when he returned to Switzerland, leaving me alone to deal with feelings I couldn't control or understand.

Then, the inverse: how every moment of wonder and pleasure and thrill I'd felt for the last few months had been because of him. Because I'd had him in ways I hadn't even known I'd wanted.

I wasn't sure it was normal or even healthy to be so completely wrapped up in another person – now I know it was neither—but I also couldn't stop it, not least because it would mean a return to that feeling of before. For good or bad, I was tied, soul bound, to Caspien. It was terrifying and electrifying all at once. I was alive and in love, and the future we could have – that I would convince him we could have – stretched out before me, endless and shimmering.

I couldn't wait to tell him about the golden ticket burning in my hand, about all the ways I was going to make him come this summer, about how I was going to be everything he needed and wanted. I couldn't wait to tell him I loved him.

I was in love. And I was still young enough and naïve enough to assume that was all I needed, to assume the power of that alone was enough to protect me from everything else.

But Cas had been right; I knew nothing of what love was supposed to be.

Unwilling to wait another minute to see him, I grabbed the trust paperwork from my desk and flew out of the house, convinced of my place in the world and Caspien's place right next to me.

I'd thought about texting him first, but then I thought about his little gasp of surprise and the way his eyes would light up when I appeared, pushed him against whatever wall was closest, and kissed him. I thought about how easily he'd open for me when I dropped to my knees and fumbled with his belt. Of how he'd grow hard and desperate around my tongue, pleading with me even as he gripped my hair in his fist.

I ran faster.

When he wasn't in the kitchen, I went straight to the library, and when he wasn't there, I went to the music room. I went to the blue and the red sitting rooms next, though he rarely spent any time in either before deciding he must be sleeping. Cas liked to sleep in the afternoons; he'd curl up on the sofa or window seat in the library, close his eyes, and sleep as deeply as a cat.

The bedroom door had been closed.

I imagined sneaking inside and watching him asleep for a few moments before waking him. He looked different when he was asleep, the perfect symmetry of his features still and ethereal as water.

Whenever I watched him sleep, I wanted to be an artist like him. I'd taken some pictures of him on my phone, but I dreamt of being able to cast him against a page out of pencil or watercolour. The rosebud mouth and the delicate veined silk of his eyelids. Dark gold lashes against the arch of his cheekbones.

The bedroom door had been closed.

I snicked it open as quietly as I could. The smell hit me first. Sweet and pungent as death in the heat of the early summer. Heat which had already begun sinking into the walls of the old house.

It was the smell of heartbreak. The smell of dreams crashing down around me. The death of first love.

The bedroom door had been closed. And had it been open, maybe I wouldn't have seen. I would have heard and understood, but I wouldn't have seen.

I'd not registered the strange car in the courtyard outside. Expensive and grey and with a personalised registration, I would still be able to recite from memory even years later. I'd look for it everywhere for years to come.

I saw the elegant arch of Caspien's back first, butter gold in the late afternoon sun.

A dark hand gripped his waist, firm enough to bruise.

"Don't you dare come yet," Caspien ordered, voice a taut desperate whisper. "I've waited too *fucking* long for this."

"I missed you too, sweetheart..." A low breathy laugh.

I knew who it belonged to. That voice. That laugh. That hand. I knew, and I felt a gasping suffocating pain sear through my chest, a hole opening impossibly wide.

No.

No.

Please no.

"I missed *this* terribly," Caspien panted, hips rolling.

"No," I said. Not loudly, not loudly enough that they would hear me through that.

But he did. Caspien turned, looking at me over his shoulder. There was nothing in his eyes. No life. Nothing at all. But as our eyes held, I saw everything in them I would never have; hopes and dreams of a life shattering.

"Jude," he said.

"What?" Blackwell said.

I staggered backwards out of the room, along the hall and down the stairs. At the foot of them, I fell, pain shooting through my knee. I ignored it. In the kitchen, Elspeth was taking off her coat, just arriving.

"Jude, sweetheart, are you hungry? There's leftover—"

I bolted past without looking at her, past the stable and Falstaff, around the side of the house and on toward the trees on the other side of the estate. I don't remember what thoughts were careening through my head as I ran. I remember only the noise in my ears and the pain in my chest, the burning in my legs.

The hut was the same as it always was: air warm and wood-soaked and close against my skin. I thought about the last time I'd been here. The last time he'd been here with me. He'd been colder, almost like he used to be.

I'd ignored it, pretended it was just his way of making going back to school a little easier. Christ, I was an idiot.

I'm not sure how long I sat there, curled up in one corner of that hut, fists clenched and tears rolling down my cheeks, but the light had begun to change outside. The refractions from the observation holes tilting lower and lower on the wood surfaces.

Then, I heard it.

The unmistakable sound of horse's hooves. Then, soft, graceful footfalls picking their way across the long grass.

The door was pulled open.

Caspien appeared, draped in amber sunshine. My heart ached.

He wasn't wearing his usual riding clothes, but a smart black shirt and a pair of light trousers, white trainers on his feet. He stepped inside and pulled the door closed behind him. He didn't lock it.

There was nothing on his face to denote guilt or remorse; it was a beautiful mask. Doll-like and perfect.

"I guessed you would be here," he said. "Though I went to the cottage first."

I turned my head from him and tried, surreptitiously, to bring a hand up to rub the wetness from my cheeks.

"You were not supposed to see that," he sighed. Then, as though he were irritated with me, "The plan was for you to come over this evening."

I glared at him. "Oh, well, apologies for ruining your fucking plans! Sorry for missing you! Sorry for wanting to see you! Sorry for—" I cut myself off before saying it. *Sorry for loving you.* Instead I said, "Sorry for being a fucking idiot, I guess."

He said nothing, but moved to sit on the bench seat opposite, graceful as a leopard. It wasn't a large space, so when he sat our knees touched and I wondered if it was the last time I'd ever get to touch him.

"Jude, though it's regrettable you had to see that, there are things you don't understand."

I felt my face rearrange itself. "*Regrettable*? *Things* I don't understand?"

"I'm just saying that if you—"

"Do you love him?" I talked over him.

Caspien's gaze sharpened. "You asked me that before, and I answered it before."

"And I'm asking it again."

"If I give a different answer this time, will it make you feel better or worse?"

I thought about that. If he said he loved him now, it would be far, far worse.

"Was all of it a lie?" I asked him instead. I loathed how desperate my voice sounded.

"Which parts?"

"The parts with me!" I roared so loud he startled slightly. "The things you made me believe, the ways you let me have you. I don't understand how you could..." I shook my head. I couldn't speak around the ball in my throat. It felt as though I was being choked from the inside out.

Then, a terrible realisation settled over me. I stared at him in horror.

"You never stopped, did you?" I said. "Seeing him. Blackwell was always there. You were just more careful about it. I was just more stupid about it."

A glimmer of something in his eye told me I was right.

"And so, I was what? A way to pass the time? Did you talk about me with him? Laugh about me with him?"

He at least had the decency to look a little ashamed at this. Christ, the pain was blinding. I could barely draw my next breath.

"Why? Why even bother? You could have left me alone, left me out of it! Not made me care about you."

This riled him. He sat up. "I never asked you to care for me, Jude," he snapped. "And please, *left you out of it*? You wouldn't let me. You threatened me! Threatened to tell the police. You acted like a child with no care of the damage you could do!" He calmed, looking me dead in the eye. "And then you found out his name."

Everything stopped. The very air seeming to still.

"That was when it began..." I whispered, understanding everything all at once. "When you pulled me closer, when you wanted me the way I wanted you." I looked at him, stunned. He'd never looked more cruel, more cold, more beautiful. "You're fucking poison."

Caspien's gaze flickered with what looked like torment, but then he lifted his chin and stood. "If I am, then it's perhaps for the best that I shan't be around to infect you any further." He reached for the door.

Panic fluttered behind my ribs. I stood. "What do you mean? Where are you going?"

"First, to France, then Sardinia, and after my birthday, we'll settle in Massachusetts."

There was a dreadful rushing noise in my ears. "But you'll be going to Oxford. There's the entrance exam and the interviews – you'll have to be back for those."

He stopped and turned, and for the first time, his gaze flicked to the pile of paper I'd dumped on the bench when I'd arrived.

"I'm not going to Oxford, Jude."

"What?" I blinked. Not going? I didn't understand. He'd always planned to go; his place was bought and paid for, and he'd told me that more times than I could remember. "What are you talking about, not going?"

"Oxford is your dream, Jude, not mine. I was never going."

I shook my head. "No, you said—"

"I said it was where all Deverauxs went. That it was where Gideon went. That it's where he expected I'd go." Caspien's voice had turned a little hard again. "But it's never what I wanted."

"Then where will you go?" There was a desolate edge to my voice.

"I'll be studying at the Lervairè Conservatory of Music. In Boston. I was accepted last month."

"No...you can't...I can't..." Then, I couldn't imagine a life without him in it. Without seeing him, even if it were only that. Looking at him. Even if I couldn't have him, I could still love him.

For him to live in another country for years was unthinkable.

I went to him then, urgently, humiliatingly, and I crowded him against the door and buried my face in his neck.

"Cas, no. Please don't go. I don't care about him, about what you've done. I can't lose you, too. Just please, please don't leave me."

I felt him tense under me, warm body turning rigid. "Stop it," he said in a tight voice. With great effort, because I was still crushed against him, he turned so that he was facing me. "I cannot love you; surely you know that."

"I don't care." I could barely breathe. I was gasping, trying and failing to draw breath into my lungs.

"Maybe not now, but one day you will," he said solemnly. "One day you'll look back on this moment and hate me so much for it that you won't be able to fucking look at me."

I shook my head again, violently. "I wouldn't ever. Cas, I love you...I love you..." I pressed my lips, tear-stained and trembling to his mouth, to his cheek, to his eyelids. "I love you so much, please. Please don't go."

He softened. Indulging me for a few moments. I even thought he kissed me back, but I think I imagined that brief softening of his mouth. Then he pushed at me, hard, and I stumbled back.

"*Stop it.*" He was trembling now, colour leached from him, and a touch of sweat beaded on his forehead. "This is finished now. I am going to Boston with Xavier. He is to start a new firm there, and we will live in the city, close to Lervairè. It is all arranged." He was still talking when I felt the bile rise up in my throat without warning. I turned to empty it onto the floor of the hut.

"You don't love him," I said, wiping at my mouth. The words burned my throat.

"I don't intend on loving anyone," he said very earnestly. "And so it doesn't matter where I am or with whom, as long as I am comfortable and far away from this place."

Be with me then, I wanted to scream. But then I registered the word: "Comfortable?"

"Comfortable, yes. Xavier has a great deal of money, and so I shall be able to live the sort of life I wish."

"But you won't be happy!" I spat it like a threat.

At this, he frowned a little as though thinking hard. "I am not sure

I've ever been happy, Jude. So that shall make very little difference to me." He pulled open the door.

"I could make you happy, Cas," I managed, wiping at my eyes again. "If you just gave me a chance, I think I could make you happy. I know I could."

He stopped in the open doorway and turned back to face me. A sliver of sunlight was left in the hut, and it pierced through him at a downward angle like a bolt of holy light through his chest.

Once more, he lifted his chin, imperious as he met my eye. "You've always had rather grandiose ideas about what you can and can't do. Oxford will beat that out of you, I'm sure." He glanced once more at where the trust paperwork lay. "If you have a single ounce of sense in that bloody head of yours, then sign that."

And then he was gone.

THIRTY ONE

I stayed there until it was dark and then walked home. Luke was making dinner, steak I remember, and the scent of burning meat turned my stomach.

I'd gone to the bathroom to throw up again and then fell into bed and slept until the following morning. When I woke up, it was that same sensation I used to have in the months after my parents died, where for a few moments, I forgot. Where my mind's short-term memory was still rousing, and the horror hadn't yet made itself known.

I lay staring at the ceiling for a long time, wondering if he'd left Deveraux yet. I thought of calling the police and telling them everything I knew about Xavier Blackwell and his relationship with Caspien Deveraux. Cas was sixteen now, but he'd been a child when this began. That, I knew, would ruin a man like Xavier.

But I also knew it wouldn't make Cas come back to me. It wouldn't give me back what I'd lost – and that was something which hadn't even been mine to begin with. I wasn't sure what I'd been to Cas, a distraction, a game, but he'd been real to me.

There was a knock on my door around 10 a.m. Luke's head popped in.

"Hey buddy, you okay? You must be starving?" His eyes were kind and warm, and they made me want to cry again.

"I'm not really hungry."

"You seeing Cas tonight? Heard he was home."

I could only shake my head. But whatever Luke saw on my face was enough to worry him.

"Well, how's about we stick on a film or go out and do something fun?"

I didn't know what Luke's idea of fun entailed, but I was certain I didn't want to do it.

"I'm not feeling too great, actually, thought I'd just hang around here. Maybe sleep some more honestly."

He looked disappointed but I couldn't find it in me to care.

"No probs. Give me a shout if you want me to bring you up anything to eat, yeah?"

"Sure."

I was grateful when he left. When I could be alone again to think over every word Caspien had said yesterday, paying particular attention to the ones that hurt the most. Then I thought about what I'd said. The ache that came from remembering how I'd pleaded, how I'd begged him, was strangely satisfying. I deserved the shame and the embarrassment. I was so fucking stupid. So blind. So guileless.

Nausea haunted me all day. Around 4 p.m., my room started to stink, and so I got out of bed and told Luke and Beth I was going for a walk to clear my head.

They shot concerned glances at me from where they were on the couch, but otherwise said nothing.

There were no strange cars parked in the courtyard, only Gideon's Jaguar. Had they left before he returned? The kitchen was dark and cold too. No sight or sound of Elspeth bustling around.

Gideon was in the red sitting room. He stood by the large window gazing out over the estate, a glass of red wine in one hand and a few sheets of paper in the other. A letter, I could see. I watched him drink for a moment before announcing myself.

"Did you know?" I asked. My voice was rough from the crying and lack of use. "About him and Blackwell, did you know?"

He turned around slowly, his gaze tracking over me hungrily. I knew how I must appear to him. I hadn't showered. I'd left the house in what I'd gone to sleep in. I hadn't eaten in over twenty-four hours. I had managed a glass of water in the bathroom as I brushed my teeth.

Still, he didn't look surprised or even concerned.

"Jude, come in. Do you want something to drink?"

"Did you know?"

"Not until this." He held up the letter. "He's been quite clever about it. About everything, really. They both have." He took a sip of his wine.

"He should be in prison," I said though without any of the fire with which I'd said it in the past. I was tired. "He used to come here when you weren't around, you know. I caught them once."

"I'm sorry, Jude. But I did warn you," Gideon said, not sounding sorry at all.

I stared at him.

He moved to sit down, taking a large sip of his wine as he did. "I warned you that he would break your heart, and he did."

I didn't want to hear it, not from him. Because he had. He had warned me. I'm sure it was too late by the time his warning came, but it didn't make it any easier to hear.

"He said I'd hate him. That one day I'd hate him so much I wouldn't be able to bear it," I told Gideon in a strange, unfamiliar voice.

"The way I have always seen it," Gideon said as he sipped his wine, "is that we have only two choices when the heart is broken. The first is to allow it to heal. It is quite astounding what the human heart is able to overcome. Though it shall never be quite as strong as it was – its foundations will be forever weakened – it can heal. The second..."

Here, his eyes danced to me. For the first time, I saw something in them that made my blood run cold.

"...is to turn it into so impenetrable a thing, such a fortress, that it will never be breached again."

I knew what choice Gideon had made. It was more evident to me then than it had ever been. His was a fortress. It was how Cas's had been hardened, too. But I had already made the promise under the moon to love him, unconditionally. Was I to turn back on that so soon? He'd hurt me, but I wasn't broken beyond repair. I was young and strong, and I could recover.

I could make myself into something Caspien wanted. Someone who could offer him the life he wanted.

In that very same instant, a new goal emerged within me: I wanted to achieve something, something that would impress him and him alone. He would be my singular critic. I'd never have the riches, status, or even looks that Xavier Blackwell had come to him with. But I could strive for something else.

His respect.

I think even then I understood that I could never possibly mean anything to him without it. I wanted to be his equal. And if that would earn me his love and affection and desire, then all the better.

I'd brought the paperwork with me knowing that I would need a witness, knowing that Lord Gideon Deveraux would be able to fill that duty.

"Would I be able to use your phone?" I asked. Because I hadn't brought mine, it lay dead under my pillow where I'd spent the night drafting a letter to Caspien that I'd never send.

"Of course." He gestured across the room.

I could feel his eyes on me as I lifted the receiver and dialled.

Moreland answered on the third ring. He sounded pleasantly surprised to hear from me, as though he'd given up all hope he ever would.

"Eh, so I was wondering – hoping – that the offer was still open. For the trust thing. They haven't changed their mind, have they?" I stared at Gideon and watched as the very corner of his mouth turned up. As though I'd just accepted a challenge.

"Of course not; everything is still very much on offer, Mr. Alcott." I nodded until I realised he couldn't see me.

"Great. Well, then I'd like to accept it, please. Thank you."

PART TWO:
FOR NOW, I AM WINTER

"The broken heart. You think you will die, but you just keep living, day after day after terrible day."

Charles Dickens, Great Expectations

ONE

Dear Cas,

I saw the most pretentious film tonight. You'd have loved it. Everyone died, and the score was beautiful. Exactly the kind of thing you'd love. You know, whenever I watch a film where the score is beautiful, I think of you. I think of that night in your bedroom when I made you watch Gladiator for the first time and you cried. I think that's the first time I thought you might have a heart. I still think about that night now, now that I know you don't.

I've grown to think that the only good thing about you not having a heart is that it means you can't love him either. That you _don't_. Despite what I see on your social media.

Yes, I still check it every day — sometimes more than that. Sometimes I think you know I do, and you post stuff there just for me.

Secret messages you mean only for me (the heart you drew in the snow a few months ago. The close-up of the Oleander plant at Kew Gardens — I hope you didn't eat it. The New York City Library) but then I wonder why you'd post the others: Pictures of him, mainly. Pictures of the two of you? Two glasses of red wine on a coffee table next to a set of keys to your new apartment. Are you happy?

You probably think I should have moved on by now. Maybe I should have. But don't they say that the things that happen to us in the years when our brains are still developing become part of us forever? You happened to me. I grew around you. Then you left. You uprooted yourself, and now the place you grew out is just barren.

But there's still a Caspien-shaped avulsion where you once were.

I'm writing fewer of these, which I guess is a good thing. They were the only thing keeping me alive after you left. Thousands of words that you'll never read, each one a kiss I wish I could place somewhere on your body. I still miss you so much that it hurts, but every day, it hurts a little less. Every day, I heal a little more.

Anyway, I'm going to keep this one short. I really only

wanted to tell you about the film. It was called 'Tid-vattensvängen' – The Turn of Tides. It was directed by the guy who did the film about the dogs in the war.

Love,

Jude

I look back on that first year without him, and then my first few months at Oxford, as some of the bleakest of my twenty-eight years. I'd lost my parents when I was eight, and with it the sorts of experiences that most of us are guaranteed at birth; proud smiles at graduation, a tearful speech at a wedding, a hundred varieties of 'I'm proud of you, son' moments, a hundred thousand tight hugs from my mum. The kind of bottomless supply of positive reinforcement you can only get from the two people on earth who are programmed to love you unconditionally. And yet, it was those months after Caspien left me that devastated me most.

More than losing my parents. More than understanding what it meant to be an orphan, I felt the absence of him. The great chasm into which my hopes and dreams of a life with him had crashed and disappeared.

I couldn't remember who I'd been before him, and didn't know who I was now that he'd discarded me.

I felt more singularly alone than I had in my life.

Even now, there's a physical reaction in my body when I recall the number of nights I spent crying and begging some higher power to have him come back to me; something between mortification and grief. And had some terrible god appeared before me in those months after he left, and given me the option of having my parents – either or both – back or Caspien, then I'd have said his name without a heartbeat's hesitation.

I moved into Ellis Hall on September 18th, a year and four months to the day after he left me.

A week or so after my A-Level results had come in, a thick white envelope had arrived from the Oxford Admissions Board telling me I'd been accepted. I'd been dizzy from shock. I'd already paid a deposit on my student accommodation in Warwick; I'd already registered my car insurance to the address there. I'd researched the nearest library, Tesco, and parking to where I'd be staying. But here it was, an invitation to study at my first choice uni in black and white and with a tone of importance that reminded me of Caspien.

Caspien, who wouldn't be studying at Oxford. Caspien, who was now in his second year of study at one of the world's foremost music schools.

I thought of turning it down, thinking of the work it would be to unpick everything I'd already laid down in Warwick, but I knew I'd look back and regret it. After all, surely it was better he wasn't going to be there. That way, I wouldn't have to see him across a dining hall or bump into him in a corridor or bar. I couldn't watch him laugh and exist without me.

It was better.

In the end, it took me an afternoon of online admin to reroute my future an hour's drive south. I didn't expect there to be any chance of getting a place in the halls, given my late acceptance, but it so happened that a room in Ellis had opened up due to some last-minute refusals. But it would only be for the first academic year. I'd need to reapply for accommodation in year two – if I didn't get one, then I'd have to find a house share or rent my own place. This wouldn't be an issue, given that the monthly allowance from the trust fund would easily cover both.

Ellis Hall was an ancient brick building that looked and smelled like an old hospital. My room was south-facing with a single sash window, a single bed, and the single most depressing view I had ever seen. It was of the car park of a mini-supermarket and a row of large commercial bins. The worst part about it wasn't even the view; it was that the bins were emptied on a Sunday morning right outside the window.

My floor, the second, was mixed; boys and girls, single, double, triple and quad, and with a large communal kitchen and a smaller sitting room. My single room had a small toilet and basin only. Bathrooms and showers were down the hall. Single rooms were apparently like gold dust here and I was shot envious glances as I'd carried my boxes and bags into it a few days before the start of term.

I met Bastian at Freshers Week. He lived on the floor below mine and had come upstairs looking for teaspoons one lunchtime. He was tall, lean, and angular with the longest legs I'd ever seen. He was from Noordwijk in the Netherlands, and struck up a conversation with me about toast toppings. He cycled semi-professionally and wanted to go full pro, but was studying medicine at Oxford as a backup.

He spoke English fluently and came over as sharp and witty, with a way of appearing completely absorbed in whatever you had to say. I liked him instantly. Bast – as he insisted I call him after ten minutes – was single but had left his high school sweetheart called Emmeline back in Noordwijk. A mutual decision, apparently. One that he didn't seem to be crying himself to sleep over.

"What about you? Single? In love? Celibate?" He had come over to my room one night about a week after we'd met in the kitchen. We had bought some beer from the supermarket outside my window and were drinking it on the floor by the small electric fire as we listened to the university radio broadcast. They were playing Coldplay.

"I think technically I'm all three," I said without any humour.

"Ah," he nodded, knowingly. "What was her name?"

There was a decision to be made suddenly. Did I want to answer questions about my sexuality that I was certain I didn't fully understand myself? Did I want to make a friend? Honesty was the first part of that, surely.

"His name was Cas," I heard myself saying. "Caspien."

Bast's eyes went fractionally wider. I took this to mean I didn't look like someone who was into guys. But he nodded and lifted his beer.

"So it wasn't mutual?" he asked, clearly curious.

I shook my head. He nodded again.

"So, are you into guys? Girls? Both?" he asked. I shrugged non-committally. "Nikita is hot." Nikita was Russian, from St Petersburg, and shared a quad with Bast and two other guys. He was short, muscular and dark-haired; he was decidedly not my type. "And he is..." He made a gesture with his hand toward his dick and widened his eyes.

I laughed.

"You look at your roommate's dick?" I questioned.

"He is always naked. I have no choice. I think maybe it's a Russian thing, but maybe not. What about Conn? From the third. He's gay and cute?"

"I don't know who that is."

"You do: Irish or Scottish, wears the Harry Potter glasses and is always carrying a book. He came down to borrow milk from the kitchen the other day." Bast explained excitedly. "I saw him looking at you."

"You're so full of shit." I shook my head. Conn sounded more my type than Nikita, though. If I had a type. I wasn't sure that I did. Or rather, I had a very specific, very singular type. *Boys who can't love you and break your heart for sport.*

"I'm not looking," I said and drained the last of my beer.

"No one's saying you have to fall in love, my friend, but you can have some fun, right? You're young, good-looking, and studying at Oxford. Why else are we here if not to live our best lives?"

"Get a degree from one of the best universities in the world? Solidify our future?"

He made a noise of disagreement. "That's for third-year Jude and Bast to worry about. Now, we live." I knew part of his approach was that this really wasn't what he wanted to do. He wanted to compete in the Tour de France. He had a poster of Eddie Merckx on his wall and considered cycling the most gruelling circuits on planet earth for a living his 'dream career.' It just so happened he was a brilliant academic, too.

He handed me another beer and stood up to change the radio to something more lively.

My eighteenth birthday arrived on a dark and cold Sunday. (My seventeenth hadn't been much better.)

I woke up hungover. There'd been a party in one of the girls' rooms on the third floor the night before. Booze lined up along a picnic table like a toxic pick-and-mix. I threw up into a sink. Smoked my first joint. Endured a blonde girl from Merton talking my ear off about her boyfriend back in Cardiff and how she suspected he was cheating on her, and how she wanted to get back at him. It shouldn't have been a surprise then when she threw her leg over me and climbed onto my lap to kiss me. She tasted of wine and cigarettes, and I'd never been less into anything in my life. I'd gently guided her off and stood, stumbling downstairs to my room before passing out.

When I checked my phone, there were a few missed calls and texts. Luke, Beth, Gideon, and even one from Alfie.

I called Luke back when I'd showered, eaten some toast, and drank a litre of water. My head felt like cotton wool, and the low hum of nausea was thinking about following through.

"Judeyyyyy, happy birthday, mate! You're an adult, congratulations!" Luke chirped. The sound of his voice settled some of the melancholy inside me, made worse by the hangover.

"Yeah, feels great," I groaned.

"Partying hard, were we?" He chuffed in faux disapproval. "Hangovers only get worse from here on out, buddy. Ha, remember how shit you felt after a single glass of champagne at Cas's birthday?"

I hadn't prepared myself to hear his name, and the sound of it spoken so casually stunned me a little.

"Mhm," I managed.

"So, what are your plans today? Anything nice?"

I hadn't told any of the others it was my birthday. I was certain they'd want to take me drinking again. Though at that point, I was starting to wonder if it might be the only thing that would help.

"Not sure, maybe I'll head down the pub later. Order my first legal drink."

"Brave lad, oh wait, here's Beth wanting a word." My sister came on to wish me happy birthday and tell me how proud Mum and Dad would have been of me. I wasn't sure that was true; weak and lovesick and becoming far too dependent on alcohol. The pit of sadness widened inside me the second I hung up the phone, and I filled it with the only thing I could think of.

I texted the Ellis group chat to tell them they'd better not be too hungover because it was my eighteenth birthday today, and I wanted to get exceedingly pished again later.

Then, because I was some kind of pain enthusiast, I pulled up Cas's Instagram. There was a video posted last night. He was playing piano in a large, bright apartment – their apartment my mind supplied – with views out over the city. He wore a white shirt too big for his frame (my mind told me, helpfully, that it was Blackwell's) and a pair of loose check pyjama bottoms. He looked painfully beautiful. Painfully far away. Painfully not mine.

I cried for a half hour after.

I got more drunk that night than I'd ever been in my life and woke up beside a girl whose name I didn't remember, guilty and ashamed. That same shame and guilt I was beginning to associate with sex.

It was the worst birthday I could remember.

It was the start of a pattern. I had lectures two and a half days out of five, and an afternoon of this was tutorials: smaller groups and a professor would meet in a room – normally, his or her office – and discuss rather than sit and be lectured at. I had two of these on a Thursday afternoon. One was Post-War European literature with a very stylish, very intelligent Greek woman called Professor

Gerotzi. The other class was one I'd picked at random from the list but which turned out to be one of my favourites: film criticism run by the youngest professor Oxford had ever had. Mr. Alexander: a youngish, good-looking, American who'd won an Oscar for best original screenplay at twenty-four for a war film called 'Butchers and Heroes'. He was a guest lecturer for the academic year, and I'd been lucky to get into his class by all accounts.

Our assignments for Alexander's class involved mainly watching films. Some we'd have to watch online using the university's access codes as they were often 1960s Bolivian things no one had ever heard of. Other times, we'd go together as a class to the local cinema and watch a showing of something popular and terrible.

On Thursday after tutorial, I'd meet Bast, Nikita and Irish Conn (who was straight as a flagpole and absolutely not interested in me) with a couple of the girls from 1st in the Lord Avery and get plastered, laugh, and try to fill the hole in my heart with cheap rosè wine.

It would work until I got back to the dorm, where morose and alone with my own thoughts, I'd have a wank to hazy thoughts of his mouth and tongue and the sounds he'd make when he came. After, I'd lie warm and sated for about three minutes until the bone-cold ache rushed in again, quick as a rising tide. Sometimes, I'd think about the scene in his bedroom I'd walked in on, a piercing pain in my gut so sharp it could take my breath away.

The best thing to do, I'd found, was to drink enough so that the moment my head touched the pillow, I'd sink into undreaming sleep.

I drank, and I forgot. And then I remembered, and then I drank again. It was a perfectly acceptable cycle for a student. Everyone went out drinking; no one thought anything of it if you got so drunk you couldn't remember getting home.

Alcohol wasn't perfect, it couldn't keep him out of my head completely, but it came bloody close. And next to Bast and Nika and Irish Conn, alcohol became an understanding and consistent friend to me that first year.

It was easy to get out of going home to Jersey that first December. I had two papers due the first week back, (Bast and Conn were going home until after New Year but Nika was staying) and with Luke and Beth enjoying their new childless life again, they didn't seem too fussed when I said I'd stay at school over Christmas.

I'd miss visiting with Gideon. He'd been a steady friend that first year, even if his little tokens about where they were and what they were doing pecked at my heart like carrion. But now that I was away from the place, the thought of going back there made me feel physically ill: like returning to the scene of some horrendous accident. Some place where a terrible trauma had been done to me.

I couldn't face it: that long drive up to the house, the view of his bedroom window from mine, the library, the hut. No. I couldn't do it. I wondered how many months I could avoid going home. Right then, I started thinking of an excuse for Easter and summer.

TWO

I ran into Finn in February, my sixth month there, when I'd been hungover and on my way to my third interview that week for a part-time job.

I didn't particularly need a job; the stipend that was deposited into my bank account each month from persons unknown was enough to feed, clothe, and water me (and by water, I mean get me drunk). But most of the people I knew here had part-time jobs of some sort, and it felt like something I should do if only to stop me drinking every night.

I'd wanted a job in the second-hand book store in Millner Close, but they weren't hiring, so I left them my CV and expand-ed my options. I'd already been turned down by a popular Italian restaurant for not having any waiting experience and the local Whole Foods because they really needed someone who could cover Thursdays – which was the only day I couldn't commit to. All in all, the job hunt wasn't going great.

"Jude! Hey, Jude!" A voice had shouted from the bottom of the steps into the Bodleian while I'd pulled up the map up on my phone for the fifth time that day. (I'd gotten it down from around a dozen since I got here.) I'd glanced up to see a tall, good-looking guy leaping up the steps two at a time.

"Er, Hi, hello?" I squinted.

"Finlay," he pointed at himself. "Finn. Finn Haldane."

The name sounded only vaguely familiar. I wondered if he was in one of my tutorials.

"We met at Caspien's birthday?"

As usual, I started at the sound of Caspien's name. I'd only been to one of his birthdays and that ...

"The distant half cousin," he added helpfully before my thoughts had caught up.

I blinked again and looked him over.

"Yeah, sure, I remember now." And I did. But the guy standing in front of me was not the slouching, skinny, brace-wearing, glasses-wearing boy I remembered from two years ago. "Did you do something to your hair?"

He threw his head back and laughed. His teeth were two perfectly straight white lines. His laugh was warm and rounded.

"Sorry, I forget sometimes how different I look."

"Yeah, I'm sorry." I scratched the back of my neck, mortified. Had a brace really changed his face that much?

"I've seen you a few times now and kept wondering if I should say hello," Finlay said, shifting a little on his feet.

"You should have." I gave him a friendly smile. "So, what have you been up to?" *Have you seen him?* Is what I really wanted to ask.

"Christ, it's been wild since Cas's birthday."

And it had by the sound of it. He told me how he'd spent last spring and summer in Namibia helping to build a school. How he'd been held at gunpoint. How he'd caught some African digestive disease and almost died. It had changed him a bit, he said. I could only nod, impressed, mainly since I'd done nothing but sit home and cry for the last year.

He was far more personable than I remembered him. Truthfully, I barely remembered him at all. But then, Caspien had been in the room the last time I'd seen Finn, and I understood now how I'd rarely noticed anything else when he was in my line of sight.

Now, he looked good. Dark auburn hair, tall with broad swimmer's shoulders, and whiskey-coloured eyes which at that moment sparkled with warmth.

"So, how you settling in? It's a pretty cool place, isn't it?"

"Yeah, good. I'm enjoying it so far."

"What college?"

"Magdalen."

He nodded. "Let me guess: English and Classics?"

"Is it that obvious?" I laughed.

"Ha, no. Once I have the college, I can usually work out the rest by looking. It's actually like some weird party trick I have."

"That go down well at parties here?"

"No, actually." He laughed, and I joined in.

"Look, I'm actually on my way to an interview now." I glanced at my phone. I was doing okay for time, but Cas's name hadn't come up yet, and I assumed the longer I hung around him, the more chances of that decreased, and I couldn't think about him now, before an interview.

"Ah, cool, where?"

"Uh, Page & Plant on Cooke Street."

"Oh, no way, I have a mate who works there, Abbie – Abigail. She's like a dep manager or something." He pulled his phone out of his pocket. "I can put a good word in for you if you like." He looked like he was doing that already.

"Oh, right, cool. I guess it wouldn't do any harm."

"What's your number?" he asked, still typing.

I rhymed it off, and a second later, my phone rang, vibrating in my palm.

"Cool, well now you have mine. We should grab a drink sometime?"

"Yeah, absolutely." I'd already begun walking away, so I turned to say over my shoulder. "Give me a shout."

I was offered the job at Page & Plant by the owner, Eddie; short, sharply dressed, and barely ever around. He had an assistant manager called Seve who ran the place and seemed to like me straight away, and Abbie who deputised for Seve when she wasn't at Uni. It was a small trendy little 'bistro with books' at the end of Cooke Street, and they'd said they could be super flexible with hours – everyone except Seve was a student. I wasn't sure if Finn had had anything to do with my getting the job, but the day after I got it, he'd texted to invite me out for a 'congratulatory drink.'

I'd said no, mainly because I'd been trying to finish up a paper due that week, but also partly because I was afraid. Afraid of Finn knowing about Cas, probably. Of him knowing how stupid I'd been, of him confirming all the things about Caspien I should have known.

A part of me wondered if Finn might be able to offer some new perspective on things. I didn't think he knew Cas well, but I thought he may still have had some unique insight that would help me make sense of things. Who Cas was. Why he'd done it. At the time, the whys of it all were more important than anything else.

I'd tried to talk to Gideon. I'd spent months after Cas left trying to get Gideon to help me understand. But Gideon seemed to want me to know only three things: how inevitable all of this was, how getting our hearts broken was intrinsic to building character, and how well Caspien was doing in Boston without me.

He was never cruel in his delivery of this imparted wisdom, but neither did he take any care to spare my feelings. (*Oh, they're spending Christmas in the Alps! They've gotten a cat! A Siberian Forest! Dreadfully fluffy! Did you see Xavier's latest case? The actress who's suing the film studio – apparently, it's cut and dry. He'll make millions from it.*)

He'd say these things as though they were friends of mine who'd moved away and I'd normally offer one-word answers until I couldn't take anymore and say something like: "Can we stop talking about them, Gideon, please?" To which he'd reply, gasping, "Oh, goodness, yes, of course, how indelicate of me."

I hadn't responded yet to his last email. I'd only glanced over it: he'd wished me a happy birthday and told me that there was a card and small gift on the way to Oxford for me, described some minor restoration work he was having done to the first floor of the house, and then, to part, a few lines informing me that Cas had passed some important exam at Lervairè with flying colours.

I knew for all Gideon's talk, that Cas rarely called or wrote to him. The fact was a lot of these updates came via Blackwell himself, and this hurt Gideon. But still, he sounded proud of Cas's achievements.

And I was proud too until I realised I had no right to be anything of the sort.

The following Friday, Finn invited me out again for a drink. He was with some people from Pembroke – Finn was studying Environmental Research there – and his housemate, Alex. Bast was having dinner with family who were in London and who'd travelled up to see him. Irish Conn was ill, and Nika had a late paper due.

Ultimately, I said yes because I needed to get drunk, and I didn't like the idea of doing it alone. In the end, I didn't reply to his text; I just searched the bar he'd told me to meet him in – a wine bar on Little Clarendon Street – threw on my nicest shirt, dragged my fingers through my hair, and pulled my dorm door closed behind me. Finn was in a loud group seated right at the back of Marcello's, four girls and three guys, including him. As I did the numbers, I wondered if this was why he was so keen for me to come. He was one guy short.

Finn was deep in conversation with a tall Asian guy who looked like he'd stepped out of a magazine. Skin polished like glass, black horn-rimmed glasses, and wearing a long Burberry overcoat.

A glance around the others settled me a little. They looked normal. Like students, at least. I stood like a dick for a few minutes wondering the smoothest way to introduce myself when Finn looked up.

His face lit up, and he waved me over.

"Alcotttttt! You made it!" He shouted as though I'd dragged myself away from something critical to be here and as though Alcotttttt were a nickname he'd called me since forever. Which, as the others turned to inspect me, suspicious and unimpressed, I appreciated.

"Guys, this is Jude, he's a friend. Shift over, Pete." He pointed at a guy who looked to be about 6 ft 8 sitting down.

I slid in next to Pete, who lifted his chin in greeting. Finlay went around the table, telling me everyone's names – names that all seemed to end in 'Y's: Maisy, Poppy, Olly, Mary, and Cally. He introduced the guy next to him as Alex, the housemate, who was even more intimidating from this angle, and added my order to the next round Olly was standing to go get.

A half hour or so later of nodding politely and drinking too quickly, I was at the bar when I felt someone squeeze into the space next to me.

"Stick it on our tab," Finn said as the server placed a pint of Guinness down in front of me. "And two shots of tequila."

I groaned. "This is not going to end well."

"We've not even started yet." Finlay grinned. "So, you ever hear from our favourite cuntiest cousin these days?"

My entire body went stiff, and I kept my eye on my pint. I'd been expecting it, obviously, but had been momentarily distracted by the glittering newness of strangers.

"He's not *my* cousin," I said lightly.

"No, no, he isn't," said Finn. "Bet you'd still fuck him if he were though."

My head whipped around, eyes widening.

Finn was smiling mischievously. "Oh, come on. I saw the way you looked at him." He made a weird eye rolling face. *Everything you feel is in your eyes.*

Heat crept up my neck.

"So, did you know about him and Blackwell?" He lifted his own drink and took a gulp. "You ever see him about? Apparently, it was all very quick."

Caspien's back arched, the dark gold tan of Xavier's hand. A sharp pain in my chest.

I lifted the small golden glass of tequila the server had just put down and knocked it back in one.

My throat burned hot and resentful. I avoided directly answering the question. "Guess it was pretty obvious now I look back."

"Fucking Cas." Finn laughed. He was a little drunk, his cheeks pink and eyes heavy from alcohol. "I mean, what does a guy like Blackwell – hot, smart and successful – see in that little prick, seriously? Like okay, I get that he's some loaded tragic orphan – although, maybe his dad is out there somewhere, who knows – but it's not as if Blackwell's into him for the money."

Finn had no idea at this point that I also had a 'tragic orphan thing' going on.

"And I get that he's got the perfect bone structure and the moody supermodel thing." He shook his head. "But he's just a truly awful person, you know? I hated him my entire life. Probably still do. I don't know."

"Why'd you go to his birthday then?" I asked. "If you hated him?"

"Well, Gideon invited me."

"And what about Gideon?" I asked.

Finn looked confused by my question. "What do you mean?"

"Just that, well, he brought Cas up. If Cas is this truly awful person, then maybe part of that is Gideon's fault?"

I felt a little guilty saying it. I liked Gideon. I wasn't sure I trusted him, but I liked him insofar as he'd been there for me before and just after Cas tore out my heart and disappeared from my life. But I saw suddenly a moment of opportunity to learn more about the two spectres who haunted Deveraux House. I wasn't sure what I was trying to find out about Gideon, but it was novel to speak to someone about them who wasn't Luke. Someone who might be able to offer me some small sliver of *why*.

I ordered two more shots while Finn pondered an answer to my question.

"Well, Cas spent his life in boarding schools," he began. "And those places are a hotbed of fuckery. So I'm not sure Gideon really brought him up so much as dealt with the legalities of his existence, you know? Signed the appropriate paperwork, made sure he didn't murder anyone." Here, he gave me a pointed look. "Took him for dental check-ups, made sure he ate and drank, and was generally healthy. Life admin, that sort of thing. We all know Gideon should never have been landed with a kid, not with his issues. My parents say he's never been quite right and then there was the stuff with Seraphina and the guy who fucked him over. I don't really know much about any of it as it was before my time, but it was messy." Finn seemed to visibly shudder.

"Does anyone know anything about Cas's dad?" It felt as though I was stepping into forbidden territory. I could imagine Cas's outrage at the question even in his absence. At my daring to ask it.

Finn looked at me, flushed face turning thoughtful. "Someone does. Gideon probably. But he's been a hot mess for years."

"What happened with him and the guy?" I had Gideon's version, but I wanted Finn's.

"The way I heard it, he fell hard for someone when he was in his twenties. This guy stole a fortune from him and disappeared, and he had to go back to his father with his tail between his legs and beg forgiveness. He's never gotten over it. Imagine a woman ditched at the altar and the guy running off with her money; that's Gideon," Finn said with a note of derision. It was the only time I ever saw something cruel in him.

Something protective flared up inside me. Some kind of empathy for the broken-hearted. For those of us who could never quite get over that first deep break. I understood it painfully well. Perhaps it was why Gideon and I had bonded as we had these last months.

"I'm guessing you've never had your heart broken then." I glared at him. "Must be nice."

Finn seemed to sober a little, understanding seeping into his eyes.

"Shit," he said. "Fucking Caspien. Sorry, man."

I nodded and knocked back my tequila.

"Thank fuck he isn't my type," Finn groaned as he ordered another two.

"He's your cousin?"

"Listen, we're descended from royalty. Do you think a little thing like a familial relationship can hold us back?"

I couldn't help the laugh that barked out of my throat. Finn laughed too, and the mood immediately became lighter.

"Well, yeah, thank god he's not your type then, I guess," I said after the laughter faded.

He picked up his glass and shot me a very specific kind of look, one that could have meant all manner of things, really, but just in case I wasn't sure, he said: "You *are* though."

THREE

Hilary term started in the last days of a bleak and cold April. I had three papers due that week. I'd worked on them through Easter break while picking up extra shifts at P&P. (I'd again managed to avoid going home to Deveraux) and felt confident as I submitted one early Monday afternoon to Professor Alexander.

I'd always enjoyed writing academic essays. It used a different part of my brain from the creative stuff, even if there was still an element of the creative about it. I enjoyed reading, and so it felt like a natural extension of that to write about the subjects, books, and theories I liked reading about.

The best thing about Oxford so far was the freedom I felt being able to read and write and learn about things that interested me as opposed to being told by a decades-old school curriculum. The scope of the curriculum here was infinite. It stretched from Beowulf to Dickens to Hemingway to Roth, and for the most part, allowed me to move in any direction through the history of English Literature that I wanted based on my own curiosities. The work wasn't hard, not yet at least, but what was harder to adjust to was the fact that everyone here was smart.

I wasn't the smartest student in class anymore; I was slightly above average at best and middling at worst. But there was some comfort to be found in that. It allowed me to keep my head down, listen, and learn. I didn't have to lead discussions like I did back home. I didn't have to impress anyone. I didn't have form that I had to maintain. Each paper I submitted was a new chance to improve and show progress.

Oxford was a beautiful setting in which to learn. To sit and read some of the greatest works of literature, poetry, and prose ever written in a city steeped in what was a near-mythological wealth of history was a privilege. Some of the greatest minds that had ever existed had studied here, and I was lucky I got to do the same.

I thought about the nameless donor a few times a day. Though he'd still never confirmed it, Gideon was the form they often took in my head. Now that Cas was thousands of miles away and out of his life, and mine, I couldn't understand why, if it was him, he couldn't just tell me so. I'd mention my gratitude to the benefactor often so that if it was him, then he'd know.

Since I'd not been back to Jersey since starting university, we continued to exchange emails – Gideon didn't text – where he'd ask me to tell him in extreme detail about my life here. He'd loved studying here. Had said this was where he was his happiest. Occasionally they invited old cohort's back for ceremonials and he never missed a single one. I wondered if this was where he'd met the person who broke his heart, though I was always a little too scared to ask him that.

He'd still feed me tidbits of news about Caspien and Xavier, though it was far easier to skip over these when they were written down.

I was in the King's Arms on a Wednesday night with Nikita and

Irish Conn when Finn texted to invite me for a drink. I'd seen him a couple more times since our first drunken night in the wine bar, where he'd told me I was his type, though he'd never made any kind of move on me, and I still hadn't decided if I wanted him to.

Me:

I'm in the Kings with a couple of friends. Come in.

He didn't respond, so I wasn't sure if he would, but twenty minutes later, he strolled through the door, completely unfazed by the strangers who glared at him suspiciously as he approached.

"Guys, this is Finn," I said by way of introduction. "I know him from back home."

This settled them. Nika grabbed a stool and sat it down between himself and me and pointed at it. Then he offered to buy him a drink.

"I'll get these," Finn said. "What's everyone on?"

When he returned to the table with their drinks, plus a shot each, any lingering doubt about him vanished. It was apparently that easy to win over my two friends. Bast had a late shift at the bike shop but was due to come later.

Finn was easy to like. He didn't dominate the conversation, was interested in other people's stories more than he liked telling his own, and was generous with his debit card. He paid for another two rounds before Bast showed up, by which time we were all amiably drunk.

I was at the bar getting my first round since I'd got here when Bast sidled in beside me.

"Yes. He definitely wants to fuck you," said Bast. We'd talked about Finn before, about how I wasn't sure if he was into me in a sexual way or if he was just a naturally flirty person. "Or, he wants you to fuck him. Whichever way you prefer."

I laughed a little nervously. There'd been no one since the drunken encounter on my birthday, which I didn't like thinking about. Not to mention, I had no clue which way I preferred. Was I a bottom or a top? Finn would be the first guy I'd ever properly been with, and I felt drunk enough to find out. Drunk enough to forget how Cas was supposed to be the first. The only.

When the end of the night came, Finn walked back with us. Bast was the one to invite him up, the offer of some beer in his room that we were all welcome to share. In Bast's room, Finn sat close to me, warm thigh pressed against mine, eyes catching mine whenever I looked at him.

He *was* good-looking. Not in the same way Cas had been, but no one was good-looking in quite the same way he was – his other-worldly beauty was almost frightening, but Finn was attractive in more than looks. He was one of those people who didn't seem to carry an ounce of anxiety inside him, had an easy manner and was completely comfortable in his own skin. He reminded me a little of Alfie. Which made me realise that it came from a place of privilege, of never really wanting for anything. Or rather, never being deprived of anything.

Finn was real, solid, and when he smiled at me, there was no artifice in it.

He found me coming out of the bathroom, the one down the hall on the first floor shared by half the dorms. He was leaning casually against the wall as I stepped out into the hall, his legs crossed at the ankles, hands in his pockets.

He gave me an easy smile. "Your friends are cool."

I moved to lean on the wall opposite. "Yeah, they are."

He seemed to be considering something, then said, "So, I've been dropping hints since the day outside the Bodleian that I'm into you. I'm just not sure if you're picking them up. So I thought I'd just ask."

Warmth rippled across my chest and down. Life flooding into the cold parts of my body.

I liked how it felt.

"Was that a question?" I asked.

Finn laughed a little. "No, I guess technically it wasn't." His eyes, still sparkling, turned more determined, and he pushed off the wall and came toward me. When he was close enough that I could smell his shower gel, I straightened up and pressed myself back against the wall. Finn looked at my mouth and then leaned in and kissed me. It wasn't hard, but it was determined. There was no subtlety in it; it was the sort of kiss that left no doubt about what he wanted. I couldn't say now whether I kissed him back, or if I simply allowed him to kiss me.

He was warm, firm, and slightly taller than me, making me feel somewhat cocooned. Did that mean I'd be under him? That he'd be the one fucking me? Was that how it worked? I was sure suddenly that I didn't want that. To be fucked.

I hadn't known what I was before, but it seemed now I knew what I wasn't.

When he pulled back, he met my eye directly and said, "That was, though."

"I'm not a bottom," I blurted. "I mean, I've never...I don't want to do that." I felt embarrassed, unqualified, and very young as the words left my mouth, and when Finn laughed I wanted a void to open up beneath my feet and swallow me into it. But his eyes were kind.

"I'm vers. But we can do whatever you want, Jude. Fuck, I wasn't even expecting we'd fuck tonight."

"Oh," I said, still embarrassed.

"I'd actually really like to suck your dick," Finn said. "If you'll let me."

I could only manage some version of a nod.

My dorm was as I left it earlier that day. Empty glasses by the bed – a habit I've still not grown out of – dirty clothes strewn across the carpet, textbooks open on the desk on the pages I'd last been reading. My laptop was on the unmade bed where I'd been watching a Belgian film at lunchtime. I flitted about scooping things up and reordering things while Finn sat at the desk chair, relaxed but rapt, watching me.

"I don't give a shit about your room, Jude," he said at last.

"Eh, oh, I know, but still."

He waited silently for a few moments while I continued before he lost patience and stood. He took the empty glass from my hand

and set it down on the desk, and then tugged me gently across the room to my bed. Nudging me to sit on the edge of it, he moved to settle between my legs and reached for the button of my jeans. His face was open and soft, a small fire of desire in his eyes that sparked something to life inside me.

"You have a really nice dick," he said as he stared at it, hand slotting around its base. He leaned in and sucked it into his mouth without any further commentary.

I'd had three people suck my dick at this point in my life. (The girl I'd woken up next to on my birthday didn't count, mainly as I couldn't remember whether she did.) Each of them had distinctly different techniques. Finn's, I decided, was the most enthusiastic. He seemed to enjoy it more than Ellie had, more than even Caspien had – though Cas's was by far the most skilful. Just like when he'd kissed me in the hallway, Finn was determined in this too, and so I came shockingly quick.

He swallowed my climax with the sorts of sounds that made me think of a particularly tasty meal. I'd fallen back onto the bed, and when he was finished, Finn came to lie on his back next to me.

When my mind cleared and the fog of climax had lifted, I said languidly, "That was nice, thanks."

He laughed. "Fuck, that's the most depressing compliment I've ever gotten." He punched me lightly on the shoulder.

I laughed back. "No, I mean, it was great. Really good. I enjoyed it a lot."

"Stop talking, Jude."

I was silent for a minute or so. "You want me to return the favour?"

"I actually don't," he said.

I twisted my head to look at him, but he was still all easy smiles and soft eyes.

"I meant, I don't need you to. I get so fucking turned on when I'm sucking dick." He gestured at his body. The zip of his jeans was down and his cock lay soft and spent outside of it.

"Hot," I smiled.

"Yeah, you are."

I punched him on the shoulder and we laughed again. It felt nice. Comfortable and easy.

We went back to Bast's party a short while after, still laughing about something stupid. We sat a little closer together, caught each other's eye a little more often, and brought each other a drink when one of us went to the box of beer on the window sill.

It set the tone for how it would be between us: comfortable and easy. We were mainly friends, but every now and then, need would flare up between us and we'd tug each other into empty rooms at parties to get each other off with our hands or our mouths.

Who instigated it would vary, but it would almost always lead to Finn on his knees with his eyes closed in bliss and his fist around his cock as he swallowed mine and we both tried not to make too much noise. Not that it mattered. Everyone knew. It was as open a secret as there was. I knew everyone was well aware of what we'd been doing when we'd come back into the room together, flushed and thirsty.

Sex, the full kind, never really came up. Or at least, that's how it felt to me. We were attracted to each other, but after sating our desires with our mouths or hands, the rush of lust would fade, and we'd leave these encounters satisfied. I didn't know if Finn slept with other people – we never talked about it – but it wouldn't have bothered me if he was. What I had with Finn, casual and easy and comfortable, was more than enough.

My heart wasn't ready or willing to take on anything else. Caspien's memory was too big, too powerful, too all-consuming for there to be room for anything else. He was a ghost, and what I was living through then was a haunting. When I closed my eyes, and often too when I was awake, I could still feel his lips on mine and the touch of his breath on my neck.

One Sunday afternoon, I was in Milner's Books, and a girl passed me who reminded me so much of him that it ached. I couldn't understand what it was because her hair was dark, almost black, her eyes round and brown.

But after following her for a little while around the store, I understood what it was. It was the line of her neck that led up to her delicate girlish ears, and the way she held her head. Eventually, she caught my eye and smiled. Surprisingly, I hadn't creeped her out.

For a second, I thought about giving her my number, asking her out for a drink. But then I remembered Ellie, and how her eyes would look like Ellie's did that day when I ended it. When Cas came back into my life, I didn't want there to be someone else I would have to hurt or leave, so I could have him.

I smiled back, then turned and hurried out of the shop and back to my dorm. I bought a bottle of vodka on the way and drank it with a stolen carton of orange juice from the common kitchen I promised to replace the following day.

When I think back now, I know that part of what stopped me crossing that line with Finn was that I didn't feel confident yet in my own sexuality. I didn't understand it enough to know what to do with it. There hadn't yet been a need for me to define myself as bi or gay or anything else. I'd slept with girls, but I knew that didn't mean I was straight. I'd loved a boy, and yet somehow I knew that didn't mean I was gay.

Had someone asked me outright, I'm sure I'd have been able to come up with an answer, but I was still uncertain enough that it prevented me from taking things to that next level with Finn.

Though I was unsure if I wanted to fuck him, I was certain I didn't want him to fuck me. And I didn't know whether that was to do with orientation or preference or even Finn himself.

So, it was a scab that I left alone. We played around with each other, easily and indefinably, but always respectfully. No definitions, no rules, and no expectations.

And this worked perfectly, up until it didn't.

FOUR

To:	caspienthe_ghost@gmail.com
From:	Jalcott.mag@ox.ac.uk

Dear Cas,

I'm going home tomorrow. Home to Jersey. Home to Deveraux. And I'm terrified.

Did you know I haven't been home since I left for Oxford? I'm not sure how you would know. Maybe Gideon tells you some things about me — I admit that some-times I tell him things I hope he'll pass on to you. Even if it isn't true. (I absolutely love it here, I'm doing really well in all my classes,

I've been seeing someone).

My last exam was yesterday and I feel pretty positive. Even if it did feel weird sitting there in that stupid outfit. Oxford has all these strange, ancient traditions that don't make sense anymore but everyone gets really excited about. The term names is just one of them, but I'm used to that now. The point of it is to make the students here feel like they're members of some secret club that only the very clever or very rich get to be a part of.

Though since I'm neither, I think it's all a bit pointless. But I think the exams went well. I actually think I'm a person who is just good at exams. How I was able to get the grades I did in my A's when I was still mourning you, I'll never know. But I did. And I'm mourning you a little less these days, so I guess we'll see....

I'm also waiting to find out where I'll be staying next year since they reallocate dorms for second years. I'll miss sharing the dorm with Bast and Conn and Nika — though they're all moving as well — but somewhere new might be fun, too.

So, I'm writing this at my desk, on my last night in this place. I won't miss the early morning bin collection.

I'm scared of seeing Deveraux again after so long. I'm scared about how empty I'm going to feel when I get there, how alone and sad it will feel again without you. It's different feeling those things here: a lot of people at Oxford are alone and sad. More than I think the University's Mental Health Committee would care to admit.

I want to go to the birdwatchers hut at least once,

I think. I'll let you know if I do. Sometimes I wonder why I'm not angrier at you. I mean, I am angry at you, really angry. But, I don't know, I think mainly I'm just sad. Mainly, I just miss you. I miss you all the time. I keep waiting to feel angry, and maybe if I saw you I would be angry with you. I don't know. I think that I'd just want to hold you, touch you, kiss you.

Fuck, I miss you so much, Cas.

Love,

Jude

The last day of term was 21st June, almost two years and a month to the day Caspien left me, and I could avoid it no longer. I had to go home. The halls were deep cleaned over the summer, and since I wouldn't be returning to my single room on the second floor, I had to pack everything into two large boxes and a suitcase before I left. I put both into the back of my car and began the just under two-hour journey to the ferry at Portsmouth.

I'd decided to take the car home and leave it there for the coming year. I'd need it to get around the island, and I'd barely used it since I got here as everywhere was walkable, I was really just paying the permit for the privilege of being able to look at it parked in the car park at the dorm.

I had almost three months off. Three months at home. I felt ill with dread at the prospect. Last summer had been awful, and I'd been little more than a walking zombie the last school year; I'd ignored almost every invite Alfie and Josh had given me, no matter what it was, and never bothered going to prom.

Since I'd been in Oxford, I'd exchanged all of four texts and a few

Instagram messages with Alfie. Only one with Josh since September. Josh, I knew, was currently in France playing for a rugby team I couldn't recall the name of.

In any case, I was sure Alfie would want nothing to do with me if I did reach out when I got home. And I wouldn't have blamed him.

I'd considered hanging out in Portsmouth for the weekend before catching the ferry on Monday morning, but the hotel prices were insane, and when I got there and saw how packed the beach and every café and bar were, I was glad I hadn't.

If I was looking forward to anything about going home, it was the idea of speaking very little to very few people. I planned to sleep a lot, read a lot, and maybe take a few solitary drives to the beach if the weather held up.

It's a ridiculously long journey across the channel on the ferry. I slept some, ate an overpriced sandwich, finished a book, and slept a little more. It was 7:30 p.m. when I drove off the boat and onto the island. Around 8:00 p.m. when I reached the gates of Deveraux. Luke came bounding out of the cottage the moment I pulled into the driveway, face bright and happy as a puppy, practically hauling me out of the driver's seat and into a hug I hadn't known I'd needed.

"Missed you, Judey," he said, his voice sounding oddly vulnerable.

"Yeah, me too. Sorry it's been ages."

"Hey, you're busy with uni, we get it. You're here now," he said, releasing me. "Got any bags?"

"One and a suitcase. Some boxes in the back seat." I grabbed my rucksack from the passenger seat while Luke lifted out the boxes. Beth was standing, arms folded, at the front door. She looked happy to see me too, I thought, opening her arms wide and pulling me into a hug.

"Good to see you. Did you eat yet?"

I shook my head. "Shitty sandwich on the boat."

"There's curry," she said and suddenly I could smell it, homely and fragrant.

My mouth watered with want. "Sounds amazing, thanks."

She nodded and wandered down the hall to the kitchen.

Luke followed me upstairs, dutifully carrying my boxes and setting them down in the corner. My room was exactly as I had left it, though with a new bed set I hadn't seen before and there was a model plane half built on my desk.

I glanced at Luke and raised an eyebrow.

"Harry bought it for me for my birthday," he explained. "Been really into it, actually."

"Makes sense." Luke was exceptional with anything that required the use of his hands. A lot like Cas had been, in fact.

"You need the desk, though? For your uni work?"

"Nah, it's fine. I don't have too much on, just some books to read and films to watch. A single paper if I want to get ahead of myself, but I can use the Library at the big house."

He nodded, gaze turning thoughtful. "I know Gideon is looking forward to seeing you. Saw him this morning."

"Yeah? I'll pop up and see him tomorrow or Tuesday." It felt like something I had to fortify myself against, not him exactly, but what he might tell me about Cas.

I saw Luke hesitate a moment, consider something, and then, as though my thoughts were as open to him as they were to me, he said, "You ever hear from Cas at all?"

"No," I said. "Never."

Luke's mouth turned down on one side, commiserating. I thought he would say something else because he stood there with that sad look on his face for a few moments before he just nodded.

"I'll let you get settled. See you downstairs, buddy," he said, closing the door.

As soon as he was gone, I fell back onto my bed and stared at the familiar crack on the ceiling.

I slept surprisingly well that night and woke the following morning feeling fresh and rested. It was one of those bright white summer days the island was famous for, sparkling with light and heat but with the faintest of breezes coming in from the channel.

I drank a glass of water and ate some cereal at the back door while staring at the lake.

I remembered the day I'd fallen in, and I wondered what I'd do if he came riding up towards the cottage like he had that day. What would it be like to see him again? I could bear it if I knew he thought about me sometimes. If he stood eating breakfast thinking about me for even a moment, then I could bear it, I thought.

By the time I came out of the shower, Luke and Beth were awake and in the kitchen, each making individual breakfasts by the look of it. It's obvious to me now what was months away from happening then, but at the time, I was too self-absorbed, too completely wrapped up in my own heartbreak to notice anyone else's.

"I'm going to take a walk around the estate," I told them without waiting for their response.

I grabbed a book and my sunglasses and headed outside, taking the path leading me towards the birdwatcher's hut and away from the big house. I'd avoided it since that day, but as I'd lain awake the previous night, I'd decided I would face it today. Maybe there was some healing or closure to be found there. Something that would make everything with Cas make sense, finally. Even if it was to understand that there was nothing to make sense of. Even if it was to accept the fact that he'd been with me purely as a distraction. Purely to prevent me from focusing on Blackwell. I needed to accept that. I needed to move on. It was enough now.

I'd been moping over him for two years, drinking when my feelings got too much to handle, and refusing to give myself over to the possibility of being with anyone else. I'd wanted to become something of an equal to Cas so if we ever met again, he wouldn't see that weak, stupid boy I'd been then, and what had I done so far? I'd been accepted to Oxford, sure. I'd made it through a single year.

But who was I? What was I?

I was certain I would have nothing to impress Cas with if he had walked back into my life right then. I hadn't reached the hut, but maybe I didn't need to go there at all. There was nothing there but bad memories, and I had enough of them living in my head.

I stopped walking, pulled out my phone and shot off a text to

Alfie to tell him I was home if he fancied catching up. Then I turned and walked in the opposite direction.

I arranged to meet Alfie in a sports bar in town. Beth had offered to drop me off on her way to meet a friend for dinner. He was already there when I arrived and had snagged a pool table beneath a large screen showing an England versus Sweden friendly that no one was really paying attention to. He greeted me with a big friendly smile, didn't mention how many of his texts I'd ignored, and offered to get the first round of beers. Josh was still in France so it was just the two of us.

"So, how's Oxford?" he asked after he'd broke.

"Yeah, it's tough. But kinda cool too, you know? Still feel like an outsider, but next term should be better." I missed my shot and lifted my beer. I was pretty terrible at pool, and Alfie knew it, though he still said 'bad luck' every time I missed.

"Exams? You get them at the end of first year?"

I nodded, "They went okay, I think. Won't find out until end of next month, though. Then resits if I've messed up."

"You'll be good, mate – you've always smashed exams."

"Hope so, hope so. Cannot be arsed with resits."

He talked about his business development and management course, which he was doing part-time while working with his dad, and told me that he and Georgia were still going strong. She was doing an internship at the States Assembly of Jersey, working in the Lieutenant Governor's office.

After he beat me at all three rounds of pool, we got a table near the bar and carried on talking. It was nice. I almost felt like my old self again, the Jude before Caspien, nights before I had to get wasted in order to sleep.

"So, what are the girls like at Oxford?" Alfie asked, eyes keen.

I'd had enough to drink that the idea of telling him I liked guys too didn't feel too terrifying. But he hadn't asked that, so I figured I'd keep it to myself.

"Yeah, they're alright." I nodded. After pondering it a moment, I said, "I went home with this girl on my birthday though and I swear, Alf, I can't even remember her name." This made him laugh, though it still didn't feel very funny to me.

"You ever hear from Ellie?" he asked.

"No," I said, and he left it there with a grim nod.

We parted ways at closing time with promises to stay in touch. I apologised for being shit at replying to texts and swore to be better, but Alfie waved it off and said we'd catch up at Christmas or when I was next home. I booked an Uber and waited for it on the corner where the main road out of St. Aubin met the pier.

On Sundays, they held a vintage market there, and I thought I might pop down for a bit the following day. For the first time in a year, I felt a looseness spiralling through me. That weightlessness that came from hope and possibility, from knowing that good things lay ahead, from knowing that I *could* be happy again if I wanted. I'd had my heart broken badly, and for a while, I'd limped along, but today, I'd realised how far I'd come from the person I'd been the day in the birdwatcher's hut.

I'd *been* healing, even if it hadn't felt obvious to me. I was stronger now than I was before Caspien. I'd suffered, I was battle-scarred, but I'd survived.

I slept better that night than I had in months.

FIVE

I went to see Gideon on Monday. He was upstairs, clearing out some of the unused rooms for the restorers coming in to do some work. As I went to find him, I'd paused outside Caspien's bedroom door, frozen as if in time, wondering what would have happened had I not opened it that day.

The plan was for you to come over this evening, Jude.

What had his plan been exactly? To break my heart in the library? To bring Blackwell out like a surprise guest star in what I'd believed to be our love story? Would that have made it easier? It would have been equally as bad. Maybe even worse.

I longed to open the door, see how he'd left his room, and look for clues about whether he ever planned to return.

"You can go in if you like," Gideon said gently. I turned to see him coming toward me.

I moved away from the door and shook my head. "I thought I heard something inside." The lie wasn't a good one, and I could tell Gideon didn't buy it. "How's it going?" I asked him, forcing myself to smile.

"Good to see you, Jude," Gideon said, pulling me into a hug. He was dressed down, a look I'd never seen on him before: navy trousers and a cream shirt, both linen and dust-coated. Dust was in his hair, and he was wearing a pair of black round-framed glasses. He looked loose and relaxed, handsome even.

"Can I help? Elspeth said you're clearing out?"

"You don't have anything better to do?" he asked, eyebrow arched. "It's summer. Surely there's frolicking or partying or drinking to be done?"

I shrugged. "No frolicking planned for today."

We worked at stripping sheets from covered furniture and combing through old tall boys, armoires, and sideboards. One of the rooms upstairs had been his father's study and looked to have been closed off for decades. There were old letters, newspaper clippings, ballot papers, political documents. Gideon was technically a Marquess, having inherited the title from his father, but both his grandfather and father had been life peers too, and we found old voting records, law amendments, and MP correspondence. Gideon had a story about almost each piece of paper I showed him, and he kept a lot of the yellowing pages I came across ("They'll be worth something to someone, Jude!"), directing me to place them in one of three large boxes he'd labelled: 'Correspondence', 'Lords', and 'Deveraux House'.

The furniture was all antique, though not all of the same vintage; some looked as though it were over a hundred years old, others more modern art-deco pieces, but all of it looked like it would fetch a fortune at auction. Of course, I knew Gideon was rich, but

I thought the value of the house and its contents had to be tens of millions alone.

After a couple of hours, he stood up, dusted off his trousers, and announced he was peckish.

"Ask if Elspeth will bring our lunch out to the eastern pavilion, will you?" Gideon asked as we reached the bottom of the stairs. "It's much too hot to eat indoors."

"Sure." I wandered off in the direction of the kitchen as he went towards the red sitting room. After using the bathroom, I went down the backstairs to the kitchen, surprised to see Luke sitting at the large dining table with a delicious-looking sandwich in front of him. He was talking about something related to squirrels as far as I could tell. Elspeth was sitting opposite, head resting on her hand and a soft, warm look on her face as he spoke.

I took a moment to study her. Until then, I'd never thought of her outside her role as Gideon's housekeeper, but she was pretty, if a little plain. A kind manner, genuine smile and a sweet-sounding voice. There were some similarities between her and my sister, I noticed then. The colouring; that pale hue that usually came with red hair and a dusting of freckles. Except where my sister was prone to scowling, Elspeth was always smiling. Friendly and open, where my sister could be standoffish and reserved. I tried to guess her age, and put her at maybe a few years older than Luke if that, though she looked younger now.

The smile Elspeth was giving Luke at that moment was not one I'd ever seen on her before. Smiling at him indulgently as he ate the sandwich she'd no doubt made for him. It made me want to step back out of the room and leave them alone.

But I stepped fully into the room and said, as loudly as I could, "Well, that sandwich looks like a bit of me."

Elspeth sat up straight, as though she'd been caught out. Luke just smiled his normal smile at me and took a huge bite of the sandwich before rolling his eyes in pleasure.

"I can make you one, Jude, sweetheart. You want cheese on?" She was standing now.

"Yes, please. Gideon's going to have his on the patio. I'll take it out."

I slid into Elspeth's seat and reached across to snatch a crisp from Luke's plate. There was nothing guilty in my uncle's face, nothing to suggest I'd walked in on anything I shouldn't have. So I pushed it from my mind. If there was anything to be seen, then it was that Elspeth had a crush on Luke. Which wasn't completely out of the question. Luke was what women considered earthy and handsome: ruddy-cheeked and sparkling eyes. Everyone liked Luke: women, men, old, young. Even Caspien had liked Luke, and he loathed almost everyone.

For the next few days, I helped Gideon clear out the suite of rooms on the first floor; it was dusty, boring work, but Gideon was talkative and funny, and we'd take breaks and eat delicious lunches made by Elspeth on the patio.

At the end of the week, he was going to Italy; he had business just outside of Florence, and I was already wondering what I would do for the rest of the summer. I had some money in the bank from the benefactor and P&P and I thought about taking the ferry to St. Malo and maybe staying there a few days on my own, but I knew it could be extremely busy this time of year and the thought of pushing my way through crowds of sweat-licked people wasn't hugely appealing. I decided I'd just get through some of the books on my TBR, go on a hike around the cliff walk, cycle over to Sorel, maybe meet up with Alfie again.

It was Thursday, the day before Gideon was due to leave for Italy, and he was talking about the hotel he would be staying at. It was an old house that had once belonged to the Borgias. I'd not been paying particular attention beyond this, slouched back on the seat with my eyes closed and enjoying the heat of the sun on my face. I was feeling content. Happy almost. The sadness of last summer like a fading memory.

Perhaps this was what made him say it.

"… before Thursday when Caspien and Xavier are due to arrive."

My eyes sprung open under my sunglasses, and I sat up too

quickly.

"You're seeing Cas? In Florence?"

Gideon nodded, taking a sip of his white wine. "Mm, they're in Venice right now; dreadful place. But they are travelling and will be in San Marino when I am in Florence, and they wish to come and meet me there." He was watching me carefully.

I was glad of my sunglasses, though I'm sure he could see my face had drained of colour. There'd been no mention of Cas or Xavier this entire week while we'd been clearing out. Now, the sound of his name and the image of them travelling across Italy together and in love made the rent across my heart open up. That newly healed fissure was pulling apart again, painful and raw.

"I do hate that you're still fighting," Gideon said gently, as though somehow that's what this was.

"That's not..." I said, a little stunned. "We're not *fighting*, Gideon?"

He waved that off, dismissive "Oh, you know what I mean. I wish you were still friends. It was so nice having you around when Cas was home, having you both at the house, having you playing toge—"

I stood abruptly, chair scraping across the concrete angrily. "We were never fucking *friends*, Gideon."

He flinched, startled by my outburst. I'd never raised my voice to him. Never swore, or lost my temper with him, despite what I'm sure now was his every attempt to get me to.

"We were never friends," I said again, calmer. "That's not what we were. I was some way for him to pass the time, that's all. Something he could play with until Blackwell could whisk him away to that comfortably luxurious life in the States."

"Jude, I think that maybe if you spoke to him you'd see that—" Gideon began, placatingly.

"No." I cut him off. "Don't. I don't want to hear it, Gideon. I don't want to hear any more words of wisdom about broken hearts or theories about what it is Cas actually wants and needs. What I want is to pretend he doesn't fucking exist. What I want is to wake up in the morning and forget that he's out there living a life with someone else." I was saying too much. It was dangerous to say this much. "Do you have any idea what that feels like? Knowing that? Knowing that while I'm here, alone, looking at all the places he used to exist in, he's just...off somewhere else with someone else? While I struggle to figure out who the fuck I am now and what I'm supposed to want now, he's thriving and happy and *comfortable*." I sneered the last word. "So please stop telling me about where they are or what they're doing or how perfect their fucking life is, Gideon, because I don't want to know. It's enough. This," I hit my own chest with a soft fist. "What he left behind is enough, okay?"

I left him staring after me as I stormed out and back to the cottage.

Friday, Beth was out for the night, so Luke and I cooked and ate alone. While he tried to make small talk, I grunted one-word answers and barely looked up from my plate. After dinner, I offered to do the dishes, but he waved me off and told me to take a beer outside to the garden, saying he'd come out when he was finished.

When he came out a short while later, he brought me another. He took a seat next to me on the outdoor sofa, got comfy, and held out his bottle for me to knock mine against.

"Really nice to have you back home, Judey," he said, taking a large gulp.

"Is it?" I was feeling like the worst sort of company. Yesterday's stand-off with Gideon and the quick resurgence of my self-pitying attitude could not have been easy for Luke to deal with, especially as he and Beth had also had a silly argument this morning – the cause of what I didn't know – which had resulted in the slamming of the front and car doors just after 8 a.m.

But still, he sounded genuine when he said it.

"Sure it is," he sighed. "House feels empty these days."

I thought about how there was supposed to have been a baby running around and how Luke might feel about the fact that there wasn't.

"How are you and Beth doing?" I ventured. "With everything."

I hoped he knew what I meant.

When he gave me a sad kind of smile, I knew he did.

"It's been hard, buddy," Luke admitted. "Beth still thinks there's something she did wrong which isn't right. But I think maybe it's easier for her to blame herself than to believe it was just bad luck, you know?"

I nodded, feeling out of my depth on the subject.

"She's had it rough, though. I wish I could do more for her."

I looked round at him. Luke was one of the greatest people I knew: strong, dependable, loyal. He always looked to help others before helping himself.

"You have, too," I said.

He smiled sadly and ducked his head. "I'll be alright. Feels nice having you around, though; grateful you decided to come home this summer." There was no accusation in his tone; it wasn't his style. When he turned his body on the seat to face me, I guessed where we were going next.

"So, you fancy telling me what's been going on with you?"

I shifted under his scrutiny. Turned my head to look out at the lake, avoiding his eyes. "Just uni stuff; it's a lot tougher than I thought it'd be."

"I'm sure it is," he agreed. "But that's not what I mean."

I looked round at him.

"Something's been going on since before Oxford," he said evenly. "In fact, I reckon since about when Cas left."

My breathing shifted, heart rate spiking a little.

He watched me and waited and when it was clear I wasn't going to say anything he let out a sigh. Then he stood up and wandered back inside the house. He was gone a couple of minutes before he reappeared, holding something in his hand that looked like a folded piece of paper. He held it out to me as he sat back down, face soft with understanding.

Confused, I took it from him. It looked like a piece of lined paper torn from a notepad. For a moment, I thought he was trying to tell me something so serious he'd had to write it down. I unfolded it clumsily.

As the words were revealed, I was sure I felt my heart stop.

It was my own handwriting. Angry and messy, scrawled forcefully on the page.

I glanced at Luke in horror, cold sweat spreading over my entire body.

His face was calm, utterly free of judgement, but still I trembled.

"I found it under your mattress after you left for Oxford," he said. "I figured it was one of your stories. You hadn't shown me any of them in so long." He smiled fondly. "You used to write about King Arthur when you were younger, then it was aliens, so I was curious what you were writing about now." He looked down at the piece of paper. "Felt wrong after reading that."

My gut twisted, dread curling upwards.

Luke shifted forward then, urgently. "Not wrong, shit, Jude, that's not what I meant. I meant guilty – I felt guilty about reading something you'd meant for him. I'm sorry I did that. It was private."

There was a noise inside my head, like a rushing of water. It filled my ears and my chest, and it made it hard to think, breathe, to speak.

"I..." I managed. "He...we..."

"I remember when you spoke to me about Ellie, about how you felt about her," said Luke, gentle and soft like he was scared I was going to bolt. "You said that being with her felt like lying. Was that why?" He pointed at the piece of paper. "Because you felt that way about Cas?"

I nodded, still unable to speak.

"You loved him?"

I nodded again. Some desperately sad look moved into his eyes because he knew, then. What I'd lost.

"Oh, buddy," Luke whispered, moving across the sofa and pulling me into a hug. Like every time he did it, something loosened in me, and I let go.

After it was over, I sat up, scrubbing a hand over my face. "Christ. What is it about you hugging me that makes me do that?" I muttered, throwing an accusing glare at him.

Luke chuckled softly. "Sorcery?"

"Yeah, okay, Gandalf."

"I reckon I could pull that off, you know. Grow this bad boy out a bit." He stroked his beard a few times and made a pompous, self-important face.

"It's definitely grey enough," I smiled, and he pretended to look insulted.

Then it was sombre again, silence swelling between us loud and huge.

"So ...you're gay?" he asked very carefully.

I looked at him. "Would that bother you?"

He made a weird face. "No. Not a bit."

"I actually don't know... there's been girls too. So I guess I'm bi?" I felt very out of my depth talking about it, my own sexuality. It also felt weird talking to Luke about it. "Beth?" I asked him, a new kind of panic spreading through me. "Did you show her this?"

He shook his head. "Course I didn't. It's not for me to tell her your secrets – or whatever this is. Christ, I wasn't even going to mention it to you."

"Why did you?"

He looked uncomfortable. Shifting in the seat, he threw a glance over towards the big house, then back at me, and then, finally, at the letter I was still holding. "Because I hated not knowing what was going on with you. Last couple years...you've felt so...far away. And I hated that. And Beth and me...I suppose we were still trying to deal with the baby, and so it was easier to pretend it was normal A-Level stress that was going on with you that summer. But it wasn't, I knew that. I knew it was Cas." Then, a look of mild embarrassment came over his face. "Truth is, it feels like I've been losing you a little every day since we came here."

I tried to protest this but he raised a hand, gently, urging me to let him finish.

"I hope you know that from the moment I met you, I thought of you like a little brother, and then when you came to live with us, it was like I had a son, too." Luke never referred to my (Beth's and mine's) parents' deaths as what it was. To him, it was always '*when Jude came to live with us.*' '*When you came to live with us.*' "A clever, moody, funny son who surprised me every day with how brilliant he was."

"Oh god." I cringed.

"What? I'm being sincere here!"

"I know, that's why it's so awful." I covered my eyes with my hands and sank back into the chair.

Luke laughed, but he persisted.

"But when we came here, it was like this new part of you started growing, a part I couldn't understand or help tend to, you know? Seemed like Gideon and Cas were the only people who got to see that side of you, and so I lost my best friend a little, it felt like. But you were mainly happy, and so I was happy."

His expression was painfully earnest and I felt as though I might cry again.

"Then Cas left, and you were so bloody sad, mate." He took a deep breath. "Judey, before I found that letter, I could only guess at what Cas meant to you based on what I saw with my own eyes."

Heat spread out from my chest and up to my cheeks at that. At how obvious I must have been. *Everything you feel is in your eyes, you know.*

"And when he went off to America with...well, that lawyer fella, I wanted you to talk to me about it, but I understand why you didn't. You loved him, and he left, and that sort of thing is hard to talk around, I imagine. But I need you to know that I'm here if you ever do want to talk about it, about anything at all. I never want you to feel alone, okay? Or that you might not have a place here."

He was talking about the letter now. The words I'd put in the letter. I knew how they must have sounded, what Luke was worried about, what he must have been worried about every night since I left for Uni. That I'd do something stupid. That I'd hurt myself.

"I know, Luke," I said. "I appreciate that. And you don't have to worry about me; I'm doing okay. I'm better, I promise."

He reached out his hand and settled it on my shoulder, squeezing it a few times.

"Good. I'm glad to hear it. But if you aren't, that's something you know you can talk to me about, right? No matter what, I'm here for you."

"I know," I said again. "Thanks."

We sat in silence, sipping our beer and watching the sun set behind the lake.

"I'm starting to think it was a bit like Ellie and me," I said after a long time. "With Cas, I mean. I cared about him more than he did about me. And that hurt." I knew it was reductive, but it wasn't untrue.

"I think maybe Cas still has a lot of growing up to do," said Luke sagely. "He's smart about a lot of things, knows more about a lot more than some people twice his age." Here, he pointed at himself. "I reckon when he's made a few more mistakes, he'll realise what he had in you."

I raised an eyebrow. "You think he'll come crawling back?"

"Christ, no, he wouldn't crawl for anyone," Luke said, and we both laughed. "But he'll walk in that weird upright way he has, right back to you."

I hated the tiny flare of hope that lit in my chest at that. Though, of course, Luke had no bloody clue what he was talking about. Cas wasn't coming back to me. Because Cas had never been mine to begin with.

"He does have a weird walk," I said.

Luke nodded in assent. We were both silent for a long time after that, the weight of our losses heavy between us. I folded the letter and put it inside the copy of *Ibsen's Ghosts* I was reading.

"So, you know Elspeth has a massive thing for you, right?" I said, desperate to change the subject to something lighter.

Luke blinked at me in complete shock. "What? No, she doesn't, shut up."

"Oh, but she does. She make you lunch every day or just Mondays?"

I left him spluttering embarrassed denials as I stood to go get us another couple of beers.

SIX

I'd been deemed capable enough to return to Oxford and started Michaelmas term as a second year with the kind of confidence and buoyancy I could only have dreamt of the previous year.

My passing grade for my first year was 72.8%, which, across four papers, was better than even I thought I'd done. I'd been advised via an email (the day after receiving my result) that my second-year accommodation was in Longwall Quad. It was closer to many of the buildings where my classes were, and as second and third years were guaranteed single rooms, it was an all-around improvement. I was appointed a cosy, low-ceilinged room set into the eaves on the third floor, far away from anything resembling an industrial bin. The space reminded me a little of my bedroom at home. It was smaller than my dorm last year at Ellis, but a large arch window made it feel bigger.

Bast was first to text me. He'd gotten a

single, too, but was in St. Swithun's with Nikita. Irish Conn was in New Buildings, which, as the name suggested, was a new build development a five-minute walk from campus, which everyone had wanted. Personally, I preferred the older buildings, bin lorries and single-glazing aside.

After unpacking, I lay on my bed and stared at the old wooden rafters above. I was glad to be back. Though this summer had been healing in ways I hadn't expected, I could feel myself starting to feel penned in. The last few weeks, Beth and Luke had stopped bickering in hushed voices in other rooms and started doing it out in the open, in front of me, forcing me upstairs or out for a drive. I'd driven to every beach on the island and sat in every coffee shop at least once.

After his return from Italy, I'd gone to see Gideon where he'd pretended that my little outburst the day before he left hadn't happened. He'd brought me back a bottle of Limoncello in an extravagant frosted glass bottle. He hadn't mentioned Cas once. Despite what I'd said to him the day of my explosion, I'd wanted to know. *How was he? What did he say? Did he ask about me? What was he wearing? Did he seem happy? In love?* All these questions burned on my tongue as I asked him instead how Florence was and whether he went to see Michelangelo's David. ("Oh, Perseus with the head of Medusa is far superior, Jude! And the Abduction of a Sabine Woman. Glorious and ghastly!") He even offered to take me there himself to show me. I tried to imagine it. Gideon and I, in Florence together, drinking in little cafés and eating dinner in fancy restaurants. Would he expect me to carry his bags for him? His water and fan? Would people think I was his son or his lover? Either way, it seemed like something he'd said off the cuff and had no real intention of ever doing. So, I'd just nodded and said, "Tell me when, and I'm there."

He told me he was going to be staying at his house in London for a while to allow for the renovation work to take place – he couldn't abide the dust. Asthma! he'd said, dramatically, like it was the name of a new broadway musical – and told me I was welcome to visit him there whenever I wanted.

I'd only been to London once as a child. It had been Christmas time, and my parents had taken me to see the lights at Covent Garden and then to a performance of the Nutcracker. So I said maybe I'd come visit him around Christmas.

It would beat going home to Jersey to listen to Beth and Luke fight.

Finn texted me a few days after term started. It was late Friday night, and I'd just gotten home from my first shift back at P&P. I saw his text when I came out of the shower.

Finlay:

Your friends are here. Where are you?

Me:

Where's here?

Finlay:

Call yourself a Classics student? Is that even proper English?

Me:

Definitely proper English. How drunk are you?

Finlay:

Not too drunk to suck your cock

Me:

We're still doing that?

Finlay:

I'd really like to, yes

Me:

Would you now

I was lying on my bed, wrapped in a towel, with the window cracked open to let the fresh air in. The room, being in the roof space, was hotter than the one in Ellis.

Finlay:

I thought about your cock a lot this summer

I wasn't sure that was true, but it still caused a little niggle of guilt to pull at me since I hadn't thought of Finn once that I could remember.

Me:

I don't believe you.

Finlay:

You still at Ellis?

I tried to think of the last time I'd gotten off, and couldn't, which made me embarrassed and a little worried. I was eighteen years old, a second year at Oxford, and the last time I'd gotten off was so long ago that I couldn't remember it.

Me:

Longall. Third floor. Room 4.

Finn sent back a string of aubergine emojis, a few tongue emojis, and a string of raindrops.

And so things with Finn picked right back up where we'd left them a couple of months before. And just like before the summer, full sex remained just slightly out of my zone of comfort or interest. I was definitely getting closer to being okay with the idea of it, and Finn himself was the reason for that. As my nineteenth birthday came and went and the coursework of my second year started to pile, I was more grateful than ever to have him there when I needed him.

One night, Valentine's Day night I think, after once again sucking my soul out through my dick, he nosed at the skin around my balls and then lower, near my hole and said, "You ever gonna let me in here?"

I stiffened a little. Looking down at him, I asked, "Is that what you want?"

He gave me an incredulous look as if it should be completely fucking obvious.

"I mean, you want to fuck me?" I clarified. "You don't want me to fuck you?"

"Jude, I'll take whatever you're willing to give me, and I do, but for some reason you're still squeamish about this, and so I'm trying not to spook you."

I sat up, blushing a little. "I'm not squeamish," I said.

"Okay, but you're something, I'm just not sure what." Finn smiled easily. "You saving yourself for your wedding night?"

"Oh, fuck off."

He laughed before his eyes turned serious again. "Look, I'm not pressuring you. And you don't need to figure shit out before you're ready or whatever. I'm easy."

I believed him. There was nothing underhand about Finn; with anyone else, I might have sensed the lie in a statement like that, but not Finn. I just didn't know why I was so hesitant about it. I'd slept with girls. Okay, two, but I hadn't overthought that to this degree. Deep down, I suspected it was related to Cas, but I didn't want to even attempt to figure out what.

"Anything you want to talk about?" he asked, sidling up so he was next to me on his bed.

"You want me to talk about my feelings?" I asked, eyebrow raised.

"Fuck, no. Just like...whatever you're stuck on with this." He waved between us. "Maybe I can help." He gave me an odd kind of look. "You're not a virgin, are you? I mean, you've had sex before? You had a girlfriend in high school, right?"

"Yes, I had a girlfriend. Yes, we had sex."

"Okay, thank fuck for that."

I hit him lightly on the chest.

He laughed before his eyes roamed over me appreciatively. "Look, I'd love you to fuck me, I'd love to fuck you, but all this is good too. I guess I'm just trying to understand where your head's at. You're a bit of a closed book, Jude Alcott."

I frowned at that. "Someone once told me that my eyes gave everything away."

He studied me then, hard. Not in the lusty way he had before but as if he were sincerely trying to figure me out. He stared into my eyes, then at my mouth, then back up to my eyes again.

When he leaned over me, noses almost touching, he whispered, "Oh yes, I see it now. Clear as day. You want to get fucked, hard."

I shoved at him, and he tipped back over, laughing.

"Dickhead."

I wasn't even going to go. Finn hadn't properly invited me. But then, we didn't really do that – make firm plans with each other. But it was his birthday, and maybe I was trying to take things to the next level by turning up and showing him I cared. Plus, at the very least, we were friends, and it seemed the decent thing to do.

I'd shot off a text to ask Bast to come with me about a half hour before, and he'd agreed, meeting me outside P&P, with a six-pack of Scrumpy Jack and a big smile. He was more sociable than Conn and less conspicuous than Nikita, who a lot of people were afraid of for some reason. Bast was the perfect wingman.

Seve had given me a bottle of wine for Finn – who he knew via Abby – and let me go early since the place hadn't been busy, Marta throwing me a murderous glare as I pulled my jacket on and ducked out of there. It was raining. That consistent, weighty rain that seemed to drop from the sky in puddles so that I was sodden by the time we got to Finn's place.

"I'll find a girl and leave you to it, my friend," said Bast as we headed up the stairs of the house on Fromme Street, a sky-blue townhouse Finn shared with four others, including Alex.

A few people were huddled together on the steps outside, two umbrellas shared between them, smoking weed. I smiled as I passed, though I didn't recognise any of them. Inside, some awful dance music played over the sound system as we made our way through the house. Bast spotted someone he knew from the bike shop in the sitting room, so he went over to say hello while I went to the kitchen.

There, I found Finn, leaning against the fridge, while talking to a tall guy who was built like a rugby player. I couldn't tell if he was flirting or not, and I couldn't decide how I felt about it, so I hesitated just out of their eyeline a moment before deciding to just dump the wine and go mingle. But then the rugby guy turned, Finn, a second later.

A look of shock moved over his face, which I assumed meant that he *was* flirting. And that I'd interrupted.

"Jude? I didn't …you're here…" He paled, panic pouring off him in waves as he stammered. I glanced at the rugby guy again and tried to give a reassuring smile.

"Yeah, bar was dead so Seve let me go." I shrugged and held out the bottle of wine to him. "Happy Birthday."

He stepped forward to take it. "When did you get…here?" He was looking over my shoulder and around the room. I thought he was looking to see who I came with.

"Literally just now. I came with Bast. You okay?"

He slammed the bottle of wine on the counter, took me by the arm, and manhandled me toward the utility room, practically shoving me inside. It was a small windowless space filled with cleaning products, dirty laundry, and unopened boxes of wine and beer. I looked at him, wide-eyed.

"Look, it's fine, I don't give a shit if you're trying to fuck him, Finn. You know we're not like that." Maybe I'd come here with some other notion, but clearly that was stupid and I was actually pretty okay about it.

Finn gave me a tired sort of look.

He said, "I'm not trying to fuck him, Jude. I just don't know what you're doing here."

I felt my cheeks heat with something. "Eh, because it's your birthday, and I thought we were friends." He'd been posting about this party on his socials for the last week. I'd assumed he hadn't invited me because *he'd* assumed I'd be here anyway. Clearly, that old saying about assuming was spot on.

"Friends." He snorted. "Yeah, okay."

I frowned. "What's that supposed to mean?"

"Nothing. Forget it. It's supposed to mean nothing." He was still skittish, but now he seemed annoyed, too. Vaguely, I wondered if he was on something. But he didn't *seem* drunk or particularly out of it.

"Look, sorry, I didn't think before coming. I should have texted—"

"You know I care about you, right?" Finn said, startling me. "I mean, I've made that abundantly, and some would argue, *pathetically* obvious." He laughed a little. Okay he was definitely drunk, I could tell that now. But it wasn't the sleepy, flirty drunk I was used to. This was something else. Bitter. Thorny. "Does being with me make you feel close to him or something? Is that it? Or are you using me, because you think if he found out, he'd be pissed off about it? Or fuck, maybe it's for some other reason you don't even understand."

He didn't need to clarify who 'he' was. I knew.

It felt like he'd slapped me across the face. Had that been what I was doing? Was I using Finn as some way to get back at Cas? Stopping short from fucking him because it might be too much for

Caspien to forgive me for. Embarrassment came first, then shame.

I struck out, blind and defensive. "Fucking hell, Finn, if you didn't want me here you should have just told me."

"I didn't *invite you*, Jude," he said coldly. "That should have made it clear enough."

I didn't understand what had caused this shift in Finn from who he'd been when I'd last seen him. But he was right: he hadn't invited me. I shouldn't have come.

I nodded. "Yeah. Okay, I guess I'll go." I moved toward the door but stopped and looked at him again. He still looked on edge, like he was frightened of something and though I couldn't understand why, I was terrified right then that it was me.

My voice was soft when I spoke, "Look, I don't really understand where this is coming from, but I care about you, too. And I'm sorry if you've felt like I don't. I'm sorry if you've felt like I've been messing you around, but it's not..." I shook my head. "I just thought you were okay with how things were. Sorry for...coming."

Sorry for everything was what I'd meant. I gave him a sad smile and pulled open the utility room door.

My heart stopped.

Caspien stood at the kitchen counter, pouring wine from a bottle into a glass.

I blinked a few times, convinced it was my imagination. He couldn't be here, he *wouldn't* be here. But it was him. My heart knew it. My body knew it.

I could have closed the door, turned, and gone out the back door. But I couldn't move. I only understood one thing: pure fear. My whole body shook with it.

And yet, I couldn't take my eyes off him. I drank every inch of him in, thirsty for what I'd been deprived of for two and a half years. His hair was shorter at the back and sides than I'd ever seen it, though long and messy on top. In profile, I could see his cheeks were pinked and his skin a little too pale, his frame leaner than it used to be. I could barely draw breath from how much I longed to go to him, touch him, hold him.

I suppose he must have sensed the weight of that longing because he stopped pouring and lifted his head, going very still suddenly before very slowly turning around. I saw his eyes widen slightly, before his expression went very deliberately, completely neutral.

I tried harder than I ever had to let my eyes show him absolutely nothing at all.

Behind me, I heard Finn let out a sigh, then a quiet curse, and suddenly I understood everything.

Cas's eyes never left mine, his stare pinning me where I stood. His eyes were ice blue in this light, his mouth a deep pink slash on his face. I waited for him to say something, anything, because I was utterly unable. Then another fear hit me; was *he* here? Had he brought Blackwell with him tonight?

I had to get out of there.

Tearing my eyes from Caspien, I forced my feet to move. I strode past him and out of the kitchen, down the hallway out into the rain. I caught someone's arm as I pushed through the crowd of smokers on the steps, but I didn't apologise, and I didn't look back.

I don't remember the walk home, the rain soaking through my clothes and my skin, running into my eyes and mouth. I just walked. I stopped at the off-licence, bought a bottle of vodka and kept walking.

By the time I got to the dorm, my hands were shrivelled and my clothes weighed a ton. I turned on the small electric heater and stripped out of them, drying myself with minimal effort, before collapsing on the floor against the bed.

I drank straight from the bottle, burning hot mouthfuls that made me want to wretch after every swallow. After the fourth or fifth mouthful, it got easier. I'd come so close. So close to being okay. To moving on. To getting over him. Had he known and timed his re-entry so perfectly it was almost funny? If tragic heartbreak could be funny.

It had been months since I had last done it, but with another mouthful of vodka, I closed my eyes and remembered it all.

I let every painful memory flood back in, like a dam bursting and the swell rushing to the front of my brain, pouring over the walls I'd built.

I missed him. I missed what we'd had. The lie we'd had. The lie he'd *let me* have.

I missed how fucking special he made me feel when he looked at me – not some orphaned boy no one really wanted – but someone special. Special enough that I could be worthy of someone like him.

Deep down, I knew he was an awful, spiteful, empty person and I had the scars to prove it – but when he'd looked at me, when he'd let me touch him and hold him and have him, it was like—

I swallowed another mouthful. Dark, twisted arousal ebbed unwanted inside my boxers. I drowned it away with vodka, as I scrubbed at my eyes.

The thing that scared me most was that I was going to belong to him like this forever. He'd carved out a part of my heart and soul for himself and nothing except him would be able to fit inside it. It was him or it was nothing. It was him.

I hated him for it. Wanted to hurt him as badly as he'd hurt me.

I thought terrible thoughts, like going back to Finn's and kissing him in front of Caspien, of dragging him upstairs and making him scream loud enough that Caspien would hear.

Maybe I'd force him to watch, maybe I'd—

The knock on the door was loud enough to hear over the hum and rattle of the convection heater and the radio. I reached over to turn the volume down on the speaker. It was always my first thought. That someone was coming to give me hassle the way Beth always had when I'd have the music up too loud. No one had ever done it here, but the instinct was still there.

I wanted whoever it was to fuck off and let me get drunk and maudlin in peace, and so I sat unmoving, hoping they'd do just that. They didn't.

The knock came again, just as steady and determined as the first.

I grabbed a pair of sweats from the clothes horse and yanked open the door.

Caspien stood on the other side, relaxed and utterly bone dry.

He was wearing a dark trench coat, leather gloves, and a look of complete petulance.

He stared at me a long time, before he said, "Well. Are you going to invite me in?"

SEVEN

"I wasn't planning on it, no."

This appeared to amuse him. "Why not?"

"Because I don't enjoy having poisonous, deadly things in my living space."

"Christ, I thought you were reading classics and literature, not drama." He pushed past me with the same entitlement he'd always had, like he owned every space he existed in, even my dorm room.

Again, I considered running. Walking out, closing the door behind me, and going far far away.

"Close the door," he said as he began to pinch off his gloves.

Steeling myself with a deep breath, I closed the door.

He unwrapped the scarf he wore and tossed both it and the gloves down on my armchair. It wasn't a large space, the dorm room, and he was already far too

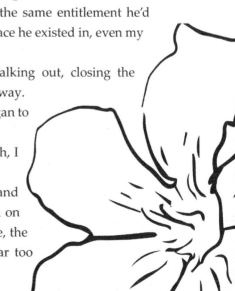

close to me. It seemed absurd that he was there at all, after all this time; how he'd just strode back into my life as easily as he'd strode out.

I stayed near the door. His scent was already on me and I didn't know what I might do if he got within arms reach. Fortunately, I'd set the vodka on the desk, which was by the door, and so I reached out for it and brought it to my mouth.

Caspien watched.

"Drink?" I asked him.

"I'm not convinced that's what that is." He said, looking around, mouth twisted in what I read as distaste.

"How did you even find me?"

He looked at me and frowned. "Were you hiding? I was quite aware you were at Oxford, Jude."

"I meant here. Now."

"Oh. Well, Finlay told me of course."

I wondered what else Finlay had told him. Suddenly, those thoughts I'd had about having him find out about Finn and I were less fantastical and far-fetched. What *would* he do if he knew? Would he care? I suspected not.

"Of course, he did." I took another drink.

He said nothing, glancing around my room again as though he wanted to burn it, or clean it.

"What are you doing here, Cas?"

"In England? At Finn's party? At your dorm? Be specific."

My fist curled around the bottle. "Here. In front of me. Why are you here, right now?"

I saw some of his composure slip a little. "You ran off. I wanted...I didn't expect to see you there."

"I suppose that makes both of us." I glowered. The anger helped keep away some of the other thoughts scrabbling for attention in my vodka-soaked brain. *Go to him. Hold him. Kiss him. Fuck him. Love him. Love him. Love, love, love ...*

"I was visiting Gideon in London, and then I had to be in the area," he explained vaguely. "I told Finlay I'd drop by and wish him happy birthday."

"That's really lovely and all, but it doesn't explain why you're here. In my dorm. Why I'm having to look at you."

"Are you and Finlay fucking?" he asked as though I hadn't said anything at all. I couldn't tell how he felt about it; it was said with only the barest hint of curiosity.

"What has that got to do with you?" I asked.

He shrugged. "Nothing, I suppose."

"Then why ask?"

"I am curious, is all."

"Didn't you ask Finn?"

"He said that you were friends."

I smiled. "Then that's what we are. Friends."

Caspien stared at me for a few long moments before he came toward me. He reached out and took the bottle of cheap supermarket-brand vodka, brought it to his lips, nose wrinkling slightly as he did, and took a large gulp. After he'd swallowed, he let out a gasp, wiping the back of his hand over his mouth.

"If you're going to drink yourself to death, the least you could do is make sure it's something decent," he said, disdainful, as he held the bottle out to me.

"Yeah, well, we can't all afford to drink $500 bottles of wine with dinner." I regretted saying it immediately. He'd posted the picture on his Instagram a few months ago. I didn't go there almost as much as I used to, but him knowing that I went there at all made me feel ill.

He spared me the mortification by saying nothing.

"What, your trust fund isn't enough to cover a bottle of decent wine?" He lifted an eyebrow.

"What the fuck are you doing here, Cas?" I pressed. "You came all the way over here to ask me about Finn and make snide comments about my drinking, really?" After everything that had happened, that's all he wanted to say? "You could have called to do that."

A beat. "And would you have answered?" he asked, his voice was softer. But I hardened myself against that because it wasn't real. Imagining his voice being soft was my mind inventing things I wanted to be true.

"Yes," I admitted. "But that would be a mistake: everything about you was, is, a bloody mistake." I thought I saw him flinch a little at this.

"You finally hate me then."

"You tell me?" I asked, slamming my bottle down on the desk. "What are my eyes saying, Cas? Do I hate you?"

I could *feel* the alcohol in my bloodstream now, hot and fervid. I was taller now than the last time we'd been face to face, and from this angle I could see the faintest trace of circles beneath his eyes, a dullness in them that had never been there before – even when they were hard and cold, his eyes were always bright and sharp. His lips were pale and dry, but I'd never wanted to kiss them more.

"No," he said, looking into my eyes. "You don't hate me. You wish you did, but you don't."

I grabbed his arms and pushed, walking him backwards until he hit the wall. The smell of him hit me the way it always did, sharp and clean like the whitest freshest snow.

"I fucking hate you," I hissed, quietly.

"You've always been a particularly bad liar, Jude. I'd have thought all these hours spent with Gideon might have taught you a thing or two, made you better at it, but it seems not."

I used my body to press him into the wall, almost groaning out loud at the feel of him against me after so long. My dick grew hard instantly, the feel of him everything I'd lost and seemed to have found again. Even if it was just for moments.

I said, "You shouldn't have come here."

His eyes dropped, slowly, to my mouth. He said, "Yes, well, it seems I have rather a propensity for making mistakes."

My head was buzzing loud, my blood as wild for him as it always was. But to have him here, pressed to me, body warm and real, felt desperately vital in some way. A fierce, urgent thing beneath my skin. The potential of it breaking loose frightened me.

I brought my hand up, intending to brush it over his cheek, shift that section of hair back so that I could see all of his face, but I couldn't do it. Was too afraid of touching him. Of what it might unleash. Instead, I thumped my fist against the wall beside his head. His breathing was fast and hard but he didn't flinch, as though he expected it.

"Jude," he said.

He wasn't touching me, not voluntarily, not anywhere on my body; I was pressed against him, and he was merely allowing it to happen. But when he said my name, Christ, whenever he said my name, it felt like the most tender caress.

Against all reason and better judgement, I dropped my head onto his shoulder, turning it so that I could press my nose against his neck and inhale. I nosed gently at the skin, breathing him in. I waited for him to mock me, push me away, or tell me to stop, but he did neither. Instead, he angled his head to give me better access. I breathed deeper.

Then I felt his hand on my dick. I groaned.

Drunk on both him and the cheap vodka, I pushed into it. I was already rock hard, but his hand on it loosened the last of my fear and resolve. I grabbed his face and turned it toward me, thrusting my tongue into his mouth. It opened readily, warm and hot and sweet as I remembered.

I kissed and bit and breathed him in, rough with his mouth, before I dragged my lips down over his chin and his jaw and his neck. Caspien fumbled with my waistband, sliding his hand inside my sweats as he panted. Before he got his hand around my bare dick, I gasped and pulled back.

I don't remember how my hand got to his throat, but it was there, wrapped around it, as I held his head against the wall.

"What the fuck are you doing?"

His mouth was a ruin. Red and wet and asking to be fucked. His eyes were glazed over with something I remembered painfully well. Lust.

"I'd have thought that rather obvious, no?" He stroked my length, thumbing the tip in a way that sent sparks shooting through my balls.

I squeezed his throat tighter.

"Cas," I warned. "This isn't going to stop at a wank, or even a blowjob. If you don't stop." I didn't want him to stop. I let out a desperate moan as his perfect fingers traced lower, over my balls.

"What are you going to do?" he taunted. "*Finally* shove your dick in me?"

The image blasted itself across my frontal lobe. Cas bent over, open and begging. Me shoving into him over and over and over. Punishing him for everything he'd done. Taking from him what I'd wanted for so long. What I deserved to have. Drinking up his pleas for me to slow or stop and ignoring every single one. There was no hesitation or confusion about what I wanted when it came to *him*. There never had been. I was almost feral with the certainty of what I wanted from Cas.

I sprang back, away from him, alarmed by the realisation.

"You need to leave," I said, turning from him. I went to the desk and lifted the bottle again, all but pouring it down my throat. It burned. Everything in me burned. Dangerous and unstoppable, on the cusp of something incendiary and uncontainable.

I turned to see him lounging against the wall where I'd left him, watching me, breathing a little quick. It was a long time before he spoke.

"I think about it sometimes," he said. "Your perfect dick. About how it would feel in me. I do regret ending things with you before trying it out."

"Shut the fuck up," I said but my breath was coming in hot, heavy pants.

I'd imagined seeing him again so many times, hours and hours of walkthroughs, of contemplating what I'd say when I got the chance to look him in the eye, how much better I'd be. How this time I'd stand up tall, how I'd not embarrass myself again. I'd be in control, sensible, cunning.

But, once again he'd reduced me to a fucking animal. From beaten and broken in that birdwatcher's hut to this. A fucking predator.

Caspien pushed off the wall, but instead of going toward the door to leave, he came toward me – slowly, his calculated gaze fixed on mine.

No, I wasn't the predator. *He was*. He'd always been the one hunting me. I'd only ever tried to survive him.

"Sometimes I wish you'd done it that day. Instead of crying and begging the way you did," his mouth twisted with contempt. "I wish you'd held me down and fucked me – who knows, maybe things would have turned out differently if you'd behaved like a man instead of a little boy."

Something snapped.

I slammed the bottle down, heard it topple and glug onto the carpet, and reached for him. He seemed to weigh nothing as I threw him on the bed. He made some half-hearted attempt at fighting me at first, but then I felt his body go pliant and loose, opening itself to me. I think he took his coat off himself, or it shrugged off his shoulders as we tussled. I reached for his belt, black and thin around his slim waist, and pulled at it before tearing down his trousers. He wore black briefs, neat and tight against his body which I also tore at with a feral need. Layers. He wore a shirt and a pullover, and we both fought the fabric off his body.

When he was naked but for his trousers at his ankles and his shoes and socks, I flipped him over so that he was on his front and grabbed him by the hips to pull him up towards my mouth. I'd never done this before, eaten someone's ass, and I don't recall it being a conscious thought even then. It was only need, a crushing overwhelming need to taste him and open him, get him wet and ready before I fucked him. I spat and licked and shoved my tongue into him over and over. My fingers, too, pushing and spearing in and out. I watched him writhe and pant and twist, and I gave him more than what I thought he could stand if the noises he made were any indication.

I tried not to think about Blackwell, about how intimately he knew this part of Caspien's body, but it was impossible and so I licked and ate and sucked at every part of skin I could reach. Jealousy and possessiveness fought with lust and arousal, which only made me rougher.

I forced him to fuck my mouth, pulling hard on his hips as I made a meal of him. When I felt him reach for his dick, I grabbed his hand and held it in mine before slapping him hard on the side of his ass. He stopped moving then.

When I leaned back to look at his hole, I saw it was red, open, and clenching desperately.

I pulled his legs out from under him and he pitched face forward, then I climbed onto him, yanking down my sweats. I was painfully hard, throbbing and hot. I looked at his hole: I was going to ruin it.

"I don't think I'll use a condom, you know," I said, running my cock over his gaping hole. It was thick and red and angry against the faded golden tan of his ass, an ass which was pinked from my mouth and hands. "I think I'll fuck you raw. Make you go back to him with my come inside you."

He made a desperate whimpering noise against the duvet. I leaned forward and dropped another mouthful of spit into his open hole.

I felt more powerful than I ever had in my life. I'd never felt so divinely righteous, so mighty, so completely in control of my own fate as I did then. Caspien under me and helpless, unable to say no, suffering me. It should have terrified me. And there was a low-level hum of terror at what I was prepared to do to him whether he wanted me to or not. I loved him, desperately, and he'd taken that love and turned it into this, turned me into this.

Or had this always lived inside me, dormant and ready to be unleashed? Whatever it was, he held the key to its cage. Only him.

Either way, I understood that there was a side of myself that existed only in opposition to him, a side that, when I was alone and tried to understand it, felt so separate from my conscious mind that I imagined it was what possession felt like.

I leaned forward and fisted, roughly, a handful of soft golden hair, pulling his head back to meet me.

"Tell me to stop, Cas," I hissed in his ear. The head of my dick pulsed against his hole and I was sure I was asking only so I could refuse him. But I said again, "Tell me you don't want this."

His face was flushed with desire, and his eyes bright and alive as stars. He looked both furious and utterly resigned.

And in a voice that would haunt my dreams, he said, "Make it hurt."

And, like always, I obeyed.

EIGHT

That night now is like a fever dream to me.

I remember, vividly, the sensations. The pleasure. Endless and extreme. The things I did to him, the things he let me do. I had not known I was capable of them. They were filthy and depraved, and I never wanted to stop. Lust and alcohol and pain and desire coalesced, turning me inside out, so that I was a red raw mass of animal with a single goal. Take. Fuck. Survive.

We passed out, and my next memory was of me thrusting inside him again. I had rolled over in my sleep and took him; his body was soft and pliant and covered in me. He opened for me readily, his mouth and hands reaching for mine in the dark as he came awake. I came inside him again.

This. This was all I needed. All I wanted. All I'd ever wanted. I needed nothing else to survive but this, and I slipped back into sleep while I was still inside him.

When I woke again, the room was cold and milky white, and he wasn't in the bed.

I sat up to find him sitting at my desk, writing something. He was dressed in only his shirt and trousers, completely absorbed in whatever words he was scratching into what looked to be my notebook.

"Don't bother," I said, and he startled, turning. "Whatever you're writing, don't bother."

He looked down at the words, then tore out the page and crumpled it in his hand.

"You were seriously going to leave without saying goodbye?" I asked in a cracked voice.

Caspien stood, coming toward the bed to sit beside me. The neck of his shirt was open, and I could see early shadows of bruising on his throat. I didn't feel powerful looking at them. I felt sick. Though maybe that was the cheap vodka.

"Do you feel better now?" he asked, not answering my question. "Now that you've gotten it out of your system, will you move on?"

I blinked at him, speechless. Then, fury, hot and sharp. "Are you fucking kidding me?" I said, sitting up. "I had fucking moved on! *You* came here. To my university, to my dorm. You provoked... whatever that was. I had moved on."

Christ, I wanted to be who or whatever I'd been last night again. I felt small and childlike, like the Jude from the birdwatcher's hut. I thought about pulling him to me and forcing him to take me again, but whatever dark spell had been cast over me had been broken by the daylight.

"Oh, please," he said. "The constant updates you let Gideon feed you – though, why you'd believe anything he tells you is beyond me – the drunken phone calls, the Instagram stalking. Messing around with Finlay." Of course, he knew, and he sounded as though he wasn't in the least bit jealous about it. "Jude, it has to stop. You're here, at Oxford, living your bloody dream. Stop living in the past, or whatever fantasyland you now inhabit: be sensible, please."

I felt the mortification incinerate me. I turned my face to the wall, unable to look at him. There'd been a couple of times where I'd slipped and tried to call him. Where I'd been weak. Twice, maybe three times. The last time had been more than six months ago. He'd never answered.

"You should block my number if you don't want me to call," I said miserably. At least he didn't know about the emails. That ghost account only I had access to.

"And what if you ever need me? For something important?" he said, like it was the most obvious thing in the world. Like the way I needed him now wasn't.

I wanted to scream: *This is important. How I feel now, today is important. How much I want you still is the most important thing in the fucking world. How certain I am that I'll break down and cry the moment you walk out that door is fucking important.*

But I couldn't bring myself to say anything at all. He let out a tired-sounding sigh and stood, moving to where his sweater was balled up on the floor. As he pulled it on, the fabric of his shirt rose up, and I froze.

There were bruises scattered over his ribs and the dips of his hips.

I climbed out of bed and went to him, lifting up his shirt to peer at the patchwork of purple over his skin. His wrists too. Vomit and shame rose in me.

"What are you doing?" He snapped, but I felt him stiffen. He tried to turn his body away from me, but there were more on his lower back near the base of his spine.

I ignored him, pushing his shirt and sweater up to examine him fully. There were a few more at the top of his back, and something which looked very much like a bite mark on the space where his shoulder and neck met. Finally, he managed to pull away from me. He turned, a very strange look on his face.

"I'm so sorry..." I whispered, deeply ashamed.

I'd hurt him. I'd *really* fucking hurt him. Last night, I'd wanted to hurt him, and I'd done it. I'd marked his skin in bruises in what, some twisted attempt to make him feel pain? Was this who I was? What I was? I sickened myself.

Caspien blinked a few times, looking lost, but then he swallowed and righted his clothes, tucking both his shirt and sweater into his trousers before doing up the belt.

"I told you to make it hurt," he said without meeting my eyes. "I'm hardly going to hold it against you now." He pulled on his long dark coat and dragged a hand through his hair.

"That's not the same," I said, very seriously. "I didn't mean for it to be like...that. Cas, I'm —"

"It's fine," he said. His voice was impatient now, clearly wanting to move on from it. But how could I?

But then he said, "I'd like for you to stop seeing Finlay."

I reeled a little. "Excuse me?"

"I don't like the idea of it. Imagining you and he together is..." He thought about the word. "Unpleasant."

"Unpleasant," I repeated. I'd wanted him to know, to hate it and to ask me to stop. But not like this. So casually.

"Yes."

"Well, I wouldn't want to do anything to make you feel unpleasant, now would I?"

He looked at me suspiciously before nodding. "Right, okay, good. I have to get back to London – I've a flight home to Boston very early tomorrow morning."

Home. Home to Boston.

That wasn't his fucking home.

"So, that's it," I said, panic and fury making my breathing hitch. "You're just gone. Again. Back to Boston."

He was typing something on his phone so was only half-looking at me. "It's where I live, Jude."

"Why did you come here last night?" I asked him. "You never answered me when I asked. Did you come here just to fuck me up again? Is this really all some big game to you?"

He stilled, lifting his head to level a smirk at me. "I fucked you up? Oh, I have some bruises which say otherwise, sweetheart."

The guilt almost floored me, but his tone felt like a slap in the face.

"Look," he said patiently. "Both of us had a fun time last night.

Nothing more than any other student does after a party on a Saturday night. Not everything has to be laden with meaning, Jude. You don't have to have an existential crisis over some rough sex with an old friend."

I could barely believe my ears. I was beginning to suspect he practised this. That he spent hours picking over the right words so they'd do the most damage. Our history, our connection that ran bone deep to me: it was carved into my fucking soul. But to him, I was some fun way to spend a Saturday night. He *was* poisonous. I'd been infected with him, and every time we were face to face, he'd twist his tainted blade that little bit deeper.

"I'm not going to stop seeing Finn," I said because it was the only thing I could think of to say that might piss him off. "I like him, he's great at blowjobs and I don't see why I should stop doing something I enjoy just because you asked me to."

He glared at me, nostrils flaring ever so slightly. "You once stopped masturbating for a whole week because I asked you to."

My balls clenched from the reminder. "Yeah, well. Things change."

"You said you were friends," Caspien reminded me in a low, threatening voice.

"We are."

"So, then you're friends the way we were *friends*?" When I said nothing, he took a step closer, smirking again. "You do realise that you don't have to stick your dick in the holes of all of your friends, don't you? It's not a prerequisite of friendship."

"Why do you even care? You're not jealous, surely?" I knew he wasn't. I knew he felt nothing like jealousy about my being with Finn, but I was drowning, so I clutched at anything I could.

"I care because you're being an idiot."

"Well, now, that is a prerequisite of friendship with you, so you can't really blame me for that one." I thought this very clever and smiled at him triumphantly.

He, however, did not look amused.

"You could have anyone," he said. "There are thirty-six colleges in this university and you could have had anyone – male or female

– and you chose Finlay. What am I supposed to glean from that, do you think?"

"I couldn't give less of a fuck what you glean from it, Cas. It's nothing to do with you."

He lifted his chin and looked me square in the eye. "Well, I'll tell you, shall I? I think you chose the one person you knew it would disturb me most to learn of you being with."

"*Disturb you*?" I almost laughed. "Explain to me what is disturbing about it, Cas? Explain to me how it's any more disturbing than you being with *him*? With the person who groomed you as a fucking child?!"

He blanched, though I couldn't tell if it was from the loudness of my voice or the words.

"Lower your bloody voice," he said very quietly. "They are not the same."

I lowered my voice, seething as I said. "No, you're right they're not the same. One is illegal. Blackwell should be in fucking jail."

"Finlay is my cousin," he said.

"Barely. What else?"

He studied me. "I had no idea you cared about him so much."

"I don't fucking care about him!" I shouted again. "That's not the point!"

I realised what I said too late, of how easily I'd walked into his trap. Anger and despair and that ever-present stupidity around him had loosened my tongue, unravelling me before him again.

Caspien looked satisfied. "You're fucking him because you think it will hurt me, even though you know that isn't possible."

"Of course, I know it isn't possible; you're a fucking shell of a human who cares about no one but yourself."

He wasn't even mildly offended by the accusation. He looked almost satisfied, blissed out, even. His eyelids fluttered a little as he brushed a hand through his hair and took a step back from me. I heard his phone vibrate, and he glanced down at it.

"My car is here," he announced.

"Wonderful," I snapped, moving to pull on some clothes. I'd been standing arguing with him naked. Not that I cared. I'd barely even noticed.

He opened his mouth to say something, that cruel red mouth that haunted my fucking dreams, but then closed it again. I could barely believe this was how it was ending: no, it had already ended. Whatever last night was, it wasn't the start of anything; I knew that.

I tried not to think about how long it might be before I saw him again.

He picked up his gloves and scarf and moved to the door, where he stopped and turned back.

"He won't believe you," Caspien said. I gave him a confused look and he went on. "If you get any silly ideas, and think telling Xavier about this will achieve something, he won't believe you."

I hadn't thought about it. The idea of telling a soul about what had happened last night was the furthest thing from my mind. It was mine, ours. I wanted to wrap it up and keep it hidden from prying eyes. So that when I was alone, I could unwrap it carefully, examine it for things that didn't exist: soft eyes, gentle pleas, tender touches. Giving any part of it to Blackwell made me want to murder something. I'd destroy it first.

"I've spent a lot of time convincing him of my mortification over your little childhood crush," Caspien was saying, "that telling him about this would sound so farcical he would laugh in your face. So, truly, I would not advise it."

I felt breathless and embarrassed.

"Childhood crush," I managed through the knot in my throat.

"Hmm." He nodded, looking at his phone again. "I'd like you to consider my request regarding Finlay. I don't think it's unreasonable to ask you not to fuck my family members, it's a matter of manners, surely?" he said reasonably.

I went toward him fully planning to manhandle him out of my room by force if he didn't go voluntarily. I wouldn't hit him, ever. But he made me the kind of violent I wasn't sure I could control. Last night had proven that.

He looked a little nervous as I approached him, but I saw his eyes dip to my mouth, too. He licked his tongue over his lips and let out a soft breath as he let me crowd him into the door. It had the same effect it always had on me, his submission. Fireworks went off down my spine and my cock stiffened, pulsing and hungry for him.

I pressed it into him. Imagined forcing him around, tearing down his trousers and thrusting inside him raw. I felt a little of whatever haze had overtaken me last night settle on me again as I lowered my mouth to his ear.

"Don't come here again," I warned. I felt his entire body tremble, and my soul glowed from it. "In fact, the next time you're stupid enough to come into any room I'm in, then I'm going to assume that you want me to fuck you again, how about that?"

He let out a small, desperate whimper.

"You can stand there spouting whatever poisonous lies you want, Cas, but your body never lies to me." It was a gamble; I knew that. But when I slid my hand between his legs and felt how hard he was, it felt as though the score line had nudged ever so slightly in my favour. "You want this."

I was careful not to say 'me' because then he could reply saying it was a mere physical, chemical reaction. Something out of his control.

But he was turned on; that much couldn't be disputed. I stroked my thumb over his length, then cupped his balls. He shuddered.

It took every ounce of willpower I had in me to step back from him then and let my hand drop away from his dick. He sank forward as though all that had been holding him up had been me. His face was flushed and beautiful. He lifted his head and stared at me in something like awe, before he stuck out his chin.

"Goodbye Jude," he said in an unstable voice, that to me sounded like bloody birdsong. Then, with a final lingering glance, he pulled open the door and walked out of my life again.

NINE

To: caspienthe_ghost@gmail.com

From: Jalcott.mag@ox.ac.uk

Dear Cas,

You left me again today.

It wasn't as bad as the first time. Or maybe I'm just getting better at losing you. Or maybe it's because this time felt different. The way you looked at me as you left this time said: this isn't done. I think it did, anyway. I've always thought we were tied together somehow. I've thought that a lot since you left. That my place on this earth, the whole purpose of my existence, was to be next to you. Like destiny or kismet or the red string of fate they talk about in Chinese mythology. Something will always bring us back to each other. I believe that, Cas, I really do. I don't know what brought you back to me last night, but it's given me some hope that you'll come back to me again.

Last night has been coming back to me in fragments. The sounds you made. Some of which I ignored, others I couldn't hear through the suffocating need I had for you.

I know I should feel ashamed of the things I did to you. But I also feel like a deep itch has finally been scratched and that there was something so undeniably right about what I did to you. What we did to each other. It wasn't how I imagined it would ever be between us, but maybe it was right. Maybe it had to be like that if it was ever going to be anything at all. I'd still do it differently if I could.

I remember you asking me to make it hurt, and even worse, I remember wanting to.

Christ, Cas. I thought I had almost rooted you out, and now I can feel you again, coming back to life inside me. I know you care. Deep down inside somewhere, I know that you must care what happens to me. You said that you won't block my number because I might need you for something important and I've been wondering what you meant by that. What kind of thing would you deem important enough? An alibi? Money? Danger to my person? After you left the first time, I thought about hurting myself. Would that have been important enough? I've never uttered that out loud to another person, I don't think I'd utter it out loud to you — though Luke read it in a letter I'd written to you — and writing it here feels okay. Like the purging of an intrusive thought.

I told you that I hated you, but you were right, I don't. I love you.

I think I'll always love you.

P.S I haven't stripped the bed yet.

Love,

Jude

Alone again, the nights began to blur back into the drunken loneliness I remembered so well from before – but with one notable difference. There'd been a loosening of a knot buried so far inside me that only he who was a part of me, had been able to do it.

I felt free of something. That uncertainty that had held me back from Finn was no more. The line had moved.

Or rather, I had crossed it.

I couldn't remember what I'd been afraid of to begin with; I could fuck a guy. I'd proven that I could.

I just needed to prove that I could fuck a guy who wasn't Cas.

Code was one of only three nightclubs in Oxford city centre. It was known for its live bands and £2 shot menu. Other than that, it was a vile, sticky place that needed the sort of deep clean they gave mortuaries and hospitals after a pandemic. It was about a fortnight after Cas had left again, when I found myself at least five shots deep and talking the ear off some guy from Corpus Christi about how shit I thought Tarantino was.

Adam, tall with dark eyes and a full, fuckable mouth, agreed. Nikita had gotten some coke from a girl on his floor and I had learned last year that I had a low – okay, very low – tolerance for the stuff, so doing even half a line would mean the others would come check on me every five minutes to make sure I wasn't having a heart attack. This particular night, thanks to that coke, I was feeling better than I had in months. If not years. I was already planning on asking Nikita to ask whoever it was to get me a batch big enough to get me through the rest of the year.

Fuck, maybe I could complete my degree high as a fucking kite. Maybe I'd never need to come down again.

"You're so fucking hot," Adam said, leaning into my ear.

As far as I'd been aware, I was talking about *The Hateful Eight*. Or rather, the piece of shit, waste of everyone's time and money, that was Quentin Tarantino's *The Hateful Eight*. I grinned at him, not at all fussed about leaving our discussion of the film there.

"Thanks, so are you," I knocked back the bright green shot Bast had put down in front of me, the sixth of the night by my count, and leaned in to kiss the mouth I'd been staring at for the last hour.

We were in a darkened booth by ourselves, though I'm not certain I'd have cared if we weren't, not that night, not with the fireworks going off under my skin. He sucked on my tongue like he might suck on my dick, which, coupled with the way he slid his hand between my legs, had me hard in his grip. Although since coke also made me hard, it could have been that.

"Mmm, really wanna fuck you," he said as I broke off the kiss.

For some reason this made me laugh. "Um, yeah, I don't do that." I lifted my beer and drank. Or at least, I thought it was mine. The table was cluttered with abandoned drinks.

"You tried it?" he asked.

I shook my head, and Adam's eyes lit up in the dark.

"Fuck, it's so good. Bet you'd love it." He put his mouth to my ear. "I'd finger you so fucking good first."

I blinked at him, letting the image settle as I looked at his hands. Strong-looking. He was in the rowing team, which showed in the muscled outline through his t-shirt. I tried to imagine my legs spread and him between them while his fingers slid inside my arse. What was the big deal if he wanted to fuck me? Maybe I should try it? Maybe I'd love it. Maybe I'd been missing out all this time and—

Some drunken guy toppled into our table, knocking over glasses and spilling beer bottles. I stood quickly to avoid the runoff.

"Seriously, mate?" yelled Adam over the music.

"Fuck, shit, I'm sssorry," the drunken guy said while his friends rushed in to help him back to his feet.

"Christ, Peter," the guy's friend said, levering him up off our sodden table. I looked at the friend, who was smiling at me apologetically. My mouth opened with surprise.

I hadn't seen Finn since Caspien's appearance at his party, though, he'd texted me the next day.

Finlay:

> Sorry about last night. I was a dick.

Then, an hour or so later when I hadn't responded.

Finlay:

> I should have told you he was going to be in town.

I hadn't hadn't known what to say. My head had been too full of what I'd done with Caspien that I'd barely remembered Finn existed.

I felt ashamed of that now as he smiled at me awkwardly and slightly embarrassed. His gaze bounced to Adam, still grumbling about spilt drinks at my side. He apologised again, before guiding his drunken friend away from us.

"Fucking first years," Adam said, standing. I didn't bother correcting him. "I'm going to dry this off; be back in five. You want another drink?"

"Rum and coke," I said without thinking. I watched him go, broad shoulders and big arms, which I suddenly remembered I wasn't into.

I looked across the club to find Finn talking with one of his house-
mates who wasn't Alex. I now realised the drunken guy was his tall
friend Pete, who I'd met a couple of times.

As I stared, his housemate turned his head toward me, a disap-
proving look on his face. Finn glanced over once, and then I saw
him pat his mate on the shoulder and move off toward the stairs
that led up and out of the club. It was a split-second decision that
involved very little thought. I grabbed my jacket from the corner of
the booth and went after him.

Finn was a little way down on the opposite side of the street when
I caught up to him, one hand in his pocket and the other scrolling
through his phone.

"If you're looking for a Grindr hook-up right now, this is gonna be
awkward," I said as I reached his side.

He stopped, eyes going a little wide at the sight of me. He said, "I
deleted the app."

"Shit, things are serious."

"Yes, very. We're getting married in the south of France next
summer."

"Sounds idyllic. What does he do?"

"Bottom."

I laughed at that. Then an expectant silence filled the air.

"Look," I said.

"Listen," he said at the same time.

I gestured for him to talk first.

"I'm sorry I was a dick at the party. I said some stuff..." He looked
very embarrassed suddenly.

"It's fine," I said, and I meant it. "I guess sorry for turning up
when you didn't want me there."

Finn shook his head. "It wasn't that I didn't want you there, Jude,
fuck. Of course, I did. But when I knew he was gonna be there, I
didn't want to put either of you in a weird situation."

"Thought you hated him?" I asked. "Why'd you even invite him?"

He gave me a look. "I didn't. But he said he was going to be in
Oxford; he invited himself. I'd have much rather had you there than

him." He shifted awkwardly on his feet, kicking at a slightly raised pavement slab. "I don't know what the deal with you and him is."

"There isn't one," I said. "There isn't a deal. We're...nothing."

Finn lifted his head, some inscrutable look in his eye. "You sure?"

"Did he say something?" I asked him, unsure how I felt about it if he had. I knew he'd never tell Finn we'd been anything.

Finn frowned, then shrugged. "He just asked why you were there, how I knew you. I said we were friends." His voice was a little strange as he said this. "Then he asked me where he could find you. Should I not have told him?"

"No," I said. "I mean, yeah, it's fine. He'd have found me anyway."

"Anyway, I'm sorry I made shit weird..." he said, looking at his feet again.

I shook my head. "You didn't, I promise." I was still high, and there was a gentle simmer of arousal in me, and Finn was looking at me like he always did before he'd take me into his mouth.

But more than all of this, I heard Cas's voice: *I'd like for you to stop seeing Finlay.* Well, fuck that. Fuck him.

"So, you care about me?" I asked him. I saw a note of alarm creep into his face. "At the party, you said you'd made it abundantly and *pathetically* clear that you cared about me."

He cringed, cheeks reddening. "Fuck, did I? Right, well I'm off to walk into oncoming traffic." He moved off, and I reached out to pull him back. Pulling him close enough that a tilt of my head would bring our lips together.

"I liked hearing it," I said.

He smiled, almost shyly, and began playing with the button of my shirt.

"What about the hot as fuck rower you left behind in there?" He nodded in the direction of Code.

"He likes Tarantino," I said.

"Fuck, that's disappointing."

"Tell me about it," I sighed. "So...do you have anything good to drink at your place?"

As his eyes lit up and he nodded, I wondered if I should feel cruel.

Finn liked me, cared about me even, and I suspected though I liked and cared about him too, that I was doing this for all the wrong reasons. But under the drizzly skies of Oxford that night with the borrowed euphoria from the coke in my veins, I only cared that I *could* do it.

That I could do whatever and whoever the fuck I wanted to without Caspien's permission, and that included Finn.

TEN

Finn's room at the house on Fromme Street was about four times the size of my dorm, with a set of doors leading off to a small balcony large enough for a single chair. A large king-size bed in a metal frame was set against one wall with a flatscreen TV on the wall opposite, and there was an ensuite with a bath and a shower

It didn't smell like an old library, either, and I suddenly wondered why we mainly went to my dorm when we did this.

I sat on the bed with the bottle of wine he'd slid out of the rack downstairs while he fiddled with the remote until the TV played some EDM playlist as was his preference. He rolled a joint and went to the balcony to smoke it. We passed it between us, along with the wine, until I felt so light-headed I had to sit down again.

"So, you ever gonna tell me?" he asked after we'd been silent a while. The joint was long gone and he sat against the headboard as he took sips from the bottle of wine. I was lying sideways near the foot of the bed.

"Tell you what?" I asked, though I had an inkling I knew.

"You and Cas," he said. "What the fuck did he do to you?"

What the fuck did he do to me? I laughed at this. Because for some reason, it was funny to me then, what he'd done. What I'd allowed him to do. It was fucking hilarious actually. It was a joke, or I was.

"What's funny?" Finn asked, a faint smile on the side of his mouth. I covered my eyes and laughed harder, so hard that my chest, stomach, and throat hurt. But then, I realised, I wasn't laughing anymore.

Finn was beside me quickly, voice a little panicked as he said, "Fuck, Jude, are you crying? Shit. Okay, shit. Fuck, Jude."

"I'm fine," I said, wiping my eyes with the back of my hand. "I'm honestly fucking fine." I looked at him and smiled. "Promise, I am."

"Okay..." He looked like he didn't believe me, so I surged forward to kiss him. He hesitated only a moment, as though suspicious of how quickly I'd recovered, but then he let me push him back onto the bed and kissed me back.

"Jude," he murmured as I reached for the button of his jeans. "You sure?"

"Just let me do this okay, we're going to fucking do this," I said as I moved down his body, tugging off his jeans.

"You're not gonna hear me complaining." He laughed, breathless as he began to undress.

I sat back and did the same, pulling my shirt over my head before standing to take off my jeans.

Finn's body was long, limber, and lean with dustings of dark brown hair where Caspien was completely hairless. Soft and lightly muscled where Cas was delicate edges and lean angles. I pushed all thoughts of Cas away as Finn turned over and pushed himself up on all fours and presented his arse to me.

"There's lube and condoms in the drawer." He gestured vaguely to the bedside table. I guessed the decision about who was fucking who had been decided, and I pulled open the drawer. "Fuck, hurry up," he said impatiently as I rolled the condom over my dick which was, despite the alcohol and drugs, extremely fucking hard.

I thought about Adam The Rower saying he was going to finger me open before fucking me and I squeezed the lubricant over both my fingers and my dick, before sliding my pointer finger at Finn's hole. It was so fucking warm in there, burning hot, and my dick pulsed.

"Christ, yes, fuck." Finn gasped, arching his back up and out and into me. He looked good like that, really good, and I wanted to be inside him more than I cared about opening him up so I was glad when he begged me to do just that. "Just fuck me, Jude, just do it—"

I slid inside him in one single slow thrust, falling onto his back to kiss and nip at the nape of his neck.

"Finn, shit." I closed my eyes and tried to breathe through the tumult of pleasure that was racing down my spine, through my balls, to the head of my dick. We stayed like that a second, mainly so Finn could adjust to me, before he began moving himself in short, shallow thrusts back onto me.

"You feel…" He panted. "Holy fuck, you're so fucking big, Jude, fuck."

"Sorry," I breathed against his neck, and he laughed.

"I'm not," he said, turning his head to kiss me on the mouth. "Now fucking do it. Split me open."

Finn was as good at being fucked as he was at giving blow jobs; loud and incredibly enthusiastic and as I fucked him I felt hope rise in my chest so big I could barely draw breath. He hadn't ruined me. Cas hadn't ruined me. I could do this. I was doing this.

But then Finn pulled away so that I slid out of him and turned onto his back to bring us face to face, and I saw a look in his eye that I recognised. A want and desire that went beyond what we were doing now. One that harboured hopes and dreams of its own, ones I knew I couldn't fulfil. It was the same look Ellie had given me. It shouldn't have surprised me, he'd told me already – *I care about you, surely you know that?* – and yet it did. But hearing and seeing and knowing it were entirely different things, and I understood with a horrible certainty that this was how I looked at Cas.

"What's wrong?" Finn asked, blinking. He leaned up to kiss me, sucking hard on my lip as he brought me inside him again. "Look, I don't care," he whispered.

I pulled my head back, separating our mouths, and held myself very still.

"I don't care," he said again. "It's Cas, right? You think you're in love with him or something?"

It was the wrong thing to say at completely the wrong time.

"I...I don't know what's wrong with me," I told him.

He smiled, reassuringly. "There's nothing's wrong with you, Jude."

But there was something immediately wrong with me, at least. My softening dick slid out of him. Finn sat up, hair mussed and cheeks pinked, a dawning hopeless realisation on his face.

I moved to sit next to him on the bed. I felt wholly sober and very, very alone.

"I'm sorry," I said, covering my face with my hands. "Fucking hell. I don't know why I'm like this. I'm a mess."

Finn was quiet for a bit. Then he said, "I happen to think you're pretty great, actually. I think Caspien the Cunt likely just fucked you up a little bit, that's all."

I looked at him. "Christ, this must be the worst sexual encounter you've ever fucking had."

He grinned. "Actually, guys cry over their exes all the time just before fucking me. It's like a skill I have."

"Another one? Like guessing the subject from the college thing?"

"Exactly." He laughed. Then he gave me what looked like a sorry sort of smile. We were quiet a long time after that. Just the sound of street noise three floors below.

"We messed around a little bit a few summers ago," I offered, some interminable amount of time later. "It was never serious, not for him. He was seeing Blackwell the whole time."

"What a fucking prick," Finn seethed.

"Your party was the first time I'd seen him since. He came to ask me to stop seeing you. Said the least I could do was not fuck his relatives. Something about manners."

I felt Finn vibrate with rage. "So, what, *he* doesn't want you but he doesn't want anyone else to have you either?"

"Actually, he said that I could fuck anyone *but* you. He thinks I chose you deliberately to piss him off."

Finn made a strangled, frustrated sound. "He is quite literally the worst fucking person on earth. I hate him. Like, I loathe that little shit." But then he turned to me. "Wait, did you? Choose me deliberately?" I couldn't tell how Finn felt about this. There was a gleam in his eye that suggested he might actually like it if I had.

"Not consciously, not at the start, at least. Tonight, though." I looked down guiltily. "Tonight, I think I was trying to prove something to myself. Or to him."

Finn thought about this, then gave me another of his easy smiles. "Okay, so please don't judge me for this, but what if I told you I didn't care? What if I told you I'd very happily lie back and get fucked by you, so you could prove something to yourself?" He nudged his shoulder into mine. "Or Cas. We could go the whole way and film it for him. Oh, Christ, please, let's do that. The next family function would be a dream come true."

I laughed, but it felt hollow, perhaps because I was hollow. Empty of that hope that had taken hold of me for a moment as I'd thrust inside Finn. I brought both hands up, dug my fingers into my eye sockets, and let out a groan.

"You know what? Maybe you're just not that into me," Finn said with a small shrug.

I looked at him, shaking my head in disagreement. "I think you're great, Finn. We get on great. You're hot and what we do – I like, a lot."

"Yeah, and maybe that's not enough. Maybe to get over him, you need something else. Something bigger, something that means... more." He turned his body towards me. We were both still naked and yet it felt bizarrely normal. "Maybe the fact he's my cousin *is* an issue for you. Or maybe you're just way too much in your head about it all and you should have gone home with the rower – what the fuck do I know?"

I thought about this. I wasn't sure this wouldn't have ended in exactly the same way had I gone home with someone else. Anyone else. At least this way, I'd only disappointed a friend who I knew wouldn't advertise my issues to the entire campus.

We got dressed, drank the rest of the wine, and fell asleep talking about all the reasons we were as fucked up as we were. Finn hadn't known about my parents until that night, and I hadn't known that he'd been twelve the first time someone had put a dick inside him. I told him about the summer I'd thought Cas was mine and how I'd found him with Xavier.

I told him about the email address I'd created too; how that Caspien The Ghost email address had kept me sane the last two years and how the idea of Cas ever reading any of them made me feel ill. (He'd offered to scan them for anything embarrassing if I ever did decide to send them to Cas. I told him there wasn't a single word in there I wasn't embarrassed about.) I didn't tell him in any detail about what had happened the night of his birthday, only that I'd been so angry with Cas that it had frightened me. He blamed Cas for all of it, of course.

As I left the following morning, it was obvious that what we'd had before was over and done. We couldn't – I couldn't – move forward with him, and there was no going back. We'd stay friends throughout our time at Oxford together, and even now we still keep in touch, but that night was the last time we were ever intimate. I'm certain, though, that it had less to do with Caspien's request and more to do with the fact I'd finally figured out what it was I wanted from Finn: friendship.

But had things gone differently with Finn that night, had we decided to try being together properly, then Nathan certainly wouldn't have happened.

Nathan, someone else who would change how I looked at myself and the world.

Nathan, who was everything I thought I wanted and needed: everything Caspien wasn't.

ELEVEN

I was getting up to leave my Thursday afternoon film criticism tutorial when Professor Alexander said, "Jude, would you mind hanging back a minute?"

Nikita threw me a look over his shoulder that I couldn't decipher, before saying he'd see me later. The others filed out without comment. I'd no clue what it could be about; I'd handed in my paper on Tarkovsky on Tuesday and so assumed it had to be about that. It wasn't the best thing I'd ever written, but I also didn't think it was 'a quiet word after class' bad either.

"I just need to send an email," he said and I nodded, turning my attention around the office.

As he typed furiously on his keyboard, I perused the shelves by the door. There were well-worn books about film theory and autobiographies of long dead directors. I slid out a pristine copy of Quentin Tarantino's *Cinema*

Speculation and flipped through it, vaguely curious about what he might have had to say. I imagined Professor Alexander got a lot of books like these as gifts and likely hadn't read half of them.

"You can borrow it if you like," he said.

I slid it back and shook my head. "Not a big Tarantino fan, honestly," I said. I likely wouldn't have said it in front of the class, a bit too risky in front of a group of rabid film critics, but I didn't mind admitting it to him.

He smiled. "Me either. Fucking loathe him."

I liked him already but I liked him more immediately.

"So, is it about my paper? Was it that bad?"

"Ah, no, actually. I thought it was decent." He scanned his desk and flicked through a pile until he found what he was looking for. "Sounds like you hate Tarkovsky, too." He held up my paper. It had notes down the margins but a 'pass' marked on the top right corner.

"He's another overrated nightmare, yeah."

"Really, eeeesh, big talk."

"If there are any more of his films on the watchlist for this class can you tell me now; I'm going to put in a transfer request."

Alexander laughed. "There's one more, but it's better, I promise. No horses were hurt in the making of this one."

"That wasn't even the worst part. I went to see it with a friend, he's Russian, and he hated it more than me. Even Russians can't stand his films."

"Okay, I get it, I get it. Jeez, no need to hurt my feelings." He put his hands out, surrendering.

"You really like him that much?"

"I do." He looked a little apologetic about it. "But it's fine. You wrote a good paper about all the reasons why I'm mistaken. No, I actually wanted to talk to you about something else, apologies if it sounds a bit bizarre."

"Bizarre?"

"You're from Jersey, right?"

"Yeah. Well, not originally; I lived in Devon until I was eight. Then moved there."

He was nodding. "Well, I'm writing something. A speculative period piece about the occupation; I have a couple of production companies interested in it. I guess I'm looking for an 'in'. Someone local who might be able to show me around." Here he smiled at me, and I understood I was to be his 'in'. I wasn't sure what kind of bizarre I'd been expecting, but it wasn't this.

"You want me to be like a guide?" I didn't know that much about the history of the island, but I didn't want to look stupid in front of my professor by telling him so. It didn't occur to me that if I agreed to this then I'd look even more stupid when he realised I didn't.

"Nothing like that. I just thought it would be helpful to see the island through the eyes of someone who lives there. I've booked a house for the summer – not sure what your plans are? I don't expect you to give up your entire break or anything."

"Oh, I'm not worried about that." I was worried because I hadn't planned on going home that summer at all. I wasn't sure how to tell him that though, so instead I asked:

"Where's the house?"

"Northeast of the island, Fliquet?" He posed it like a question.

I nodded. "Nice spot."

"You can say no, Jude," he said with a smile I'd soon learn made up a whole catalogue of smiles Nathan Alexander possessed. Smiles he could whip out for any and every situation. "I told you it was a little bizarre. I heard you mention it the other week and thought I'd ask, but there's absolutely no obligation here. I promise."

"Oh, it's fine. I just wasn't sure about my summer plans yet, that's all." Even that sounded rude to my ears, but Nathan didn't seem to notice. He was still smiling as he moved to sit back at his laptop.

"Okay, well I'm gonna be in Jersey for a few weeks over summer and if it turns out you're there at the same time, and don't mind showing me around a little, then you can let me know. How about that?"

"Yeah, okay." I nodded. "Sounds good."

"Perfect, okay, well. I'll see you on Tuesday."

It turned out I saw him before that.

It was Sunday morning, and I was on my way back from an all-nighter at the flat of the girl Bast was sleeping with. There'd been alcohol, weed – a lot of both – before I'd passed out on an uncomfortable leather sofa in the large airy hallway. I'd caught sight of myself in the mirror as I'd taken a piss and promised to stay off the weed for a bit. I looked like utter shit.

After splashing some water on my face and checking that I had my phone and keys, I slipped out of the flat without even looking for Bast or Nika.

On Merchant Lane, the scent of cooking bacon stopped me in my tracks, and I followed it inside a little deli where I ordered two bacon rolls and a large tea, intending on inhaling both and proceeding to sleep until Tuesday morning. But when I pulled my mobile out to hold it to the keypad, it was dead, my screen black, and my phone long drained of any battery. I looked at the tall, bespectacled, arty-looking guy behind the deli counter with a desperate pleading look I'd be ashamed of later.

He said, without a single shred of sympathy, "Shit, that's unfortunate."

"I'm just up the street," I began. "Let me take this now and I'll come back this afternoon and pay? What time do you close?"

"We close at 3 p.m. Go get some cash, and I'll keep this warm for you."

I wanted to fucking cry. I was so hungry, the smell of bacon was flooding my nostrils and tastebuds, and I knew that even if I went home, I had no clue where my bank card was and I couldn't wait on my phone charging. I could only imagine what I looked like. Hungover, unshaven, and starving with wild, bloodshot eyes and a mop of unruly hair. This arsehole seemed to be enjoying it too.

I knew there'd be no food in the kitchen at the dorm either. I looked at the brown paper bag, greased spots of bacon already seeping through the sides, and the large brown cup of steaming hot tea. Salvation is what it looked like.

"I'll get it," a familiar American voice said from behind me. I whipped around to see Professor Alexander holding out his card towards the cashier. "Stick it on my order, Bailey."

Professor Alexander was dressed for running. Black shorts, black fitted running top, cheeks flushed and healthy, curls damp on his head. He looked exceptionally good, startlingly so, actually. I was a little stunned by it so early in the morning.

He gave me a cheery, friendly sort of smile as he took me in. "Late one was it, Alcott?"

"Um, yeah, I was...out and yeah," I stuttered. "And my phone died."

His silver eyes gleamed with something like amusement as he moved to swipe up my order.

"I honestly don't know how you kids do it." He held the cup and the small brown bag out to me.

"Usual, Nathan?" Bailey, Keeper of the Bacon Roll asked. If the overly familiar way they'd addressed each other wasn't clue enough, when I glanced at him to find him plotting my death, I got the picture. Bailey had a crush.

"Yeah, thanks," Professor Alexander said without looking away from me. I took my breakfast from him gratefully.

"Thanks, sir. I'll pay you back."

Alexander's eyes crinkled at the corners as he laughed. "Sir, is it?"

"Shit, sorry," I groaned, cheeks flaming. "I don't know why I said that. Professor, I mean.

"Nathan," he corrected. "That whole professor thing makes me feel weird most of the time, but here in a coffee shop on Sunday morning?" He shuddered visibly. "All kinds of wrong, Jude."

"Right, got it," I said.

The shop was getting busier now and I was starting to feel increasingly worse the longer I stood there. I was well past hungry and the thirst had me about ready to topple over. I was sure I'd regret craving a grilled bacon roll altogether when I thought back on this incident but right now I wanted to take it home and shove it down my throat in one go.

"I'll be off, then. Thanks again, Prof – Nathan." I held up the bag and cup of tea and grinned stupidly before scurrying out of the shop and back home towards the dorm.

They were, admittedly, the best bacon rolls I'd ever eaten and after finishing them and gulping down the lukewarm sweetened tea, the lingering embarrassment over my run-in with Professor Alexander was all but wiped out by how blissfully full and satisfied I was. I slept for twelve straight hours after.

I'm not sure when I realised Nathan was attracted to me, when I understood that his rapt attention whenever I spoke in class – and furtive glances when I didn't – was more than just scholarly interest in his student. But certainly it was sometime into Trinity term of my second year, after the coffee shop and after he had announced to our close-knit film studies class that he wouldn't be returning next term. (A couple of the girls had actually cried during that class.)

He'd only been due to stay for one academic year, but had extended when a job he'd had lined up in London had fallen through.

He'd told us after one of our trips to the local cinema, he had an apartment in Brooklyn to get home to and a dog his sister had been keeping for him, and a job on a play (with a well-loved actor) off Broadway, that he was expected to start in November.

If not for all this, he said, he'd absolutely stay. He couldn't tell us about his replacement yet but he said she was exceptionally cool and we'd love her way more than we'd ever liked his pretentious American ass.

He'd been decent enough never to mention the bacon roll incident. On the Tuesday after, I'd set a slice of vegan banana loaf and a large iced black coffee on his desk with a note that said, 'Bailey said this was your usual – thank you '. He'd lifted his head and given me that gleaming American smile and a nod, and that had been that.

Until one night in the Upper Camera library I'd been typing away so long on my laptop that my hands had gone numb. I stopped to shake them out. It was late on a Friday, and I had a paper due on Medieval language on Monday. I was working at P&P all weekend, so this was the only time I had left to finish it without having to pull an all-nighter on Sunday. I hadn't eaten yet, though it was about 8 p.m.

Suddenly, a cheese and pickle sandwich appeared in front of me along with a bottle of water still chilled from the fridge. I twisted in my chair to find him standing over me, avidly reading my laptop screen. He was tall, so he needed to crouch over me in order to see the screen.

"Eat something," he said, eyes still fixed on the screen. "You've been here four hours and haven't eaten."

My brain was too overloaded, too exhausted, to think about asking how he knew how long I'd been here or that I hadn't eaten. I opened the sandwich – from the vending machine on the ground floor, I noticed – and ate it in four large bites while Nathan read my paper over my shoulder.

As he read he said, very close to my ear, things like, "good point", "ah, so smart", "really good", and "clever boy."

"You need to stop buying me food," I joked when I'd finished the sandwich and drained half the bottle of water.

"And what if I like feeding you?" he said softly.

I turned my head to look at him. The library was quiet – not empty – but quiet. On Friday nights, most people had better things to do. *I* would normally have better things to do. But it meant there was no one in the immediate vicinity to see Nathan turn his head and bring our mouths just a breath away. His eyes dipped to my lips and I felt something stir nervously in my gut, then lower between my legs.

Want.

Different in nature and flavour from the want I'd had for Finn's mouth or his dick, and closer to the kind I'd had for Caspien. It was just the forbidden nature of it, I told myself. It was the knowledge that I could never really have it. It was knowing that a boundary existed that couldn't be crossed. It was, ridiculous as it sounds, safe.

But still, the abruptness of it frightened me. I hadn't known I'd felt that way about Nathan, not to mention he was my bloody professor, and that part had come on me very much like it had for Caspien. Sudden and breath-taking.

I stood abruptly, slammed shut my laptop, grabbed my bag and ran out of the library as fast as I could.

TWELVE

Nathan said that asking me to be his guide in Jersey had nothing to do with his attraction to me and everything to do with fate dropping me in his lap when he was writing a screenplay about the occupation of the island. I was a gift, he said more than once.

He'd been drawn to me before he knew where I was from ('those big green eyes that look at everything the world has to offer you with an edge of terror'), and the synchronicity of it only proved that we were meant to be something to each other.

After the night in the library, buckled from embarrassment, I skipped my Tuesday film criticism class. And then the Thursday tutorial after that. I'd made up some lie to Nikita about not feeling great Monday night, followed by a dentist appointment on the Thursday, but I was going to run out of plausible excuses soon enough. Honestly, I was fully prepared to fail the class and resit something in the summer, after he'd gone, to make up my grade.

But on the Friday, a week to the day after the incident, I was reading the back of a microwave meal – it was the third one I'd picked up so far – at the Waitrose chilled section when I felt a presence come to a stop next to me. I slid the packet back and picked up another.

"Definitely the moussaka or the cottage pie," the presence, who had a distinct American accent, said.

I stiffened, instantly aware of every part of my body. Turning my head I wasn't surprised to see him watching me with one of his easy smiles. "Be easier on the tooth." Silver-grey eyes sparkling.

My stomach dipped as I opened my mouth to attempt some excuse.

"Sir, hi, hello...I," I stammered like a bloody imbecile.

He rolled his eyes. "Oh, man, not the *sir* again." He reached into the fridge compartment for a garlic loaf, and put it into his basket. "I'm actually glad I ran into you because I've made a lot – too much – spaghetti Bolognese. If you'd like to join me for a bowl?"

My mouth opened, closed, opened again. "You want me to have dinner with you?"

"I mean, if that's weird, I could leave the room, and you could eat. After all, the goal is just feeding you. I don't technically need to be there."

Unexpectedly, I laughed. There was a nervous fluttering in my stomach, but I was ravenous with it. I wasn't sure what the fuck I was doing, but I found myself nodding.

"I really like spaghetti Bolognese."

Nathan had rented a basement flat only a five-minute walk from the university. It used to be a B&B, he told me as he led me down the stairs and into a cosy little vestibule where we took off our shoes. He opened the door into a large low-ceilinged living/dining space, a vine green kitchen nestled at one end. The place looked newly renovated, though it had a lived-in feel: papers piled on the dining table, books and a laptop on the coffee table, and a pot of delicious smelling Bolognese steaming gently on the hob.

As he turned on the oven for the bread and boiled the kettle for the pasta, I took a seat at the dining table and listened as he explained how his quarter Italian heritage was to thank for the ragu sauce.

I accepted a glass of wine and set the table with the mats and cutlery he set down next to me, while he plated up the food. It felt bizarrely comfortable. I liked him as my professor, probably because he wasn't like the other professors. He was half their age for a start, and he didn't so much teach or lecture as chat about films he liked and why. And as we had dinner, it felt much like it did in class. He made me laugh, he was interested in what I had to say, and it was only after stuffing my face with the best spaghetti Bolognese I'd ever had, and was a little loose from the wine, that he asked why I hadn't come to class this week.

I groaned, hiding my face in the crook of my arm. "Because of what happened in the library."

"And what happened in the library, Jude?"

I lifted my head to peer up at him. He was sipping casually from his glass, a wry smile on his mouth. He was extremely good-looking, mature, and successful. And as incredible as it was, he appeared to be flirting with me. But he was also my professor. And it was as though I'd only just remembered that last part, and that I was here, alone, having dinner with him, because suddenly, the easy, jovial atmosphere had sharpened to a very fine and deliberate point.

I said, "Come on. You know you're...well, hot."

"Do I?"

I let out a nervous chuckle. "I mean, surely yeah, you do. Half the girls in class are in love with you, a couple of the guys too. And then there's Bailey at the coffee shop who's been plotting my death since you bought me a bacon roll and who I had to lie to so I could get him to give me your order."

"You lied? Not Jude Alcott." He was grinning now.

"I just said you'd asked me to go there for your usual, that he'd know what it was. I thought there'd be less chance of him messing up the order on purpose."

"Wow. How very Machiavellian of you."

I smiled, proud of myself.

"So, that's a lot of people you claim are in love with me. What about you?"

Without thinking, I almost said, '*I'm in love with someone else*,' but I thought better of it.

Instead, I said, "Nah, I don't think any of them are in love with me."

Nathan laughed and stood, lifting both our bowls and forks. I followed behind him with the side plates.

"I can do the dishes," I offered. For some reason, this made Nathan look at me with what I thought was fondness before he gave a slight shake of his head.

"I have a dishwasher. Go sit down."

I sat on the sofa sipping my wine as he finished up in the kitchen. "Do you miss New York?" It was a nice flat, but I imagined his place in Brooklyn to be something he might miss.

"Uh, yeah, I do. I miss my dog. I miss craving Japanese food at 4 a.m. and being able to walk two blocks with him and get it."

"What's his name?" The coffee table had a photo of him with his dog. It looked old and large, with a pointed dark nose and lighter around the head and ears.

"Ivan."

I shot him a look as he came to sit next to me.

"*Ivan's Childhood*. Tarkovsky, of course," I laughed. "Could have guessed that."

"It's a good name."

"Terrible film, though," I smirked.

"Okay, what's your favourite film then, wise guy?"

I shrugged, "Don't have one."

"Coward."

I laughed again. "I really don't. I like films – I like them a lot more since I joined your class, but they don't move me the way books do. I can never quite suspend my belief enough to lose myself in them completely."

"The way you do when you're reading," said Nathan.

"Exactly."

"I think that's a perfectly acceptable point of view." He nodded and reached across to top up my wine. "Unlike your stance on Tarkovsky, for example."

I wasn't aware of how comfortable I was, how much I was enjoying myself with him; I'd somehow spent an entire night without thinking of Cas. And then it was close to midnight, and the wine bottle was long empty. The conversation had reached a natural lull, and though he'd certainly given me looks throughout the night, I wasn't truly one hundred percent sure of how to read the situation. I was nothing special, whilst he was a smart, talented Oscar–winning professor. I was going to need to have it spelt out for me before I'd make that kind of a fool of myself.

"Shit, I didn't even realise the time," I said, standing. "I should get going."

He didn't move. He sat with his legs slightly parted, arm resting along the back of the sofa and a look on his face that I'd have to have been blind not to understand. When he widened his legs a little more, eyes never leaving mine, I couldn't help my eyes dipping to the space between his legs.

My film criticism professor was hard. Really fucking hard.

There were fourteen individual points noted in the policy concerning relationships between students and staff. I knew because last Friday, after the library incident, I'd gone home and looked it up. I knew that under 'definitions' that policy included every individual working within the University under a formal contract (such as visiting academics). I also knew that since Caspien, I hadn't wanted anyone as much as I wanted Nathan Alexander in that moment. It seemed like too good an opportunity to pass up on.

I was an adult, but that didn't take away from the fact that the burden of responsibility in this sort of thing sat with the staff member, not the student. There was something in the statute about harassment towards staff which Nathan could maybe level at me. But he'd invited me here, to his house. He was hard. There was no way I'd misread this.

Nathan's voice jolted me out of my thoughts.

"Jude, I don't want to do anything that makes you uncomfortable." He sat up, suddenly more serious. He had read my overthinking as something else.

Fervent, I shook my head. "I'm not uncomfortable, I promise. I'm not. I just wanted to be really clear about what this was. If it's what I think it is, I mean. Honestly, I'm a little shit with this kind of thing."

"What kind of thing is that?"

I shrugged awkwardly. "Knowing when people are into me, knowing if it's what I think it is or...something else entirely." I saw Cas's face then. *I never asked you to care for me, Jude.* "I always get it wrong somehow."

Nathan slid forward so that he was perched on the edge of the sofa.

"Then let me spell it out for you, Jude Alcott. I haven't stopped thinking about you since the day in the coffee shop. I've never wanted to take someone home just to shower, feed, and cuddle them to sleep before."

I felt my cheeks heat, renewed mortification at the memory.

"That's what did it? You mean, I sit in your class twice a week and try to impress you with my studiousness and intellect, and me hungover, unwashed, and starving was what got you?"

"Aw, you try to impress me?" He looked charmed. "I don't look at my students that way in the classroom; there are rules about that kind of thing, you know." One side of his mouth twitched.

"But outside of the classroom is fine?" I raised an eyebrow.

"We were two consenting adults who met in a supermarket and decided they wanted to have dinner together."

"You're still my professor." I wanted to gag myself.

"Well, in about eight weeks, I'm not going to be your professor anymore, Jude. And this is definitely something we can revisit. I like you, and I'm happy to wait if any of this feels uncomfortable – that's the last thing I want."

He was serious, I could tell. He would wait for me. I found it... thrilling. And to my absolute disgust and horror, I got an inkling of what Caspien must have felt like with Blackwell.

Except that Caspien was a child then and I was an adult.

I was an adult and if Nathan wasn't worried about what might happen should we be found out, then I decided I wasn't either.

It gave me the final push I needed. I lowered myself to my knees so that I was on the rug between his open legs, and then I kissed him.

His lips were gentle and soft and the scrape of his short facial hair against my cheek as he tilted his head sent a delicious rush of arousal to my dick. Despite the undercurrent of fear about who he was, it already felt far less confusing than being with Finn had. I reached up and dug my fingers into his hair, grabbing at the chestnut brown curly top and pulling his head closer. When he moaned, lust spread over my body, all the way to my fingertips.

Nathan's mouth tasted of wine and dark cherry, and I sank into the kiss so completely that the memory of another kiss, one that tasted of birthday cake and champagne, was all but forgotten.

We kissed for a long time that night – it was all we did – and I lost myself in it. He was an exceptional kisser. He kissed me as if I was something he'd longed for, something he wanted desperately. Kissing Nathan Alexander is something I miss even now. His mouth was always warm, always welcoming, always soothing away the aches and wants lingering there for someone else.

If I could have chosen a love, one that would have made me a better version of myself instead of worse, then I'd have chosen Nathan. But we don't get to choose these things. I'd learned that lesson already, and I'd learn it a few more times still.

But that night, hands and tongues and tender smiles unfurled something new and hopeful into my heart.

When our kissing reached some critical point, it was Nathan who pulled back, smiling down at me as he brushed a hand over my cheek. I didn't want to leave. I didn't want to go home to my dorm where I'd pick apart everything about Nathan and set it out so I could compare it with Cas.

I wanted, almost desperately, to sleep next to him so I could wake up and see the sun on his face, so I could kiss him with the warmth of it on his lips. But he never asked me to stay, and I didn't want to beg, so I kissed him at the door and said goodnight.

As I walked home under the same moon that had listened to my promise to love Cas unconditionally, I was almost convinced I was free from it. From him. From Deveraux, from that heartache that had been living deep inside me for so long.

That delusion didn't last very long.

THIRTEEN

In the end, I managed to convince Nathan to hire a proper tour guide. I could show him a good time (I said with a wink) but not the places where the Germans had built their first bunker on British soil. I'd found it was much easier to admit not knowing much about my island's history after he'd had my dick in his mouth.

But I agreed to go home, at least for the three weeks he'd be there. Luke was ecstatic and had already made plans for us to go fishing and do a couple of the west coast walking trails. Gideon was in Italy again, and from there, he'd be going back to London – where I was still welcome to come visit him if I was at a loose end (I hadn't gone over Christmas after all – and Deveraux was still under renovation.)

It would be a different kind of summer without Gideon or Deveraux, and after the second-year exams I'd just emerged from – the hardest and most stressful of my life – I was looking forward to going home.

I was looking forward to showing Nathan my home.

For the last few years, home had felt like a memory I didn't want. A series of reminders of something I wanted back so intensely that it was painful. But those reminders had followed me onto Oxford, too, and that was because Cas didn't live in a place, he lived inside me.

But as I headed home that summer, Cas was barely even on my mind.

I got home on a Thursday night, the last week in June, and sensed the atmosphere between Beth and Luke the moment I stepped inside the cottage. Luke had picked me up at the airport, his mood light and animated, but which disappeared the second he walked through the door. Beth was at the dining table on her laptop, surrounded by piles of paper and with her phone in her hand, glancing between both screens. I knew she'd got a big promotion at work in April, and it was more demanding of her time and attention than her middle management sales job had ever been before.

"He's home, Beth," Luke said when Beth didn't look up from her phone. His voice was strangely cold. Not a tone I'd ever heard him use on her before. I looked at him, but he was turned and peering into the fridge.

"Hey," she said, standing to throw her arms around me for a quick hug.

"Alright? Still working?" I gestured at the table.

"End of the month performance." Beth sighed. "There's a management meeting tomorrow."

"I see." I gave her an apologetic look.

"You hungry, Judey?" Luke was asking as he took something out of the fridge that looked like leftovers.

"I'm okay, actually, had a burger at the airport."

I wanted to get out of the kitchen, where the air felt precarious and tense. Upstairs, I made a half-hearted attempt at unpacking before giving up and lying down on my bed. Nathan was arriving on Monday evening; he was currently packing up the flat in Oxford, and the last of his boxes were being picked up on Monday morning to be shipped back to New York.

He wasn't a great texter. He preferred to talk on the phone, which I, expressly, did not, but I dialled his number anyway, and he answered on the fourth ring.

"Hey, you," he said. "How was your propeller flight across the channel?"

"Loud. Creaky. Very bumpy."

"Fuck," he groaned.

I'd discovered about a week prior that he hated flying. So much so that he'd only been back to New York once in two years, and that was because his favourite aunt had died. He'd considered not going home for this either, but there was a reading of a will he'd had to be present for after. He'd planned to take the ferry across to Jersey until I told him it was a ten-hour journey. The plane was an hour. 'Yes, but not a real plane', he'd argued. I'd then shown him a picture of the plane's engine, which seemed to relax him a little.

"It'll be fine," I said. "They don't even fly that high, so if it comes down in the sea, it won't make too much of a splash."

"I'm hanging up on you now."

"I'm joking," I laughed. "It was fine. Smoothest hour I've ever spent in the air."

"Okay, I'm going to choose to believe that."

He told me about the dinner he had with some of the faculty the following night, which he was quietly dreading. He didn't socialise much with the rest of the department, I knew. They'd been stand-off-ish with him when he'd first arrived: he was convinced they saw him as a young American upstart with nothing to commend him but a shiny statuette. The fact he wasn't even thirty yet only made it worse.

"They'll be bricking it. The loss of the hot, prodigious Oscar–winning lecturer is going to be quite the loss to the teaching body," I said. "Speaking of which, did you remember to pack it?"

"It's already gone. Wait a minute, you said hot."

"You know I think you're hot."

"Yeah, but I worried it was because I was your professor. And since I haven't technically been that for two whole days..."

"I think *technically* you're still my professor until the last day of term, which is Saturday, so..."

"Oh, you're right, which means Monday you'll be seeing me man to man for the first time."

I snorted at this. "Man to man?"

"Yes, what? It will be." He was laughing, too. I could hear him settling, as though getting into bed or stretching his body out on the grey sofa of his living room. "Have you been thinking about it?" he asked, voice low and rough.

It had been almost six weeks since the night we first kissed, and we still hadn't had sex. It had been everything except sex, and he'd never pushed or pressured for anything more. Though I could tell how much he wanted it, he'd never done anything to make me feel uncomfortable.

I'd told him that aside from my high school girlfriend (this he'd found unsurprising and very cute), there'd been one other person I'd been serious about. He understood that this person had taken some part of me I wasn't sure I would ever get back.

But patience had its limits. And I was reaching my own: I wanted him. We'd discussed preferences, what I did and didn't think I could do, what he was able to teach me. *Everything*, he'd whispered one night. *We'll find out what you like and what you don't, and we'll work everything out together. Please don't worry, baby.*

And there was that. The nickname.

It seemed ridiculous to me that I could be anyone's 'baby'. And yet, when he said it in that lazy American accent, I didn't feel ridiculous. It made my cheeks heat whenever he said it, but I didn't hate it. Not at all. I liked how it made me feel. I liked how Nathan made me feel.

"Have you?" he asked again.

"I've thought about it, yeah," I admitted. "But can we wait until I see you to talk about it?" I didn't want to talk about it over the phone. Not because I was embarrassed, but because talking like this over the phone, especially while lying here, was too close to a reminder of what I'd once had with someone else. And I was thinking about him less and less each day that went by. Nathan had begun filling some of the empty spaces he'd left behind.

"Sure, we can, baby," he said easily. "Everything okay? How's your sister?"

"She's okay, busy with work, I guess. But Luke's glad I'm home."

"Are you going to tell him about me?"

Nathan knew that Luke knew I was into men. And I'd wondered about how to tell Luke – whether to tell Luke – that one of my professors was coming to the island for three weeks, and that I was going to be spending a lot of time with him. I considered leaving the professor part out and just saying he was someone I'd met in Oxford, without any specifics, but it felt too much like lying.

"Would you be okay with that?"

"Of course, I would. I'd like to meet him if you'd want that."

That idea filled me with a thin thread of horror. Luke and Nathan face to face, man to man, trying to have a conversation. About what? Luke didn't watch pretentious films, didn't read, didn't know anything about New York. And Nathan knew nothing about gardening or the natural world and hated action films. But then I remembered that Cas and Luke had gotten on very well despite all of the reasons they shouldn't have. Everyone liked Luke, and Luke liked most people.

"Let's see how the telling him I'm seeing my professor goes down first."

"Ex-professor."

"I don't think that's a thing."

"It will be on Saturday."

On Saturday night, Luke invited me out to the pub. It was one of those warm summer nights when the air felt baked and fragrant and the birds were lazing in trees too tired to fly. We walked down the long drive to the bus stop and took the bus down towards the beach.

Luke's local was the friendly little gastro pub that sat halfway down the main road to the beach. The manager was a client of his, and he brought over two pints on the house after we'd found a table outside in a shaded section of the beer garden.

"Can't beat it," Luke said as he wiped the foam from the head away from his lip.

He looked older, I thought. Lines dug deeper into the weathered grooves of his forehead and sides of his eyes, new lines that hadn't been there when I saw him at Christmas. He was still handsome though, suntanned skin bright against the dark of his hair.

"It's good," I agreed.

The beer was satisfying, cool and fizzing against my dry throat. I normally went for something stronger – I was normally trying to get drunk – but the last few months, I'd been drinking far less to get drunk and more to enjoy the warm mellowing it offered to my muscles. A glass after dinner with Nathan, a single, cool beer as I read in my dorm. Maybe I was growing up.

The silence swelled between us, and I knew it would be as good a time as any to tell him about Nathan. But Luke spoke first, ripping out the ground from beneath my feet as he did.

"So Judey, I wasn't sure the best way to do this, to tell you this, but I figured it was best to just come out and say it." He took a large deep breath, resigned and tired sounding. When he met my eye, I could see his own shimmering with something I recognised. Pain. Heartache. "Beth and I, well we're gonna be getting a divorce."

FOURTEEN

It turned out that my sister had met someone else – someone at work. Daniel, his name was – it had 'just happened'.

Luke said she'd been 'different' for the last eight months or so, though I knew things had been different between them since before that. Since the baby, I think. Though deep down I wondered (and feared) if maybe they'd been different since I came along.

A few months ago, he'd seen a message on her phone and confronted her, and it had all come tumbling out. I could tell he was devastated. A gloominess in him that had never been there before, like a light had gone out.

I should have been sitting there while my sister explained this to me, but Luke and I had always been closer, so I listened as he explained how she would be moving out, away from Jersey, in fact, in the next couple of weeks.

I felt such a rush of betrayal and hatred for her that I wasn't sure how I was ever going to look her in the face again.

"I think the baby changed things for us," he went on, sadly. "I wanted the baby more than she did, and then when she had to go through that, I think she blamed me a little for it."

"It wasn't your fault. These things happen."

"Yeah, I know. I think logically she knows that too, but we feel how we feel. We can't logic our way out of feelings, you know?"

I thought it might be one of the most astute things he'd ever said.

"Does she know you're telling me?"

He shrugged. "I told her I would be, as soon as you were home," he said. "I didn't want to do it over the phone. Not with your exams on."

I sagged with gratitude.

"How come she's still there," I asked. "How can you even look at her?" I knew I was being extremely biased, but I couldn't find it in me to care. I felt as betrayed as Luke did.

"I've been sleeping in your room," he said. "Been on the couch the last few nights."

"Christ, Luke." I sighed and sat back, folding my arms. "Right, well, that's not happening again; I'll take the couch." Nathan would be arriving on Monday anyway, so I could stay there.

"Don't be stupid. It's alright." He reached out and squeezed my arm gently. "It's not for much longer."

"Actually, it works out okay because on Monday I've a friend coming over. He's renting somewhere in Filquet, so I can stay there with him." I wasn't sure what tone I was using, but it was enough to prick Luke's curiosity. His expression lightened a little, and a small smile peeked at the side of his mouth. I felt my cheeks and ears grow warm.

"A friend, is it?"

I tried to keep my face neutral. "Yeah, from Oxford."

Luke nodded, still smiling.

"Okay, so he's like a guy I've been sort of seeing."

Luke's eyes went wide, and he nodded again.

"Christ, okay, he was sort of my professor."

This made him sit up straight, eyes darkening.

"I promise it wasn't anything weird, okay maybe it's a little weird, but he's young, older than me but still young; he's twenty-eight. He's like a guest professor. They have these slots each academic year where they invite people in to teach certain subjects. Last year, we had that historian from the telly in; she does all those shows about the Tudors. Well, he was like that. So not like a real professor."

I was rambling. Luke was still frowning.

"I swear, Luke, he's great. He is. And he's not teaching there this year. He's going back to New York in September. But we've been careful, and he's really great; I promise he's not like some weirdo pervert or anything," I explained.

Luke considered all this for an uncomfortably long time before he said, "So, what happens then? In September? He's just buggering off back to America and leaving you?"

I had not prepared for this line of questioning, so I had nothing right away. I stammered a little before saying, "I'll visit."

Nathan and I hadn't discussed anything of the sort. Which only then struck me as a little odd. Had we both already defined this as some sort of summer fling? Was that what I wanted it to be? I'd not thought beyond this point with him. Maybe that's why it had been going as well as it had.

"Hmmm." The noise was Luke's trademark sign of disapproval, and my heart sank a little. "Well, I'm not sure about all this guest professor stuff, seems like a professor is a professor and a student is a student and so he should have known better if you ask me."

I was immediately on the attack.

"Oh, for fuck sake, Luke, I'm a bloody adult. It's not like I'm Cas shagging a thirty-two-year-old lawyer when I was fifteen."

Luke's back went ramrod straight. "What?"

"Oh, come on, you didn't think he'd run off with a guy he'd just met, did you?"

"I didn't give it all that much thought. Never met the fella he's with. You're saying he was how old?" Luke's face had gone very pale. "When Cas was...you're sure?"

I gave him a look. "Extremely."

Luke curled his fist atop the table, eyes black as pitch suddenly. He took an angry sip of his pint. "Does Gideon know this?"

I gave a helpless shrug. Then sighed. "Anyway, this isn't about Cas, and Nathan isn't Blackwell. He's the furthest thing from it, Luke. I promise."

Luke stared at me for a long time. "Okay, Judey," he said at last. "If you know what you're doing, then I'm alright with it." His mouth softened, not all the way to a smile, but away from the hard grim line of a moment earlier. "You seem happier, buddy."

I smiled. "I am."

But then, I remembered. My smile fell.

"I actually don't know how I'm supposed to look at her, Luke."

He reached out to squeeze my arm again. "Hey, she's your sister, and she's been through the mill of it too." He lifted his pint and drained the last of it. "I don't want you to hate her on my behalf. Christ, I don't hate her, Judey. I just feel like I've lost my best friend, you know? It's been pretty lonely these last couple years with you gone and Beth being, well, so far away too. Now I've lost her. I'm just not sure who I am without her, kinda scary being single again. Jeez."

I felt an enormous swell of guilt about that then. About running away at the first chance I got. About staying away at every opportunity after. But it had been necessary. I'd known no other way to cope.

"Sorry," I said anyway.

"You've nothing to be sorry for," Luke said.

"Yeah, well, I'm sorry for not being around when you've been going through this." I took a sip of my lager.

"You've been off living your life. Getting a degree at Oxford. Shagging your professors."

I coughed out my beer. It landed over both of us. Luke was grinning – almost happily – as he wiped it off his arm.

The following morning, Luke was out, working somewhere on

the grounds, and Beth was in the kitchen making breakfast when I walked in. I hesitated, thinking about turning around and going back upstairs. But she'd heard me come in and turned to look at me.

I took a moment to just look at her: she looked better than I'd seen her look in a long time. Well-rested and tanned, her hair in long healthy waves down her back. I hated her a little more for it.

The look she gave me seemed to contain multitudes.

"He told you then," she said with a sigh.

Without a word I walked across the kitchen to pull out a mug, and began to fill the kettle. I set it onto boil and stood at the kitchen sink, my back to her as I looked out the window.

"Jude. Please look at me."

I wasn't sure I could. My knuckles were white, and my jaw clenched so hard it ached.

"I'm your sister," she said. I wasn't sure what that was supposed to mean, but I turned around.

"Yeah, and Luke's your husband. What's your point?" I said harshly.

"These things just happen, Jude. It's no one's fault."

"Well, it's certainly not Luke's fault. *You* let this happen, Beth. Luke loves you, adores you. Luke is the best fucking man I know, that most people know, so it is someone's fault – but not his!"

She smiled. A sad, twisted thing I didn't like at all. "Christ, he's just bloody perfect, isn't he? You've never seen him as anything else."

"So, what you're going to try and convince me you running off with someone else is somehow *his fault*?" I asked her, incredulous.

"No, no, of course, not. But I think if you meet Dan, you'll like him." She smiled hopefully.

I blinked at her, dumbfounded. "Seriously? You must be off your bloody head if you think that's ever going to happen." I turned back to making my tea. She was quiet while I did it. While I poured myself some cereal, while I dragged out the kitchen chair and threw myself down into it. I ate a few angry spoonfuls while she finished slicing fruit behind me. To my surprise, she pulled out a chair and sat across from me. I wanted to get up and leave the room, but I was as stubborn as she was. I didn't look at her.

It didn't matter that Luke didn't want me to hate her on his behalf because I hated her on my own. The gap that had closed a little after she lost the baby rumbled open again. I was glad she was moving off the island. Glad I wouldn't have to see her make a new life with a man who wasn't Luke. Luke, who was as close to perfect as a man could be. Luke, who was too good for my sister.

Luke was the one who'd been there for me and now I'd be there for him. Beth would be like every other family member I never saw. I could see her pleading eyes skirt to mine every now and again, but I ignored them.

I finished my cereal without uttering a single word to her, lifted my bowl, put it in the dishwasher, and walked out of the kitchen.

FIFTEEN

"I'm sorry, baby," Nathan said, when I told him about Luke and Beth's divorce.

He didn't think it odd that my loyalties were with Luke and not my sister. He said he'd feel exactly the same if he were in my shoes. He knew how close Luke and I were, and he thought the notion that blood was thicker than water was nonsense.

His parents had divorced when he was twelve, and he maintained it had fucked him up in a very specific kind of way, a way that had made him a tiresome over-achiever. ("You're all grown up though, so you're gonna be fine.")

Nathan had rented a tranquil, white-stoned cottage with a herb garden about a twenty-five minute drive from Deveraux. At the bottom of the garden was a wooden gate, beyond which me-andered one of the five scenic cliff walks on the 'What to do in Jersey' page of the official tourist website.

The house was in a nice spot, perfect for writing a screenplay.

I picked him up from the airport on Monday and drove him to the Airbnb. I'd driven past the cottage on my driving lessons and recognised it immediately as the place after the blind turn.

He'd decided not to hire a car. I'd told him most places on the island were within cycling distance and offered to drive him anywhere he needed to go.

He'd arrived at the arrivals gate with two large suitcases: every item of clothing packed for his return to New York in three weeks' time. After retrieving the key from the lockbox and lugging them out of the car, we'd dumped them inside the hallway and explored the cottage.

It was smaller than ours at Deveraux; one bedroom with a small study area at the top of the stairs with a view out over the cliff walk. A well-equipped kitchen, a full-size bathroom, and cosy bedroom with a king-size bed which Nathan had promptly pushed me down onto and kissed me senseless.

"Fuck, I missed you," he said against my lips.

I kissed him back hungrily. "I missed you too," I said.

After dinner we took the bottle of wine out to the garden where we sat at the small bistro-style table and listened to the waves crash against the cliffs below. After I'd told him about Luke and Beth, he'd told me about the faculty dinner. One of the history professors had gotten drunk and come onto him, though no matter how much I begged, he wouldn't tell me who. Something about his integrity hanging on by a thread.

When the bottle was long finished and we were both tangled up together on the sofa exchanging soft kisses, he lifted his head and looked down at me. There was some kind of an implicit understanding between us that tonight it would happen. I'd packed a small overnight bag and brought it with me when I picked him up from the airport.

"Have you decided?" he asked softly. His fingers traced the side of my mouth and down to my jaw. I was very hard. We both were.

I swallowed, cleared my throat, and said as bravely as I could, "Yeah, I think I want you to fuck me."

His eyebrows only went up a little. "You *think*?"

"No, I mean, I know." I looked straight into his eyes when I said this. "I've thought about it a lot, and I need to know if it's for me. I've been dancing around it for a while now. And I want to try it with you. I mean, obviously you'll do it properly, not like some knobhead rower from Corpus who likes Tarantino."

"Obviously." There was a playful lilt to his mouth.

"So…will you?" I asked him.

"I don't think there's anything else I want more, Jude," Nathan said and pressed a kiss to my lips.

"Not even another Oscar?" I grinned.

He thought about it. "I honestly think two is too many."

I laughed.

Nathan did know how to do things properly; I'd been right about that. He'd taken me into the shower, both of us standing in the roll-top bath as we crowded under the overhead spray. After washing himself quickly, he told me where to clean and how – thoroughly and carefully seemed to be the main thing – and left me alone to do it. I was to come back into bed when I was ready.

He opened me slowly and carefully with his fingers first, saying things like '*good boy*' and '*you're perfect*' and '*so beautiful, baby*' as he did. He'd suggested I ride him so I could control the penetration myself, but the idea of it felt too…exposing, too performative, so I lay on my back, pulled my legs up and wide, and thought of England.

He wasn't as big as I was, but he was still bigger than the fingers he'd used before. Despite Nathan pushing in slow and gentle, I was certain I was being split wide open. It was excruciating. We had to stop several times so he could remind me to breathe. I was convinced I'd never, ever, put myself through it again. Until suddenly, and shockingly, the pain turned to pleasure. A sharp, breath-taking kind of pleasure that seemed to come from a place deep inside me I hadn't known existed before.

Nathan saw when it did, and he began to move, slow at first and then faster. But the sensation soon went back to pain, and then see-sawed from pain to that strange searing pleasure and back again so that I became dizzy and overwhelmed from it.

When he began to drive into me, I could only cling on. He kissed me and fucked me and told me again that I was good, perfect, beautiful. I gripped the muscle of his shoulders and buried my face in his neck, and waited for it to end. There was some pleasure, fleeting and piercing, and the weight and scent of him all around me was arousing, but I knew I was supposed to feel more than that. I wasn't a bottom, I decided. It was good that I knew, that Nathan – perfect and gentle and respectful Nathan – had been the one to teach me that. He came a short while later, collapsing on top of me before quickly pulling out and rolling off me to lie by my side.

"Fuck, baby, that was incredible." He was still panting as he tore off the condom and discarded it by the bed. It took him a moment to come back down to earth. Then he sat up, concern creasing his forehead. "Shit, did I hurt you?"

I shook my head. "No, not really." I sat up and glanced down between my legs. It felt strange there, loose and wet from the lubrication and penetration. Used. I didn't like it. "Let me just go to the bathroom really quick." I made a stupid comedic show of not being able to walk just to make him laugh.

Inside the bathroom I used the towel to clean myself – I hadn't come, hadn't been hard the entire time he fucked me – and ran the cold tap until it was a noisy gush. Then I sat wincingly down on the toilet seat and let the usual post-sex melancholy settle over me.

So I wasn't a bottom. It didn't need to mean anything more than that. Nathan wasn't a strict top, and so it didn't matter. He'd already said it didn't. He preferred to top, but it wasn't a deal breaker for him. I'd fuck him and it would be fine.

Had I really been expecting to like it? No. Was I surprised that I didn't? No.

So why did I feel disappointed? Like I'd lost something? Like I'd failed at something crucial.

Okay, yes, maybe I'd been thinking there'd be some great pivotal shift inside me after I did this thing, which would knock me off the path I'd been on since the moment I set eyes on Caspien Deveraux. Emerging from the chrysalis of heartbreak into someone new and whole and changed. Someone who didn't need what he'd needed before.

But it hadn't happened. I was the same. And, somehow, he had slithered his way back into my head so that it felt like he was in the room with me. Sitting on the edge of the bath, staring at me with cold blue eyes, quietly satisfied that I'd failed. Not only at this stupid self-imposed sexual awakening but at removing him from my heart and soul. I loved Caspien, still. I wanted Caspien, still. There was a twisted kind of solace in understanding that had tonight gone differently, those truths would likely still have remained.

Nathan was everything I should have wanted. Everything I should need, but I sat there knowing that what I wanted and needed was something else entirely. Someone else entirely. That's the only way I was going to feel whole. That was the only way I was going to heal. By having him. By realising what it was to be wanted by him. To be loved by him. And since I knew it was impossible, because he wasn't capable of it, that knowledge was a new but familiar kind of devastation.

And the terror and hopelessness I felt at having to live like that for the rest of my life, wanting and loving someone who was entirely incapable of wanting and loving me back, was the worst fucking thing imaginable. A great suffocating panic rose in my chest so that I struggled to breathe for a moment. My chest felt tight, and my head was loose and weightless on my neck. I put my head between my legs and forced myself to inhale and exhale, slow and steady, for a few minutes.

Then I heard a soft rap on the door. "Baby, are you okay?" Nathan's voice was hitched with concern.

I stood and turned off the tap, glancing in the mirror to make sure I didn't look how I felt. I opened the door.

While I was in there, he had redressed in a navy T-shirt and black shorts. His curled hair was wild, like he'd been pulling at it.

"Yeah, sorry, sat down and couldn't get back up." I grinned. "Someone pounded my arse into oblivion."

This time the joke fell flat.

"Jude," he said.

"I'm fine, promise." I kissed him. Quick but firm. He followed me back into the bedroom where I went to my bag to pull on a pair of sweats and a t-shirt. I could feel him staring at me from the doorway. Could feel his concern rising.

"I need you to tell me you're okay, Jude."

"I already told you I was fine," I said, a little firmer than was necessary. To make up for it, I went to him, sliding my arms around his waist. "I'm okay. I'm good. But I think, well, I'm not a bottom."

He pulled back to look down at me. "What?"

"I just think...well, it's not for me. It had absolutely nothing to do with you, but it's just, yeah. Not my thing." I gave him an apologetic look.

"That's why you're being like this?" He sounded relieved. "Because you didn't like it?"

I shrugged.

"Shit, baby." He pulled me into him and nosed at the hair on the top of my head. He had a couple of inches on me, and this was a common position to find myself in. Pressed against his chest as he stroked my head with his jaw or his nose. "You scared me for a minute there."

"Sorry," I muttered into his chest.

"No, I'm sorry you didn't enjoy it, really I am. I wanted you to like it."

"I'm not saying we can never do it again ever." Though inside, I was hoping I'd never need to do it again.

"We're never going to do anything that makes you uncomfortable, ever," Nathan said. "I told you, it's not a big deal for me. I like you far more than I like topping, Jude. How you feel when we're together is more important than which sexual position I fucking prefer." He sounded a little angry, but it wasn't at me. He kissed my head again.

What on earth was wrong with me that I wasn't satisfied with this? Here was a man holding me to his chest and telling me my comfort was important to him, my feelings were important to him and yet my fucking soul ached for someone who'd thought nothing of either. I hated myself as much as I hated Cas in that moment. For who he'd made me. For what he'd stolen from me.

Maybe I couldn't give Nathan all of me, all those parts that had been broken or stolen and now belonged to Cas, but I could give him what I had left.

It wouldn't be enough, obviously, Nathan deserved better, and he'd come to realise that soon enough.

And he did. In fact, sooner than I thought he would.

SIXTEEN

We waited a few more nights until we tried again, this time in reverse. It was immeasurably better. Nathan was, I was coming to understand, a brilliant lover. No matter the position or the act, he had perfected the ways in which to make his partner feel good. I revelled in those nights; his touch, his mouth, his cock – as long as it was not inside my hole of course – brought me to orgasm over and over again. But more so, I loved our days together that summer.

He'd hired a tour guide he found on the tourist website for three full days, and he'd invited me along with him to learn about how the island survived five years of occupation by the Nazis. We took day trips to Guernsey and Alderney, too. We'd spend days at the cottage where he'd barbecue us lunch and make me wear nothing but his shorts as I lay out on the grass and read something he'd hand me and deem 'mind-expanding.' It was always works of American literature, and it gave me a perverse kind of pleasure to know that Caspien would have hated it. Brett Easton Ellis, Upton Sinclair, and Steinbeck were Nathan's favourite writers. *Moby Dick* was his favourite book, which I'd already read. I'd pushed back on his other favourite book, *Infinite Jest*, because I'd watched a YouTube video once about the most un-readable books ever written, and this was number three on it. 'We only have three weeks together', I said at the time. 'I'd rather not put myself through this now.' He'd laughed and made me promise to read it one day. (I've since read it, and I emailed him a few years ago to tell him. He hadn't been surprised to know I'd hated it.)

I'd call and check in with Luke every other day, but mainly, I stayed away from the house as I didn't want to face Beth. I couldn't understand how Luke was able to do it. Now I know it was his last hope that she'd change her mind, realise how much she loved him, and stay. It didn't work.

Toward the end of Nathan's second week on the island, he insisted we go out for dinner. He wanted to take me out on a date, he said. I'd been nervous at first, for reasons I wasn't sure I could explain, but which I didn't have to because he seemed to know anyway.

"I'll keep my hands to myself, I promise." He smiled as he pulled me in for a kiss. Nathan made a lot of promises, and so far, he'd kept every single one. I knew this wouldn't be any different. "You're not out here, are you? Just to Luke?"

I nodded, the word 'sorry' on the tip of my tongue, unspoken. He'd chastise me for apologising for things that weren't my fault. He said I shouldn't apologise for feelings I had, or didn't have, and for things I had no control over. There was no reason to be sorry for these things; it was just who I was. And who I was, was perfect.

I wasn't sure my not being out in Jersey fell into any of those categories.

"So then tonight, we're just friends. Or I'll go back to being your professor." He winked. "I'm whatever you want me to be, baby."

"Friends is fine," I said, smoothing down a stray hair at the side of my head. It was too long, that mid-stage where the curls would thicken and become close to untameable.

He stood behind me at the bathroom mirror and grinned at me. "Besties it is."

I laughed and turned to plant a kiss on his mouth. I'd rather have stayed home, but I figured this was another thing I could give him to make up for all the things I couldn't.

He'd booked a table at one of the more expensive restaurants along the beachfront. I'd never been inside it before but I knew Luke and Beth had come for their anniversary once. It was that kind of place. Marble floored and glass-fronted, though the large windows were pulled back tonight so it was open to the sea. A waiter showed us to a cosy table overlooking the seafront.

We might be posing as friends, but it really wasn't the sort of place you'd come with a mate. I felt a little conspicuous as I looked around. Most of the tables seemed to be straight couples, though some were groups. There were no tables where two men sat across from each other.

Nathan, sensing my growing discomfort, shot me an encouraging look. If he thought I'd have allowed it, he'd have reached across for my hand to give it a reassuring squeeze.

I'd driven so I ordered a sparkling water from the waiter who'd sat us down while Nathan ordered a white wine. We perused our menus – made up of mainly seafood – and discussed what we'd share. As we gazed out at the sea, I began to relax.

"Hi there, are you ready to order?" the waitress said, interrupting our quiet conversation.

I turned and sat bolt upright. Ellie stood smiling a blinding hospitality smile at me. Her face faltered with shock, before she glanced at Nathan, back at me, and then at Nathan again.

"Ellie, hello, how are you?" I said, overly polite. "I didn't know you worked here?"

"Um, yeah, it's just for the summer." It took her some effort to force her eyes from Nathan to me. "I'm home. For the summer. How are you, Jude?" She was flustered, I could tell. Shifting this way and that, on her feet. Cheeks pinking from embarrassment or something close to it.

"Ah, ok. Yeah, I'm good. You?"

She smiled even wider. "Yeah, really good."

"How's Edinburgh?"

"Great, yeah. I'm loving it. How's Oxford?"

"Hard." I laughed. "But great, yeah. I'm enjoying it. It's a great place to learn." I glanced at Nathan to find him watching the exchange with increasing amusement. He lifted his wine to take a slow taste and raised his eyebrows at me, playfully. He was enjoying this.

"I'll bet." Ellie looked at Nathan again, who was still looking at me.

"This is Ellie," I told him. "We went out in high school." I'd only told him there was an Ellie, not that I'd broken her heart and made her hate me because I couldn't stop thinking about the boy who'd gone on to break mine.

He turned his dazzling American smile on her. "Ellie. Of course, nice to meet you. I'm Nathan."

"You too," said Ellie, dazzled. "So, are you both ready to order?"

I suspected she'd asked to switch sections after that because for the rest of our dinner she was on the opposite side of the restaurant, hidden mainly behind a low wood-panelled wall. I was glad of it. Glad I didn't have to make polite conversation as she brought out each course. As she explained the cheeses and the sauces. Though Nathan I'm sure would have enjoyed every second of it.

He'd said it had been adorably awkward.

Later that night, as we walked along the beach, he'd asked me to tell him about Ellie. Whether I still thought about her. Whether I'd loved her. I'd told him the rest.

"She's exactly the sort of girl I imagine you with," said Nathan. "Naturally gorgeous, girl-next-door type." She was gorgeous, still; thick dark hair she'd now cut to just above her shoulders, warm brown eyes that sparkled when she smiled, a dusting of freckles over her forehead and nose.

"You imagine me with girls?" I raised an eyebrow at him. "I think you're doing gay wrong."

He laughed. "You know what I mean. She fits you. Actually, she's almost like the girl version of you."

I stopped walking and turned to him. "Wait, is this your way of trying to get me to dress up as a girl for you?"

"That could be fun," he said. "Schoolgirl? I'll be your teacher."

"Obviously," I said.

It was an idyllic three weeks. Nathan inspired me to write again; something beyond emails to a ghost – I hadn't written a single email to Cas for months.

I watched him work for hours in various places all over the cottage. Gold-rimmed glasses framing his face, brow creased in concentration, fingers flying over the keyboard. He'd stand up, stretch his back and neck, and hand me his laptop as he made himself another pot of coffee.

He was talented, I already knew this, and I thought the script he was writing would win him another Oscar (it hadn't), but just watching someone sit there and knit together a story from nothing but a few tunnels and some old photographs was like alchemy.

If Caspien is the reason this story exists, then Nathan is the reason I am writing it.

"Come to New York with me," Nathan said, a few nights before he was due to leave. We lay in bed, sweat cooling on our bodies, all windows of the cottage opened, two bottles of wine swimming in our blood.

"And do what?" I asked, sleepily.

"Be with me."

I laughed. "You have to work."

"I've been working here and being with you here. I can multi-task fairly impressively."

"That's definitely true. That thing you do with your mouth *and* your finger at the same time," I groaned. "Impressive."

He moved to sit up, his skin peeling away from mine as he did. "But I'm serious. Why don't you? Term doesn't start until when, October 13th?"

"I'm helping out with Freshers so I said I'd be back on the 3rd."

"So, that's more than two months. You'd love New York."

"I'm sure I would." I turned to him. "I promised Luke we'd hang out for a bit this summer and I've spent a lot of time here, fucking my professor since I got home."

It was meant as a half-joke, half-distraction, but some sad look bled into his eyes and I knew I'd missed the mark. He smiled a cheerless little smile.

"Okay. I get it." He leaned in and kissed me softly and slipped out of bed.

I heard the shower turn on and I sat up against the headboard and stared out of the window. The sea was a calm landscape over the cliffside, moon glittering silver on its surface. He came back about twenty minutes later, body dappled with water and his sculpted back and shoulders pinked from the heat. I watched him pull on some clothes, outdoor clothes.

"You're going out?" I asked.

He shot me a tender smile over his shoulder. "Just for a walk down to the beach."

Guilt and sadness swelled in me like the tide.

"Do you want me to come?"

"No, baby."

"Nathan, I'm..." I tapered off because I knew what I was about to do. I was about to apologise for something I couldn't help. For how I felt. "I'm sorry," I said regardless.

With a sigh he came and sat down on the bed near my feet.

"There's nothing you need to apologise for, Jude."

"No? So why do I feel like shit?" There was something thick and hot in my throat.

"Because you're a good person who cares about people."

"So are you. You're inviting me to New York with you, because you care about me, and I'm saying no because..." I really was going to bloody cry. Christ, I was pathetic.

Nathan reached out and put a hand on my thigh. "…Because you know what it will mean if you say yes. And you're not ready for it to mean that. Not yet."

My shoulders dropped with relief. He got it. He got it, and he didn't fucking hate me for it. Or at least, I didn't think he did.

"Do you hate me?" I asked.

He frowned and shifted forward, closer, and held open his arms. I went into them and let him hold me.

"You know I don't. Jude, sometimes you're so fucking childlike, it scares me a little." He said, "I think I hate the person who hurt you, but then I remember that he was a child too."

"I hate feeling like this. But I don't know how to stop," I admitted. "I wish I could just love someone else. I wish I could just love you. You're so much better than him." I *was* crying now. Stupid, childlike, tears I knew I would be ashamed of later.

Nathan only held me tighter. "Love doesn't work like that, baby." He laughed gently. "But for what it's worth, I wish you could too."

Hurting Nathan was the worst thing I've ever done. Worse than Ellie. Because Nathan I'd gone to for all the right reasons. Nathan I could have easily had a future with; a happy one filled with growth and love and everything a healthy relationship should be.

I just decided that I didn't want it.

I had no one to blame for what happened between us but myself. I suppose I could blame Cas, but by then I'd decided to start taking responsibility for my own emotional shortcomings.

As it was, I'd taken the goodness Nathan offered me, sucked him dry, and returned to some dark dead place like the emotional vampire that I was.

As we said goodbye at the airport, he'd turned to me, that beautiful smile on his face even then, and told me I could always call him if I needed him. No matter how far in the future it was. If I changed my mind, if I decided I wanted to see New York after all, I could call. He'd always answer.

And this went on to be true, he always answered when I called.

We've met up once or twice through the years, whenever he came to London or when I went to New York, but whatever spark had been there when I was his guileless, wide-eyed student had been well snuffed out by what was to come soon after.

He's married now, to another screenwriter he met working on a hit TV show – it actually became a bit of a cultural phenomenon. They have twin boys and two dogs and live in Santa Barbara; their Instagram is something of a viral sensation from what I can gather. He looks happy.

We haven't spoken in a few years, but he did send me a card and gift (a framed photo he'd taken that summer of me reading at the beach) when I published my first book.

The book's dedication page had read: *For Professor Alexander; I guess he was finally good for something, huh?*

I'd named the book after Tarkovsky's film, *The Sacrifice*.

SEVENTEEN

After Nathan returned to New York, I returned home. Luke and I spent a few days fishing, as I'd promised, but the strain of being under the same roof as Beth came to a head about a week later.

It was a Sunday afternoon when Daniel turned up at the door to pick her up. She was in the garden hanging up washing, and Luke was out, so I opened the door to him, still half asleep and vaguely hungover.

Daniel was about as different from Luke as it was possible to be. He was lanky and tall with short red hair and the complexion of a bottle of milk.

"Uh, hi. You must be Jude. I'm Daniel," he said awkwardly before shoving out his hand. I stared at it. He dropped it back to his side while I continued to stare at him in bewilderment. "Is Beth home?"

I could only blink, astonished. *This* was who my sister was leaving Luke for? After staring at him too long, I left him standing there as I went to the back door.

"Your less good-looking bit on the side is here," I said. "Seriously, that's what you broke Luke's heart over? No accounting for taste, I suppose."

She looked mortified for a minute, then furious as she charged toward me.

"How bloody dare you."

"How dare I? How dare you? Inviting him to the fucking house?"

"Don't bloody swear at me, and this is *my* fucking house!"

I glowered. "Actually, it's Gideon's house, Beth, and we live here by virtue of Luke working for Gideon, so I think it's about time you pissed off out of here and left us in it in peace."

I saw the rage (and hurt) trembling under her skin, and I thought for a moment she might hit me. I probably deserved it too. But she just pushed past me and went inside.

I sat outside and flicked through my phone resolutely refusing to step foot inside until she was gone. There was an email from Gideon that I hadn't read properly when I'd seen it come in last night. There'd been no mention of Cas – I always scanned the content for this first. He was still in Italy, due home to London in a couple of weeks. Did I want to visit? The altercation with Beth had made the idea appealing suddenly. While I hated the idea of leaving Luke alone, I needed to get out of there before my sister and I came to blows. Before I said or did something that would likely result in us never speaking again.

I emailed him back and said I'd come to London before heading back to Uni, and asked him to tell me when he'd be home, and I'd book a flight. I told him in very vague terms about what was happening at home, Beth and Luke's separation, and how hard it was at home right now. It was later that night before he replied.

He was sorry about Luke and Beth. I skipped most of the diatribe about love and heartache – I already knew what he'd say about this – and skipped to the last paragraph: his house in London was empty, and I could go whenever I wanted. I just needed to let him know, and he'd let the concierge know to have the place stocked for me.

I told him I just needed a key and an address. The key, he said, was with the concierge. The address he'd put at the bottom of the email along with a link to a map url. I clicked on it to see his house in London was a flat in the borough of Kensington and Chelsea. The street was one of those Georgian rows, all white and blonde brick façades with a large green park in the middle. I'd have that to myself for a few weeks before Gideon arrived?

I closed the email and immediately pulled up flights to London.

I did not pack light. I wasn't planning on returning to Jersey before I went back to Oxford for the start of term. Luke was dejected when I told him I was going, and I felt guilty about that, but my mind was made up. He understood. Luke always did.

I suggested he take a break, a long weekend off if he couldn't spare a full week, and come to London and hang out with me there. I gave him all the details and told him I'd already suggested it to Gideon, who'd said he'd love to see him, too. I even said I'd go to Kew Gardens with him. He dropped me off at the airport looking sad but smiling through it, hugged me tight, told me to have a good time, and said he'd think about coming over for a few days.

I didn't hold out much hope.

London was a hotpot. Stifling, bubbling hot, with too many people.

I took a taxi to the address from Gideon's email, fumbling with my money in sweaty hands, only to find the taxi accepted debit cards. The driver helped me out with my bag and suitcase by dumping them unceremoniously on the pavement of Wilton Place and drove off.

I stood trying to find number 128 for a moment before a tall black man in a long smart coat came out of a door and down the gleaming white steps to ask if he could help.

"Um, yeah, is this 128? Wilton Place?"

"It sure is, sir."

"I'm staying here. I mean, at a friend's place. He lives here, but he's not here right now. He said there'd be a key?"

His eyes twinkled with delight as his mouth stretched into a grin. "You must be Jude. Gideon told me to look after you. Come on."

His name was Kuende, but I was to call him Ken.

The building was a long row of individual townhouses which had been split into flats. Number 124 was the concierge station, where absent owners (Russian Oligarchs and English Lords) could leave keys and have deliveries accepted, visitors granted access, and keep a general eye on the place while they were out of town.

Gideon's property was a large duplex which was accessed on the ground floor. Ken carried my suitcase to the front door, unlocked it, and led me inside to the entrance hall, where he set it down.

"There is one key for the front door, and for the bi-folds in the kitchen. One is for the mailbox in the concierge station." He held up a small one. "But when Lord Gideon is not here, I collect the mail and leave it here for him." He pointed at a neat pile on a console table.

"Oh, okay, well, I can do that then. No worries."

Ken told me there was a black phone in the kitchen and sitting room that connected to the station, which I could use whenever I needed something. I wasn't sure if that meant first aid or takeout food, and I didn't want to ask, so I just nodded. Then he left me alone.

The place was impressive. Huge doorways, high ceilings, and wide open rooms, large windows that looked out on the leafy streets of Chelsea. The kitchen was on the basement level, and stretched the length of the house, front to back. Beyond the wall of folding doors was a garden, and dominating the space was a pool. Even I knew a pool in central London was a rare extravagance. The pool wasn't overly large, but it wasn't small either. Feeling bold, I slipped off my trainers and ran at it fully clothed, plunging into the cooling depths.

As I emerged, I realised I had a huge stupid smile on my face.

After stripping out of my wet clothes, I hobbled around the house, dripping wet, until I found a bedroom at the back of the house that I liked and which I was certain wasn't Gideon's. Then I went for a shower in the ensuite and changed into something light. The house had air con, but I hadn't figured out how to work it yet.

Gideon had instructed someone to fill the fridge, and I found continental meats and cheeses, bags of salad, orange juice, milk, eggs, and an assortment of vegetables. I made a salad and poured a glass of wine I found in a separate wine fridge. I sat at the kitchen table and watched an episode of Taskmaster on my laptop while I ate.

I felt strangely content. At ease. Almost, but not quite, happy.

The next few days were similar. Lazy and warm. I woke late, ate, read, and floated in the pool. I turned pink and then brown. It was as close to near bliss as I could imagine. I wondered why Gideon ever left London. Imagined the sort of life I would lead if I were him. I missed Nathan and wished I'd known about this place before he'd left because maybe we could have come here together. I'd seen a few gay couples roaming around London when I'd ventured out for supplies, and put myself and Nathan in their places.

And then, because I was still me, I imagined me with Cas instead. Holding hands while we wandered the Waitrose food aisle, sitting eating a sandwich together on a blanket in the park, walking an excitable dog down the street. And the dark cloud would roll over me again.

I could barely stand thinking about the night in Oxford when he'd come to me. I'd just about convinced myself it hadn't happened, that it was just a dream I'd had. One that had left me with a yearning so deep that not even Nathan hadn't been able to touch it.

Cas was so offensively loud in my mind one night that I drunk two bottles of red wine and passed out on the sofa in Gideon's living room. When I woke up briefly in the middle of the night, groggy and dry-mouthed, I saw him standing over me. He had such a soft, tender look on his face as he looked down at me, that I went back to sleep with a smile on my face.

"There you are," I muttered before passing out again.

I woke up the morning after, sore everywhere on my body. Bright, brash, sunlight streamed in through the windows.

I wasn't sure where I was, or what day it was, but I was very, very sure I was going to be sick. I made it to my bedroom, then to the ensuite, where I threw up lungfuls of bilious red liquid in loud, terrible gushes. It was the worst hangover I'd ever had. And to this day, I've never had worse. I can't even look at red wine without wanting to heave, even now.

I blamed this on Caspien, too.

I'd dreamt about him, I remembered as I sat miserable on the bathroom floor. Of him standing over me, of him talking quietly, of his voice and the sound of him breathing.

I threw up again.

Then I went to lie down on my bed and passed out.

When I woke up, it was 3 p.m. I'd lost almost a full day. I'd make up for it by going for a walk, flush out my lungs and body with fresh air. My stomach protested with hunger, but I wasn't confident anything I put in my body would stay there. I got out of bed and showered, dressing comfortably and loosely, and went to get a bottle of water for the walk.

I came down the stairs into the kitchen and froze. My entire body felt made of liquid – liquid I was going to throw up all over Gideon's marble floor.

Cas sat at the breakfast nook, his laptop open in front of him and a tall glass of something luridly green next to him. He turned, giving me that very same, very uncharacteristic softness he'd had in the dream I'd had last night.

Except it hadn't been a dream. It had been real. He was here.

EIGHTEEN

He *looked* like a dream. His hair long but styled, bright gold in the late afternoon sunlight. He wore a loose, cream-coloured striped shirt, the neck open and a delicate gold chain nestled against his throat. Shorts showed off tanned legs I knew were dusted with fine gold hair. Then I noticed his arm. Bandaged in a sling tied across his chest; I'd thought it had been resting on the table.

"What happened to your arm?" I said as a greeting.

He blinked, clearly expecting another question, and tried hiding it beneath the table.

"It's actually my hand," he said evenly. "Two fractured metacarpals."

I went toward him, or rather, my feet did. He closed his laptop and turned his body toward me as I took a seat at the nook.

"You won't be able to play piano with that," I informed him.

He still had that same soft look on his

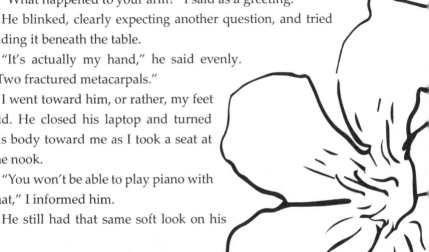

face as he looked at me. I didn't know what it meant, what to do with it.

"No," he said with a small, bitter smile. After a moment, he slid the green drink across the table to me. "It will help if you can keep it down."

"What's in it?"

"Best you don't ask."

"Poison?"

It was a joke, but he tilted his head, acknowledging the reference. It wasn't as unpleasant as I feared: the consistency was the worst part; thick and gloopy, viscous as it slid down my throat. But almost the moment it settled, I began to feel some magic at work. The roiling in my stomach calmed a little, the nausea abating. I stopped sweating, though my body was still very hot.

"You'll be wondering why I'm here," he said at last.

"Uh, sort of, yes. Gideon never told me you were coming." I told myself I wouldn't have come if I'd known.

"It was very last minute – he doesn't know I'm here yet. And I didn't know you'd be here until I found you on the couch last night." At this, he looked away, and I couldn't decide which part he was lying about. When he met my eye again, he said, very sincerely, "If you want me to go, I will. I can stay at a hotel; it's not a problem."

I should have told him to go. The last time I'd seen him, I was an animal. I'd made threats that I was ashamed of now, and I was afraid of what I might do. I knew I shouldn't want him anywhere near me, not again. But I was Jude. And Jude loved Cas. And so I also knew I would never tell him to go again. I regretted many things that had happened between us, and would regret a lot more before we were done, but none more than telling him to go that day in Oxford.

"This is more your house than mine; I can go."

"I don't want you to," he said quickly. I thought I detected a note of panic in his voice. "We're adults. Surely we can live under the same roof for a few weeks without killing each other?"

A few weeks? He was staying that long? I swallowed.

"It's not killing you I'm worried about, Cas." I knew he understood my meaning because his breathing hitched very slightly. "Where is he then? Will he be joining us?"

His breathing changed again before he shook his head and looked down at the table. "No. I...we...He's still in Boston." I'd never heard him speak with as little certainty before about anything. Certainly not about Blackwell. Stupid hope rose in my chest.

"What happened?" I asked. "Have you split up?" I was amazed to learn that I didn't know what I wanted the answer to be.

"No. Nothing like that," he said. "Everything's fine." The words rang completely hollow and I hated that I bloody cared.

I stood on slightly unstable legs. "Okay, well, I need to go for a walk and clear my head, I still feel bloody awful." Feeling half-dead but exhilarated at the same time. His presence still had the same effect on me it always had clearly. "I'll be back in a while."

I was at the stairs when he called out after me. I turned. He looked so beautiful sat there, some godlike figure draped in cream and gold and light: too perfect to be real.

I needed air, a lot of it.

"Thank you," he said, smiling that soft bloody smile again.

I almost fell over. Had he ever said thanks to me for anything before? If he had, I couldn't remember it, couldn't remember his mouth ever shaping into those words before.

I muttered something inaudible and bolted up the stairs and out of the front door. I was halfway down the street when I realised I hadn't a clue what he had even thanked me for.

When I got home a couple of hours later, Cas was making dinner. Chopping lettuce one-handed as chicken, mouth-wateringly, roasted in the oven. I hadn't been aware he cooked. The sight of him there, his back to me, soft classical music playing while he prepared dinner was so completely out of one of my fantasies, that I couldn't move for a moment. I just watched.

He was dextrous with a single hand. Even when he rinsed a large tomato and set it on the board, he was able to cut down its centre and slice it into fine segments.

"You could help," he said without turning. "I'm working at a handicap here."

"I don't know, I'm quite enjoying watching you struggle." I went towards him and took the knife from his left hand. Cas was left-handed, and I thought about how lucky it was that this wasn't the one he'd hurt.

"How'd it happen?" I asked as I began to slice a bell pepper.

"I was playing tennis," he answered smoothly.

"With Superman?"

He snorted. "No, it was an awkward fall. I put a hand out to break it and broke my hand instead." He was pulling open the door of the oven to check inside. "Ten more minutes, I'd say. Are you hungry?"

I'd had a burger and chips at Five Guys about a half hour ago. "Yes, starving."

"Good," Cas said.

"How did you even get it in there one-handed?" I said as I pulled the chicken out of the oven ten minutes later.

"With extreme skill."

We let it rest and set the table, an easy silence weaving around us as we did. I sliced bread while he poured water. He handed me the knife and asked for a few slices of the breast while I took a large leg. I caught myself just looking at him: Cas was here. We were here together. How had this happened? I tried not to think about fate, and kismet, and the universe sending me signals and focused on my chicken.

"You need me to cut that for you?" I asked as we sat down to eat.

He shot me a glare, the first I'd seen since this morning, and I smiled. Then he proceeded to cut his chicken one-handed.

He could cook. The chicken tasted wonderful, succulent and flavoursome, but I was getting full quickly. Not wanting to offend him, I kept eating.

"So when do you return to Oxford?" he asked, conversationally.

"Beginning of October. I volunteered to help out with Freshers Week."

"Christ, why on earth would you do that?"

I shrugged. At the time I'd offered, I hadn't known what I wanted to do with my summer, only that I wanted to spend as little time as possible at home. This was before Nathan's offer.

"Freshers are always fun," I said.

"Were you?" he asked. "A fun fresher."

He couldn't possibly have known what he was asking. Couldn't possibly have any understanding of how broken I still was the September I'd arrived in Oxford. Yes, I'd drunk-called him a few times, but they were hang-ups. He didn't know the depth of my misery.

I stared at him as I shook my head. "No, Cas. I was a fucking miserable fresher."

His hand stalled for a moment, before he continued eating. A slightly more uncomfortable silence filling the space between us.

"So what does your hand mean for school?" I asked him.

His jaw clenched almost imperceptibly as he reached for a piece of bread. "I will lose a semester. Most likely two."

"Shit." I stared at him. I knew his music degree was a year longer than a standard university degree here; I'd looked it up, meaning he had two years left at the conservatory even before breaking his hand. "I'm sorry."

He looked at me, a slight frown on his face. "Why? You didn't do it. It's my own fault."

I didn't think falling over was anyone's fault. "Is it painful?"

"It's fine."

I made a hearty attempt to finish my plate. Though I hadn't even filled it the way I normally would, I had to put down my fork when I'd only cleared about a third of it. I gulped my water and sat back.

"What are your plans while you're here?" he asked me, lifting his own glass to take a small sip.

"I haven't made any. Figured I'd split the time between lazing around the pool and doing some touristy stuff."

"This is your first time here? London, I mean."

"As an adult. I came with my parents when I was little."

I thought I saw a note of pity on his face before he blinked it away.

"You should go to the British Library, I think you'd like it," he said. "It's in St. Pancras, and Bloomsbury isn't too far from there: there's a string of bookshops. And perhaps the V&A. It's been a few years since I've been there, but it's a good way to spend the day – they have a nice café and gift shop. I don't know if you love the theatre, but The Globe is *definitely* worth seeing in the summer too, no one wants to watch King Lear in the rain. But avoid the Tower at this time of year, it's like Piccadilly Circus, which I would also avoid. Unless being in the centre of a litter of pigs is your thing."

I wanted to do all of those things, I decided. Even Piccadilly Circus.

I'd probably regret it, but what was one more regret in the catalogue of Caspien related regrets?

"What are your plans? Want to come tourist-ing with me?" I stuffed a bit of chicken in my mouth just to have something to do with my hands. "Stop me falling prey to any embarrassingly obvious traps."

He looked at me a long time as he considered this, an unreadable expression on his face.

"If you like," he said at last.

The following day we went to the Globe: they were showing a matinee of Henry IV Part One. I'd looked it up the night before and suggested it to him as we each lay sprawled on one of the sofas in the living room. The Olympic swimming coverage was on TV, but we were only half-watching it - me on my phone and him with a book open on his thigh that he hadn't picked up since I'd come into the room.

We were a little late arriving and so had to squeeze into the open-air theatre quietly. I'd wanted to take the Tube, but Cas had given me a look as though I'd suggested we go swimming in the Thames instead and asked Ken to call us a car.

The place felt ancient and I spent a lot of time not watching the play, instead looking up and around at the old wooden structure and imagining people hundreds of years ago doing the same. Tiers of covered oak seating circled the almost gladiatorial-style ground floor, the place was steeped in history. Finally, I forced myself to watch the play, as Cas was doing intently beside me.

Shakespeare wasn't my favourite; I knew this was basically blasphemy as an English Literature student, but I found him dense and waffling, and it took too much effort to concentrate while reading him. That performance to this day was the best I'd ever seen his work performed. Something about the location and the actors, maybe they too delivered their best work given the stage they were on. Their inflections caused soft ripples of laughter from the audience where they were supposed to, the delivery with the sharp edge of wit it was written with. It felt like I got it, finally. It was only that day that I realised Caspien's horse had been named after a central character in the play. I'd looked at him when the character had staggered on drunk, during an early scene.

"Where is he?" I asked as we wandered north across Southwark Bridge after. "Falstaff."

"Boston," he said. "He's at a ranch outside the city. I try and ride him on the weekend but it's not always possible."

"Oh, so what, he went on a plane?"

"Yes, they have an equine section between first class and business. There's hay and sugar cubes, and the cabin crew brush them down every two hours."

It took me longer than it should have.

He laughed. "Christ, your face."

"You're a dick."

"And you're just as gullible as you always were."

I stopped walking and stared at him.

Cas stopped and turned to look at me.

He sighed. "It was just a joke."

"Which part?"

"About the horses. They put them in their box stalls and onto smaller planes. Sometimes they tranquilise them."

But he knew. I knew he did. *You're just as gullible as you always were.*

"I still shouldn't trust you, though. Is that what you're trying to tell me?"

"I wasn't trying to tell you anything; it was a stupid joke, Jude." Then, very seriously, he said, "Your eyes are different, you know."

I said, "I don't know what that means."

"I can't tell what you're thinking as easily as I used to."

Good, I thought initially; it was good that how I felt about him was no longer ringed in neon, flashing loud and obvious. People were trying to get past us on the bridge as we stood there, staring at each other, but I hardly noticed them.

"I'm not the same person I was when you left." *When you left me,* was what I meant.

"No," he said. "No, you're not."

I wasn't sure what to say to that so I started walking again.

"Are you hungry?" I asked him once I was by his side again.

"A little."

We chose a sushi place near Monument. It was too bright and too busy, and I was glad that conversation would be difficult. His words were still rattling around in my head. My eyes were different. He couldn't tell what I was thinking as easily as he used to. Initially, these had seemed like good things, so I didn't understand why it was now causing a stir of panic and worry in my chest.

But then, I did.

There'd been comfort in knowing how well he could read me, how well he knew me, because it was provenance of what existed between us. He knew me the way he'd know a book he liked or a piece of music he knew by heart.

He knew me well because I was his, and now that he didn't...

Cas sat with his back to the window and his broken hand resting on top of the table. His sunglasses were tucked into the neck of his shirt, white again today, and the exposure of the sun from the open theatre had pinked his cheeks and nose. Cas was always distractingly lovely to look at, but especially so in the summer. It was how he'd been when I'd first seen him, first loved him, and in my memories, he was always this way: sun-kissed and glowing with the heat of the warmest season.

In Jersey, he'd looked like a delicate and fragile summer bloom. In London, he took on a different aura: expensive and cosmopolitan. The insouciant way he held his water, the glint of his Cartier watch, the gleam even of his fingernails. He was grace and extravagance, oozing good breeding in a way that made me feel self-conscious. Would people assume we were a couple? If so, that he was roughing it with me?

Did I want them to think that? My head was a noisy clatter of anxiety and doubt.

He seemed not to notice my internal turmoil – perhaps since my eyes no longer gave everything away – while he talked about the play, other performances of it he'd seen and where, all while using his chopsticks to feed himself green sesame tossed salad and sashimi.

Soon, I fell into that familiar trance of watching and listening to him move and speak. That commanding way he'd always had of holding my attention, of being the only thing I could see, of being the sun to my Icarus.

The next day, we went to the British Library. A vast, jaw-dropping space that felt like a portal to another world opening up in front of me. I remember the entrance hall unfolding into a labyrinth of walkways, escalators, and stairwells all framing the huge six-story King's Library tower: a stretch of glass-fronted bookshelves ran the height of the building and stood as a centrepoint.

I've spent a lot of time here since, writing and reading, but this first visit with Cas was like walking into some modern temple of worship where the book and the word was a deity. Even the smell to me, that great Library smell I'd always loved, was more potent that day in the cool rows of the British Library.

He took me to the treasures gallery first, which he said we wouldn't be able to do properly in a day but was the best place to start. He pointed me to the original set of Shakespeare's folio of plays and the Magna Carta, before moving off to wander by himself. I took this to mean I should too.

I gravitated towards a section showing manuscripts dating back to the ninth century; including a gold engraved Qu'ran from North Africa published in 876. I'd teared up at the original handwritten copy of Wilfred Owen's war poem, with Sassoon's tender annotations on the margins. Owen had been a child – when I was swimming in the sea and sunbathing with my friends, when I'd been falling in love with Cas, he'd been in a hospital bed in France writing about the pointless horror of war.

I lost a few hours wandering the collection before finding Cas pondering an original sketchbook of Da Vinci's drawings.

"This place is amazing," I said. "Did you see the Wilfred Owen section?"

He nodded, still looking at the sketches behind the glass. "Devastating."

I looked down at the sketches he seemed to be completely absorbed in. They weren't overly impressive to me, but I knew that wasn't the point.

"Do you still paint?" I asked him.

"Not really." Then, he seemed to remember something. "What did you do with the portrait I painted of you?" He asked it in a way that presumed I'd done something destructive with it. For an instant, I thought about lying.

"It's still on the shelf above my bed at home."

There was a flicker of surprise in his eyes. Then, like he too was recalling what else happened that day, his mouth parted, and the faintest blush spread across his cheeks. He turned away.

"We should go now if we want to make it to the bookshop," he said and walked toward the gallery exit.

NINETEEN

The following day was a Saturday and to avoid the even busier Saturday crowds the city was famous for, we decided to stay at the house. I woke late, having slept well, to find Cas already showered and dressed, sitting in front of his laptop in the nook again and watching something with earphones in.

As I crossed into the kitchen, he slid them out.

"I made pancakes," he said. "There are some in the fridge for you if you want to heat them up."

I looked at him, impressed. "Is there anything you can't do one-handed?"

"Play piano." He slid one ear back in.

"You want a refill?"

I pointed at his coffee cup. He nodded and moved to stand, but I crossed the kitchen to take it from him, and he sat down again. On the screen of his laptop was a guy playing piano energetically in front of an audience. Cas appeared to be

laser-focused on it, the fingers of his uninjured hand air-tapping the keys on the table. I felt a stab of pity in my chest for him. I imagined it would be like going blind and unable to read Braille.

I grilled myself some bacon, reheated the pancakes, and filled his coffee cup before sitting down next to him.

"You still don't drink it?" he asked as he lifted his cup. He'd closed the laptop and was focused on me instead.

I shook my head. I loved the smell of coffee but found the taste repulsive. At some point in my third year, among the late nights and deadlines, this changed. I consider myself now to have a worryingly dependent, low-level addiction to it.

I lifted my sweetened tea and sipped. "Can you go into the pool with that?" I nodded at his hand. There wasn't a cast on it, just a splint, cushioned with white padding, his finely shaped fingers wrapped up tight inside it.

"I think so."

"But I probably shouldn't, like, throw you in?" I smiled around a mouthful of perfectly cooked pancake.

"Not if you value your life, no."

I chuckled. "Finals of the swimming are tonight. Shall we watch?"

"If you like."

"They're on late, so we can have dinner first."

"Do you want to go out, or shall I cook?"

"You've cooked a lot since you got here."

He shrugged one shoulder. "I don't mind it; I do it at home. I enjoy it."

Home. I hated the sound of that. Of the idea of him cooking for Blackwell after a hard day of being a despicable prick. I looked down at my plate. "Where would we go if we went out?" I asked

"Well, what would you like to eat? I could ask Ken to make reservations at Isabel or Scott's." He was already lifting up his phone. I didn't know who Isabel or Scott were.

"I'm not fussy. I'll eat anything."

"The last time we went to Scott's, we saw Ryan Foster, the actor, not the MP," Cas said. "Isabel isn't as good as it used to be since

Jean-Georges poached their head chef." I was beginning to get a picture of the sort of places Cas was used to eating with the prick.

"Okay, well, maybe we can order some takeout and stay home?" I suggested. "I really don't feel comfortable in those kinds of places anyway."

He paused his scrolling and looked up at me. "Why ever not?"

"I just...don't. They're not my kind of place, Cas."

This seemed to confuse him, but after a moment he said, "Then you choose somewhere, I'm happy to go wherever you like."

"I'm honestly more than happy to stay in. But I don't want you to cook again, so let's order in."

"I really don't mind cooking, Jude."

"I know you don't, but tonight I fancy something disgustingly unhealthy, like pizza or kebab."

"Kebab?"

The horrified look on his face made me laugh.

"Pizza then."

"Pizza." He nodded. "Okay, then."

We spent the day by the pool, sun burning and tanning our water-stippled bodies. He wore blue and white striped Ralph Lauren trunks that sat high on his thighs, reminding me of how soft the skin was there.

I spent more time in the water than he did, jumping in to cool off when the heat got too intense. He sat, cautious and careful at the edge, before slipping in up to his waist and keeping his hand on the side. I knew he could swim, I'd seen him that day at the beach, but now he floated along the side like a child who couldn't might.

I was happy to fetch and carry our snacks and water for the day while he sat under the large parasol and read his book. (A biography of Jean-Paul Sartre he'd bought at the British Library gift shop.) Later, when the sun had dropped behind the buildings opposite, we went to our rooms to shower and change. He was in there so long that I went to check on him and found him fast asleep on top of the bed, a bath towel draped over his hips.

I watched him sleep for longer than I should have. The golden flick of his eyelashes resting on his sun-browned cheek. The slight part of his lips, the small frown on his face as though angry at something or someone, even asleep.

The intensity of my feelings for him in that moment, so acute and unyielding, transcended everything that had come before. He was still the boy I'd loved three, four summers ago, but that love had matured inside me like wine in a barrel, and it was more robust and vinous than it had ever been.

I'd learned so much in the years we'd been apart. I'd studied in one of the greatest institutions in the world, I'd met friends and lovers who had changed me inexorably with their wisdom, generosity, and kindness, and yet, in the loving of this person who had never offered me any of these things, I was still unchanged. Nothing existed when Caspien was next to me; it had always been that way. I needed nothing else, wanted nothing else, and I never felt as whole or as completely alive in the world as I did when he was with me.

I didn't understand it, I'm not sure I wanted to. But there could be no other person for me, now or in the future. He was it. For better or worse, he was it. But as much as I loved him, as much as I wanted him, I was frightened of him, too. Of the power he had over me and how completely I belonged to him. For longer than I'd had him, I'd been without him: yearning and longing for him so fiercely I could barely think past it. I couldn't remember what it felt like to have him in my arms, which scared me too. I was sure – I'd always suspected – that he'd been created and put solely on this earth to torture me with what I could never have.

I couldn't understand where Blackwell was, why he hadn't rung him or why Cas hadn't mentioned him, and I hated the see-saw of hope and despair that yawned within me from this. They were fighting; I'd gathered that much. But I couldn't understand why Blackwell hadn't been calling and begging him to come back to him;

how had he even let him go across an ocean without him? Because I was sure if he were mine, I wouldn't.

I closed the door and let him sleep. Then I went to order pizza.

The following day, Bast called me. He was in London. He had seen a few pictures I'd posted on Instagram and called to check how long I was in town. He was in town with his girlfriend, or ex-girlfriend, or however he was defining her this month. It was difficult to keep track. I knew they were open, slept with other people through university, but were also very committed to each other. (They'd settled down, married after university, and were still happily married.)

Cas and I were heading toward the Tate when he called, but I'd told him I'd be free in a couple of hours if he wanted to meet up for a drink then.

"A friend from Oxford's in town," I said as we moved down the queue toward the entrance. "He wants to meet for drinks after."

"Oh," Cas said. "No problem. I can drop you off on the way home. Where?"

We still hadn't used the Tube. Cas had used Wilton Place's chauffeur service each time we'd gone out. If I didn't know better I'd think he had agoraphobia. But no, just very specific standards of public transport.

"Um, not sure yet. I'm to let him know when we're done here. But I thought you'd come?"

Here, he turned to me. "You want me to come with you? To meet your friend?"

"Yeah, why not?"

"In Jersey, the idea of me hanging out with your friends was the worst thing you could imagine."

"Yeah, well, you were pretty awful then. I don't mind you as much now." I grinned as I nudged his shoulder.

A strange expression flickered over his face. "I'm fine to go home by myself, Jude. I'm not depressed or anything."

I made a face. "I didn't think you were? What?"

"I just mean, if you want to go meet a guy, then, I'm fine with it."

"Bast is a mate," I said, trying to gauge if he really would be fine if I went to meet a guy. "It's nothing like that. He's got a girlfriend. She's with him, and I haven't met her before, so it won't be weird or anything."

I saw some muscle in his jaw relax. "Oh, alright, then," he said again.

They'd been at Buckingham Palace, so we met them in the middle at an ale pub in Westminster called, imaginatively, The Buckingham. The inside was one of those dark, wood-panelled places where they sold an extensive range of craft beer and over-priced fish and chips and boasted of being 'A traditional London pub' on their website.

Cas looked about the place like a cat might, alert and wholly unimpressed, before we made our way to the bar.

"What are you drinking?" I asked Cas as I scanned the craft beer.

"Gin and tonic." It was posed almost as a question.

After ordering our drinks, we made our way toward the back of the pub and the beer garden, towards where the sunlight was pouring in through the open doors. I spotted Bast immediately, tall as a poppy, head and shoulders above everyone else. He stood up when he saw me, a huge grin on his face as though it had been years since he saw me, not weeks.

"You made it!" he beamed, pulling me into a hug. "This is Emmy, Emmy, this is Jude." His girlfriend waved and smiled but didn't stand. I turned to Cas.

"This is Bastian, Bast. We were in a dorm together our first year."

Bast put out a hand to Caspien, which he shook politely.

"Hello. Caspien, nice to meet you."

Bast's reaction was immediate. I saw his eyes widen as he looked at me, then Caspien and then back again, abject delight moving over his face.

"Caspien? Wait, are you two—"

"Cas's partner is in Boston," I said, cutting him off with a look. "We've just been catching up. I'm staying at his uncle's place for a couple weeks. I didn't know Cas was going to be around."

I was over-explaining, I knew. Bast's wide-eyed look turned to one of mischief. He'd been drinking, his eyes with that glazed, sparkled look they'd get after a single beer. He was infamous for being unable to handle his drink despite being bigger than all of us. I wondered suddenly if this was a good idea. Bast knew a lot about Cas and me. Too much.

We sat down, and Bast introduced us again to Emmeline, a pretty blonde with distinctly Germanic features. Emmy told us about what they'd done since arriving on Friday: a few gigs, a theatre show, and a couple of comedy clubs. Caspien drank his gin and tonic quietly and quickly before ordering another from a passing server. I was certain it wasn't table service, but a few minutes later, a G&T appeared next to him.

"So this isn't your first time in London?" I asked.

"No, we've been a few times, we love it here," said Emmy. "We were talking actually about how we would like to live here after our studies. But it is so expensive for property that I don't know if it's possible."

I glanced at Bast because I knew he wanted to move to northern France after Oxford, where all the best cycling routes were.

"Yeah, I reckon I could live here," I said instead. "But the prices are definitely crazy. You should see Gideon's place. Christ, it's insane. There's five bedrooms, a concierge, and a pool. I'm actually dreading going back to my dorm at Longhall."

"Hey, maybe you'll get New Buildings this time."

"Ah, one can dream." I lifted my glass.

"To no bin lorries," Bast said, touching his pint to mine. "So it's just the two of you at this huge house with a pool?" Bast had a pointed gleam in his eye.

"Yeah, just us. You could have stayed if I'd known I was going to be here, actually. I'm sure Gideon wouldn't have minded." I glanced at Cas for confirmation. He said nothing, and I couldn't read his expression. He wore his sunglasses as he drank his G&T with his good hand.

"Are you at Oxford too, Caspien?" Emmeline asked.

"No, I go to school in the States."

"Really, how cool. Where?"

"Lervairè Conservatory of Music."

"He's a pianist," I said.

They both looked at his hand. Emmeline's mouth rounded.

"Not at this precise moment, obviously," Cas said dryly.

"What happened?" she said, sounding and looking devastated for him.

"A fall."

"And your partner? American? From Boston?"

I felt Cas go very stiff next to me. "He's from London, but has a law firm in Boston. We moved there a couple of years ago."

"Ah, how lovely." Emmeline smiled as though it really was the loveliest thing she'd ever heard. Bast flicked me a look, knowing it wasn't.

Just then, someone tried to squeeze past us, a little too forcefully, so that Cas was pushed into the table. Where he'd positioned his hand meant it was thrust between his body and the table. He gasped in pain, his drink tipping over across the wooden picnic table.

"Hey, would you bloody watch it?" I rose to my feet, saying a little too loudly, a little too aggressively: "He's fucking injured."

"Shit, sorry man, sorry bud," the guy said to me and then to Cas. "Sorry, man."

"Are you okay?" I sat down again and looked at his hand.

"I'm fine." Caspien hadn't even looked at the guy; he was just staring at me from behind his dark wayfarers.

I offered to get him another drink, but he stood and announced he'd get it himself as he needed the toilet. I watched him pick his way through the crowd before Emmeline took our order and slipped off to the bar. When we were alone Bast levelled a long look at me from across the table.

"Don't even bother, Bast."

He threw his hands up. "I never said anything."

"Okay, good, don't."

He waited a few beats. "So, have you fucked him yet?"

I rolled my eyes as I downed the last of my pint. "No. Of course not."

He made a thoughtful noise. "Fuck, he is pretty, isn't he? I see it, Jude, I get it."

"Get what?" I frowned. "You're not even a little bit into men?"

"Hey, I've always said I could be for the right man. And he has the look."

"What look?" I was curious despite myself.

He shrugged. "Pretty, rich, English. It's a shame you're only two out of three. Or you could have been the right man for me."

I laughed.

"Will you make a move on him?" he asked after a moment.

"No of course not, he's with someone."

"And if he makes a move on you?"

My heart lurched. "He won't."

"But if he did? Maybe he's lonely, maybe he's in a sexually un-fulfilling relationship with his lawyer – they are bad lovers, I hear. What then?"

"He's not going to try to fuck me, Bast. The last time was..." I shook my head. "A mess."

"You were just a boy! You can't be too hard on yourself. Next time will be better," he said jovially.

I didn't even know what part of that to argue against. I'd told no one about the night in Oxford, so for all Bast knew, the last time we'd been together was before he'd broken my heart. That night in Oxford lived somewhere deep inside me that I'd never shown to anyone – anyone but Cas. Partly as I was ashamed, but mostly because it was ours: Cas's and mine. And I wanted to keep it that way. And he'd never mentioned it, hadn't even made reference to it in the last seven days we'd spent together.

It was as if he'd completely forgotten about it.

To Bast, I said, "He isn't going to make a move."

Before he could refute this, he gestured with his eyes over my shoulder. Cas sat down next to me with a fresh G&T in his hand. Over the next two hours, I watched him, quietly impressed, as he sunk another five without showing a single hint of drunkenness.

Until, that is, we got up to leave.

TWENTY

Bast and Emmy had tickets for some adult comedy show across the river, so as they got ready to leave I called Ken with the location and asked him to send a car for us.

I wasn't sober, but I wasn't even close to the sort of drunk I'd get on a usual night out with Bast at Oxford. I could tell Caspien didn't like Bast. He barely cracked a smile at his stupid jokes, let alone laugh at them, and he'd answer his questions with as few words as possible. I put it down to a personality clash; Bast was loud and rambunctious where Cas was reserved and cool.

The more he drank, the more his mood darkened, turning morose and a little detached, compared to how he'd been the last few days when it had just been the two of us anyway. But since I'd never really spent a lot of time with Cas around other people – Gideon and Luke aside – or ever seen him drunk, I put it down to the social situation.

"You want to wait outside for it?" I asked.

The sun hadn't set, and there was a shaft of bright sunlight on us, so he still wore his sunglasses. If I'd been able to see his eyes, I'd probably have noticed just how drunk he was, but because I couldn't, it was only when he stood that it became obvious. He reeled backwards into me so that I had to steady him with my body and arms. He sat back down.

"I think I might be drunk," he said, sounding as sober as a judge.

"Oh, thank fuck for that," I said. "If you'd drunk that much gin and were still sober, I'd have doubted your physiology."

"Help me, will you?" he said and stood again.

I slid an arm around him and guided him through the maze of bodies, holding him a little tighter as we descended the short flight of steps. His body was loose-limbed and warm and I tried not to focus on the feel of him this close again, of the weight of him, or how he needed me in this moment, even if it was only to hold him up.

Outside, the streets were busy, and so I led him to the wall of the bar and sort of propped him against it before moving to stand next to him. When I felt his head loll onto my shoulder, I tried to pretend it was the most normal thing in the world.

"Your friend is a bit of a wanker," he remarked.

"Is he? Most people like him."

"Most people are idiots."

I chuckled. "He's a good guy, just a little excitable around new people. Like a Labrador puppy."

"He's a chauvinist."

"Christ, okay," I frowned at him. "Gin makes you cranky. Noted."

"He spoke over his girlfriend at every opportunity, used sexist language at least twice, and thinks far too much of himself."

"No one's perfect."

"You are."

I looked down to check the sarcastic smirk on his face, but it wasn't there. His mouth was a straight line, but since his eyes were still hidden behind his sunglasses, I assumed he was smirking with them.

I laughed and said something like, "Ha, okay, no more alcohol for you."

He muttered something I couldn't make out, and then I was certain I heard him snore.

So Cas was a sleepy drunk. I'm not sure it's what I expected; I'd always imagined him turning more deadly and poisonous than usual.

The car arrived a short while later, and I had to guide him over to it with my hand around his lower back before helping him up into the back of the black Range Rover. He slid across the seat and slumped against the window. I reached over to snap his seatbelt into place before sitting down and doing my own.

When we arrived at Gideon's, I had to shake him gently awake, which caused him to startle so violently it was as though I'd given him an electric shock.

"Hey, it's okay," I soothed. "We're home."

He snapped off his glasses and for the first time I saw the red, glassiness of his eyes. There was something like wariness in his eye as he looked at me.

"Okay," he said and nodded once before letting me help him out of the car. He seemed to momentarily sober as we climbed the steps, but as soon as we were through the door, he fell into the side table.

"Let's get you to bed," I said, taking hold of him again to lead him down the corridor toward his room. It was larger than the one I was using, and at the front of the house overlooking the leafy street, navy and golds and greens, which felt like him.

After sitting him down on the bed, I closed the curtains, casting the room into half-darkness. I turned on the bedside lamp on the far side of the bed and then moved to switch on the one next to where he was sitting.

Cas sat very still, with his hand resting on his thigh as he stared at a point on the wall. When I moved in front of him, he looked up at me, blue eyes oddly focused despite the clear intoxication in them.

"Here, I'll help you with these." I knelt and began to unlace his trainers – I'd tied them for him earlier, too – slipping them off his feet. His ankles were slight and hairless, I knew, knobby pointed joints leading down to smallish feet. "Why don't you undress and get into bed?"

I'd help him if he needed me to, but stripping Cas out of his clothes felt like something I needed to prepare myself for, and I wouldn't put myself through it unless it was necessary.

Suddenly, he leaned forward, and I thought, terrified, that he was going to kiss me. Instead, he leaned his forehead against mine and breathed me in. His breath was gin-sweet and hot, and I tried to steady my own.

"I miss you," he whispered, so softly it felt like an exhale.

I froze, unable to breathe or move, pinned there by the hint of desperation in his voice. If I hadn't watched his mouth move, I'd have assumed I imagined it.

"Cas," I said, closing my eyes. It was too much, too overwhelming, too impossible.

"Jude, please," he said and tilted his head to bring his mouth closer to mine.

I'd not known that kind of power existed within me to refuse him, but clearly, over the years, some layer of self-preservation had grown over me, over my mind and my heart, so that I was able to gently push him back. I stood.

"I'll get you some water and aspirin for when you wake up." I went to his bathroom and, refusing to look in the mirror, let the tap run while I searched in his toiletry bag.

Along with his creams and lotions, I found three pill bottles. One, a very well-known pain medication I knew he shouldn't have taken while drinking. The other two, I wasn't sure of until I read the label. They were for depression and anxiety.

My whole world tilted on its centre in that moment, re-ordering, things falling out that I didn't understand. I shoved them back into his bag and zipped it up, feeling uneasy, guilty, and like I'd invaded his privacy. Would he want me to know?

I thought no, he wouldn't, and I'm sure if he were sober, he'd have come running in here by now, furious that I'd gone through his things.

I knew there were all sorts of things for headaches in the main bathroom, so I went there to find something for his head instead.

When I returned, he was lying down on the bed on his back with his eyes closed. I set the water and pills down next to him and moved to go.

"Will you stay?" he asked, opening his eyes. "Just lie next to me. Don't worry, I won't try and kiss you again." There was a bitter twist to his mouth as he said this that changed the meaning to: *Don't worry, I won't lower myself to trying to kiss you again.*

Nodding, I rounded the bed, and got on the other side, and lay down next to him. He sat up, took a few loud gulps of water, and lay down again so that he faced me. I shifted onto my side to face him.

His eyes were closed.

We weren't touching, weren't even particularly close – it was a very large bed – but it still felt intimate. It would have been the perfect moment to ask him about the pills, about what was going on with him and why he needed them, how he was really doing. But I didn't dare. I was afraid, not only of him, but of what it meant. Was he sad? Was he in pain? Because if he was, then it changed everything, and I didn't know what to do with the new reality it left me with.

I needed him to be happy. Because part of my grieving Cas, instrumental, in fact, to my grieving him, was knowing that he was happy with the choice he'd made. Was knowing that he'd chosen that perfectly comfortable life with Blackwell on the other side of the fucking world and regretted nothing. I didn't want to hear that it had been a mistake, because then it would mean we'd both been miserable for no fucking reason.

"I think about it," Caspien said. "The night in Oxford. Probably more than I should."

A deep tremor rolled through me. There was guilt and a deep aching sadness, but it warred with white-hot shameful lust.

"I'm sorry," I said.

He opened his eyes. "I'm not."

I stopped breathing, caught in the blistering intensity of his gaze. He was drunk. I couldn't trust anything he said or did while he was like this, but it didn't stop me from wanting to.

"It wasn't..." I began.

How on earth did I begin to explain my feelings about that night to him of all people? "It's not how I ever imagined it would be between us. I'm ashamed of it, of who I was that night. I just..." *wanted you so much. Hated you so much. Loved you so much.* I suspected he knew all of this, and since I swore I'd never offer these things to him as easily as I once did, I shut up.

"How did you imagine it?" he asked.

Perfect. Tender. Life-changing.

I tried a smile. "You don't want to know."

He looked like he might ask me to tell him anyway. But he said, "You don't look at me the way you used to."

Because I'm afraid to, I wanted to say.

"Well, thank god for that," I said instead.

A strange, lost look flitted over his face before he shut his eyes and began to breathe evenly and slowly, slipping into a drunken sleep.

I lay there watching him for a long time, thinking over his words and his behaviour and what it all meant. He was here last minute without Blackwell; he was telling me he missed me, he had tried to kiss me. He'd said everything was fine, but all the evidence suggested the opposite. Was he thinking about leaving him? What did it mean if he was? I wouldn't even dare to hope.

I decided that the following day, I'd ask him outright what was going on with him. I wouldn't mention the pills I'd seen in his bag, but I'd make it clear I was here for him, that I was a safe pair of hands if he needed them, if he wanted to talk about anything.

I woke in the very early hours of the morning to find the bed next to me empty. As I made my way to my own bed, I heard noise downstairs. He was at the counter, stirring something steaming in a mug.

"Hungover?" I asked.

He looked up and shook his head. "I don't get them."

"Never?"

"No."

"God really does have favourites, huh?" I poured myself a glass of water and stood next to him to peer into the cup he was still stirring. It smelled citrusy.

"Lemon and ginger tea," he said before lifting the cup and wandering back towards the stairs. Without looking back, he said, "Goodnight, Jude."

TWENTY-ONE

I woke late that afternoon. After showering, I made my way downstairs to find the kitchen empty. Unlike other mornings, there was no sign of food having been recently cooked or any evidence that he'd been here, so I assumed he was still sleeping.

I made myself a quick brunch of cheese omelette, bacon, and toast and went to sit out by the pool. It was another stifling day, with no breeze to speak of and very little cloud, and I soon fell asleep on one of the loungers by the pool.

When I woke up an hour later and he still hadn't appeared, I went inside to wake him up. His room was empty.

A momentary panic gripped me that he'd gone back to Boston without even saying goodbye, but when I checked the bathroom and saw his toiletry bag was still there and pulled open the wardrobe to see his suitcase, I relaxed.

It was another two hours before I heard

the sound of the front door opening, a muffle of voices, one of which was Ken's, the other Cas's.

I'd been half-watching a film in the living room and got up to go meet them at the door. Ken was carrying three plastic shopping bags while Caspien was carrying a fourth.

"...down to the kitchen for you?" Ken was asking.

Caspien spotted me as I came out into the hall, and his face was a mask of inexpression.

"It's fine, Ken. Jude can carry them down," he said. "Jude, take them will you?" I obeyed, watching as Caspien handed Ken a folded £50 note.

"You should have said, I'd have come shopping with you." I was putting away the groceries while Cas lifted them out of the bag and set them on the counter.

"I was at an orthopaedic appointment," he told me. "I went shopping on a whim; we needed a few things."

I stopped what I was doing and turned to him. "What did they say? Is it healing alright?"

"Seems like it."

"Did they tell you when you'd be able to play again?" I asked. "Piano, that is, not tennis."

His mouth twitched with a small smile. "I'll need to wear the splint for another eight weeks or so." He'd played every day when we'd been in Deveraux. I couldn't imagine how he was feeling.

"I'm sorry, Cas."

"Stop apologising for it," he said sharply before saying he was going to take a shower.

We made a dinner of halloumi, couscous stuffed peppers, and salad, and ate it with a bottle of rosé wine.

He hadn't mentioned last night while we cooked, hadn't even indicated he remembered it, but something in the way he avoided touching me or making eye contact as we moved around the kitchen, told me that he did. My own nerves were frayed from trying to pretend it hadn't happened. I'd not stopped thinking about it all day: of how softly he'd whispered that he missed me, of how close he'd been to kissing me, of how he thought more than he should about the night in Oxford.

We'd been eating dinner in a taut silence when the thin string of my patience snapped. I couldn't take it any longer.

"Can we ta—" I started.

"So, have y—" he began at the same time.

"No, it's fine, you go," I said.

"I was just going to ask if you'd heard from Luke," he said.

I blinked at him. "What?"

He lifted his eyes from his plate. "You said he was thinking about coming over."

"Um...No. I haven't spoken to Luke."

"Okay," he said. "What were you going to say?"

"Forget it."

His expression flickered, and he went back to eating. After a few moments, he said, "Are you looking forward to going back to uni?"

I dropped my fork onto my plate and scrubbed a hand over my mouth. Beside me, Cas flinched.

"Seriously? You're asking me about uni right now?"

He looked lost. "We haven't really talked about it. I was just curious about whether you were enjoying it."

I let out a hollow laugh. "I don't know how you do it, Cas, I honestly don't."

"I've no idea what you're talking about."

"You're exactly the same as you've always been. This is all just another bloody act: this version of you." I waved in his general direction. "The one cooking me dinner, asking me things like you care about the answers, telling me you miss me. Who are you with him? Which version does he get? I'm curious."

Carefully, he set his cutlery down and picked up his napkin to wipe his mouth. "I'm not sure why you're being like this; it was just a question. You've wanted to go to Oxford for as long as I've known you, Jude; I wondered if it was everything you hoped it would be. That's all."

"Sure. That's all." I lifted my wine glass and drained it before reaching for the bottle.

"Is it not going well?" He looked almost worried about me. "Are you doing alright there?"

"I stopped seeing Finn by the way. I fucked my film studies professor instead."

Sparks of *something* flared in the ice blue of his eyes. Thrilled, I went on.

"He came to Jersey for the summer to write a screenplay, and we spent it together. It was perfect. Actually, *he's* perfect. He asked me to go to New York with him. I'll probably go over at Christmas," I lied.

"I'm pretty sure professors don't fuck their students during the summer holidays," he said. "So excuse me if the word *perfect* feels like a bit of a contradiction."

"He was my ex-professor when we fucked." The term sounded absurd then. "And he was a guest."

"Oh, well, that makes all the difference." His tone was unpleasant as he lifted his wine. "I'm sure the Oxford University Council will see it exactly like that."

I felt anger surge in my chest at the implication, followed by a distinct note of fear. "Remind me what age you were when you met that famous celebrity lawyer of yours, again?" I snapped. Cas sipped his wine but said nothing. "Nathan's one of the best people I've ever met – a million miles away from that fucking pervert you ran off with, so you can piss off with your threats and snide remarks."

Cas was watching me very closely, breathing very quickly.

"I see," he said at last.

"What do you bloody see?"

"You're in love with him."

I stared at him, speechless. Then, I began to laugh. Near hysterical laughter that sounded insane in the echo of the kitchen.

"Oh, I fucking wish," I said when it had died in my throat. "I fucking wish."

With a last contemplative look in my direction, Cas stood and carried his plate into the kitchen. I watched him tip the food waste into the small compost bin and then set the plate on the counter so he could open the dishwasher.

The laughter had died off, and in its place, sadness and regret swelled inside me. I hadn't wanted this. I'd wanted to talk properly, to show him that he could trust me and talk to me about whatever was wrong.

How had I made this about myself? I was acting like a child again. I carried my own plate over and scraped the leftovers. He'd begun clearing the rest of the table, and I watched him for a bit before moving to help.

"I can do it, Jude," he said without any heat.

"Yeah, I know you can."

Still, I helped him. When the kitchen was a white expanse of polished marble again, we stood awkwardly at opposite sides of it, looking at each other. The words I'd thrown at him at the table sat weighty in the space between us.

"Well, I think I'll go to bed," he said, though it wasn't even 8 pm. "I'm tired."

He went.

After he left, I poured another glass of wine, but it had turned to poison on my tongue, so I poured it down the sink and tried to fight what was clawing against the inside of my chest. But I was tired. I didn't want to fight anymore. It felt like I'd been fighting him, us, for years and I was done with it.

I turned and charged upstairs and down the hall toward his bedroom. I didn't knock as I opened the door and went inside. He stood in front of the mirror in the bathroom, and he whipped around as I approached him.

We reached for each other at the same time, and as he gasped into my mouth, I took his face in my hands and kissed him hard. I backed him up against the sink, careful not to hurt his hand, as I slid my hands into his hair and tasted his mouth for the first time in a lifetime. It was an antidote. Except he was my poison, too.

"Tell me again," I said.

He made a small, desperate noise as I bit his lip roughly. Holding his chin, I forced him to look into my eyes. "Tell me again that you missed me."

"I missed you," he breathed, reaching for the button of my shorts.

The desperate way he nipped at my jaw went to my head, both of them, and I pulled him out of the bathroom. We undressed ourselves, though I helped him pull his T-shirt over his head and unfasten his sling, before I pushed him back on the bed.

As he lay sprawled there, panting, naked, and hard, I tried to consider what this would mean, how much it was going to hurt when he left me again – because he would, it was what he did, and decided I didn't care. I was Jude. He was Cas. This was *us*.

What was one more battle scar on my heart when the war was this glorious?

I also decided that, this time, I would take my time.

I kissed every inch of skin that I could reach with my mouth, dotted kisses along every dip and rise of his body, swallowed every gasp he let slip past his lips, pressed my mouth over his heart, and made unspoken promises against his skin. *I love you, I love you, I love you.*

"Jude," he said breathlessly. My name spilled over and over again from his mouth as he writhed and begged and reached for me with his hand.

I kissed along his collarbone and down his inner arm, all the way to his injured hand, where I kissed the exposed part of his palm. He fisted my hair, and I looked up to find his gaze sparkling with some intense emotion I couldn't name. I wouldn't say it out loud again; I wasn't strong enough not to hear it returned, but I tried to say it with my eyes, with my hands, with my mouth. I crawled up his body to kiss him on the mouth again, and he kissed me back deeply, devouring my lips as though he was starved. He pushed at my chest and nudged me onto my back, climbing over me so that he was facing away from me, the nodes of his spine popping out as he bent his head and swallowed my dick. I arched up into the perfect sweet pleasure of his mouth, moaning his name.

"Cas, fuck, that feels..." I broke off into a groan as he pushed me deeper into his throat. Tight heat swallowing over the head again and again, driving me insane. When I heard him choke on it, I stopped thrusting and pulled out. The apology never made it past my lips.

"Do it again," he said, forcing my dick down his throat again.

It felt so good I was seconds away from coming, but somehow he knew when to pull back just enough, when to loosen his throat just the right amount, to keep me teetering on the edge. I grabbed his thighs, and pulled him backward so I could reach his hole with my mouth.

The instant my mouth touched it he sat bolt upright, back arching so beautifully that I was momentarily distracted. Elegant lines and smooth golden skin scattered with little delicate freckles. He was gorgeous from every angle, the most beautiful person I'd ever seen, ever touched, and my lust swelled in my chest. He leaned forward again and took me into his mouth, but since I wanted this to last, I needed him not to. I slid myself out from under him and positioned myself behind, bending Cas over on all fours so he was facing the bottom of the bed, and took his hole to my mouth again.

"Jude," he moaned, wanton and loose, pushing back into my mouth. "Jude, that feels..."

"Good?"

"Incredible, Christ, so bloody good. Don't stop."

I set about it again. Spreading him open with my hands as I fucked my tongue inside him, spearing that perfect tight heat over and over. By degrees, I felt him loosen and widen around my tongue, the small hot space opening like a hungry mouth. He shifted his head so he rested on his shoulder and then used his hand on himself frantically, gasping with pleasure beneath me.

I pulled back and sucked my finger into my mouth before pushing it inside him. The noise he made was filthy, depraved, and he arched his back deeper to push back onto it, fucking himself with it. My mind was utterly calm, utterly clear, and utterly focused on every breath of his pleasure. I wanted to make him crazy from lust, from need, from how much he wanted me. My cock was hard and leaking at the head as I pulled my finger out and ran it teasingly over his hole.

Cas whimpered. "I need you inside me, please Jude, please."

I needed it, too. I pressed a kiss to the base of his spine and then both cheeks as I asked, "Do you have lube? Condoms?"

"There's lotion next to the bed."

There was. Some large medicinal-looking tub with a doctor's prescription on the side. I pulled off the lid and thrust my fingers in. It was the consistency of soft wax; I scooped some up and rubbed it all around his opening before spreading the rest over the head of my cock. I knew we should use something, but since we hadn't the night in Oxford, and since Nathan and I always had, and since Cas didn't seem to care, it faded from my list of concerns as quickly as the thought entered my brain. I covered his body with my own, cocooning him under me, and reached out to settle my hand over his to intertwine our fingers, and then I pushed inside him. He took me easily, the strange waxy lotion making the slide smooth and easy. I pressed my mouth to his hair, his temple, and then to the space below his ear.

"Fuck, Cas." I groaned.

He whined, delicious and soft, and then turned his head to find my mouth, kissing me with his own wide open, tongue desperately seeking mine.

"You're...so...big," he gasped. "I love it so much. I love how you feel inside me. Christ...Jude..."

"I know." I kissed him. "Fuck, you were made for me, Cas, I swear you were. You feel so good. So perfect." I kissed him again.

He made another soft whimpering noise, and then I was all the way in, pulsing against the tight space inside of him. I felt his heartbeat move with mine, and with the cadence of it in my ears and in my chest, I began to move. Slow at first, gentle at first, careful at first, but soon I couldn't help myself. I sped up, fucking him rougher, quicker. I shifted, sitting back so that I was kneeling, and used my hips to thrust up and into him. This changed the angle of my dick inside him and it had a breath-taking effect, he let out a loose, throaty sound and sat up, using his good hand to stroke himself as he fucked himself down onto my dick.

It felt incredible. I wrapped an arm around his body and pulled him against my chest. Holding the base of his throat and his hip, I rutted up and into him even faster, deeper, until he was moaning and thrashing in my arms.

"Oh my god," he gasped.

I moved my hand from his hip across to his dick, taking over where he was half stroking. It was burning hot and perfectly hard, and I began to jerk him off as I continued to thrust. The strangled noise from his throat told me he wouldn't last much longer.

He came loudly a few moments later, over the bed sheets, as well as my hand before he forced my hand off his dick, sensitive now.

"Keep fucking me," he said. "Don't stop."

"Cas, I'm going to..."

"Do it. Inside me, Jude, I want to feel you come inside me."

The orgasm rose like an earthquake, shooting through me from the bottom up, rocking my entire body, before I exploded inside the warm grip of his body. Still coming down from his own, he milked me from the inside, soft clenches of his body around my dick so that it felt like it would never end.

After, I slipped out of him, along with a warm rush of come, and fell back onto the pillows. He didn't do what I expected him to, which was go directly to the bathroom to find something to clean us with, instead moving to lie down next to me. He lay on his back at first before I reached out to stroke a finger down his side, then he turned to face me.

Bliss settled, warm as milk in my veins as I waited for the familiar melancholy to settle over me. But as I gazed into his eyes, and as he smiled that small hesitant smile at me, I knew the feeling wouldn't come this time.

"Well, that was...something," he said, still smiling. It wasn't a smile I'd ever seen on him before: almost shy. It made my chest ache.

I smiled back at him. "It really was."

There was no warning before he did it; he just rose up and leaned over me, kissing me very gently on the mouth.

I knew the bliss couldn't last. I knew I didn't have him. That he couldn't love me. But my mind and body didn't care. So great and absolute was the pleasure I felt in that perfect moment. I wanted to bathe in it, in him, gorge myself so that when he left me, I would be able to sustain myself on it for the months and years to come.

TWENTY-TWO

I woke up the following morning with Cas pressed to my front and my nose buried in his neck, the scent of his hair the breath I took. I kissed the skin at the line of his hair as I pushed my morning erection against the firm heat of his body.

He woke slowly, stretching and groaning like a cat. He turned onto his back without opening his eyes, pouting until I captured his pout with a kiss.

"Morning," I whispered, kissing my way down his sleep-warm chest. I dusted him with kisses, sucking one nipple then the other into my mouth before continuing lower.

We'd fucked twice more last night before taking a dazed, languid shower together where I'd washed his body then his hair before sinking to my knees and sucking him off again. I wanted to do it again now.

"Good morning," he gasped as I reached

his thigh, kissing the inside of it. He spread open his legs invitingly but let out a small noise of complaint. "I'm sore everywhere. What on earth did you do to me?"

I lifted my head to say. "Fucked you senseless."

The blush that crept across his cheeks was the most disarming thing I'd ever seen. "I've never had much sense, so I wouldn't count it as a major accomplishment, Jude."

I rolled my eyes and dipped my head to suck his warm sleep-soft cock into my mouth. He winced, but his eyes flashed with heat.

"I honestly don't know if I have the energy," he said.

I let him drop from my mouth. "You don't have to do anything, just lie there and look pretty." I smirked as I pushed his legs up and buried my face in his hole. Slowly and with focus, I ate him out until he couldn't resist anymore. He used his hand to get himself off, and when I could see he was on the verge, I sat up and opened my mouth so he could direct the head of his cock into it.

"Fuck, I love how you taste," I said as I kissed him, pushing his own come into his mouth with my tongue.

He whined a protest against my lips but opened his mouth and swallowed what I gave him hungrily. Then he pushed me onto my back and returned the favour.

Some binding had come loose, a line in the sand washed away, the Rubicon crossed. Because we could not, and did not, hold back after this. I touched him when I wanted to, where I wanted to, pulling him into me while we cooked to kiss him stupid, snatching the book out of his hand while he read on the sofa to pull him to his back and swallow his dick.

He instigated less – though I knew this was because of a reluctance to display certain emotions and not because his desire was less than mine – because when I initiated, I was always rewarded with an enthusiastic and deliciously submissive Cas. He knelt and bent and spread himself for me willingly. And each time he came, it was always hard and completely, and with a look of almost shock on his face. It was fucking adorable.

I got so lost in him (and us) that I forgot all about the things I'd wanted to ask him; the pills in his bathroom and the reasons he was in London, when he'd leave me again. Nothing else existed outside of us.

I knew I should be careful. It was almost identical to how it had been in those days before he'd left me for the first time. I would have moments of clarity and begin to think straight and sensibly for a bit. But then he'd appear and smile that shy smile at me, say something or do something so completely unlike the Cas I thought I knew, and I would forget again.

We'd been sleeping together four days and nights when he took a call on his mobile, bringing him back to bed in a strange mood. I assumed it had been the pervert. I wanted to ask. I'd been thinking all the time he was on the phone that when he came back we'd have the talk, but when he'd come back to bed, he'd pulled back the covers and went down on me. He'd turned me on so hard and so fast with his tongue and his hands (he'd gotten even better at the thing he used to do with the slit at the end of my dick) that I was moments away from coming. Then without a single bit of prep, he climbed on top of me, pulled me inside him, and rode me into oblivion. He'd been focused, determined, and almost angry, which had been incredibly confusing.

I hadn't been thinking straight either because I sat up, grabbed him tight around the waist while I spread and drove up and into him and asked, "Does he fuck you as good as this?"

His eyes had blazed with arousal as he shook his head.

"I want to hear you say it."

"No. He doesn't...fuck me like this. Oh, shit, Jude." He came, gasping and untouched, a few seconds later.

The following day, I was doing short laps in the pool while he watched from behind his sunglasses on one of the sun loungers. I could feel his eyes on me, appreciative and lustful. I'd never considered myself a vain person, but with him watching me, all of the things people had often told me about my appearance suddenly seemed very important. I climbed out of the pool and stalked toward him, crowding over him to kiss him, ignoring his huffs and complaints about getting him wet. When I pressed my palm to the front of his shorts, I was thrilled to find him half-hard.

"Sunglasses or not, I can see you ogling me," I whispered at his lips.

"My eyes were closed actually," he lied. Against my mouth, his breath was coming in quick gasps. When I kissed the side of his neck, his pulse raced against my lips.

"Mmmm sure they were." I straightened and reached out a hand. "Come into the water with me. It will cool you down."

He lowered his sunglasses. "I don't think what you have planned for me in there is going to do anything of the sort."

"Busted."

I reached down and grabbed his good hand, and he let me pull him toward the pool. He watched me jump in before he lowered himself in at the steps. Once he was in, I immediately went toward him and crowded him against the side. He slung his arms carefully around my neck – he was wearing his sling less, but I was always careful with his splinted fingers. We kissed under the heat of the sun, the cool blue of the water lapping at our bodies as I lapped at his mouth and his jaw, and as he played with the hair at the nape of my neck.

"I love this," I whispered. "Being here with you. No one else but us."

I was prepared for him not to answer, but very softly, as though someone might overhear him, he said, "I do too."

I was tempted to spoil the moment by asking him to stay with me, to leave him, to never go back to America, but I bit my tongue and hugged him close instead. We floated out into the middle of the pool, kissing lazily and deeply under the all-seeing glare of the August sun.

Later, we drank a bottle of good wine in the garden before wandering, tipsy and silly, down the street to a small Italian restaurant for huge bowls of pasta, which we ate on a small table outside. He talked about his favourite restaurant in Rome, about his course at Lervairè, about his cat – Laurent – before we walked hand in hand by the river while the sun set. I'd never been more content, not since I was a child and I knew what it was to be blessedly unaware of how painful life could be.

He looked radiant under the witching hour light. Over the last few weeks, his skin had turned a deep Grecian gold, bringing out the vibrant and dazzling azure blue of his eyes. He'd smiled more than I'd ever seen him smile, and day by day, his hand bothered him less. He was happy.

When I bought him a white rose from a seller on the bank of the Thames, he rolled his eyes but looked adorably flustered.

"You're ridiculous, you do realise that?" he said as he took it from me.

I smiled, unapologetic. "Oh, I know. You've told me enough over the years."

His smile faltered, but then he moved his rose to the other hand and re-took my hand. We'd come to a stop to watch a boat pass by, a large river boat, which seemed to be hosting a party on board. The music was loud enough to hear where we stood.

"What if I asked you to dance with me?" I turned to him. "How ridiculous would that be?"

He flicked his eyes to me, no doubt to see if I was serious. I was. He laughed and shook his head. But he danced with me, slow and wary. I'd never been more in love with him in my life. I'd never been more happy in my life.

That night when we made love, I thought my heart would burst.

"Jude," he gasped, clinging to me. "Jude...fuck, it feels so good. You always feel so...good." I kissed every part of his face I could reach, touching his lips just as his orgasm shot through him. He held me so tight it was as though he was afraid I might disappear, and I wanted to tell him that I never would.

"I'm yours, Cas," I told him. "You're mine, and I'm yours. *Always*.

Tell me you know that, tell me."

"I know, Jude," he replied, soothingly. "I know."

Since the pattern of my life had always been the same, I should have expected what was to follow. Events never turned slowly, or gradually; my tragedies were always great and sudden and complete. And this one would be no different.

TWENTY-THREE

The day started like all the others had since we'd begun this again. The scent of Cas's skin in my nose and the heat of him spooned against my front. He turned in my arms and kissed me softly. "I'm hungry," he whispered, then slipped out of bed.

I groaned and twisted onto my back, watching as he pulled on a pair of shorts and a T-shirt. "What time is it?"

"After twelve. Shove some clothes on and come down and eat. We can always come back to bed."

"Or you could just let me eat you here?" I did some mildly disgusting thing with my tongue.

He laughed and shook his head. "I promise I'll make you something far tastier."

"Oh, I highly doubt that."

He yelled something about being insatiable and disappeared out of the room. I should have been able to sense what was coming by the weather: it was

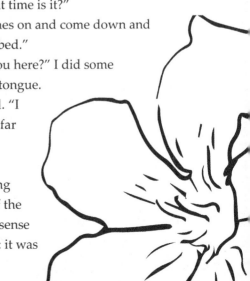

the first overcast day of the whole summer, a watery-looking grey sky that felt heavy and foreboding. I remember thinking I should put the cover over the pool.

When I arrived downstairs, Cas had set the nook, and after checking whether he needed a hand with the cooking, I did as he told me and sat down and waited. It was some egg concoction he called 'Turkish eggs': perfectly poached eggs on a bed of garlicky yoghurt sprinkled with chilli flakes and drizzled with oil. Toasted buttery sourdough on the side. It was the best thing I'd put in my mouth since him.

"That was incredible," I told him after I'd cleared my plate. "How did you learn to cook so well?"

"YouTube," he said as he popped a piece of yoghurt-soaked bread into his mouth. "I don't have much of a social life, so I watch a lot of cooking videos."

I was about to ask him why he didn't have much of a social life when I heard voices from above. At first, I thought it was Ken, dropping something off, but he wouldn't have come in without ringing us first. Then I heard Gideon's voice.

We both turned as he came down the stairs.

"Ah, here they are!" he said, beaming at us.

He wasn't alone, and I begged, *pleaded* with the universe, for it to be Ken behind him on the stairs.

But, of course, the universe had never been that kind to me. It had never been kind at all and it wasn't about to change its habit at this point. Blackwell came down the stairs behind Gideon and took in the sight of us both sitting there together. A cloud rolled over his face to rival the one outside. Dark and violently thunderous.

Beside me, I felt Cas stiffen, before he sat down his fork and stared at his plate, making no move to get up and greet them.

It occurred to me then that we hadn't showered. I still had him on me, he was still covered in me, and a delicious sense of satisfaction spread over me despite how awful this was.

I'd finished eating anyway so I slid out of the nook and stood to carry my plate to the sink. When I turned, Xavier was by Cas's side, smoothing a hand over his hair even though Cas still wasn't looking at him.

Frowning, I looked at Gideon.

"Jude, I'm so delighted you're still here. I was just saying to Xavier that we should all go to dinner tonight at Isabel. It's this fabulous restaurant in Mayfair. I'll have Ken call them and reserve us a table. How is eight for you?"

I couldn't think of anything worse. I thought about telling him that Isabel wasn't as good since Jean-Georges had poached their chef, but I was too focused on Cas and how I couldn't decide if it was my imagination or not, but it looked like he had ever so slightly leaned into Xavier's touch. I made my excuses and left the three of them in the kitchen.

I stayed in my room the entire day, pacing, biting my nails, and reliving the last five days in excruciating, painful detail until I thought I might go crazy. I came out to find Gideon by the pool reading the *Financial Times.*

"Where's Cas?" I asked him.

"They've gone out," he said before folding the paper and setting it down on the small metal outdoor table. He looked at me very intensely. "I expect they've a lot to talk about."

It hadn't rained yet, but the air felt muggy from the threat of it, thick and opaque. Resolutely ignoring his gaze, I sat down and pulled out my phone. I thought that I should text him and make sure he was okay.

"I've booked the table for tonight," he said.

"Great," I muttered without looking up.

It was several moments before he spoke again. "Jude, you know, after last time, I really did hope that you'd have been more careful with him."

"I don't know what you're talking about."

He let out a loud sigh. "He isn't going to leave him; surely you know that."

I froze.

Gideon uncrossed his legs and sat forward. "Caspien is a realist,

Jude. He's always been the same. He's also extremely stubborn, and will never ever admit to having made a mistake. Even if that means a life of unhappiness."

I pounced on that. "So he is unhappy? With Xavier?"

"Of course he is, but it hardly matters. He's made his bed, and he's far too prideful to consider getting up from it. He's also far too smart to leave Xavier Blackwell on the promise of something as fleeting and pointless as happiness and childish notions of love."

"That's the most stupid thing I've ever bloody heard." I scowled. "Everyone deserves to be happy, Gideon. Everyone."

"And when were you last happy, young Jude?" Gideon cast a sad smile over me.

I stood.

"This morning," I said and left him sitting there.

They came back about a half hour before we were due to leave for dinner. I'd been coming out of the bedroom as Cas passed to go to his own, Blackwell I could hear talking to Gideon in the living room.

I moved in front of him to block his path. "What the hell's going on?" I whispered, urgently. He'd not responded to any of my messages.

He let me press him against the wall but glanced nervously toward the living room.

"Jude," he shook his head.

"Did you know he was coming?"

He gave me a look. "Of course not."

"Cas, I don't know if I can do this, stay here and watch you with him." I buried my face in his neck, and he let me, his body going soft under my touch. Recognisable, frantic lust raced up my spine.

"Please don't leave yet," he asked me, his voice a little desperate. "I don't think...just please stay a little longer." He pressed his mouth to mine, and I nodded, touching my forehead to his.

"Okay."

I felt him relax a little. He pulled back and gave me a tender sort of smile. "I need to go change for dinner."

I watched him retreat to his bedroom and close the door. When I walked into the living room, Xavier turned, some dark cloud coming over his features as he glanced in the direction of the bedrooms. I gave him a forced smile and went to sit across from him on the couch.

"Oh, why don't I go fetch us some aperitifs," Gideon said, standing. Then, quite purposefully, he disappeared from the room and left Blackwell and I alone.

His stare was as black as I remembered it, a void as deep and dark as his name, though it sparkled with something sly. Like he was enjoying a joke I didn't understand.

He was still objectively good-looking; healthy deep tan and black thick hair, chiselled jaw dusted with dark stubble. It wasn't hard to understand Cas's attraction to him. Now or back then. Gideon's neither. I imagined reams of women and men falling over themselves to gain Xavier Blackwell's attention.

Personally, I'd never loathed another human more except maybe the man who'd killed my parents.

"How have you been, Jude?" he asked, relaxing into the couch a little more. His gaze was intense as he stared at me, and I wondered if he looked at everyone the same way. If it was just me, did that mean something? I'd had a glass of wine, so there was a boldness in my veins as I stared him down. I was also an adult now; when the last time I'd seen him I'd been a frightened little boy.

"Pretty fucking wonderful until you showed up," I replied.

The look in his eyes didn't change, but he let out a small huff of laughter. "Cute. I can see why he likes playing with you."

The chill spread from the top of my head all the way down to my toes.

"What the fuck is that supposed to mean?"

Before he could answer, Gideon came flouncing back into the room carrying a bottle of champagne. He pulled four glasses from the drinks cabinet behind the couch and proceeded to pour us all a glass. Cas arrived a few moments later looking freshly showered and wearing a black shirt and trousers, which were cinched in quite dramatically at his waist. His sleeves were rolled up, and strips of thin gold hung from his wrist and neck. The only colour he wore was the white splint around his right hand. The effect was an almost feminine look, chic and classic. I knew I was staring, but I didn't care.

He lifted a flute of champagne and downed it in one. "Can we go now?" he said, looking at his watch. His manner was easy, casual, and I wondered where the panicked, desperate Cas from the hallway ten minutes ago had gone.

I can see why he likes playing with you.

The staff at Isabel seemed to know Gideon well, shaking his hand and ushering him straight past the people waiting to a circular table near the centre of the high-ceilinged space. I felt uncomfortable almost immediately. It wasn't the sort of place I'd ever come on my own, stuffy and formal, and with lots of gold and mirrors for people to look at themselves in. I watched as Xavier pulled out Cas's chair for him, bending to kiss the top of his head as he sat in it. I took the seat directly opposite and lifted the wine list, determined to get very, very drunk.

When Blackwell chose Cas's wine for him, I put it down to his very obvious snobbery, but when he ordered his starter and main course for him too, I felt my face rearrange itself. The glasses of wine and champagne only emphasised the other emotions swirling inside of me.

"Maybe he doesn't want the lamb," I said, causing everyone to look at me, including the waiter.

Cas shot me a warning look, while I glared at the pervert across the table.

"He always has the lamb when we come here," Blackwell told me dismissively. "He'll have the lamb."

"Yeah, well sometimes change is good. Variety being the spice of life and all that." I dropped my eyes to my menu. "What do you think, Cas? I think the fish looks good? I'm going to have the fish, I think."

"And I'll have the short rib," said Gideon, handing his menu back to the waiter.

"So it's two lamb, a fish and a short rib." The waiter was looking at Blackwell for confirmation and it only pissed me off even more.

"That's it," the pervert smiled. "Thanks."

Gideon began talking about some opera he'd seen in Italy which I tuned out, focused only on the stiff way Cas sat and the very determined way he avoided looking at me. I couldn't work out why it was strange; all I knew was that it was unlike any version of Cas I'd ever seen before.

The Cas I'd known these last few weeks had been some version of this one here: dulled, careful, almost hesitant. A far less dangerous version of the boy I'd known at Deveraux. Like a knife that had gone blunt.

Blackwell liked the sound of his own voice, that much was evident over three very rich overpriced courses, and so it was hard to find an opening in the conversation where Caspien might have entered it. But even when the talk turned to subjects I knew he was interested in, he said very little. I counted six or seven words in total throughout the starter and main courses. He drank his wine, ate his food and spoke only when someone asked him a direct question. He was nervous, clearly, and I could have put it down to my being there – me, the guy he'd been fucking for the last few days – sat across from his oblivious partner if not for the thing niggling at the outer edges of my understanding.

By the time the dessert menus were set down in front of us, I was drunk. I couldn't, wouldn't, hold myself back a moment longer.

"You going to order his dessert for him, too?" I said as Xavier picked up the menu card and scanned it. I set my own menu down. "Why don't you order mine for me, too, while you're at it? Go on, try and guess what I like." I sat back in my chair and stared at him over the rim of my wine glass (some £400 bottle of white that tasted like water by this point). When he levelled a nasty look at me, I knew the meaning wasn't lost on him. To my right, Gideon let out a jittery laugh while Cas cleared his throat.

"I don't want dessert," he said. "I think we should get the bill."

"I'd like dessert," Blackwell said, his eyes not leaving mine.

My voice was lively when I said. "Me too; I bloody love dessert."

I ordered the most expensive thing on the menu, though I could not now tell you what it was, and ate it slowly while glaring at the piece of shit sitting opposite me.

Gideon waffled on about French cheese while Cas drank his wine. When he set it down and stood, saying he was going to the bathroom, he turned his body and knocked his splint against the glass. It toppled his red wine straight into Blackwell's lap. The pervert shot to his feet, eyes dark and voice violent. "You stupid, fucking idiot," he growled at Cas.

Cas, before my eyes, shrank back, face paling with fright.

I shot to my feet. "What did you just fucking call him?!" I was rounding the table towards Blackwell, but I felt Cas pull me back.

"Jude, please don't," Cas said, but his voice was very far away.

We were about the same height, Xavier Blackwell and I, and about similar builds, though I suspected he was fitter. I didn't care.

"What did you call him?" I asked again.

People were now staring, but I didn't care about this either.

"Oh, for the love of god, sit down, *little boy*," Blackwell said, dabbing at his crotch with a napkin.

"Little boy?" I laughed, coldly. "Oh, well, then I should be careful you don't try and fuck me, I suppose."

He froze at this, lifting his black glare to mine. It was murderous. He took a slow step toward me, and Cas pushed himself between us.

"I would urge you to be very, *very* careful what you say next," he said implicitly.

"Darling, let's go, please. I think we should leave now." This was Cas, his voice soft and soothing. I'd never heard it like that before, and I could only blink in horror when I realised he wasn't talking to me, but Xavier.

I watched in a daze as he slid a hand around Blackwell's waist and pulled him away from me, away from the table, and out of the restaurant. When I came back to my senses, I charged after them. I heard Gideon shouting my name as I went.

Outside in the street, I saw Cas opening the door of a black taxi, Xavier practically shoving him inside. I called out to him, running a little way after the taxi, but it pulled out into the busy London traffic and was soon lost to the lights and engine noise. I flagged down my own, and gave them Gideon's address, playing over every second of the dinner in my head. I knew what I'd seen, what it meant, and I felt ill from it. Furious at myself for being so fucking blind. It had been in front of me the entire time. How had I so readily ignored it?

I thought about the hollow sound of his voice when he'd told me everything was fine, when he'd told me how last minute his coming to London had been, when he'd told me in too much detail about the tennis match where'd he'd broken his hand. Imagining Blackwell's face, I punched the seat of the taxi, ignoring the way the driver watched me in his rear-view mirror.

I'd kill him for this. I was going to kill Xavier Blackwell. He'd put his hands on Cas, *my Cas*, and I was going to murder him for it.

TWENTY-FOUR

Though they'd gotten a head start, they weren't at home when I got there, sending me into a spiral of panic.

I called his phone, which rang before going to voicemail. I rang it seven or eight more times before it went straight to voicemail without ringing at all. When I heard the front door opening, I ran toward it only to find it was Gideon.

He shot me a pitying look. "Come and have a drink with me, Jude."

"Where is he?" I demanded. "Where are they?"

Xavier hadn't had a suitcase when they'd arrived earlier, that thought had only occurred to me when I'd gone to Cas's room to see if they were there. That meant he had a hotel or a flat somewhere in London. That's where they'd gone.

"I think it's best if you calm down before you do something you regret."

He laid a hand on my shoulder as he passed, fatherly almost, and went into the living room.

"How am I supposed to calm down when Cas is somewhere with *him*?" I needed to tell him, though I was sure Cas would hate me for it. I followed after him, speaking quickly as anxiety rose in my chest. "You don't get it, Gideon, I think he's going to hurt him. I *know* he is. I think Xavier was the one who broke his hand. I need to get to him, Gideon. You don't understand."

He was pouring something dark into a very small wine glass. Port. Gideon never missed his after-dinner glass of port.

"Oh, Jude, there's very little I don't understand." When he turned, he had a very strange smile on his face. He took a small, careful sip of port. "You know that by now."

I stared. "You knew? You *know*?"

"I know that love is a complex beast, violent and passionate, and that to give oneself over to it so completely is not without sacrifice."

"Oh my fucking god, not now with this shit. What are you talking about?" I went towards him, black with fury. "This is Caspien! Cas! Your nephew, and you knew that Blackwell was…that he…" I couldn't bring myself to say it. "You knew?"

"After how deeply he hurt you, you cannot possibly tell me that you're not somewhat satisfied that this is the bed he now lies in?"

It felt as though he'd punched me.

I shook my head, flabbergasted. "No. Of course I'm not satisfied. What is wrong with you? What the actual *fuck* is wrong with you?"

Though I was shouting now, my angry tone didn't seem to perturb him in the slightest. He carried his port to the armchair and sat down, crossing his long legs.

"You know, when I first met you, I thought you would make such a perfect playmate for him. But I'm beginning to think that I miscalculated."

I didn't want to hear this. Not now. Gideon going off on another one of his philosophical tangents about love and heartbreak. I'd heard it all before. I dialled Cas's number again.

"When I saw how you looked at him that first day at the house,

I thought you'd be perfect for Cas to learn his lesson on. Bright-cheeked and wide-eyed; impossibly dazzled by him. Christ, I knew how you felt about him before you yourself even did. Caspien is almost impossible to resist, but you did, Jude, for far longer than most. For far longer than Xavier did." At this he chuckled, some hollow mean little noise that seemed to come from his throat. Cas's phone had most certainly been switched off by now.

I turned my full attention to Gideon.

"What are you talking about? You said you didn't know about him and Xavier. The day I came to you, after he left, you told me you didn't know they were together until you'd read his letter."

Gideon sipped his port and gave me a complicated look. "You think Caspien left me a letter? Caspien would never explain himself to anyone, least of all to me. As soon as he was legal, old enough not to need my blessing, he left. But it was hardly a surprise. I could see it coming the moment they met. You see, studying the minds of men is something of a hobby for me. Xavier's wasn't too difficult to figure out. Besides, Caspien was very much his type. I simply put Caspien in his orbit and the inevitable happened, just as I knew it would."

I gaped at him in horror a moment before the fury rushed back in.

"Caspien was a fucking child!" I spat. "You sat back and allowed him to be groomed and abused?"

"Oh, I think you're being a little dramatic," Gideon said, calm in the face of my storm. "Cas was sixteen. Xavier is handsome, rich, and adores him. He's given him a wonderful life in Boston, you should see their apartment, his wardrobe, the car he drives. Caspien is fortified enough to survive a few disagreements in order to live the life he's been given. In fact, thanks to my guidance, I'm certain he can survive just about anything. I think you need to give him a little more credit, Jude."

There was a loud noise in my ears, and a heat in my blood I wasn't sure I could control.

"Your *guidance*?" I said, voice thin from rage. "Your guidance is the reason he's in a relationship with a violent fucking predator." I went to him, crowding over him. "Now tell me where he is before we find out how many *disagreements* you're able to survive, Gideon."

For the first time, I saw some alarm in his eyes. Not for Cas though, of course not, but for himself. How fucking stupid I'd been. I'd allowed myself to be taken in by him, just as Cas had always warned. I'd allowed myself to be dazzled by a façade of eccentricity and flightiness. It was an act, all of it. He was septic; a pernicious, vindictive danger who should never have been allowed to look after a child.

"Where are they?" I said again, the warning clear in my voice.

"Xavier has a house in Holland Park," he said, at last.

"I want the address."

I ran to the end of Wilton Place and hailed another taxi. It took too long, and as the driver tried and failed to make conversation with me about all manner of nonsense, it was all I could do not to scream for him to shut up and drive faster. At some point between Belgravia and Earls Court, it began to rain, fat heavy droplets which battered the roof and windows of the taxi. I'd not worn a jacket, but it was the least of my worries as I shoved my card in the slot and bolted outside and down the street to number eighty-six.

It wasn't as grand as Gideon's, but Blackwell's London house was a three-storey, opposite a park in central London, so even my outsider point of view knew it meant money.

I banged on the door and rang the bell a few times before I could hear movement behind the door.

Blackwell opened it, changed from what he'd worn at dinner into a crisp white T-shirt and dark sweatpants. He looked confused to see me for a moment, then angry. He was about to close the door in my face when I lunged, crashing into him full force, so we both went sprawling back into the hallway.

I'd never hit anyone before – or since – but when my fist collided with his face, I worried that I'd never be able to stop. The force knocked his head back on a tiled stone floor so hard I heard the impact. It shocked him into a daze, because he just lay there a moment while I hit him a few more times, my fist pummelling his face.

When he gathered his wits, he tried to grab my arms, then when that failed, threw a punch into my side.

"I'll fucking kill you!" I was saying over and over and over. "I'm going to fucking kill you for hurting him...I'll fucking kill you!"

Just then, Cas appeared at the end of the hallway. His eyes were red-rimmed and his hair wild as he looked at me in horror. Worse than that though, was the confirmatory swelling over his right cheek and eye.

The momentary distraction was enough for Blackwell to shove me off and get himself to his feet. He began kicking me, though since he was barefoot, he used his heel to drive down into my abdomen and my legs. I barely felt it. Reaching out to hit his thighs and legs, all I heard was the sound of Cas shouting, screaming, at him to stop. He pulled and grabbed at Xavier, trying to force him off, but Blackwell was unhinged with fury.

Finally, Cas threw himself on top of me, becoming a shield between Blackwell and me. Even that didn't stop him. He reached in to grab a fistful of Caspien's hair and attempted to drag him off, which only made Cas scream louder and cling to me harder.

"Please, Xavier, stop," he was shouting, pleading. "That's enough, you've hurt him enough, please, stop. Please."

The sound of Cas's begging made me feel ill. Angry and ill and determined that the moment he let me up, I was going to kill this man. I'd go to prison for this, happily. How fucking dare he reduce Cas to this. How *fucking* dare he?

Eventually, Blackwell's kicks slowed and stopped, and then the hallway was filled with the sound of our laboured breathing and the traffic noise from the street.

Blackwell straightened, T-shirt torn and bloody now, as he stared down at us both with absolute contempt. His face wasn't quite as messed up as I'd hoped it would be, but I'd burst his lip and given him enough bruising that he'd have to explain it. I still couldn't feel the damage he'd done to my body, though it would be enough to linger for weeks after.

He fixed his hair and then reached out a hand. Cas hesitated only a moment before he took it, allowing him to pull him up and off me. He brought Cas close, brushing his hair back from his face almost tenderly, before kissing him on the mouth. My insides felt like they were made of water.

Finally, Blackwell turned his stare to me.

"I could have you arrested for that," he said.

On weakened legs, I stood. "And I could have you arrested for abusing a fifteen-year-old boy. Who do you think will spend more time inside a prison cell, you vile prick?"

I thought he might hit me again, in fact, I'm sure he meant to but Cas gripped onto him, holding him back

Blackwell said, "How about we add slander to that charge sheet too while we're at it?"

"Slander my fucking arse. I saw you with my own eyes; he was *fifteen*. Not to mention what you've been doing to him for months, if not years. Think your reputation would survive that, Mr. Celebrity Lawyer?" I took a step forward, fists clenching again. They throbbed from the fight, but I'd happily beat them to a pulp on his face.

"Is that so?" Blackwell rubbed a hand over Cas's back, and I felt something hot rise up from the pit of my stomach into my throat. "Caspien, sweetheart, if you wouldn't mind setting your friend straight here, before that mouth of his gets him into something he can't get out of."

I knew what Cas was going to say before he even opened his mouth. I knew it, but it still felt like he'd thrust a knife straight into my chest.

"You're mistaken, Jude," he said. "I was fifteen when Xavier and I met, but I was an adult before we were together. It's dangerous of you to insinuate otherwise." Like he was being rewarded for speaking his lines well, Blackwell kissed him, this time on his temple.

"Now, I'm going to be a gentleman and let you say your goodbyes." This, he said to me. "But if you contact him again, or come near him again, or if I so much as hear a whisper on the wind as to Caspien's legality when we were first together, I will ruin you.

Then, I will ruin your sister and your uncle. And then, in my spare time, I'll make it my business to ruin everyone else you care about. Do you understand me, Mr. Alcott?"

I could barely breathe, let alone speak. I glanced at Cas to find his eyes shimmering with unshed tears. That terrible ugly bruise mottling around his right eye.

"Good. Now say goodbye and then get out of my fucking house," he said before striding down the hallway toward the back of the house.

When I heard a door close, I grabbed Cas's hand and pulled him out of the front door and down the street.

"He's a fucking psychopath." I was saying as I pulled my phone out of my pocket. "I'm phoning the police. You should have let me kill him, I wanted to fucking kill him."

I felt Cas stop walking, the dead weight of him pulling me to a halt. He reached for my phone and snatched it out of my hand.

"Don't be ridiculous, Jude. You're not calling the police."

"Why is it ridiculous? He's a nutter, Cas. Like an actual lunatic. He should be in prison."

"And he'll say you came to his house and attacked him, and you'll be arrested. There are security cameras at the front door."

"So, then, I'll be arrested. But when they find out what he's been doing to you, they'll get it."

He stared at me, bewildered. "Sometimes it's like you're still a bloody child. That's not how the world works, Jude. For Christ sake, please tell me you know that? You think they'll just believe whatever you tell them?"

"So then *you* tell them." I stepped closer and lowered my voice. "The truth about him, how old you were." He looked away from me, unable to meet my eyes. "Look, I know why you said it in there, in front of him, but if you were safe, away from him, you could tell them the truth."

It took some effort for him to look at me. "It wasn't like that, you know it wasn't. I wanted it, I wanted him."

This, I wouldn't hear. Couldn't. "Maybe that's what he's made you believe, Cas. But it doesn't matter, you were a child who didn't know any better, he was a grown fucking man. He took advantage of you, I know you know that."

"I'm not...going to do that." He shook his head. "I wasn't...no."

I reached for his hand, the one Blackwell had broken, and held it up by the wrist. "And what about this? He did this to you, didn't he? There wasn't a fall or a fucking tennis match, was there? He did this. He hurt you because he's a violent, despicable piece of shit."

He looked down again, muttered, "It was my own fault."

"You had bruises in Oxford that night, too." I said. I'd remembered in the taxi on the way here. I'd thought they were mine, and he'd let me believe it. "Older ones. They were his, weren't they? Not mine. How long has he been hurting you, Cas?"

He tried to pull his hand away. "Stop it, Jude."

"Stop what? It's why you came to London, wasn't it? Because you were afraid of what he might do to you if you stayed. You're afraid of him. Why are you protecting him?"

I saw his throat move as he glanced around the dark street, frightened eyes wide and panicked. "It's not what you're saying; it's not always like that..."

"It should *never* be like that, Caspien." I gestured to where the bruise around his eye was darkening more every minute we stood there. "What about that? For spilling his fucking wine?"

He looked at me as though I couldn't possibly be that dense. "No, Jude. Not for that."

I stiffened. "He knows about us."

"Turns out, I'm not quite as clever as I think I am..." he said, obliquely.

"So then he knows. That'll make it easier to leave him."

Cas shook his head. "No. Jude. Nothing has changed. I chose Xavier, I chose him, and sometimes we have to see things through to the end."

I'd never heard anything more ridiculous in my bloody life and the look on my face told him so.

"What bloody end? When he hurts you so badly, you end up in

the hospital? You can't play piano, Cas! Because of him. Tell me what the fucking end is. Help me understand what that looks like because I'm struggling to see past the bruise on your face and the broken fingers and the fact he's a fucking predator."

"Okay then, I leave him, and then what? In your head, where everyone gets exactly what they want, what exactly is it you have planned for us? Where do we go? Where do we live? Because I won't ask Gideon for a single penny, and I've not a penny to my name until I turn twenty-five, so what is it you see happening here?" He was talking quickly, rashly, saying these things as though they were fantastical and not as though I'd spent years imagining them in very great detail.

"You come to Oxford with me," I began. "People change schools all the time and they do teach music at Oxford. I've got enough from the trust fund to pay for a flat somewhere for us, or we can house share. I'll work too. Whatever I need to do. I'll finish this year and then do my honours while you finish, or I can just get a full-time job, and then when you're done, we can go anywhere you want, do anything you want. I don't care as long as I'm with you."

He looked taken aback at the level of detail I'd supplied him with.

Still, he shook his head. "You make it sound like you'd be happy. But you wouldn't be, not with me. I don't make anyone happy, Jude. In fact, I've a great deal of skill in making people quite miserable, you included. Or had you forgotten?"

"You're looking at it wrong," I said. "You make me so fucking happy when we're together, Cas. You. These last five days with you, I was happier even than I was that summer. You know why? Because you were happy, too. You can deny it, but I know it's true: you were happy. I could see it. I could fucking *feel* it. We were happy together, and so that proves we can be. Look, I don't know what Gideon's made you believe, but you deserve to be happy. Letting people love you is okay."

I knew I shouldn't, not again, but I couldn't stand the thought of him not knowing I still felt the same.

"I love you, Cas, I always have. I've loved you since the moment

I saw you, I think. Even when I thought I hated you, I loved you. I don't think I know how not to, so please don't go back there. Don't choose that, choose me. Stay with me. We'll go to Gideon's, pack our shit, and leave. Together."

He looked tormented. "You've no idea what you're asking."

"Yeah, I do. I'm asking you not to go back to someone who fucking hurts you," I said. "You're not safe with him."

"And you're not safe with me," he said. "I'm poison, remember? Like that Oleander plant you found that day in the arboretum. Best to rip out at the root." He gave me a small, bitter, Gideon-like smile.

I shook my head and went to call that nonsense.

"No, you were right," he said. "Really, it was the most insightful you've ever been. It's true. I am. I ruin everything I touch. Christ, my own mother loathed me. I ruined her and I'll ruin you as well and I don't want that. I don't want to be the one to ruin you, Jude. Not you."

He was pulling away from me now, physically, emotionally. The rain had stopped, but it started again then, a light patter at first before it became a rushing torrent.

"Please, Cas," I said to him. "Don't do this again, please don't do this."

"Go back to Oxford and try to be happy, Jude. That's the only way this goes. I promise you it's for the best."

I was shaking my head. He was looking at me the same way he had in the hut that day, except this time it felt worse, a fatal wound I would never heal from. Not again.

"If you go back there, if you choose him now, then we're done. *I'm* done. I can't watch you do this to yourself. I won't." The threat was the only thing I had left, a last desperate grasp at a drowning thing.

"Please try to be happy," he said again as he took a step backward.

"I mean it, Cas, we're not doing this again."

He was further away now and he had to raise his voice a little to be heard over the sound of the rain. There were tears in his eyes, as there were in mine. "But this is what we do, Jude. It's what we've always done."

"Not anymore. It's over. Don't come to me again."

He smiled, sadly, and nodded once. "Finally, he learns."

Then he turned, and walked back quickly the way we'd come. I stood there for a long time after he turned the corner, the rain pounding against me the only thing that made me feel alive.

Gideon was where I left him. I didn't bother talking off my squelching wet shoes as I walked past the living room, soaked to the skin.

"I wondered if he might actually listen to you this time," he said from the dimly lit room.

Stopping in the wide doorway, I stared at him, loathing and heartache a ton weight on my chest.

"I think you've always been like this, haven't you?" I said as I went toward him. "Even when you were a child. Maybe your parents loved your sister more, or maybe someone stole your toys as a child or maybe you had no bloody friends to play with, so you began playing with people instead. Is that it? You were already this person well before you got your heart broken. I'm pretty sure of that now."

I never let him answer, though I wasn't certain he was going to.

"You know, Gideon, I don't think I ever trusted you, but I liked you. I cared for you. I even thought you were the reason I was at Oxford, that you were the person making my life that little bit better, I think even up until tonight, I still thought that. But now I know it can't have been you. Because you, Gideon, don't care about people. Not even your own flesh and blood, your sister's son, who you promised to raise and love. Even he was a plaything to you. You ruined him. So much that he thinks he *deserves* the kind of life he's living now with that piece of shit. You tried to ruin me too – I guess time will tell whether you did or not." I went to walk away before I remembered something else I wanted to say.

"I'm sorry that someone broke your heart, Gideon, really I am, because there's no pain on earth like it. But I've survived heartbreaks too and I still have a fucking soul. I'm still capable of love. And the fact that you're not tells me one thing, you're weak. Weak and sad and bitter and that's the reason you're going to die alone."

His face was a mask, and I realised then that it had always been. "We all die alone, Jude."

"Oh, there's a very special kind of alone for people like you, Gideon," I said and went to pack.

To:	caspienthe__ghost@gmail.com
From:	Jalcott.mag@ox.ac.uk

Dear Cas,

This is the last one of these I'm going to write. Part of me thinks it's been an entirely unhealthy pursuit, part of me thinks it's having been able to talk to you like this all these years, like you've been here with me, that's kept me sane. Especially this last year.

Maybe it's a bit of both: I've learned there are very few absolutes in life. Or love for that matter.

I finished my degree. An upper-second. Not a first, but they say an upper-second from Oxford is like a first from most other places, so I'll take it. I'm taking some time off to go travelling; Nikita, Bast and I are heading to South America. Then, we plan to head north and up into Canada. If we run out of cash or get arrested, then I'll call you — I assume that would count as 'something important?' We've planned on staying away for a few months, but we'll see when we get there. I'm excited, first time abroad and all that. Should be a laugh.

Luke and Elspeth are engaged, and they're moving away from Deveraux and across the island to look after Elspeth's mum, who's had a stroke. You might have already heard that from Gideon.

I haven't spoken to Beth in over a year; she moved to Manchester with Daniel and they're running an online recruitment business. At least I think that's what it is.

I don't really want to mention this next part because it makes me feel ill, but it feels weird not to: it's all I've been able to think about since Finn told me. He wasn't saying it to be mean or anything, Finn isn't like that. He assumed I already knew. He assumed I'd heard it from Gideon. (Finn doesn't know I haven't spoken to Gideon since the night in London. I don't plan to either. What was it you said that night in the rain? Rip it out at the root? Well, I've done that. With both of you.)

Anyway, I suppose commiserations are in order. Finn said you married him. In Italy, Verona I think. I'd honestly been unable to process much after that. I still get angry and sad when I think about it, when I think about you with him. About what you think you deserve. I hope there wasn't a prenup and that it was for the money. Or for the house in Boston. I hope you're happy, though I suspect you're not. (This isn't the comfort I wish it was, trust me.)

I still love you. I think I always will. But it's like my parents, I'm never going to stop loving them, I'm only going to get better at living without them loving me back. So I'll be okay again at some point. I'm trying to be happy, like you asked me to be. It's harder some days than others, but I also know that it will get easier.

I think that's all I wanted to say.

I'm sort of sad that this is the last one: maybe I'll write a postcard from each city I visit? Keep them all and put them with everything else I've kept. The copy of Dracula you borrowed that day at the beach, the drawing of Falstaff I stole from your sketchbook, the piece of music you'd been writing that day that you threw away — I can't read music so I don't even know what it sounds like — the receipt from the night we went to dinner in London, the letter I wrote you when you left me the first time. I forget what else is in there, but there's a lot of stuff in that box. The picture you painted of me is in a box in Luke and Elsbeth's loft until I decide where I'm going to live after. I'd like to go back to London — visit those places we went together, again. I think I could be happy there. I managed to save a lot thanks to the mysterious donor, so I might be able to afford it.

Anyway, that's all.

P.S — I didn't mean what I said that night in the rain. You can always come back to me. You can always call me. I'll always answer, Cas.

Love,

Jude x

PART THREE:

THE SACRIFICE

"Suffering has been stronger than all other teaching, and has taught me to understand what your heart used to be. I have been bent and broken, but - I hope - into a better shape."

Charles Dickens, Great Expectations.

ONE

EIGHT YEARS LATER

I woke early and found Jasper already in the kitchen, stirring a pot of porridge on the stove.

"Sleep well?" he asked cheerily.

"Not particularly," I admitted before slipping out the back door to go for a run.

Running, I'd found some particular kind of solace in over the last couple of years. It was my only form of exercise. In London, I'd do it late at night or very early in the morning, before the pavements were filled with commuters, and let my legs move as though completely separate from my conscious brain. I could plot and plan entire chapters and scenes like this, deconstruct books I'd read or films I'd watched, or some days, like today, I'd play out what my life might have looked like had Caspien chosen me that rainy night on the pavement of a street in Holland Park. I did this rarely these days, but when I did, I gave myself over to the fantasy utterly.

I'd play out an endless variety of futures we'd never gotten to live together. We were happy. Our lives were always happy, and filled with contented days like those we'd spent in London that summer.

I ran to the cottage, which was shut up and long empty. It was locked, but I peered in through the living room window to find the couch where Cas had first used his mouth on me left behind. A small TV cabinet was barren and dust-covered. I rounded to the back and found the garden overgrown and abandoned. The clothing line was bare but for a few wooden pegs aged and bleached by the sun swinging gently in the wind.

It wouldn't take much to bring it back, I thought. It could be lived in again. I still dreamt of it frequently. Its old brick walls, thick window ledges, the scent of the forest that blew in when the back door was open, and the gulls flying overhead towards the cliffs. I'd had moments of happiness here, bittersweet and fleeting, but still, I yearned for the place like a lover yearns for their beloved.

Next, I ran to the birdwatcher hut, a harder route through the trees and over small hills and a hazardous forest floor. It was in worse condition than the cottage, certainly. A corner of its tin roof lifted up like a dog-eared book page. Moss collecting along its surfaces like lesions. I had to prise open the door to get inside, its frame swollen from rain, but once I did, I wanted to leave almost immediately. I couldn't bear its smell or the way the shadows on its walls reminded me of heartache and loss.

Had anyone ever been inside it since I'd last been here?

Had he ever come here? Thought of me here? Yearned for me here?

I pushed my way back out and ran a different route back to the house, thirsty and breathing hard. The kitchen was empty, and I poured myself a glass of water and took it back upstairs. As I passed the music room, I could hear the TV, the sound of American accents, something that sounded like a true crime show.

Upstairs, I showered and dressed, and went down to see about some breakfast. It was still early, just after nine, according to the kitchen clock. I was toasting some bread to have with jam when Jasper appeared, carrying a food tray.

"Coffee's still warm. I can make you something if you want?" He offered, setting the tray down. "We've eaten."

"Toast is fine, don't worry about it."

He shrugged and proceeded to wash up the two porridge bowls and rinse out the cups.

"How is he this morning?" I asked as I sat down at the dining table and took a bite of toast.

"Same as usual. He was asking about you, thought he'd dreamed you being here."

"He said he's only got a few weeks left. That true?"

Jasper dried his hands on the dish towel and came toward me, taking a seat opposite.

"To be honest, he should probably be dead already. He was given a few months at the start of the year."

We were in October.

I nodded, grim.

"He never visits either, you know," said Jasper. "Caspien."

The sound of his name felt like a scar being prodded at. An echo, a phantom pain. I didn't know what to say to that, so I took a sip of coffee.

Jasper continued. "He calls. I've spoken to him on the phone a few times, asks a lot of details about his treatment and condition, but I've never seen him in person."

This could mean everything or nothing: I'd never understood Gideon and Cas's relationship then and I wasn't going to attempt to understand what it was now.

"Does anyone else visit him?" I asked.

"Um, his old housekeeper, Elspeth. And Luke. Shit, that's your uncle, isn't it?"

I nodded. Luke was how I'd first heard about the cancer. Because I'd ignored Gideon's emails, deleting them without reading, which had come suddenly again at the beginning of the year. Then Luke had confirmed it. The handwritten letter had come via my agent a few weeks ago. On Deveraux House stationery, in a gorgeously swishing hand.

"Nice guy, Luke," said Jasper.

"The best."

We sat drinking our coffee in easy silence, but I could feel Jasper's eyes straying to me every now and again.

Finally, he said. "Was it about him then?"

I looked at him.

"*The Sacrifice*. I read it. Was it about Gideon?"

I took another sip of my coffee and considered how to answer that.

"It was about a soldier who went to war for someone he loved. Gideon's never loved anyone."

I could tell it wasn't the answer he expected. Or wanted.

"Sounds like he never knew love. How would he have been able to give it?" Jasper said almost defensively. "Maybe he'd have liked to have been loved. Imagine dying without knowing what it feels like to be loved or to love someone. He's just a sad old man who's going to die alone."

"He's not alone. He has you."

Jasper smiled a sad smile. "I don't love him."

I hated how his words made me feel. Pity again. Pity for Gideon. I didn't come here for this. I stood and dumped my plate and cup in the sink. I came here for what he promised me: answers.

And I was going to get them.

Then I was going to leave him to die alone and unloved just like he deserved.

He was sitting up in bed watching something on TV. He brightened when he saw me, but the look on my face gave something away, and he reached for the remote and switched the thing off.

"Jude, good morning; how did you sleep?"

"Fine," I said as I took a seat on the same chair I'd sat on last night. "Now, why am I here, Gideon? What is it you have to say to me?"

His expression faltered as he moved to sit up a little. As he shifted, one of his pillows slipped out and tumbled to the floor. I moved to pick it up, and helped him rearrange himself into a more comfortable position. I could feel him staring at me as I did this. From here, he smelled like rotting flowers.

"Thank you," he whispered gratefully.

I sat back down. Waited.

"You never answered me last night when I asked when was the last time you'd seen him," Gideon asked carefully.

I studied him, wondering why he cared, wondering whether to tell him. In the end, I didn't see what harm it would do.

"Surely he's told you that?"

He shook his head. "He will not let me utter your name. It's the only condition he has when he calls. The first time I asked about you, I did not hear from him for an entire year."

My body was clenched so tightly it trembled. "The last time I saw him was in London. Eight years ago."

Gideon's mouth fell open.

"We had nothing left to say to each other. Besides, I told him it was done, we were over. Then, to let me know just how done we were, he married his abuser."

"So then you do not know?"

"Know what?"

"That he left him. Two years ago. They divorced, quite messily. Caspien was ruthless with him – he had an exceptional lawyer, a far better one than Xavier. Caspien has been living in London; he has a role with the London Symphony." Gideon sounded proud.

I couldn't breathe.

He'd left him. Two years ago. He was living in London. Where I lived. He was living in the UK, and he hadn't contacted me?

I'd not given him conditions. I'd been absolute: don't call me again. It's over. We're done.

I felt a terrible heaviness in my chest.

"It doesn't change anything," I managed, though I knew it did.

"Of course it does, Jude," said Gideon.

I wanted to change the subject. "If he's been living in London, why does he never visit? Jasper said he's not seen you in years."

Gideon's mouth flattened. "Because he refuses to come here."

"The house?"

"Yes. And the island. It has too many memories for him. When I was still well enough to travel I saw him in London, but he hasn't been back here since...well years. In truth, things have been strained since..." He looked at me. "Since you, Jude."

"Oh, it's my fault is it?" I said. "Let's not kid ourselves. You two had a messed up relationship long before I came along. I've fuck all to do with it."

"True. But what I...he...what we did to you was the breaking of us." He sank deeper into the pillow. "We were never the same after you left us. It was too great a thing for us to move past."

"Well, thank god for that," I scoffed. "At least you two weren't able to fuck anyone else up the way you did me. That's something."

He gave me an agonised look. "I've so many regrets, Jude. How I looked at the world then, how cruelly I used you. Both of you."

And so now we had it. The reason I was here. To absolve a dying man of his sins. But I wasn't a fucking priest and I'd long ago been cured of my bleeding fucking heart syndrome.

"Yeah? Well, I wish it was as simple as that, Gideon. But it's not."

He nodded, magnanimously. "I know. I know a few words aren't going to magic away the pain I put upon you for my own ends."

He turned, pulling open the second drawer of the tall chest by his bed. From it, he pulled a brown envelope and closed the drawer again. He pulled out a couple of wads of paper and rifled through until he found what he was looking for. Then he held it out to me, gesturing for me to take it.

I had to get off the seat to reach it. Sitting back down, I scanned the page. I had guessed what it was; Gideon's apology.

"I hope you'll agree it's generous. Of course, Caspien will own the house, but he has expressed his desire to have it entrusted to the history and culture department."

"Money," I said when I'd finished reading. Of course, he was giving me money. A lot of it, too.

"I'm dying, Jude. And I cannot take it with me. I have very little family to speak of, and I have accounted for them in the same way they've accounted for me these last few months. Elspeth and Luke shall have something, Jasper too, of course, but I'd like the majority of my estate to be shared between you and Caspien. Since Caspien has his own money, he shall be seen to regardless, so I wanted to make sure you were comfortable after my passing."

That word struck like a blade inside me.

"Comfortable," I echoed.

"I should like you not to have to worry about money, to be able to write for as long as you want to without living costs being any kind of burden to your art. You have an incredible talent, Jude. I'm so proud of what you've achieved."

I couldn't believe what I was hearing. I stood from the chair, walked toward him and threw the copy of his will onto the bed.

"I don't want your money, Gideon."

He'd expected this. Was calm as he said, "Jude, I understand how proud you are, but when I die I should like to know that you are com—"

"If you say *comfortable* to me one more fucking time, I will burn this mausoleum to the ground with you inside it."

He closed his mouth. Looking up at me with pitiful eyes full of death.

"Money isn't comfort to me, Gideon. Comfort is going to sleep with the person you love wrapped up in your arms. It's knowing the people you love are safe and happy. Comfort's not choosing a piece of shit grooming abuser over someone who would have spent every day trying to make you happy. Comfort is knowing you deserve happiness and to be loved. That's my comfort, Gideon. He was my comfort, and I would have been his, and you're part of the reason neither of us has it. So keep your fucking money. I'm not interested in it."

I turned on my heel, determined to leave this house and never come back. There was nothing new to be learned here.

I was done. Finally done.

"He chose you," Gideon said.

I turned, furious. "No, he didn't. You messed him up so royally that he thought a violent relationship with his fucking abuser was what he deserved."

"You don't understand," he said, sounding tired. "Though neither did I at the time. Even though it was right in front of me."

He broke into a fit of terrible, wracking coughs. Concern dragged me back to him, and I helped him drink a few shallow mouthfuls from his water cup through the straw.

When it was over, he was still breathing hard, but his eyes were as focused and determined as ever.

"He chose you, Jude. Over Xavier and over himself. He chose you."

"Gideon, let's leave this alone," I said calmly. I felt guilty now for my outburst. He was bloody dying. Couldn't I show some empathy for Christ sake?

"No, Jude, you need to understand. You're right to hate me, because it was my fault he had to choose at all. But he chose you, Cas chose you."

"Gideon," I said again.

"You were never to know. He didn't want you to know," Gideon said, coughing. "But he wanted you to have it, to have Oxford, to be happy without him."

Everything around me, and in me, ground to a sudden terrifying halt.

"What are you talking about?" My voice was dangerously thin. An almost whisper.

"It's right that you hate me, Jude, it is, but I cannot leave this place without telling you what he did. What he did for you, because he chose you, because he *loved* you."

I staggered back from him, from the bed, reeling. My head was both very loud and very quiet at the same time.

"No, no, that couldn't have been..." I'd spent years trying to figure out who had done it. Who'd cared so fucking much about my life, my future, my expectations of myself, to have done that for me. Three years ago I'd even hired a private investigator. He'd said it was a dead end. There was nothing, not a trace of this mysterious altruist who had ensured I'd gotten to Oxford. *Oxford is your dream, Jude*, he'd said that day in the hut.

"Who else?" Gideon asked raspily. "Who else, Jude?"

At some point, I'd thought maybe it had been the person who'd killed my parents. Some great epiphany had caused him to attempt to make up for it. But if that was so, why hadn't he done the same for Beth? I'd thought, even after everything I'd seen to the contrary, it had indeed been Gideon. I'd thought about Luke too – that he'd hidden some money away from my sister just so he could do this.

But not once, not in any scenario, had I thought it was Cas.

Cas was cruel and capricious. He cared about no one. He was heartless and selfish. I'd meant nothing to him.

"I don't understand." I was shaking my head, refusing even now to believe it. "How? It doesn't make any sense. He had no money; he didn't inherit until he turned twenty-five. He told me this. It's why he couldn't come to Oxford. It's why..."

"His father," Gideon said. His voice was solid now, the gaspiness from his coughing fit gone. "Some time after his sixteenth birthday, he was contacted by a lawyer. His father wanted to meet him, begin some kind of relationship with him, pass to him some paternal endowment; I was not party to the details. There was a DNA test, Caspien insisted, and when the provenance of the claim was verified, Caspien agreed to meet with the man."

I'd sat down on the chair again, but my legs still felt weak, my heart thumping like a drum in my chest.

"I asked Xavier to facilitate the meeting, to represent Caspien's interests." At this, he looked guilty again. "I was told the meeting did not go well. That Caspien said he had no desire to speak with the man again. I was also told that the endowment was refused."

Here, he looked at me. Here, I understood. Here, the truths I had always accepted as fact, rearranged themselves entirely.

"I was later given to understand that Caspien had, in fact, accepted the money. That he had set up a trust fund to be administered by a third-party firm to cover the cost of an Oxford education, a car, private dental and health care and the general living costs of a student for the duration of that education."

"It can't be true."

"Why not? Because you've convinced yourself he never cared for you."

I had. I had convinced myself of that. But only because it made things easier to bear.

"It's a theory, one you've made up in your head."

"Yes. That I then put to him and had him confirm," said Gideon. "He threatened that if I ever told you, he would have Xavier destroy me and take every penny I had. Cas knew how you would feel if you ever learned the truth."

"Did Blackwell know?"

"Of course, he did. He knew exactly how Cas felt about you."

How Cas felt about me. I felt scraped out and raw, hollow. I didn't know what I was supposed to do with this. How to feel.

Then I remembered.

"You said he left Blackwell two years ago."

Gideon knew what I was asking, what I now understood. "As soon as he turned twenty-five."

I won't ask Gideon for a single penny and I have not a penny to my name until I turn twenty-five.

"He stayed with him until he inherited his own money," I said as everything slid into place.

"He married him so he could take half of what he owned," Gideon supplied. "Six years. Any marriage under five makes the splitting of assets a little trickier."

Cas. What the hell did you fucking do?

I wanted to cry. Hit something.

"He loved you, Jude," said Gideon. "He chose you. He chose you when he was sixteen, in the only way that made sense to him. He thought Xavier was a different kind of man then, yes, but when he knew that he wasn't, he chose to protect you instead of himself."

I shook my head. "No. He could have left with me then, Gideon. In London. He didn't have to go back to him. I would have forgiven him for anything, I'd have loved him through anything. He didn't choose me then."

"Xavier would have ruined you, Jude," Gideon said. "He wanted to keep you safe and happy. That was in Oxford, far away from Xavier. And him. He wanted you to live your dream..."

"He was my fucking dream, Gideon!" I shouted. "Him! He made himself miserable, forced himself into a life with that piece of shit for what? For what?" I tore at my hair and scrubbed a hand over my mouth.

Gideon looked sadder than I'd ever seen him.

"For you, Jude. For you."

TWO

I left Gideon, drove the rental car to St. Helier, and found a bar as I contemplated what he'd told me.

I knew I shouldn't believe it.

It would be easier not to; if I didn't believe it, then nothing had changed. Cas still chose Xavier, the man who killed my parents was my mystery sponsor, and Gideon was still a conniving, insidious prick who was lying about this just like he lied about everything else. But if it was Cas, then it meant I didn't know him. Not as I thought I did. He wasn't the person I'd always believed him to be if he could do this.

But when I turned it over, examined it, it made more and more sense that it was Cas. Cas was the only person it *could* be. I went back and forth between believing Gideon was a liar, and believing everything Cas had done for the last ten years had been for me.

A lightbulb moment had me go to

my phone's contacts and dial a number I hadn't dialled in years. The receptionist answered with a cheerful greeting, polished and professional.

"Moreland and Wright, Kate speaking, how may I help you?"

"Hi, I'm an old client of Mr. Moreland's. I had a question about a legal matter he dealt with for me a few years back."

"Can I take your name, please? I'll check if Mr Moreland's available."

"Jude Alcott," I said and told her I didn't mind waiting.

Moreland greeted me the way he always did. Apologetic and friendly. "You know I can't give you a name, Mr. Alcott. I'd love to, but I can't."

"I know. But how about I give you one, and you tell me if I'm right?"

Moreland sighed.

"Caspien Deveraux," I said. I could have sworn I heard his breathing change. The smallest, fraction of a hitch down the line. I'd given him a few names over the years, but never this one.

Finally, he said, "Mr. Alcott, we've discussed this, many times. I can't disclose my client's name to you without being in breach of the confidentiality clause contained therein. I'm sorry."

"Yeah, okay. Thanks." I hung up and ordered another drink.

I thought about going to Luke's, putting it all to him to see how plausible he thought it was. But I knew he'd say it was Cas. Of course, it was. And I wasn't ready to accept that.

So, several hours later, I called an Uber home, banging on the front door and ringing the bell until Jasper answered. "Oh, it's you. I thought we were being fucking invaded or something."

Ignoring him, I marched into the red sitting room and went immediately to the drinks cabinet. It wasn't the horn of plenty it used to be in here, but I found a large bottle of sherry, dusty and forgotten, near the back, which I scooped out and uncorked.

I drank it from the bottle.

Jasper eyed me warily from the doorway.

"He was worried you flew back to London. But I told him your stuff was still in your room." He folded his arms huffily. "You being like this isn't good for his health you know."

"I've no idea what you're on about." I fell back on the hard sofa and slid my legs up onto the glass coffee table.

"Drunk and disorderly. Shouting. Storming out and coming home at all hours of the night."

I laughed at that. "Okay, mum."

Scowling, he came into the room and perched on the arm of the sofa. "If you're going to be such a moody fucking prick, can you just pack your shit and fuck off? Let the guy die in peace."

"He wanted me here."

"Yeah, I know, Jude. I've listened to him go on and on about you for months. Cas too. So he was a horrible cunt to you, he was a terrible father to Caspien, but he's trying to make amends which is a lot more than some people do, so just give him a fucking break, will you?"

"Give him a break? Piss off, Jasper. You've not a fucking clue who he is, what he's done." I lifted the bottle and drank.

"Actually, you learn a lot about a person by wiping them clean of their own shit and blood, by watching them rot away in front of you."

"He's a manipulative liar," I said, but the anger had subsided at the image he'd painted of Gideon. "He always has been. This is just another one of his fucking games." He'd designed this in such a way that I'd be left with this even after he died. Never knowing the truth.

"Yeah, maybe. Maybe it is." He shrugged. "Maybe it's all another big fucking lie to get you and Caspien together so he can die knowing he undid the worst mistake he ever made." He stood, looking down at me with a measure of scorn I thought I might deserve. "How fucking awful of him. What a piece of shit he'd be for that."

Jasper strode from the room without looking back, and I proceeded to get very, very drunk. I passed out with Caspien's name on my lips and the distinct sound of his voice in my ear. I woke and drank some water from a glass by my bedside, before falling back to sleep.

I dreamt of him, willowy and dressed in black, smelling of sea salt and fresh moss.

I was in his bedroom, lying on his bed, as he sat down on the edge and smiled at me. It was a real smile; the London smile. I dreamt of the night we walked along the Thames as the sky turned from summer orange to indigo to deepest black.

You're ridiculous, you do realise that?

I know, I'd said.

When I woke, dry-mouthed and disoriented, I didn't know where I was. The bed felt different from my own. There were no iron bars to cool my feet against, and the mattress was softer than I remembered. I looked up at the ornate ceiling and recognised the rose cornicing.

Deveraux. I was in Deveraux. In Cas's mother's bedroom.

I sat up and looked around. No. Not his mother's, his.

I was in his bedroom, in his bed. And I was completely naked.

What in the name of fuck had I done? A glance under the sheets gave me my answer. Mortification spread up from my chest, where my depravity had dried and flaked.

I groaned. I remembered nothing about my night, how much I'd drank – a lot, evidently – before coming into his room and …

Christ. I sat up.

"You're awake, then," a voice said from somewhere to the left.

I turned and saw to my utter shock, Cas sitting on the window seat, legs curled up and a book in his hands. I scrubbed my eyes, because I was imagining things, obviously, I was still asleep, obviously.

But still, he remained. He wore all black; turtle neck jumper, smart trousers, and polished smart shoes. A brown coat was draped over the chair next to him.

"Cas? Fuck. What...are you? Doing here?"

He stood up from the window and came toward me, sliding his hands into his pockets. He looked painfully gorgeous. Older, touches of it in and around his eyes, but beautiful still. That same delicate beauty I always associated with him. His face had lost a lot of the hardness it used to carry, now sad where it would once have been cruel. I tried not to think about why that was.

"You called me," he said.

"No, I didn't."

Cas took another step toward me. "Last night. Yes, you did."

No. Last night, I'd gone out, come back, gotten very drunk. More drunk than I'd been in years, and then, I...oh god.

I didn't know what to do with this. I certainly couldn't accept it while I sat here, naked, covered in... and in his bed.

"Could I...Would you mind just waiting here while I go...shower and put some clothes on?"

He nodded, the faintest trace of a smile on his mouth.

Very carefully, I climbed out of bed and pulled the top sheet off to wrap it around myself before walking to the door.

I stopped and turned back, to check he was really there, before I slipped out of his room and down the hall to his mother's room. Grabbing fresh underwear and clothes, I went to the shower and cleaned myself quickly.

Cas was here. I'd called him. Something he wasn't lying about because when I found my phone – sensibly plugged in by my bed – there was indeed an outgoing call to him at 11:36 p.m. I wanted to die from embarrassment. I hadn't done it for years, drunk called him, but last night I had. What had I said?

I'd called him, then gone to his bed and had a wank in it? With Gideon and Jasper in the house? What the fuck was wrong with me?

The only upside as far as I could tell, was that I didn't appear to have a hangover. The most minuscule of mercies.

I crept back to Cas's bedroom like a criminal would retrace the steps to their crime scene, to find him where I left him, on the window seat reading his book. He stood when I entered, placing the bookmark inside and setting it down.

I drank him in again, properly. I hadn't seen him except online for eight years. He looked healthy and vibrant, his skin unmarred and glowing with life, bright blue eyes shining as they looked at me.

"I called you," I said.

"You did."

"And you answered."

"I told you if it was important, then I'd answer."

"How are you here?"

"Well, I'm living in London now. I caught the first flight over this morning."

I couldn't read the look on his face; it was tense, on the cusp of something huge, something I wasn't sure I was ready to hear.

"Gideon said you never come here, that you've refused to set foot in the place ."

He tilted his head a little like it was extremely obvious. "Well, it wasn't Gideon who asked me to come."

I went then to sit on the bed, hoping he couldn't see the way my legs trembled as I walked across the room.

"He doesn't look good."

"I know," he said.

"So… obviously, I can't remember the call. I don't know what I said…" I wanted the floor to swallow me whole. I couldn't look at his face. His perfect fucking face. Christ, I'd missed him. It almost hurt more now that he was here, standing right in front of me. Real. Almost within touching distance. His hair was long again, tucked behind his ears, and curling against the collar of the rich wool at his neck. I wanted to go to him and pull him into me, kiss him. More than anything else, more than knowing the truth about what he'd done, I wanted that.

I said, "You always told me he was a liar. That I should never believe anything he said. So…" I swallowed and looked at my hands. "So, I don't know what to believe, Cas. I needed to hear it from you." I still couldn't decide if I wanted it to be true.

"I know," he said again. "But I won't lie to you."

I narrowed my eyes at him. "You lied to me about Xavier. Then about what he was doing to you, you lied to my face about that. More than once."

He nodded. "Yes, because I never wanted you to see me like that. As something small and weak – like *he* did." I could tell this was difficult for him to say, but he pushed on. "I thought if you knew what he'd done to me then it would change how you saw me. And I didn't want that."

"It never changed how I saw you, Cas; it never could. It only made me hate him more."

He gave me a sort of conflicted look. "I know. I know that now."

I was quiet a moment before I straightened my spine and looked him right in the eye.

"So is it true? What Gideon told me. You're the one who set up the trust for me? Who paid for Oxford, my car, my fucking dental treatment?"

This, too, was painful, hard for him to say.

"Yes," he said at last.

I sat forward, elbows on my knees as I covered my face with my hands. "Fucking hell, Cas. Why? *Why* would you do this?"

"You know why, Jude."

I didn't think I did. I didn't dare hope that I did. But I could see only two reasons why he'd done it: pity or love. I loathed the idea of the first and could barely stand the idea of the second. Knowing he'd loved me all these years and yet stayed away.

"So you put yourself through years of fucking hell for what? For me?" That's what Gideon had said. *For you, Jude. For you.*

He shook his head. "No, it wasn't entirely like that. It was..." He took a deep steadying breath. "When I first met Xavier, he was different. He was older, experienced, handsome. I was entranced by the life I thought he could offer me. A life away from this place, where my mother's misery lives in the walls, where Gideon's lives out in the open in every room. I was determined to escape the moment I could. When my father came to me with his money, earned honestly by all accounts and not inherited, I was going to refuse him outright. I wanted nothing from him. He was the reason I was here and the reason my mother was dead. His name is Liam, by the way, Caspien Liam Deveraux: it's bloody ghastly. Anyway, I thought I could use his money for something good."

Here, he looked at me. "I thought it might make what I'd done to you feel less...*fatal.* I don't regret it. How can I? You did it, you got your degree from Oxford, and you published your novel. Doing that for you has been the best thing, the only decent thing, I ever did for you. For *anyone*. You're not responsible for anything that came after, Jude. This is why it became even more important you never found out. Because I know you: you would take this and make it your fault, somehow. When it was no one's but his. I made the decision to give it to you before knowing what he was. There's no fault of yours – or mine – to be found in who or what Xavier turned out to be."

"But I was to go my whole life not knowing it was you?"

The thought was unimaginable. Painful.

"That was the plan."

"Still as fucking selfish as ever, I see."

He winced. But then I saw a hint of the Caspien trademark smirk I thought I'd never see again. "On the whole, yes."

"So it was a consolation prize? 'I fell in love with Caspien Deveraux and all I got was this lousy trust fund'? A thanks-for-taking-part sort of thing? That it?"

"Some would argue you got the better end of the deal," he said. "You got the money without any of the aggravation." He gestured at himself, the aggravation.

"Yeah, well that wasn't your choice to fucking make, Cas!"

"But it had to be me, Jude. It had to be. If it had been up to you then you'd have chosen me without thinking, and I'd have broken your heart anyway, and neither of us would have learned a bloody thing!" His eyes were glittering and hard, his cheeks pink.

"So all of this was some sort of fucking lesson?"

"For me, yes, it was." He ran his hands through his hair and turned to stare out the window, breathing hard and fast. When he spoke again, his voice was softer, calmer. "I thought I could live my whole life the way Gideon has: with love being some ancillary but ultimately useless thing I didn't need. And perhaps I could have."

He turned and smiled, some hollow sad thing I could barely look at.

"But then, there was you. And everything that you are: warm and kind, gentle and sweet, and you loved me despite everything I was and everything I did, and everything I couldn't give you. Christ, I didn't know what to do with that kind of love, Jude. How to hold it or carry it or even look at it. It was terrifying. I was sure I would kill it – I tried to. But then I began to feel its absence. I missed it. I longed for it. The feel of it on my skin, and deep inside my chest and in my head whenever I felt like I might disappear from loneliness. You and that love was what I clung onto when...when he made me feel as though I was nothing. It was how I survived."

My throat and chest felt thick from the tears that threatened to spill out. "You could have left him, you could have left him, and you stayed because of me, Cas."

"No." He shook his head, firmly. "I stayed because of me, because I'd convinced myself it was what I deserved. I'd made a mistake, chosen badly, and I'd hurt you so cruelly that I could barely stand to look at you. But then in London you were...you. Different in some ways, wiser almost, but you were still you and incredibly, you still loved me. When I thought he might hurt you, I stayed to make sure he never could. I'd hurt you enough, the world had hurt you enough, and I wouldn't allow anything else to hurt you. Not when I could prevent it."

"You didn't have to protect me from that, I told you I wasn't afraid of him."

"And have everything be for nothing?" He implored. "Jude, you have to understand the way I saw myself then. It's impossible to let yourself be loved when you're as inherently un-loveable as I believed myself to be."

He sighed, loudly. "I have a lot of regrets, too many to count, but none as great as allowing Gideon and Xavier to convince me of my place in the world. I regret hurting you, Jude, I do, but I think..." He thought about this next part hard, then he took a deep breath, and said, "I think if I'd stayed with you then, chosen you then, I'd have destroyed you. I'd have turned you into something cold and cruel and bitter; a person who hated the world and everything in it. Because that's who I was then." He looked around the room, then back at me. "You were everything warm and bright and alive in this place and I would have poisoned that." Cas looked as though something very heavy had finally been taken from his aching hands.

"Maybe instead of you destroying me, I could have saved you?" I said.

Cas smiled another small, sad smile. "You did save me, Jude. So many times."

After what felt like hours he moved across the room and sat next to me on the bed. There was less than an arm's distance between us now and the proximity of him was like the sun after years of winter. Warm and vital, giving life to everything inside me.

It was him who spoke first.

"I loved your novel," he said, soft and sincere.

"Thank you."

"Was Bennett based on anyone?"

"What do you think?"

He nodded, smiling a little. "Thought so. Christ, he was awful."

I looked at him. "Misunderstood, I'd say. Easy to hate a guy like that without taking the time to understand him."

Caspien was staring at me very intensely. There was a hitch in his voice as he said, "You look well, Jude."

"I'm alright."

"Good."

"You?" I asked.

"I'm alright, too."

The long-dead glimmer of hope flickered to life again. I'd smothered it more times than I could count, but it always returned. An old friend.

"Are you...seeing anybody?"

Cas smiled, shy. Then shook his head. "No. I'm not."

I nodded. To my delight and surprise, it was him who spoke next, turning his body slightly towards me as he did.

"Jude, I know we've done this backwards, completely, and I wouldn't blame you if you wanted nothing to do with me. But we've established I'm rather selfish, and so I wondered if you might be willing...and able...perhaps *you're* with someone now, I don't know, I should probably have asked that first. But if not, I wonder if you might be willing to give me another chance. With you. We could go for dinner, or a drink: whatever you'd be comfortable with."

He was nervous. Caspien Deveraux was asking me out, and he was nervous about it.

"Are you asking me out on a date?" I asked, half-smiling.

His cheeks flushed, beautifully. "I...yes. I think so. But only if you're single, and you're going to say yes, because otherwise...well that's rather awkward. And embarrassing."

"Cas, I've been in love with you since I was fifteen. I've wanted this since I was fifteen. I'm not about to turn you down, am I?"

"Maybe you'd want to torture me a little. I don't know. I'd deserve it."

I reached out slowly and tucked a strand of his hair behind his ear where it had come loose.

"No, you wouldn't."

He leaned into my hand, eyes fluttering closed a little, before he pitched forward and wrapped his arms around me. He buried his face in my neck as he hugged me tight. I held him like that for a long time, his body warm and solid against my chest as he breathed me in. The promise I'd made under the moon flared up bright and potent inside me again.

Love him. Love him. Love him.

It was a dangerous and violent thing to love. And just like me, Cas was war-weary and battle-scarred. But together we'd heal. Together, we'd smooth away the cracks on our hearts so that they could do what they were made to do: love.

EPILOGUE

Gideon died on a Friday, quietly and without much theatre. Jude, Jasper, and I beside him as he went. We'd never used the word 'love' with each other, and that day was no different.

He still knew me by the end, which Jasper said was unusual. Still knew Jude. He'd gripped his hand and whispered another apology for his part in everything that had happened while I watched, quiet and wary, even now untrusting that he wouldn't drip his poison into the well of us.

The night before he died, I'd sat by his bedside and read to him. Jude had gone to bed, and I'd sat in the dim light, the sound of his breathing so slow and so shallow that I was certain he'd gone. But then he'd spoken.

"Caspien, you won't leave him again, will you?" he'd rasped. *"No matter what?"*

"I am not doing this, Gideon," I said, not looking up. *"If you no longer want me to*

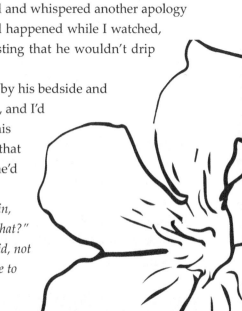

read, then I'll go to bed. But we are not discussing him. I've told you this already."

"But you will tell him you love him," he said, as though I hadn't just *refused to discuss it. "He needs to hear you say it, Caspien."*

I sighed and closed the book, lifting my eyes to the bed. *"You do not have to worry about him, alright. I plan to make him happy."* And I did. I'd never do anything to hurt him, not again.

"And you'll be happy too, won't you? You deserve to be happy, too."

"Yes, Gideon. I plan on being happy, too. With Jude. Please stop worrying about that."

"But you've told him? He knows how you feel? How you've always felt?"

"He knows about the trust. I suppose I have you to thank for that. But we are taking things slowly." I sighed, knowing that despite my protests, I was going to discuss this after all. *"I cannot walk back into his life and assume my place in it is the same as it was."*

"Yes, of course. But I think if you just tell him you love him then it will all work out, I am certain of it."

"Yes, uncle." I said because I wanted him to sleep. I wanted him to stop talking.

Upstairs, I'd gone to Jude's room – my mother's room – and stood outside the door. I was afraid to knock, afraid of what it would mean if I did. I wanted to knock, to ask him to put his arms around me, to feel the comfort of his constancy. I wanted to lose myself in that deep, unwavering comfort only he'd ever been able to give me. It had been true that his love had been my greatest comfort over the years I'd spent with Xavier. Jude, whose love was a lighthouse on a stormy sea. Jude, who'd saved me over and over and over again. But we *were* taking things slow and it would be selfish of me to go to him now just because it was what I needed.

I'd gone to my bedroom alone. Cold and large and with memories, almost enough of them to pour scorn on everything I'd tried to fix inside myself since leaving Boston.

Gideon's funeral was bigger than it ought to have been. People from the island and London, traipsing up the steep hill to the family plot to say goodbye to a man they hadn't even known. Not really.

Only myself and Jude had really known all sides of him. Perhaps Jasper, his faithful nurse – who looked at Jude in a way I disliked intensely – had seen a side to him that not even we had.

Xavier hadn't come.

Not only as I'd instructed my lawyer to advise him that his presence on the island would be considered a breach of our 'agreement.' The agreement we'd made upon our divorce, so long as he stayed away from me, the offences he'd committed against me (over the years I'd documented each one thoroughly) would never find its way to my lawyer.

In the end, it didn't matter. He'd been caught in a compromising position with a boy of fourteen; the son of a client, a very rich and very powerful client who was doing a fine job of destroying him without my input. I expected I'd get a call before the case went to trial. I had been his husband, after all. Who knew his character better than I? A pity for him that our agreement wasn't enforceable in a court of law.

At the graveside Jude stood close to me looking haunted and desperately sad, and I couldn't help but imagine how he must have looked as a child at his parents' funerals. Large, green eyes shimmering with fear and loneliness. He cried for Gideon. Gideon who'd only ever seen him as a playground where he could re-enact the pain that had been done to him. Jude's heart was an awe-inspiring thing; its capacity for love and empathy and forgiveness despite what cruelty had been done to it was beyond my understanding.

Later, when everyone had gone and Jasper had left the mansion, I found Jude in the music room staring at the empty bed, cleared now of the detritus that had kept Gideon alive the last few months. He had a lost, far-off look on his face.

I took the opportunity to watch him from where I stood unnoticed, skin pale and smooth and hair a dark forest, rich with the dying light of the afternoon. He'd changed in the years since I first met him. From a gangly pretty boy who smelled of cut grass and Skittles, to something darker and frighteningly handsome.

Jude had always been unaware of his own appeal; of the very particular kind of beauty he possessed and the power it held over the people around him. While I'd been trained very early to wield mine like a weapon, his was innocent and guileless. Deceptively clever and yet filled with an almost child-like wonder, he was a perfect entrancing mix. He was less innocent now than he was then, more hardened – by myself and Gideon – but more attractive for it.

I loved him. I'd loved him for years.

It had taken me too long to realise it, to understand it and recognise it for what it was: that thing which had ruined everyone I knew. My mother. My father. Gideon.

Jude was the *only* kind of love I'd ever known.

"Did you love him?" Jude asked when I came to stand by his side.

I stared at the deathbed. "No. I don't think I did."

He looked at me, forlorn but not surprised. "Seems unfair we both became orphans and I got Luke and you got Gideon."

"Luke is one of a very particular kind," I said. Jude was another very particular kind. "Very few of us get a Luke. Besides, my father's alive and well, remember."

"Liam," he said.

"Please, don't."

"You prefer Lucifer?"

"Immeasurably."

He grinned. My heart flipped. I liked seeing him smile. I also liked hearing him laugh, so I divulged the next piece of information for that reason only. I'd sworn to take it to my grave.

"He's a used car salesman."

Jude's mouth dropped open. "No, he isn't."

I nodded, grimly.

"Oh, my god, this is perfect." And he burst into a fit of laughter.

We stayed at Deveraux four days after the funeral before going back to London together. We'd meet with Gideon's lawyer on Monday. (Xavier's firm had been relieved shortly after our separation.) Luke and Elspeth would fly over on Sunday evening, and the four of us, plus Finn's parents, would attend the reading.

I already knew what the will contained, so there would be no surprises for me. I knew Gideon had shown Jude part of it, but there was some other detail in there he would be hearing for the first time.

At the airport exit, I stood facing him unsure what to say. Jude seemed relaxed; he'd been chatty and smiling throughout the flight.

"So," he said hesitantly. "About that date..."

Nothing had happened between us in Jersey. Nothing but lingering glances and the briefest of possibly accidental touches. *Tell him you love him,* Gideon's voice had said each time there was a lull in our conversations over the simple dinners we'd made together in the kitchen – dinners which had reminded me of our blissfully domestic weeks in London.

But telling him I loved him seemed like another selfish thing to do, and so it had never felt like the right time.

"You still want to?" I asked, a strange flutter of panic spreading over me. Had he realised he didn't? After all this time, this last week with me could very well have changed his mind. Now that Gideon was dead, no longer forcing us together, maybe he'd decided th—

"Of course," Jude said grinning. "When are you free?"

Smiling, I pulled up the calendar on my phone. "We have a concert coming up, so there's quite a lot of rehearsal." I scanned the dates, heart-dropping when I saw when I was next free. "We're rehearsing every night for the next three weeks."

"What time does rehearsal finish?"

"Around nine, sometimes later. Our conductor is...Stalin-esque."

He chuckled at this. "So, I'll wait for you after rehearsal. If that isn't too late?"

I shook my head. "No, it's fine."

"Cool. So how about tomorrow?"

"Okay, tomorrow then. We rehearse at the Barbican."

"Yeah, I know. I'll wait outside for you." He began to back off, smiling.

"Uh, there's a car coming for me," I said. "If you want a lift back into the city?"

"I actually like the Tube." He winked at me and then turned, looking back to shout. "See you tomorrow!"

I waved stupidly. Butterflies swirling and swooping in my stomach.

The following night, he was waiting inside the foyer when I came out, chatting to the doorman whose name I didn't know, though I'd been here almost a year. When he saw me, he stopped talking and smiled that bright beautiful smile at me. The one he'd always smiled at me.

I groaned as the butterflies kicked up again.

"Ready?" I asked him, hating how nervous my voice sounded.

"Yep," Jude smiled. "Catch you later, Phil."

"Phil?" I asked when we were outside.

"Yeah, he let me in to watch you for a bit."

I glanced at him. "You watched?"

"Didn't know you had a solo."

"A small one."

"You sounded fucking amazing, Cas."

I cleared my throat, a little embarrassed by his sincerity. "Thank you."

"I bought a ticket for the concert on my phone while I was waiting."

"Oh, I could have got you one."

He shrugged. "I don't mind paying for it."

It was a brisk night in early November, and Jude's cheeks and nose were already pink from the chill, his freckles like constellations across both. His eyes sparkled a lush verdant green – it was my favourite colour, the colour of Jude's eyes. I pulled my scarf up and my coat around my body.

"Are you cold?" he asked. "We can just go in here if you want?"

It was a bar I knew the players sometimes drank in, and I was quite happy walking a bit further to find somewhere we would be alone. I shook my head, and we walked on a little more.

Jude was telling me about a film he'd seen with the same kind of enthusiasm he told me about books. I'd often thought that if Jude could find a job that somehow combined both, he'd be entirely in the perfect profession. For now, he was an English supply teacher at a grammar school in North London. He'd written his book over a few years, and though it had been a critical success, he hadn't made enough money to give up teaching. Though it didn't sound like he wanted to: he enjoyed it. I could imagine him being good at it, too.

We found a quiet-looking bar in Clerkenwell, shucked out of our coats, and sat at a table near the back. Jude fetched the drinks, and I watched him go, as oblivious as ever to the looks of both sexes, a fact that only made them more interested in him.

When he sat back down, handing me my beer, he was smiling so wide I thought I'd missed something.

"What?" I asked as I took a sip.

"I just can't believe you drink beer now. As long as I've known you, it's been something ridiculous: rosé wine, gin and tonic."

"There's nothing ridiculous about either of those."

"I mean, true, I drank anything and everything at Oxford. If it had an alcohol content, I drank it. Some of the hangovers were legendary." He grimaced.

"The folly of youth."

He gave me a long, wistful look. "Indeed."

We spent the night talking about everything and anything, avoiding any topic that would sour the mood. My flat was in Soho, and Oxford Circus was on his line, so he walked me home while explaining to me why Whitechapel was the most glamorous place in London. At the door of my building, we stopped. He looked up at it and then around the bustling thoroughfare.

"Do you get much sleep here?"

We were right on the corner of Carnaby Street and Fouberts Place, and it could be loud.

"Not really," I admitted. I'd taken it for the size of the living room and its proximity to the Barbican.

"We should have gone to mine instead."

"Aren't you in Shoreditch?" I frowned.

"Yeah, but I'm in the basement. It's quieter down there."

"I had no idea you were so concerned about street noise." I joked.

"Aren't you? I think uni traumatised me for life; my first-year dorm looked onto an alley where they'd empty the bottle bins at 3 a.m." He laughed. "God, this is the worst date-chat ever. Sorry."

I caught my eyes drifting to his mouth again. I'd been doing it all night. The faint freckle he had, like a beauty mark, just to the left side of his upper lip. I wanted to trace it with my tongue again. It had been so long.

"Do you want to come up?" I asked him.

He nodded, looking a little nervous for the first time. Upstairs, he complimented the size of the living room, into which I'd managed to fit an upright piano, a reading area with bookshelf, lamp and armchair, two large sofas, and a dining table. Somehow, it still felt spacious. The bijou kitchen was tucked behind a set of glass, metal-framed doors at one end.

I left him to use the bathroom while I poured us both a drink; an old fashioned. Somewhat of a signature of mine.

"Fuck, this is good," he said as he took a second mouthful.

I nodded, watching him now with the same sort of covetous look strangers often did. Everything about him drew me in. How he smelled, the sound of his voice, his laugh, the shape of his mouth. But mostly, it was always this: the way he had of looking at me. As though I was something he needed in order to breathe. Some vital commodity he would die without.

But he hadn't died without me. He'd survived. Bloomed even.

I wasn't the same person Jude fell in love with, and though I was still frightened of hurting him, of somehow destroying that which made Jude, Jude, I was determined to show him that I *could* love him back. I would allow him to love me while returning that love.

He watched me now with a strange mix of tenderness and hunger. I'd revelled in both sides before, and I wanted them both again. And again. And again.

"Can you play something for me?" he asked, casting his eyes over my shoulder at the upright. It hadn't been where I'd expected him to go, based on the look he'd been giving me.

"If you like."

I stood and carried my tumbler over to the piano and set it on the top. I sat on the small stool and lifted the lid. A flashback, a phantom pain over the fingers of my right hand. *When I'm talking to you, you will fucking look at me, do you hear me!? The weighty top bashed down onto my fingers once, twice, three times. The pain excruciating.*

"What would you like to hear?" I asked, clearing my throat as I forced away the memory.

"Anything," said Jude softly. "I just like watching you."

"And here I was thinking piano was more of an auditory experience."

"Not when it's you that's playing it, it's not." He sipped his drink and gave me a bawdy look, which made me laugh.

"Actually, I've been working on something." I shifted on the stool, feeling a little self-conscious. Especially given he was the muse.

"You wrote it?" His eyes widened with delight.

I nodded, settling my hands over the keys.

I'd been working on the suite for over a decade. I'd started it when I was still at Deveraux, a catalogue of songs that had become our story: *The Boy. The Gardener. The Beach. The Reader. The Library. Oxford. London. Oleander.*

It was almost complete though I still tinkered on the pieces daily, adding and removing things depending on my mood, never quite happy with the sum of the parts. But perhaps there was one more piece to create, one more to add. *The Boy: returned. The Man: in bloom.*

I began to play *Oleander*: the piece I was most confident in, the one I'd worked on longest. The one I'd been lost in the night Xavier broke my hand. That night, I'd boarded a plane and left him for the first time, only to find Jude, inexplicably, waiting for me on the other side of the ocean. My lighthouse in the storm.

As the piece moved through its motions, he watched me with tears in his eyes and his heart on his sleeve. His eyes had changed, but he still looked at me the same way. As though I was his and he was mine. I wasn't afraid of that look now, I returned that look now.

When it was over, he shook himself as though coming out of a dream. He looked like he might jump to his feet and applaud.

"Fucking hell, Cas. That was...incredible."

"Thank you." I lifted my glass and moved to sit back on the couch across from him.

"I really want to kiss you," he said after a moment. "Can I?"

"You never have to ask me that, Jude."

He set his glass down and moved across the couch toward me. Then, he took mine and set it down too. When he brought his hand up to touch my cheek, I let out a small desperate noise I hadn't thought I was capable of.

"Did he ever..." Jude began, green eyes turning dark. "Without your consent? Did he ever hurt you like that?"

I'd never lie to him. But neither did I want to say it out loud, the humiliation was too great.

In the end, I didn't have to. His jaw clenched, and his mouth flattened into a line. Still, his touch was excruciatingly soft as he skimmed his thumb over my lip.

"Cas..." He pressed his forehead to mine, breathing quick. "I'm so sorry."

"Please, don't Jude." I pleaded. "It's over. I'm okay. Everything is okay now."

"Please tell me you know you never deserved it. I haven't been able to stop thinking about what you said that day. I can't." He fixed me with a firm look. "Please tell me you know now that you never deserved what he did to you."

The truth was, I was still trying to get to a place where I believed it unflinchingly. Counselling was gruelling and some days felt like walking through quicksand filled with snakes. But it was working, I could feel that too. And so while I couldn't say it and mean it today, I knew I would be able to one day.

"I'm getting there, I promise."

He squeezed his eyes closed and leaned in to kiss me. Gentle, soft.

"I love you so much. *So much.* I think I'll always want to kill him."

I kissed him back then. Hungrily. Forcefully. Pushing him backwards on the couch so I could climb on top and bury myself in his mouth. He moved his hands over every inch of me, as though checking I was real, inhaling and tasting my mouth, my neck, eyelids, ears. As though I were something tender, delicate, which needed to be treated carefully. Only Jude had ever made me feel like this.

He touched me with his eyes and his hands and his mouth and it was like we were boys again. There had never been anything other than purest unbridled love when he did this. No matter how I'd hurt him, he loved me the same as he always had. With everything that he had.

I'd been telling the truth when I told him he'd saved me over and over again; because if Jude could love me, Jude who was perfect, Jude who was the sun, then it meant I was worth loving. Gideon had raised me to be something cold and poisonous, Xavier had tried to crush me to dust, but Jude had just loved. Tender and sweet. No matter who or what I came to him as, he'd loved me. Every version of me. And I felt like myself only when he saw me. He looked at me the same way he looked at the world, with warmth and wonder and curiosity. Jude gave life to everything around him, and I felt truly alive *because* he loved me.

I climbed off and led him to the bedroom, where we undressed each other in silence. Looks speaking a thousand words. Naked, I covered him in kisses, capturing his groans and gasps in my mouth and between my teeth. After what felt like hours, he changed our positions so I was beneath him, and began to open me.

First, with his mouth, exceedingly slow and deliberate, before using his fingers with a deft and careful touch that had me begging for him. Before pushing inside me, he brought us face to face and stilled, looking deep into my eyes. His own were a dark vine green now, pupils black and wide with desire

Tracing my cheek and then my mouth, gentle and soft fingers moving over their shape, he said, "I'm never losing you again, Cas. You realise that, don't you?"

"You never lost me," I said. It was true. I was always his. Just like he was always mine. "And you never will, I promise. For however long you want me, I'll be here. I'm yours." My body wasn't used to his size, hadn't been used to any size for a long time, but Christ, it wanted him. It was as though it had been made for him.

"I'm always going to want you," he said, kissing me as he began to thrust. "I don't remember a time when I didn't."

As he fucked me, he ran his hands over my body, under it, touching and tasting. It was slow and then it was frenzied. It was gentle and then rough. He turned me inside out and emptied me clean of everything but him. I was free of everything I'd been before, rotten and poisoned, new and remade, and I would never ever go back to any life that he wasn't a part of.

He took hold of my arousal and stroked, dragging me to a point of pleasure so white-hot it felt like I was being burned from the inside.

"Jude...I'm going to..."

"Come for me, let me see you...fuck, that's it, baby. Look at you. You're so beautiful, Cas. So beautiful. So perfect. I love you so much."

It was the most intense orgasm of my life. More intense than any I'd had with him before. More so than the countless times he'd made me come in that hovel of a dorm in Oxford.

When I was milked dry, he leaned in to devour my mouth as he fucked me to his own climax. Every thrust of Jude's hips sent a spark of sensation up my spine, over-sensitivity a shocking but delicious pulse through my whole body. I was mindless from it. From him. His perfect body, perfect cock, perfect soul a balm to my own. I felt him erupt, a flood of hot healing pleasure coating the inside of me. He choked out another declaration and slid off me.

I twisted my body, throwing a leg over him to keep his cock inside me, not ready for the sensation of being empty of him yet. He belonged there. He let out a languid, sex-rough groan, before sighing dreamily.

"I don't think I'll ever get over the fact that I actually get to have you like this," he said.

I rolled my eyes at him. "I'm sure the novelty will wear off soon enough." I rested my head on his chest, the beat of his heart a steady cadence.

"Oh, you wish."

We were silent for a few moments before I decided it was time. I'd never said it before. Not once, to anyone. I didn't know if there were certain rules to where and how, but I was impatient. It was a peculiar kind of weight in my chest, and I'd been nervous for over a week now; I wanted rid of the feeling.

"I love you, Jude," I said in a strangely formal voice.

I heard it against my ear; the sound of his heart skipping its regular rhythm.

"What?"

"I love you," I said again.

He sat up, causing him to slip out of me. I was forced to sit up, too.

"Since when?" he asked. There was a strange look on his face. Confusion, I thought. Or maybe fear.

I hadn't been expecting this. Questions about it. "Um, well, for a long time. I just didn't recognise it, at least that's what my counsellor thinks, but now I know. Now I know that I love you. That I've always loved you."

"You've *always* loved me?"

I was frowning now. "You don't have to sound so utterly disconcerted by it."

"Oh, trust me, that's not what this is."

"Then what is it? Your face has a strange look on it."

"Does it?" He laughed. "I don't know, I guess now I know how I'd react if someone told me I'd won the lottery. This would be my face."

"Well, you're not doing it now."

Now he was smiling. Very big and very wide. I felt my own mouth turning up into a smile.

Without warning, Jude threw himself at me, kissing me hard over every part of my face.

"Say it again," he said when he came up for air. His grin was still pulling at the sides of his mouth.

"I love you."

"One more time."

"I'm not a performing monkey, no."

He laughed and kissed me again, and I kissed him back. But against his lips, unable to stop myself, I whispered it once more.

"You know," I said when he was relaxed and half-dozing by my side, "Gideon has left you quite a disgustingly large sum of money and a house in Tuscany so it will be like winning the lottery."

POST-SCRIPT

THE JERSEY ENQUIRER

Jersey to open London Film Festival!

The Island will be packed with famous faces this weekend as it opens the London Film Festival with the premier of a much-anticipated film. The Birdwatchers, starring Sebastian Forrest and Oliver Leister is an adaptation of the semi-autobiographical, queer coming-of-age novel by Jude Alcott, who grew up in St. Ouen.

The novel, an instant New York Times bestseller, tells the story of an orphan named Milo who is drawn into a twisted web of betrayal, lies and deceit when he falls in *love with the beautiful but cruel Nicholas.*

Adapted for the screen by the author himself, and filmed on location in Deveraux house, Oxford, and London, the film has been set to music by Caspien Deveraux, the classical pianist and composer. Deveraux is also a St. Ouen native and the author's long-term partner, as well as the owner of the 18th-century property.

The couple, who no longer live in Jersey (they split their time between Tuscany and London, according to the author's website) are said to be contemplating a move back to the Island, which could mean the doors of Deveraux will close to the public for good. The composer had previously granted care of his family's ancestral home to the Island's Historical and Cultural committee, and it has been a popular tourist attraction for the last five years. Its last inhabitant, Lord Gideon Deveraux, died of pancreatic cancer seven years ago.

This weekend will see the property transformed into a cinema hall with the author and composer, the film's stars and director, and other celebrities in attendance.

The Birdwatchers *is the third film from Oscar-winning Swedish director, Hildr Nordlund.'*

ACKNOWLEDGEMENTS

Thanks to my Beta Readers: Cara, Chelsea, Tonya, Stacey, and Clotilde; and to my Proofreading Dream Team: Cara and Kelsey. I couldn't have made it to the end of this monster without you. Thanks to J for always supporting this madness and for feeding our fur babies when I don't leave the room for days. Thanks to those fur babies for always being adorable and letting me steal cuddles when I need them (I need them a lot). Belle and Sebastian, mummy loves you lots.

Cara, you were an absolute rock throughout the finishing of this book. I cannot thank you enough for listening to my constant ramblings over what felt like every moment of these boys' lives, for the cheerleading voice notes when I needed them most, for all the crying ones too - I think my dark author heart loved those most of all. And thank you for helping get this over the line at the end there so I could go drink cocktails on a boat in the Aegean. Couldn't have done it without you. I can't wait to have a wee dram with you next year and talk about how perfect Cas is. I adore you.

Thanks to every single one of you who's been hyping this book up from day one. Making reels and edits and trailers long before you had read even a single page of this book. Your generosity stuns me! I appreciate you more than I can say, and for your patience and constant support (even through a changed release date) you have my heart – I just hope you don't hate me too much for what I put these boys through.

This book took me over a year from beginning to end, but it's lived inside me a lot longer, years in fact, and now that it's out in the world maybe it's time to let go. But honestly, I'm pretty certain that Jude and Cas will live inside me forever, and I hope a piece of them stays with you for a long time after you close the pages of this book too.

OTHER BOOKS BY
THIS AUTHOR

Hamartia: An MM K-pop x Rockstar Romance

A Dark Fall

Into The Dark

SOCIALS

Made in United States
North Haven, CT
01 July 2024

54301025R00300